Miracles

Miracles

A Novel About Mother Seton
The First American Saint

Marcy Heidish

NAL BOOKS

NEW AMERICAN LIBRARY

NEW YORK AND SCARBOROUGH, ONTARIO

Copyright © 1984 by Marcy Heidish

All rights reserved.

For information address New American Library

Published simultaneously in Canada by
The New American Library of Canada Limited.

LIBRARY OF CONGRESS CATALOGING IN PUBLICATION DATA

Heidish, Marcy.
  Miracles: a novel about Mother Seton, the first
American saint.
  1. Seton, Elizabeth Ann, Saint, 1774–1821—Fiction.
I. Title.
PS3558.E4514M5 1984   813'.54   83-25050
ISBN 0-453-00462-8

SIGNET, SIGNET CLASSIC, MENTOR, PLUME,
MERIDIAN and NAL BOOKS are published *in
the United States* by New American Library, 1633
Broadway, New York, New York 10019, *in Canada* by
The New American Library of Canada Limited, 81 Mack
Avenue, Scarborough, Ontario M1L 1M8

NAL BOOKS TRADEMARK REG. U.S. PAT. OFF. AND FOREIGN COUNTRIES
REGISTERED TRADEMARK—MARCA REGISTRADA
HECHO EN HARRISONBURG, VA., U.S.A.

Designed by Kathryn Parise

First Printing, May, 1984

1 2 3 4 5 6 7 8 9

PRINTED IN THE UNITED STATES OF AMERICA

2216153

For
Sister Philomena Kelly, Sister Francisca Hardy,
and Sister Mercedes Martinez

and especially for
Jacques de Spoelberch

You observe the carven hand
With the index finger pointing heavenward.
That is the direction, no doubt.
But how shall one follow it?

—Edgar Lee Masters
Spoon River Anthology

Part One

1

I've come to see the room:

This hospital room with the two beds and the big window and the television on the wall. The place where they say the miracle happened; the place where the child lay dying, where the novena started and the cure, they say, began.

All I can see now is sunlight. Mattress ticking. The bald blue seat of that plastic chair. I smell . . . Swiss steak? . . . Brussels sprouts? That quickflash smell of institutional food, it makes me think of bad seminary suppers—not miracles, not even loaves and fishes. All the same. Miracles are what I'm charged to think of.

They say the child was covered with sores: acute lymphatic leukemia complicated by chicken pox. Four years old, she cried for her mother, lay with arms flung wide. They say she had forty-eight hours, outside, when the prayers began: *O God, giver of all good gifts. . . .* In this room and beyond it, there would have been the rise and fall of voices, soft and cadenced, female voices . . . *the power of Thy grace . . .* voices on the air like mist, and then the ribbon, narrow, white; the ribbon that touched the body of the holy woman, touching the body of the child . . . *if such be Thy will. . . .*

"Father, no smoking here, sorry."

The image fades. The nurse's shoes retreat with a rubberized squeal. I squash out my Lucky Strike amid the rattle of bedpans and dinner trays and walk down the hall. At the elevators, I wait under a fatherly full-color photo of President Eisenhower. What have I done for him lately? I guess this is it.

I am here, on the second floor of St. Agnes Hospital in Baltimore, on behalf of the tribunal empowered to investigate the cure of Ann O'Neill nine years ago. I am here on behalf of the archdiocese, to investigate a cure said to be effected by a relic of Elizabeth Bayley Seton, who died a hundred and forty years ago. I am here because the Church has recently declared Mother Seton Venerable and may soon declare her Blessed; and then, if all goes smoothly, canonize her as the first American-born saint. And I am here to make sure it doesn't go too smoothly.

There is a postulator appointed to this cause: he tries to make the case for sainthood. I help to try to break it if I can; I'm appointed to the "devil's advocate," his assistant in the States—actually an assistant to an assistant's assistant, the way Rome works. But here in Baltimore I stand for the Promotor of the Faith, the watchdog, the check-and-balance on this process. It's my job to be a skeptic. Which comes pretty naturally to me.

My name's Chandler. Father Thomas Dreux Chandler, named for the Puritan shippers on my father's side and the old-line Baltimore belles on my mother's: French Catholic girls who seldom took the veil. I went to Hopkins to please my mother, then to St. Mary's to please myself. I could say I was drawn to the priesthood as a kid, as a dreamy-eyed acolyte, but it wouldn't be true. In fact, what impressed me most, those years, was the silver-tongued monsignor who raffled off a whitewall-tired Ford in five minutes flat. I'm no mystic. I'm a lawyer: a *juris canonici doctor*, with a degree in church administration besides—assistant chancellor of this archdiocese for the last two years. Across my desk come questions of canonical form, diocesan rule: May Mr. Feeny's father have a Mass of Christian Burial if he is first cremated? May Mrs. de Meo, mother of nine, practice birth control even if her pastor says no? The baptism with the non-Catholic godmother, the interfaith nuptial, the occasional request for marital annulment—these pose questions I know how to answer. Most of the time. Or so I've thought, till recently.

But miracles?

That word speeds me past the Church right back to sand-lot baseball—I was ten, eleven—that tough catch in the out-field, that impossible pop-up fly. I shut my eyes. I grabbed for it. I got it. And next thing I knew, the flushed coach was pumping me on the back, shouting, "It was a miracle, kid, a miracle!" That's what I think of first.

Well, it all goes back to how you're raised, I guess. My father never did convert. My mother was casual about her faith. I did have one great-aunt jingling with medals, who believed in miracles. Down on her knees to St. Jude when-ever she lost hope for one of us; down on her knees to St. Cecilia, I recall, to make me, of all things, a concert pianist. She embarrassed us, this aunt. Her ethnic piety didn't fit our style.

Nor was it our style, necessarily, to give a son to the priesthood. I was meant to be a lawyer in the world, not the Church. In college I was hardly monastic; I always had plenty of girls. I was able to renounce that pleasure. I was not able to renounce cigarettes or Hershey's with almonds. And why should I? I'm not an anchorite, an ascetic. The closest thing I've ever felt to a spiritual transport was an all-nighter I pulled in seminary, cramming for an exam in theology, second year. About three in the morning, sick from Cokes and Camels, I had an odd and curiously sweet sensation of floating, weightless, across the room. Just fatigue, I hasten to add. I heard no angel voices, saw no golden nimbus—and if I had, I can tell you, I'd have run, not walked, out of my vocation and home. Permanantly.

My vocation: I'm not sure how I realized I had one. I used to know. I don't anymore. I don't even know if I still have one at all. To be blunt, I'd doubt it. This year I feel severed from it, radically, irreparably, though unable to bleed. Un-willing to bleed. And unable, unwilling to heal. I wish I could say it's just my age—priest hits forty, turns inward, wants out, happens every day. The times are restless too: the Vatican Council set to begin soon, changes to come, we all know. I wish I could say that was it.

What it is, I'm well aware. The dreams, the bad days, I know when they began. This sense of disconnection, this low-grade despair—I can trace the onset precisely. It started when my sister died two months ago. My charming, careless younger sister: I found her. I know how she died, and why. I know that as a priest I was useless to her. I know the Church was useless to her. Worse than useless. I try to dream a path around what happened. There is no such path. And ever since I realized that, it's been this way with me.

I asked to go on retreat. I asked to go home for a while— home to the shaded white Victorian house in Roland Park where my mother still floats magnolias in a bowl in the hall. Where it seems it's still the forties and I'm not yet a priest; perhaps I'm only in from college for the weekend after all. I asked for some respite, some step toward the exit—and got appointed to this tribunal. A change. A shift in the weekly pattern. A slight digression into the supernatural: relics, magic, mumbo jumbo.

Just what I needed.

Now I sit for six and sometimes eight hours every Saturday in the basement of the Cathedral of Mary Our Queen, examining testimony on this purported O'Neill miracle. For six and eight hours it makes me uneasy. After all, this is 1961—not 1194. But Rome, we're told, wants to give America a native saint, and Rome has rigorous standards. We listen to hematologists and oncologists. We scan blood-cell counts and differentials while over our heads the organ groans, Mass is said; schoolchildren sing "Maryland, My Maryland." We sit and talk about the relics of one who may be a saint: relics which may be the dross, the lees, the vapor trail of a soul perhaps quite different from our own.

This woman whom we scrutinize and study, whose very bones have come within our circle of concern—lately she's very much on my mind. Say if her spirit did somehow enter that hospital room—speaking hypothetically, of course— what sort of spirit would it be? Would it pass with a rustle of skirts, a trace of perfume? She was a society girl once. She kept her pink dancing slippers all her life, I've seen them—are they relics too? Would her spirit bend to heal that child because she'd rocked five children of her own? She was a wife before she was a nun; before she was Mother she was mama.

Convert. Nun. Mother. Foundress.

It's a declension I cannot make with ease. What makes a miracle worker? Or a saint, for that matter, in this day and age? I'm not sure I really know. But if I did know, I somehow doubt I'd choose this woman. This Elizabeth Bayley Seton.

Of course I know the facts: know that Rome has found that she died in sanctity; that her life and her writings, closely examined, reveal "heroicity of virtue." I know also that she fits the bill for an all-American saint—born of solid American stock, on the eve of the American Revolution, foundress of the first order of American nuns, the first parochial school.

There are politics in this, I think.

But cynicism aside, I still can't see it.

She's appealing, yes—but hardly a Joan of Arc. Still, if this miracle is accepted by Rome, it's likely that she'll be declared "Blessed," and beatification is the next step toward canonization. If I have doubts, it is my charge to voice them now. And if I'm to voice them, I'll have to look more closely at her life. I'll have to wade through those voluminous letters of hers, those copious journals—and I'll have to be thorough.

At the moment that kind of thoroughness has a certain appeal. It's a shelter for my mind, a way to keep it out of the blistering emptiness that seems to beat around me now. I look at the material before me and take grim comfort in its overwhelming abundance. This will keep me busier than any retreat master could.

Especially because I cannot, so far, see the miracle worker in this miracle. I cannot see this woman standing with the stature of a saint. The most persistent image of her in my mind, superimposed over everything else, is not that of a heroine, a holy woman. It is instead the image of a supplicant: a forlorn young girl. A forlorn young girl standing in a hallway, straining her soul for a sign. A sign, not of her Heavenly Father—but of her earthly one.

2

I *think of her running,* the day of the riot, running home through the city, running down the Broad Way. I think of her pushing past the carters in her good blue dress. Around her the street streaked and spun and in her ears still came the crash of glass and, higher, harsh, the shouts: *"Grave robber, body snatcher"*—she'd heard the mob and run.

That finished it: her haven, her private hours gone. That year, that spring of 1788, she had stolen away whenever she could to the laboratory—the vast brick echo-haunted hospital on Great Georges Street, empty since the war, where in the northern wing her father had his dissecting room. She would go shyly, secretly. She would slip in through the cellar door within ten minutes of the afternoon lecture. No one saw her—she made sure of that. Her promptness mattered to her even so.

She always wore a freshly ironed dress, the green one, the blue one, the one with the ribboned perriot. She always brought with her an apple, a wedge of cheese, something to keep her so she could stay. She always walked New York's back streets, so as not to meet someone she knew. She hoped she didn't look furtive. She knew she looked un-obtrusive, small. Almost fourteen, she saw herself with an exaggerated, elongated clarity—the way girls are, that age, I've heard them in the confessional: whispering secrets as if they're sins, flooding the grille with self-conscious sighs, the smell of starch and sneaked cigarettes. At that age she knew minutely how she looked: knew her large dark eyes, her pointy French-boned face; knew how to make it dimple in the glass, flirt the lashes like a fan—how to make it a pretty face. But on the street, on the way to the laboratory, she kept her face sober and her eyes down. So she had been taught—*de-porte-ment*, *demoiselles*—but more because she dreaded being noticed, questioned, stopped. She had to be there by ten past three.

King Street to Williams: she walked through a low canyonless city clustered on the island's tip, its narrow streets twining in from the harbor; Williams to Dutch, she walked, skirts held back from the splash of wide-spoked wheels, skirts jerked back from the snouts of rooting pigs; Dutch to Fair, she walked, skirts brushing flowers that frilled through a fence, parsnips thumbing up through the earth; Fair to Nassau, she walked, cool air hurrying her on, air that smelled of water and tar and by a printer's window suddenly, sharply, of ink.

Behind her, like roofless black rooms, lay a scattering of charred foundations from the great fire of '76, when the British took the city; she heard, fading now as she moved on, the rasp and din of rebuilding. Ahead of her on Nassau Street, a pair of boys spun by with hoops, red circles slicing past the breeches of a sawyer, the gingham of a slave, the hogsheads of the Tea Water men. Up Great Georges the hoops streaked on, she in their wake, beneath the creaking Sign of the Three Biscuits, between vendors of baked pears and vendors of beach sand, *for floors! lily white!*—past the squat gray prison and the bright red gallows, and at last, rolling fast and free, careening into a knot of boys playing cricket in the Old Negroes' Burying Ground. At the burying ground she knew she was almost there; she quickened her step, averting her eyes from the tumbledown graves. From here and from the potter's field, it was rumored, her father, nightly, stole his supply of illicit cadavers. She did not believe this. She did not want to believe this. She turned away and hurried on toward the laboratory.

Across the grass.

Down the three stone steps.

In through the cellar door with the rusting latch.

She stepped inside and felt the place arch over her, shading her, branching all about her like an ancient tree, reaching off into limblike corridors, its corners and cupboards nestled like knotholes above her head. She climbed up into it; the stairs creaked softly beneath her feet.

Up past the stretchers: she wasn't afraid.

Up past the locked room: she wasn't afraid.

Up past the dead-room: she wasn't afraid, mustn't be, wouldn't be; wasn't.

The dim upper hallway, though plastered, gave the effect of being blue: the peeling walls seemed to shed blue shadows, the pine floorboards awash in perpetual twilight. She seemed to remember her mother carrying her down a hallway like this—old house, dark wainscoting, scent of coffee. She seemed to remember that house radiating out from her mother, from her skirts, her arms.

Here in this hall she could stay unseen, smelling lye soap and laudanum, listening to the building's amiable sighs and shifts and occasionally the bright ring of metal. It was all right to stay, she told herself, because this was a kind of hospital. It was all right to stay because this was a kind of school. It was all right to stay, above all, because this was her father's place, more truly the home of Dr. Richard Bayley than the five-chimneyed house on King Street.

"Observe, gentlemen, as I incise the skin . . . the adipose tissue . . . the muscles . . . the ligaments . . . and now, separating the head of the humerus from the glenoid fossa of the scapula . . ."

His voice floated into the hall from the laboratory and, suddenly elated, filled with warmth, she moved nearer the door. She could be close to him here, coming like this; this was the only way she could be.

"And now, ligating the arteries, the veins . . . observe as I continue to suture . . ."

She imagined him there, tall before the class, his lean frame poised by the table, dark head bent. She imagined his face in profile, his eyes not cold now but lit with the excitement of his lesson. She imagined the class rapt, those quick-mouthed young men and their loud feet, stilled by him. He was the sort of teacher who could hold a class on the hottest day. His scalpel wandlike in the air, he cast a spell upon the room; this she had seen through a crack in the door. He could inspire—he could scald. His voice, she knew, could sear like acid. Even so. Even so she wished to be one of them, his students; wished to be the bright one, the best one, the one relied upon for right answers.

". . . and so achieving hemostasis."

The long clever fingers. The dry ironic voice. The elegance of him. He was the first doctor in town to make house calls by carriage, an innovation all his own. She knew he had a fashionable practice—the very best people sent their servants running for him, often in the middle of the night. She had seen them herself, the footmen still in nightcaps pounding on the door, their lanterns glowing with the crests of Livingstons and Jays. She had seen her father, alert and combed, moving swiftly to the door, bag in hand. He never saw her watching. He'd leave a scent of lime cologne and leather on the air.

". . . and who can name these off—you, sir, now, then . . ."

They scrambled to answer him. She knew, she had been told, his credentials were impressive: his mentor the great Dr. Hunter of London, his partner the noted Dr. Charlton of New York. He had performed the first successful amputation of an arm at the shoulder, he had detailed the course of croup—who wouldn't scramble to answer him? Even the mutterings in certain quarters against his experiments, even those rumblings were respectful enough. *Tremendous dedication*, people said; the staunchest patriots overlooked his wartime commission to the king's troops. He was often in the laboratory till midnight, he was off with his bag before breakfast. *Tremendous dedication*, everyone said, when he was absent on her birthday. *Tremendous dedication; you should be proud.*

"I must say, gentlemen, the ball-and-socket joint is a masterpiece of design. . . ."

Listening now, she felt rich, rewarded, a piercing sense of pride within her. His voice, clear and honed, hung beside her in the hall like a silver-handled knife, a treasure she had summoned. His voice was always level, finely edged. She had never heard him shout, seen him unshaven, touched his cheek. Once, peering through the banisters at a supper-dance at home, she saw him in a flowered waistcoat, offering on the tines of his fork a love apple to a red-haired lady. Elizabeth recalled the sound of his laughter. She recalled how she had longed for his eyes to fall on her and light. They seldom did. At home. At her. She wasn't certain when she had last talked with him alone. Was it Christmas, when he gave her the earrings? Was it really then? Or was that moment something her mind had conjured, decorated the day with, devised solely for her comfort on a hundred nights since?

". . . our intent, gentlemen, insofar as we can, is to alleviate suffering. . . ."

Here it didn't matter. Here he was hers. In this secret communion with his voice, she felt connected to him as she did at no other time. In this hall his voice was warm, not distant, the way it was when he looked up from his books to find her at his study door—this girlchild he scarcely knew, what could he possibly have to say to her? In this hall she could recall and savor another evening, another supper party. That time she had again crept downstairs, crept close. That time he had seen her, a child of seven in a ribboned nightgown; and that one time he had held out his hand. She remembered the flourish, the lace at his sleeve. She remembered the chuckles of the guests, the glint of candlelight on silver. And she remembered the tinkle of the spinet as, light and graceful on his feet, he had danced with her a few steps of a schottische. Her hands in his were light; she seemed to float before him. The walls of the room, in that moment, were the color of claret wine.

Now, in the hallway, floating on the rhythm of his words, she had that moment back again. Here everything had that shine to it, stairs and sills and a shop across the street, its stepped Dutch gable shelved with amber afternoon light. From a window she heard the rattle of carriages and buskets and carts, she heard vendors call *fresh clams* and *tea rusk* and she was within it, she was a part of it, a part of this laboratory, this setting for her father and his words. Here she belonged, here in this place she knew as a watchman knows a warehouse: knew it front stairs and back, knew where the shadows lay deepest, where the sun would fall when—and by the sun she knew when at last it was time for her to leave.

Often on her way home an unbearable fatigue would slow her steps, a sense of despair settling upon her. Then she would tremble, feeling herself unmoored, drifting out across the city and the dimming sky with no one to anchor her. But no matter how she trembled, leaving it, she never felt that way the next day, back at the laboratory.

The day of the riot, the hallway was different.

The sounds were different.

There was a dense stillness outside, no calls of vendors, no voices at all; just the street's clatter and a hum, an indefinable murmur at the building's north side—the point where people mostly gathered. She had seen them there when she'd come in: a small crowd, silent. She hadn't paid much mind; she knew her father didn't. There were always people hanging about outside the laboratory: the curious, the idle, the ones who sometimes protested the dissections. There would always be people of that sort about, she'd heard her father say to his class: ignorance, you know—shall we turn to our lesson? And so that day, she'd simply brushed by them. It was only later that she remembered the sounds had been different.

The sounds of the students were different as well.

Down the hall she heard them, raucous, rough—her father must be late, they'd never hoot like that otherwise. Alert, anxious, she edged nearer the laboratory, listening for his voice, for the familiar orderly rhythm of the afternoon. The sound of muffled laughter rose from the room, overflowing it, foaming out into the hall: laughter so compelling and conspiratorial she couldn't hold back—she had to look in through the door.

It opened before her, this laboratory she had seen so often in her mind: a slice of floorboard, a streak of sunlight—the rows of tables with their sheeted forms, dusted with sawdust and slivers of melting ice. She saw a knot of students by the window, their white shirts pressed together like the fingers of a glove. They clustered around a classmate—a thin boy, bespectacled, red-faced, who was flung over a chair; for an instant Elizabeth thought he might be ill. And then she heard the malice in the laughter; then she saw what was being raised above the boy, beaten against his upturned rump.

It was an arm; a man's arm.

It was severed at the shoulder. The flesh was pale and faintly freckled. Brown hairs bristled from wrist to elbow, the elbow slightly bent. The shoulder erupted in a tangle of bloody sinew. The hand, tallow-colored, spanked the boy. It jabbed him, it goosed him until, with a yell, he broke free and bolted from the room; he brushed past Elizabeth and plunged down the stairs. Rocking with laughter, the boys wrenched open a casement, crowing as they spotted their victim below. "Hoo, Timmy, look *here*—your mama's arm that *spanked* you, Timmy . . . your mama, your *mama*." The arm, its pulpy tissue dangling, was thrust like an oar from the window.

Something sour rose in Elizabeth's throat. The place blurred, faded into a reddish mesh before her eyes. Stumbling backward, her fist at her mouth, she groped for the old dim safety of the hall. She reached it as the first bricks crashed through the windows. The sound of smashing glass filled the room; shouts rose from the street. Another hail of bricks. *Butchers!* Glass sprayed like water; the students pounded toward the door. *Grave robbers!* For a moment Elizabeth stood frozen. "Oh, Papa," she called in a whisper; then, spinning around, she ran down the hall.

Down the corridors, the shortcut passage, groping for the stairs, she ran, knowing as she did that she would never come here again; a hundred half-ripe afternoons lay tumbled behind her. Down the steps, knees trembling, out through the cellar, she skirted the mob, *oh Papa Papa*. Down Great Georges Street, kicking up mud, scattering pigs, she ran, the gabled houses slanting toward her; pushing past sedan chairs, past vendors' carts, into the Broad Way she ran, her shoes clattering on cobblestones now, and still she ran, the brownstones of St. Paul's Chapel soaring up, the white walls of the City Tavern flashing by, and now the burnt wrecked walls of Trinity Church ahead, and one more turn, and one more block, and sides aching, breathing ragged, she streaked down King Street and pulled open the door to her father's house.

The hall was still. Her father wasn't there: delayed on calls, the servants said. Above her head Elizabeth heard, just faintly, the voice of her stepmother scolding a child. The clock in the parlor chimed the quarter-hour. Her eyes fell on the pale lid of an enameled snuffbox, on oval miniatures in ivory, the silver tankard on the mantel. The house was cool, unmoved by her terror. The cedarwood secretary, the China-trade porcelains sat silent, disapproving of the wildness she had brought into the room. But what if her father went to the laboratory, what if he walked into that mob? She turned to the window, feeling her dress cling damply to her back. She fixed her eyes on the street, willing his tall figure to appear there, safe, unharmed, on his way home.

I can see her waiting in that elegant house—a small girl, tragic-eyed, she seems so vulnerable to me. Makes me think of someone I'd find waiting in a rectory parlor, one of those sad young people who come asking for "a priest." And what would I tell her—join the CYO? A week later she'd be back. Just to talk. Still lonely.

Bothersome: that image of her, vulnerable, turning to one of us for help. With saints you want it vice versa. But there she is, this girl staring out at me from that April evening of 1788, gazing from a ragged postwar city torn again by the "Doctors' Riot." There she is, dreamy daughter of a man of science, the eminent and chilly Richard Bayley: curt, correct specialist in surgery and causology of croup, with his British training, society following, Tory leanings, professional dedication, and chronic domestic neglect. A man who would not have my sympathy even in a counseling situation.

But she, this daughter—she would have gone to bed that night and not to sleep; not until she heard his voice in the hall, his step on the stair. She would have heard his study door click, locked; then she would have drifted off at last, thinking how she would tell him all that had happened. That night she went to sleep feeling safe; and waked at four, jarred, alert, feeling suddenly unsafe once more.

She waked to the unearthly glare of torchlight.

Below the window it streamed and smoked, orange, luminous, misplaced sunset colors rippling on the dark. Rising around it like a whine, like a hiss, was a wordless hum, and then there came that chant again: *"Grave robber, body snatcher"*—the voices flamed with the torches on the dark.

Elizabeth sat straight up, beaded in sweat. Her eyes moved about her room, all of it aflicker in that eerie light: the chest of drawers with its pitcher and bowl, the mirror blazing now above; her bonnet streaming ribbons from its peg, the bed's canopy arching riblike over her. *Go back to sleep*, she thought. Go back to sleep and it won't be real. "Go back to sleep," she whispered aloud, knowing she could not. She rose and lit the lamp, edging toward the window— saw the torches, saw the crowd, realized that this was not the shredding of some dream. It was the mob from the laboratory milling downtown, not yet satisfied—instantly she knew its chant, its rhythm. Her one thought was to find her father—just to know he was in the house. Her shawl around her, she clicked her door open and ran down the stairs.

Below, hall and parlor were dark. The shutters were closed. Her low-wicked lamp at familiar objects, turning them strange: a chair's clawed foot, a clock's sharp hand. Beyond them the walls seemed to float, insubstantial as the darkness itself. She moved to the other end of the house. A thread of light showed beneath the door to her father's study. He was there, he was awake. In just a moment she could call him. In just a moment she could knock on his door. Not until she needed to, of course. Not unless she had to. But now the house seemed less permeable than before.

Emboldened by his light, she pulled a hallway shutter ajar. Immediately the sound of the mob heightened; she could feel the weight of it pressing in upon her. In its midst, a face jerked forward on a pole: a lewd face, artlessly evil, drawn on a feed bag and joined to a doctor's blood-spattered white coat—and beneath it, shifting, swaying, fists and faces massed together, faces bright and stern and

~ 16 ~

thrilled. The torchlight rippled over them like water, turning eyes to sockets, mouths to gashes: nightmare faces. She suddenly remembered her cousins pulling down a bird's nest in the garden, smashing eggs almost ready to hatch. She recalled gathering the broken shells on a leaf, watching the innards palpitate. After that she had played alone.

A brick glanced off the wall. She banged the shutter closed. Pay no mind, she thought, as she did when passing rough boys on the street. The constables were there, she had seen them, *pay no mind*. Her knees felt watery even so; her palms were damp. She started toward the study, feeling a tremor of anger—anger at that door like a turned back. Instantly ashamed of herself, she stood by the door, making the anger recede. She leaned closer, listening. All she could hear was the steady scratching of his quill.

He would be sitting there at his cedarwood secretary, his books and papers arranged before him; nothing crumpled, nothing awry, ink pot and sandcaster set just so, side by side, filled just so, just so high. His desk would have the look of a tea table set by an exacting butler. His face would have the remoteness of someone gazing from a coach window. She thought of his face, the fine straight nose, the surprisingly impish cleft in the chin. It was a face that seemed crafted, carved from some strong stone; carved with the same precision he used to whittle sticks into small neat skulls. Whenever he had to wait, he whittled, he sketched, made notes; time was not for squandering. She thought of him suspended in the lamplight, outside time, tireless. He never seemed to sleep. He seemed beyond the common human things of life. It was inconceivable to her that he, like everyone else, was invisibly connected to a bed that knew the impress of his body, to a razor that knew the nap of his beard; to soap, slops, laundry. Did he appear this way to others—or was it only her? Lately she had seen the chill formality between him and her needle-voiced stepmother. Perhaps it was true: none of them was good enough for him.

Now she heard him murmur to himself as he wrote, two brief words she couldn't quite make out: *Ah, there . . . ? I swear . . . ?* And then a dry private chuckle. She thought of him smiling at her as they danced. She thought of the scent of his lime cologne, the paper-white rims of his nails. She raised her hand to knock. She would say . . . she would say: Papa, I couldn't sleep. . . . She would say: Papa, I'm scared. . . . She would say . . .

Her hand stayed suspended above the wooden panels of the door. She thought of how she'd gone into his study once when she was four, five; she had stood on a chair examining everything on his blotter. The magnifying glass. The penknife, the quills. The flat bright stones that hugged the hand and weighted his papers. She had gazed, she had sniffed; she had not touched. A speechless wonder had slowly filled her. And then she had felt the grip of two strong hands, tight and untender, around her waist. Without a word she was sped through the air and set down outside the door. His swiftness, his absolute silence had shown the force of his fury. The door had shut. She had stood weeping where she was now, out in the hallway.

Her hand drifted away from the door. She became aware of herself standing there, spilling lamp oil on the floor. *Good Lord*, he'd say if he could see her, *use your time, child, use your mind.* Her time, her mind. Her mind was filled with smoke. *Your mind, work it like a muscle.* Obediently she groped for some constructive thought: her mind produced its store of French verbs. She was good at them, she had an ear for languages. *Je pense, tu penses* . . . The house was stirring overhead. *Il pense.* A child cried, the baby wailed; her stepmother's heavy tread sounded above. *Nous pensons* . . . From the servants' quarters there were steps, clinks, whispers. *Vous pensez, ils pensent.* Behind her now: soft footfalls, a rustle. Her sister Mary appeared in the hall, her nightgown a blur in the low lamplight.

"No use trying to sleep," she said, her voice matter-of-fact. She followed Elizabeth's eyes to the study door. "He won't come out, you know."

Solid Mary with her square face and straight hair and strong workmanlike hands: a settled-looking girl with a compact figure that seemed rooted in the earth, matronly at eighteen. She did not expect things of their father—open doors, interested questions. She would not pine for him. She saw things unadorned, as they were. Elizabeth knew her sister sometimes found her flighty, fanciful; Mary's annoyed affection had been a constant in her life since she could recall, quickening the hands that had buttoned her shoes and smoothed her hair. Elizabeth, by contrast, sometimes felt impatient with this placid companion, this saver of scraps, methodical folder of Christmas wrappings. But now, as Elizabeth rattled off what she had seen, Mary seemed like a good oak table, one she could lean on, lie down on if necessary: firmly pedestaled, broad-backed, ultimately generous and serviceable.

"Mary *Mary*—"

"Ssh-sshh . . . Eliza! You feel things too much."

"I do *not*."

"Listen . . . the high constable's there, I saw him."

"But still—"

"Sshh, now—don't be scared."

Don't be scared. How many times she had heard Mary say that; how many times in all the houses they had lived in together. How many years it had been: soon after their father's remarriage, when Elizabeth was five, the pattern had been set. They had gone from relative to relative, house to house: a few months with an uncle, with a grandmother, back to their father's, and off again. All those carriages they had sat in. All those back bedrooms they had shared. Those bedrooms: she could smell them, that musty attic smell, that mix of starch and talcum. Their two bonnets on the bed, ribbons dangling. Their two heads at the window, gazing out. Their backs spine to spine in bed at night like two arms in a sleeve. So often she would wake clinging to Mary and Mary would smooth her hair and whisper: *Don't be scared.* By now she should have been used to it. By now Mary's voice should have brought peace.

In the mirror Elizabeth saw her face, a frightened white silver, the dark eyes enormous. Her mother's eyes: so they said. She stood there held by her own gaze, her white gown, the lamp. She thought she remembered her mother standing like that, white gown, smell of lamp oil—in the old house, the dim house, a house that had creaked like a comfortable chair. *Yes, my bonny.* Her mother stooping down to pick her up, silken sleeves against her skin. *Carried you mercy how you cried.* Yellow lamplight, white-white gown. *Cried the night the British came, carried you in my arms.* Bright thin voice, dark hair streaming long and loose. *Cried . . . I carried yes my bonny . . . night we'll all remember.* She could not remember it. She had been two years old. She had been told about that night, about her mother, by the servants; she knew she'd made the images fit their words. She wished she could remember more—more than crawling toward a white skirt on a stretch of sunny grass; more than strawberries held out to her on long pale fingers, soft laughter above. *Yes, my bonny.* Oh Mama. A rustle, a giggle; nothing more. Elizabeth looked away from the mirror.

"I wish . . . Papa . . ." she began, her voice full of cracks.

"Papa's right here." Mary's voice was calm.

"But he's not, not really. . . . Mary, don't you ever wish he'd be . . . he'd be . . ."

"No . . . not so much . . . not anymore."

They sat in silence, Elizabeth leaning against her sister's knees, Mary idly braiding a wisp of her hair.

"The laboratory . . . ?" Elizabeth began again.

"Wrecked," said Mary, flat.

"What'll he do, then?" She knew as she asked.

"I heard them talking." Mary frowned at a knot in Elizabeth's hair. Upstairs Charlotte Bayley's voice sang a tuneless lullaby; the sound of the cradle's rockers seemed to crease the ceiling. For a moment they could picture her above them: the foxlike face, the hemp-colored hair up in a knot, the dark blue eyes that knifed so openly at them. Mary jerked her head upward. "She wants us out—go-one." She could not keep the word from splitting open like a seam. "She'll have her way. Again. And Papa will go off again. London, he said. And we . . . maybe we'll go to Uncle Will's again. Or Grandam's. Maybe New Rochelle . . . maybe Staten Island . . . maybe—"

"Oh, *Mary.*"

"Sshh-sshh."

"I *can't*—"

"Eliza, Eliza, we've done it before."

Elizabeth thought of their uncle's big house in New

Rochelle, its wide lawn overlooking the water. That had been mostly all right; still, they'd known they hadn't really belonged. It had been mostly all right at Madame Pompelion's, too, the young ladies' school they'd gone to here in town. She could see it: the whitewashed classroom, the low pine desks. She could see herself there with Mary: two girls hesitating in a doorway, hand in hand. She remembered the tinkle of the piano there, Madame's fast French voice, *Alors, un et deux et vite vite*: dancing class, spinning Mary around till she was giddy. Madame Pompelion's: it had been all right there, but they were too old for it now.

She thought of packing the trunk again.

She thought of the forced bright good-byes.

She thought of the children who pointed at them, calling them orphans. And that lost, rootless feeling that came over her, with nausea, in the nights. And that moment waking in the mornings when she couldn't remember where she was. This was starting to sink her, pulling her down past the fear into the old melancholy. She felt herself draining away, disappearing into the dark at the end of the stairs, and as if for salvation she fixed her eyes on her sister's face.

Mary saw Elizabeth's eyes, the slump of her shoulders, the crouch of her back. She moved closer, her voice low and strong, beginning again the story she had told them so many times.

"Now, Eliza . . . one fine day we'll have our house . . . and the house will be made of rock. . . . And the roof will be made of slate. . . . And the house won't burn, won't fall down, won't change ever. . . ."

". . . ever, and we'll stay there always." Elizabeth picked up the thread.

"And we'll wake up there and go to sleep there . . ."

"And we'll hear the night watch there, every night . . ."

". . . every night: 'All's well . . .' "

" 'All's well. . . .' "

" '. . . All's well. . . .' "

They learned together, the sisters on the stairs in the dark, lulled by the rhythm of their voices, while the mob wailed outside like a storm. Slowly, softly, sleepy at last, they climbed the steps and, sitting up in Mary's bed, they drowsed and waked and said their prayers, and heard as if from a distance the crack of gunfire, a spreading silence, and dimly, dimly, the sound of a carriage starting away.

When Elizabeth waked again, it was full daylight. Sun lay on her face. She was back in her own bed, alone. The mob had dispersed. Mary had dressed. And their father had gone.

3

"*F*ather of us all" read the motto, spelled in buttons and worsted thread and hung above the shop of Huyser the tailor. "FATHER OF OUR COUNTRY" read another, baked on a pudding and written in sugar and set in the window of the baker next door. Up the length of Queen Street she could see the mottoes, and the murmur in the street rose like steam around them and the murmur rose toward her. The waiting crowd was wedged so tight, she thought you could cross the street on people's heads. Elizabeth was standing just above them in the storefront window of a musical instrument maker, with seven other people and a red bass drum and nine gleaming fifes—standing under flags and flowers to welcome George Washington to New York for his inauguration week.

Whenever she thought of it later, that moment came back to her with an intense rush of noise—the many-threaded voice of the crowd and the pealing of bells and beating beneath them, the drums. She stood listening in the window, still amazed that she had been set down at the center of this hour—an hour that, yesterday, had been idle talk blowing across the lawn.

" 'His Mightiness!' "

Her Uncle Will had roared a laugh and slapped the tea tray, setting the cups to rattling. "Damn me! George Washington wants to be called 'His Mightiness.' "

"What should his wife be called, then?" Aunt Sarah had steadied the table.

" 'Her Heftiness,' I'd say, from all reports."

A pattering of laughter greeted this, and a trilling of "Papa, you're too mean."

"Mean?" William Bayley pointed the sugar tongs at his heart. "Mean, my dears? I?" He dropped a cube of sugar onto his tongue and winked, a wink that took in all of them there on the lawn: wife, sons, daughters, and the two nieces seated at an end of the fan of chairs.

It was the first day mild enough to take their tea outdoors. From Elizabeth's cup rose a thin thread of spiced steam, mingling on the air with the smells of earth and blooming dogwood. On her plate was a muffin studded with raisins and running with butter. Against her hair, now and then, blew a flutter of snowlike petals from the trees; at her back was the safe, soft undertone of servants' voices. Long low afternoon light lay tawny on the grass, glowing on the heavy silver tea service, flashing from the spoon in her fingers, and behind her the house sprawled, loose-limbed and easy, like a great lanky squire in hunting clothes; casual, clapboard, many-roomed, shaggy-roofed, concealing its sparkling formality within. She could, on days like this, in light like this, convince herself that this was her house; she could convince herself that this was her dogwood tree, and this her teacup, this her lawn.

It was the house of her father's brother, built on land that had been in the family for over a century. Familiar house, familiar land; Elizabeth and Mary had often been sent here. This was their longest stay: just over a year now since their father had gone to London. Elizabeth watched the daffodils blowing by the path, wondering how a year could wheel so swiftly without him; without any word from him at all. She turned her mind away from him, back to the talk, but another voice was on the air now, piercing it, like a needle pulled through silk and suddenly into flesh. She had made herself forget that he was there, screening him out with the back of her hand—Wright Post, the young doctor lounging on the grass by Mary's chair. Lately he was there almost every afternoon.

" 'His Highness . . .' " he was saying. "Another title they've proposed, though Washington still favors 'His Mightiness.' Naturally Congress was appalled. . . ."

Nat-ur-alleh, Elizabeth mimicked to herself.

". . . Speaker Muhlenburg quite devilishly proposed 'His High and Mightiness.' "

"Hah! Perfect!" Her uncle slapped his thigh and spilled his tea. Elizabeth looked away from him; away from the young man's eager grin and Mary's shining face.

" 'President,' sir—that's all they'll hear of now."

"Dull! Flat as stale ale. These damned republicans! They've no sense of style, Post—no sense atall."

Elizabeth fixed her eyes on the lawn. Across its cropped expanse, like a bird attempting flight, a white napkin scudded and fluttered, dropped by a cousin gone to join a game of bowls. She fetched up the napkin, wishing to run with the boys, watching the flash of their pale shirts and hose. All these cousins were stocky like her uncle, ruddy-faced and blunt-featured—as if the Bayleys of England had appeared in these children, this father; the LeContes of France had materialized only in her, and in the father who was absent. Elizabeth fixed her eyes on her cousins. There was a triumphant clatter of ninepins. Post's voice rebounded from it like a well-tossed ball.

". . . he arrives in the city tomorrow, should be in New Jersey tonight. The preparations, they're a bit overblown—they plan to fetch him into town on a curtained barge—"

"Barge! We've lost a king . . . and gained an emperor," her uncle roared again.

"—to be greeted by the governor, the entire Light Infantry, the Grenadiers, the—"

"Not an emperor—a pope!"

William Bayley leaned over the tea tray and tapped a pewter beaker chased with small figures. They all knew these figures—a mitered pope, a hoofed devil, a king. They all knew the verses etched beneath them: *Three mortal enemies, Remember—Devil, Pope, and Pretender.* Elizabeth smiled suddenly, recalling how they'd chanted these words as children, acting out the rhyme; recalling her cousin Joey pawing the ground as the Devil; Dick as the Pretender to the throne, and poor Johnny, the baby, forced to be Pope. A ripple of laughter came across the grass, everyone remembering now, and Bayley roared good-naturedly above it, "Not 'His Mightiness' . . . 'His *Holiness*,' tell *that* to your friends in Congress, Post."

The light on the lawn was shifting. The shoreline had blurred. In the lengthening shadows Elizabeth watched her sister's yellow dress, its skirts blowing as she walked with the tall young doctor. *Pompous*, Elizabeth threw at his broad back. *Posturing ass.* Farther away now, they leaned together. *Mary, Mary, you never talk to me anymore.*

The teacup felt bony and fragile in her hand. She could break it; no one would notice. She could disappear; no one would care. She saw herself as if from a distance, sitting on the rim of this family, half in, half out. Mary's solution to this, Elizabeth saw, was marriage. Her sister was nineteen, it wouldn't be long. And she, Elizabeth, would be left sitting on this family's edges, sitting alone—this family or another, it didn't much matter. Her eyes dropped again to her teacup. Drained of the will to break it, she wandered off across the grass, shoulders hunched, the sound of talk and birds and wheels on the road receding as the twilight deepened on the lawn.

"Your wigs, sir . . . *voilà*."

Elizabeth turned. That sting of a voice. She had listened for it all afternoon.

"I was in town, knew you'd want these fetched. The city's pandemonium; dressmakers, wigmakers—all frantic. See if these are right. Here, look."

There she stood, wig boxes open at her feet as if she'd somehow sprung from them—Madam Wit, they called her, cousin, spinster, lady, linguist: Miss Molly Besley, by some grace Elizabeth's particular friend. Miss Molly stood as straight as a teacher's rod, pewter-haired, anchored in her silken skirts, holding out a pair of powdered wigs on wooden forms; in the dusk she seemed to be presenting William Bayley with a pair of disembodied gentlemen. And then, the wigs approved, the greetings done, she was standing before Elizabeth, lifting her chin in one hand.

"Mooning again, Eliza, I see."

The words didn't scald; Elizabeth knew they weren't meant to. That voice, clipped and wise, cupped warmth in its center. Everything about Miss Molly was clipped, deft, precise: every gesture, every word. "Well," she said now, with one of her swift glances, "I hear happy reports of you." Another glance. "All the same. I wonder. Let's walk."

Her step had just begun to slow this year, her seventy-first, but it was still brisk enough, a step to keep pace with. Beside Elizabeth on the dimming lawn, she rustled, smelling of lemon sachet and French perfume and the peppermints she kept in her reticule. She had the finest clothes Elizabeth had ever seen: ruched bonnets, ruffled gowns, a parasol the color of a ripening pear—all worn with such grace she might have stepped from a family of dancers. In fact she was a cousin on the LeConte side, descended from rebellious Huguenots who had gone to the barricades, then to the West Indies, and finally to the colonies. Passionate Protestants, they'd named this town they'd founded for the Huguenot stronghold La Rochelle; here they had built their houses and printed their prayerbooks and handed them down to family brides. Miss Molly had not become one of those brides, though no one seemed to know why. Elizabeth had stopped wondering about it; had stopped wondering too by what luck Miss Molly had become her friend.

". . . pandemonium, as I said." Miss Molly tapped Elizabeth's sleeve. "Just as I like it. Lively. Exciting. Your uncle would hate it. The entire city's trimmed with that name: Washington-*Washington*-WASHINGTON."

And her low rich chuckle. When animated, pleased, her face would flush. Most of the cousins never saw that flush; she did not choose to share herself with everyone. She was particular, this sharp-tongued lady with her definite opinions and bone-true insights; she chose to be. In her elegant gowns and royal-blue coach, her prayerbooks fluttering colored ribbons, she stood out from this irreligious horse-and-dog-loving family. Glamorous, pious, she had an air so different as to be exotic, as if she lived somewhere abroad. Instead she lived in her own house with her own servants, raising roses and translating theological essays from the French. In her house, Elizabeth knew, there were always fresh flowers, and candied apricots, and ivory toothpicks. And treasures: Elizabeth had seen the prayerbook from Tours, the perfume from Paris, the sketch of the mulatto maid who knew voodoo. She had seen, in the third drawer of the mahogany secretary, a braid of honey-colored hair, tied with white ribbon and labeled in a girlish hand, "Molly, 1739." Visiting that house, Elizabeth had been allowed to open the books, try the perfume, and wear under her skirts a taffeta petticoat the color of a sunrise.

Now, walking on the lawn, Elizabeth suddenly wished she were wearing that petticoat. She wished she could hear it rustle and she wished she were back in that house— wished to be waking there tomorrow, watching her cousin, straight-backed at the breakfast table, crack their boiled eggs with a duelist's single swift stroke. She wished she were where she couldn't see Mary with her suitor. Far ahead, they were crossing the path: yellow dress, white shirt, drifting among the elms. A sense of loss flooded Elizabeth once more.

". . . have you heard a word I've said, my dear? You seem to be off in the stars." Miss Molly glanced toward the elms. "Or rather the trees." Then, seeing Elizabeth's miserable face, she spoke lower, her voice kind. "Never mind, Eliza. There are a hundred things to do without her. A hundred ways not to miss her, not to feel left."

They walked in silence awhile.

"I don't suppose you'd miss her tomorrow," Miss Molly said then. "If you and I were in the city. On Queen Street. In a window. Watching General Washington arrive."

She was right.

The next day in the city, on Queen Street, in the window, Elizabeth missed no one, pined for no one. Tory or not, uncle or not, all her thoughts were fixed on waiting for Washington's procession.

Their position was choice. Their view was clear. They had seen the cannon smoke rising over the gables. They had heard the quick thudding of the thirteen-gun salutes and they had smelled the smoke, strong and acrid, above the smell of the water two blocks away. Elizabeth imagined the barges drifting on the water like great canopied beds. She imagined the procession landing at Coffee House Slip, moving up the red-carpeted stairs at Murray's Wharf. Even now it was nearing, she could feel it; the crowd in the street could feel it too. There were people wedged onto steps, onto sills, on the roofs; many had been camped there the night before—a patchwork of ginghams and silks, lace and leather, mobcaps and cockades and wigs. Above them, from a roof, a boy had climbed onto a massive chimney. He gazed out as if from the rigging of a mast, one hand shading his eyes, his cocked hat pushed back on his head. Against the clouded afternoon sky he crouched like a cast-iron weathervane, rigid, still, holding Elizabeth's eyes south-southwest. All at once he swung around, as if the wind had shifted. Eyes narrowed, mouth wide, arm flung out, *They're coming*, he called, *They're coming.*

A tremor swept the crowd. Elizabeth heard the thump of the drums. *Coming!* the boy sang out from the chimney, his voice high and clear, *Coming now!* Flags had appeared. Turning in from Wall Street, taking the corner sharp, they spilled their colors onto the breeze, blooming there so suddenly a long *ahhh* rose from the crowd. *Coming O coming* caroled the boy, and now the drums were nearer, stronger, shaking the street, and now they could be seen, banded in red, strapped in white, swinging at the soldiers' hips, and the shiny voices of the fifes rose above them. *Here!* cried the boy, his voice cracking, *He's he-ere!* Behind the dragoons, behind the grenadiers, they could just make out the top of Washington's head: white hair, high brow, his hand slowly waving a light blue hat. They saw him through the tricorns and gun barrels of his men, saw him in fragments at first, a shoulder, an elbow, a slant of wide flat nose; taller, nearer, taller still, a rawboned frame in blue and buff.

Handkerchiefs flew. Hats waved. Flags tossed. As if with snow, as if with porridge, the air filled with the petals of a thousand daisies. The street roared with *huzzas*, with *God Saves*, with Washington's name, and pealing, pealing, the bells turned the mild afternoon hard and bright with their sound. Washington bowed to the left, to the right, doffing his hat, and then he was nearing their window—Elizabeth leaned out, Miss Molly's hands steadying her, and sent her handful of petals into the air. For an instant the general's gaze fell upon her. She saw the petals on the shoulders of his fine blue coat. She saw the sheen of sweat on his large flushed face, saw the startling wetness in his bovine eyes. He raised his hat to her. She raised her hand, and he passed on.

Behind him now marched aldermen, assemblymen, councilmen, and still the bells rang out, and still the crowd called *huzza* and in the window of the musical instrument maker, Miss Molly and Elizabeth called with them. "Tom . . ." Miss Molly tapped the shopowner's sleeve. "Got a flag for an old Tory?" A flag was produced, one of the miniatures made for the day; she took it in her blue-veined hand as precisely as one would pick a rose. In her hand it waved in time to the fifing, the drumming, the bells, and above it Elizabeth saw her cousin's face, rosy and misted and, in that moment, young.

It was twilight by the time the roads were passable, Washington in residence, the boy down from the chimney. A gentle drizzle had begun. Crowds of people surged softly around them in the streets, and as the darkness folded down, they saw the town transformed—illuminated. Every window of every house, every shop, was lit with lanterns, rush lamps, candles: light spilling onto steps and cobblestones, shining on the wet streets and glistening from the railings and catching in the spokes of carriage wheels—a city of flame and air, brighter than anything Elizabeth had ever seen. She wandered through it, awed, enchanted, and for some minutes she did not realize that Miss Molly was no longer beside her.

Their eyes taken from each other by the city, they had somehow wandered apart. Elizabeth, turning, realizing, had a sudden sense of something heavy tumbling through her, as down a steep flight of stairs. She pushed through the crush, her eyes picking over the faces, *not hers, not hers.* She had never been in these streets alone at night; she had seldom been out at night at all. She remembered that inner skidding she had felt once, long before, separated from a nursemaid in a marketplace, the stalls looming larger, infinite, the moment she realized she was lost.

She pushed on. The street seemed steep. The city winked at her, leered at her, its glow suddenly garish. She wouldn't be able to find Miss Molly; not in this crowd, not tonight. She wouldn't be able to find the carriage, find her way home. The walls beside her seemed to slant, to lean. She remembered how they had blurred, that day of the riot. She thought of that other crowd, its faces, its shouts. She felt this one closing around her. For a moment she could not breathe.

She studied a sign, a wall. She let them gain bulk and substance again. There was the wigmaker's shop, there the John Street Theater; there the brownstone quoins of St. Paul's Chapel. She paused at the chapel's gate. She and Miss Molly always stopped here when they visited the city; it was a ritual with them. Wherever they had been, at the museum or the waxworks or the shops, they would come here for a half-hour's quiet on the way home. Since Miss Molly's shift from Reformed Church to Episcopal years before, this chapel had been her favorite. Perhaps she would come here tonight, just to sit down, to get her bearings. Elizabeth put her hand on the gate. Perhaps if she just waited here . . . She walked past the gravestones and opened the door.

The church was bright and still and empty, except for the snores of a tramp asleep in a pew. The ceiling, painted pale blue, and the walls, painted pale pink, made the place seem a great elegant nursery. Its clear-paned windows were backed by the darkness now, giving them a staring look; otherwise everything seemed the same as always, spare and trim—the Ten Commandments over the altar, the large gilded bookstand in the narthex. The stand, in the shape of a spread-winged eagle, held a blank-paged book inscribed with personal prayers; Elizabeth stood before it now as she and Miss Molly often did.

"For G. W.," someone had scribbled there, "Long may he reign." After a moment she took up the quill and scratched onto the page, "For M. B., that she be safe." After a long hesitation she added, "For E. B., that she be found." Then she turned and seated herself in a pew, waiting for the tick of her panic to slow.

She had waited this out before. She had felt this lost before, within the borders of sheltering houses; new houses. She remembered feeling this way that first time at her uncle's, so many years before. Her father had just remarried; her baby sister Kitty had just died, and Elizabeth had been unable to stop seeing that small coffin in her mind. She had seen it across the supper table and under the bed, seen it through plates and kettles and quilts until, whimpering into the nearest silken skirt, she had told Miss Molly.

They had been at the linen cupboard, she remembered. They were facing rows of calm white sheets, stacked before them like the pages of a book. *Where is she where is she*, Elizabeth had wailed, and Miss Molly had knelt there, lifting her chin in one hand. *Where's Kitty where's Mama*, the the wailing had risen, and Miss Molly had sat her in the window seat by the cupboard, showing her the clouds. Had she used the word "heaven"? Elizabeth could not remember. All she could remember was the smell of starched linen and the sight of those clouds and the nearness of this woman who seemed to make them appear at the end of her pointing finger. After that Elizabeth had looked for her mother and sister in the clouds, in morning skies and sunsets. And after that she hadn't felt so lost.

Now in St. Paul's, she found her eyes straying to the dark windows for that old childish comfort. She glanced at the hourglass on the pulpit, its sands run. What time was it? How long had she been here? Above her a chandelier swayed on a current of air; the tramp, cursing softly, shuffled out. She felt a fingering of fear at the back of her neck. She was here alone. She might have to sleep here alone. The goodness of the day had drained from her; her mind felt permeable as a sieve. Images floated through it, dark and old. The laboratory. Dim hallway. Sheeted cadavers. Pine coffin, Kitty's. . . . Elizabeth jerked her head up. With an effort she made other images come. Miss Molly's house. Roses. Prayerbooks. Silk. Yards and yards of it, December, afternoon light. The afternoon of the dressmaker, the fire.

That afternoon she had visited Miss Molly and found her being fitted for a gown. The room had foamed with lace, floated with satin and silk, and her cousin had stood at its center, draped in cloth the color of plums. The air had been filled with the quick snip of shears and the sharp high voice of the French dressmaker. The dressmaker's hair, in a tight knot on her head, bobbed puppetlike beside the skirt of the gown. Pins gleamed from the cushion on her wrist. Her words rushed out in a *patois* so rapid Elizabeth could not understand it; it was only the chuckling of the two women that indicated the subject was amusing.

When the dressmaker had gone, leaving the gown on a form by the hearth, Miss Molly's maid Giselle brought in the tea tray. "Appalling, how much time that takes." Miss Molly poked the form where ribs would be. "Even so, I delight in Mamselle's stories."

"Gossip?" Elizabeth hoped to hear it.

"Parables. Allegories, marvelous, the nuns taught them to her long ago."

"You *laugh* at them?"

"Certainly, they're meant to be enjoyed—here, try this tart, almond paste, lovely.

Elizabeth remembered that feeling of safety she'd had; the clink of spoons, the scent of tea, the bedroom dimming softly in the winter dusk. It was candle-lighting time. It was the hour of closing shutters, drawing blinds, of homecoming. Elizabeth remembered that she had her mouth full of almond paste, that moment they first smelled the smoke.

Looking up, they saw the plum-colored gown, left too near the hearth, take flame. As they stared, the skirt became a blazing ball, the sleeves transfigured, and in a sudden magical leap the whole gown, retaining its cut and lines, turned a breathing orange, as if for a moment it had sprung alive.

Without a sound or pause Miss Molly had dodged forward, surprisingly swift and agile, throwing a quilt over the gown and beating it with a poker—Elizabeth would always remember the sight of her, panting, striking, slugging, pummeling the dress form like an attacker. The fire had jumped, sprouting like brilliant weeds from a dropped handkerchief, the rug itself—Elizabeth stamped on them before they could reach the bed hangings. The flames out at last, she and Miss Molly gasped, staring around at the ruined dress, the blackened walls, the smoking rug. Their eyes ran; they leaned together, coughing as a dark sharp smell rose around them.

It was only then that Elizabeth noticed her cousin was trembling, as if in a strong wind. Miss Molly pressed her hands together to stop them shaking; she could not stop them. She stared at her hands as if they astonished her; then she crossed to the corner where her prie-dieu faced a simple cross. Offering no explanation, no excuse, she knelt there, letting herself down with a convulsive motion—nearly the same motion Elizabeth had seen from a woman who, having trudged miles to her father's surgery, had thrown herself down by his door. Now Elizabeth was alarmed to see this; to see her cousin's hands clasping and unclasping, as if to get a grip on prayer. Miss Molly looked aged; she looked weak. The burns on her dressing gown gave her a tattered appearance, wholly unlike her. Her lips continued to move. Slowly, almost imperceptibly, her face began to smooth out. The angle of her spine shifted. Her hands came to rest. It seemed that she was gradually casting around her a circle of steadiness, tangible as the hem of a skirt. The circle widened. It appeared to Elizabeth that Miss Molly was somehow effecting a change on the room, stilling it as she had stilled herself. Drawn to her cousin, Elizabeth moved toward the prie-dieu. She knelt there—then drew back, fearing she had trespassed. Miss Molly's lips went on moving. Her eyes remained closed. Her arm came around Elizabeth's shoulders.

Alone now on the kneeler in St. Paul's, Elizabeth sighed. She was unable to summon that feeling alone. She rose from her knees, sat back in the pew, pushing her hair off her forehead. Tears were building behind her eyes. Exhausted by the effort to be brave, she curled up in the pew; numbed, she sank into a half-sleep. And then a series of sharp steps bit the floor. A hand was on her arm. "Thank God," Miss Molly said. "I hoped you'd think to come here."

At the sound of her voice, Elizabeth was reaching for her. Miss Molly leaned over, and as she had done by the linen cupboard years before, tipped her face up in one hand.

"Home, let me . . . come home with you," Elizabeth wept. "Let me, I'll help, I'll . . ." A rush of tears blurred her words.

"How I'd like that," Miss Molly said after a moment. "A joy for me. But not right for you, my dear. Not really."

"It *would*."

"Eliza, I'm old. Yes, old: look. And soon, I think, you'd be my nurse. And by the time I got round to dying, life would have left you beached. It happened that way to me, nursing my mother. I won't see it happen to you."

"But you . . . you're the only one, the one I have . . . I haven't . . . anyone else, Mary, she'll get married . . . Papa, he . . . he doesn't care . . . for me. . . ." Her face streamed.

"You mustn't keep grieving over that, Eliza." Miss Molly's voice was kind; her hand smoothed Elizabeth's hair. "Make no mistake, I'd have a thing or two to tell your sainted father. *If* he'd materialize. But keep remembering, he's not the only father you have."

"*What?*"

"Self-pity's dangerous, darling girl; it sours the mind. If your father doesn't care for you—let God be your father. Turn that way. Take comfort in that."

Elizabeth shook her head. "It's not the *same*."

"No. It's quite different." Miss Molly put out her hand, thumbing tears off Elizabeth's cheeks with the swiftness of a boy killing ants. "Eliza, I think you must go back to your uncle's. And to wayfaring. There must be a lesson in it for you—though I fail to see just what it is. Providence can be maddeningly obscure. Still. I don't suppose it would spoil you to come home with me for a night or two. Would it."

She rose, moving to the eagle-winged prayerbook. The quill scratched. Her glance touched her cousin. That one's for me, Elizabeth thought. She's writing that one for me.

It was only a reprieve. She knew that. It was only a respite. She knew that. She knew it was only a day and a night and a day, but Elizabeth moved through that next morning with the lift of a convalescent rising from a sickbed.

Miss Molly was resting. Elizabeth was striding across her

lawn. Her mind raced. Her pulse raced. The air smelled of dew and biscuits, and something within her stirred, noting this morning as rare, never to come again. She saw everything—trees, fenceposts, gravel—so clearly she felt their outlines. She heard every sound—birds, scythes, breeze—as new. Following the lawn's slope to the shore, she saw, like cuttings of paper, a scattering of sails on the water, and nearer, a man in a dinghy with a long frayed rope on his shoulder, its threads leaping like a lit wick in the sun. The sight of these things filled her with a wordless rush of feeling. *Girls your age*, her aunt would have said; *the moon*. But it wasn't her age, it wasn't the moon. It was simply being here.

Elizabeth glanced back at the low wooden gate to the meadow. On other days she had read Milton there; today her mind would not hold still to read. Her skirts hitched up around her knees, she ran just to run, streaking up the shoreline and a steep rise of land. Below her she saw a cart lumbering out onto the road and she was running again, running toward it, wanting to ride, to move; she didn't care where.

The driver nodded at her as she hoisted herself onto the cart. Jacko, they called him, the hostler's son: a few years older than she, he was a gentle boy with a round moon face and wide light eyes. Some childhood illness had robbed him of both hair and speech; his head was smooth, his silence hung about him like mist. She had ridden with him other times out to the clearing where he cut brush; she always felt easy with him, thinking of him as a misfit like her.

The clearing was nearby, light-striped, familiar. As Jacko began to chop at the brush, she sat with her back against a tree, a bed of sun-warmed moss beneath her. Head tilted, she looked through the branches at the sky. Its depth of blue seemed to pull her toward it. She could dive into it. She could swim in it. She could see unspooling against it yesterday's procession: a pattern of cocked hats and glinting buttons. Her eyes half-closing in the sun, she let the reds and blues roll past, faster, blurring. She felt herself drifting, light and loose, above the clearing, beyond Jacko, beyond her own body. The clearing dwindled; the water spread beneath her. She was wind, she swept and streamed, and below her now was the illuminated city. She dipped lower. From this height, surely, she would be able to see her father. But as she watched, the lights of the city glimmered out. Now it was a skeletal city, a city of bone and fire-ash. She heard the beat of muffled drums. She saw in the pale street a slow procession. A man walked at its head, a tall shadow of a man, and *Father!* the gray voices called, *Hail! Papa!* she called; she could not let him go, could not renounce him yet. She had flowers to give him. He would see them, he would smile. She leaned toward him. His face, featureless and dark, brushed her like a moth's dry wings. She opened her hands before him. Ashes fell from her fingers.

Papa! she called again, but the procession had faded. The city had faded, gone to dust. Tears burned her eyes. *Find me,* she called. *Take me home.* Her tears fell on the dust, shining there, and as she watched, the shining grew. A space opened from it, but not as before. Now it was a streetless place of steepled light. The light was pure and clear and in it there were colors and in the colors there were voices, low and safe, conversing in words she could not grasp. *I can't hear you,* she said, but the voices were fading, the light itself was draining away. With all her strength Elizabeth reached for it, straining for it, thrashing for it. And then it was between her fingers, an edge, a hem, narrow and bright. She held to it; pulled herself upon it, riding, rising upon the light, and she was laughing, laughing into the wind, and she was laughing out loud, even as Jacko shook her by the shoulder.

4

She seems to have been a pious girl.

Or is that just public relations?

She seems to have been a lonely girl. Perhaps her spiritual ecstasies were due to that, more than piety.

Ecstasies. I have to smile. That sort of thing wasn't much encouraged in us, in seminary. The few who had raptures seemed to be unstable or grandstanding. Rays of light, angel voices, dilated eyes—I mistrust it all. Clinically speaking, a person in such a state experiences a form of hysteria. Psychologically speaking, a person in such a state experiences a sense of specialness. Somebody Up There likes me. Something a lonely girl might want to think.

"Psychologically speaking": I'm starting to sound like these experts who testify before us. But how else can I grasp this? How else to understand the mind of this girl: sensitive, bereft, given to emotional extremes—a girl who, if I am not mistaken, even contemplated suicide. Suicide: not my favorite topic; not the Church's favorite topic. But there's the reference in her journal—a point not to be glossed over, though its significance isn't yet clear to me.

What's clear is that she couldn't sustain the ecstasy, the transport in the clearing. Her spiritual life was too young, too green. Her temporal life was too troubled, unsure. Her father's continued indifference, her continued homeless state —clearly these caused the new downward slide. Clearly she suffered. But suffering, alone, does not make a saint.

Perhaps I've found the blot on the copybook, the flaw I've been hunting. Perhaps this will crystallize my vague uneasiness about her, this sense that she was somehow . . . weak.

And perhaps not.

I mustn't jump too fast.

Especially in this modern age of saint-making. Especially in this age when is, so much of the time, psychologically speaking.

Look at her there, two years later, sitting in the churchyard, sitting alone. It is August. The leaves lie limp and dusty on the yew tree above her. The paths around her are parched. The air shimmers with heat, the gravestones are dusty. It has not rained in two weeks. Throughout the city there is the smell of rotting wood, rancid water. On the air is the high tight whine of insects. This is the month when, some years, people fall ill after Sunday dinner and are buried before Monday tea. Some years, this month, mattresses burn in the streets and the gravediggers' spades clang long after dark. Not this year; not yet. The city is waiting, Elizabeth is waiting. And if the fever comes, she more than half hopes she will be taken. She has thought this out clearly, not just in passing. This morning she has looked at the laudanum again.

She will tell Miss Molly this. She will tell her everything—about the dreams and the bad mornings, about the trembling when she wakes and when she goes to sleep. Soon her cousin's carriage will come for her, soon she'll be there. Thinking of the visit, Elizabeth feels a flicker of apprehension. For three months Miss Molly has lain ill, out of sight, guarded by her servants. *Apoplexy*: Elizabeth has heard the terrible whispered word. But Miss Molly is recovering, recovering well: everyone says so, though no one has seen her. Certainly she must be. Certainly Giselle would not let Elizabeth come if not. Certainly she will see Miss Molly and that will stop the dreams, the shakes, this sick scared feeling; it will stop her thinking of laudanum.

As she waits for the carriage, Elizabeth's hair clings in damp frills to her forehead. Her dress, her best white lawn, is streaked with sweat and rimmed with dust. The end of her nose, unguarded by her bonnet, is tightening with sunburn. Her sister's house, where she lives now, is cooler—but Elizabeth can't bear to wait there. She can hardly bear to be there at all.

In the pleasant shaded house on John Street, the elder sister is now the owner, the younger sister the boarder. Elizabeth has become the sole poor relation. Mary has become the wife of Wright Post; a year married, still very much a bride. Evenings, Elizabeth sits with her and Wright in the parlor. She sees their hands brush over the coffee spoons. Their heads are pillowed together by the back of the couch, as if they are sitting up in bed. Elizabeth bends her head over her sewing, she stares out the window. The room grows smaller, its air too warm. Mary rises, putting out the candles; Wright's eyes trace the curve of her breasts. Behind them, head down, Elizabeth climbs the stairs; in the hot dark house, she lies awake, listening to their bed creak down the hall, its headboard, in a final spasm, clanging ecstatically against the wall.

Nights are the worst; nights and Saturday afternoons, when Wright returns early from his surgery. And this Saturday Elizabeth has fled the rapping bed frame, the whispering walls, the entire groaning gasping house. The heat outdoors is impersonal, all-inclusive. In the end it is cooler to sit here.

Over Elizabeth the yew tree spreads, offering some shade; it falls on her shoulders like a shawl. This is where she always sits, here in the churchyard of St. Paul's, here on this bench under this particular tree. She sits inside the chapel as well—she has in fact become a frequenter of the place, with her favorite window, her preference as to time of day and angle of light. It's better than the laboratory. Here she need not be stealthy, need not hide. And here she has companions.

Elizabeth and the sack women. This is the company she keeps, this is the silent company she has joined: the flock of homeless women who roost here, moving in counterpoint to the church's real life. They have their benches, they have their pews; pews they sleep in, spend more time in than the Sunday faithful. They disappear at baptisms, weddings, evensong. They reappear between times, filling the cracks of the canonical day.

Among them, among the slim-shouldered graves, Elizabeth says the prayers Miss Molly taught her; she follows the notes floating out from the organ, *Very God of very God*. Every leaf, cloud, tree, is an object of unconnected thoughts of God and heaven; groped for, fumbled with, these thoughts sometimes spill through her fingers. In her hands she has two smudged pious novels which she reads on her bench; she wishes there were convents in America like the French ones in these books—how romantic, how thrilling to run away to one, possibly in disguise. What would her father say then? Her father: she does not want to think of him, back in New York now and still so distant from her. She will not think of him. She will think of Miss Molly, she will think of her novels; she will sit safe beneath the hawthorn trees with the sack women.

One of them is settling on the bench beside her: Mag, called Magdalen by the deacon, Magpie by the constable. Mag is tall. She wears three skirts, one over the other, in flat faded colors: the reds of unripe tomatoes, the yellows of dying grass. Over her shoulders is a balding black shawl and on her head is a blue silk bonnet: clearly an item of charity. The face below it is worn, alert, dirty, canny, its age indeterminate. Strung with twine across her chest are a pot and ladle and six or seven spoons. A tinderbox hangs from her belt—she glitters in the sun. She never speaks but often sits with Elizabeth; once she shared, on the point of her knife, a roasted chestnut. Elizabeth likes her, looks for her; dreads her. She feels a frightening kinship with this woman who wears all her clothes, all her goods, this unmoored woman who has no home.

Elizabeth thinks of all the packing and unpacking she herself has done this last year. She has lived with her grandmother Charlton and her godmother Startin and also with an aunt. She has stayed again in New Rochelle and also in Newtowne and at last with her sister on John Street; she has not stayed at her father's, uninvited to her stepmother's house. Every time she has to move on, she strips her bed and sits on the mattress ticking, waiting for the coach. Every time she comes into a new back bedroom, new mattress ticking awaits her: the sight of it makes her feel chilled.

The first week in each new house, she gags over the washbowl in the early mornings, unable to stop the spiral of panic within her. She fits nowhere. She lives nowhere. She has no one who deeply cares what she dreams, eats, fears, craves. She knows now that this may not change. Her life may be a series of back bedrooms: a series of trunks, coaches, mattress ticking. She has no beaux, no prospects, no party invitations. She can see herself as a gray-faced spinster, tolerated, ignored, pointed at by another generation of children. The thought of this makes her lean over the washbowl again. The inner curves of these bowls have imprinted themselves on her mind: white at her grandmother's, flowered at her aunt's, ringed with virtiginous lines at Mary's, where she still feels ill.

It is at Mary's that she begins looking at the laudanum. There is a bottle in Wright Post's medical bag. She has heard him speak of it, her father too. A little, she knows, stops pain; a great deal addicts; too much kills. She has only looked at the laudanum, hasn't touched it. But lately the thought of it is always near, floating clear and colorless in its beaker at the back of her mind.

Elizabeth walks back to John Street now to meet the carriage, her eyes straining for the face of Simon, Miss Molly's black driver. She finds him waiting by her sister's door, smiling at the sight of her. Inside the coach she smells Miss Molly's peppermints and perfume. Something seems to lift within her; she feels lightened all the way out to the house.

Moving across the familiar lawn, through familiar doorways and halls, the feeling grows. Her step quickens as Giselle shows her to the bedroom. There are still fresh flowers, still candied apricots, still silver-framed miniatures on the mantel; everything in order, everything as always.

In the cool shaded bedroom, Miss Molly lies propped on two crisp pillows, her hair curled, her nightdress champagne silk. Giselle retreats. Elizabeth takes a chair by the bedside and leans closer. Her cousin's eyes open; her blue gaze sweeps Elizabeth's face.

"Tell me," Miss Molly says, very low, "tell me the spell for true love. Pennyroyal, sage . . . tell me the rest."

"It's me, Eliza. I—"

"Just mix it, then, I'll pay. . . ."

"It's *me.*" Elizabeth's voice is smaller. "I wrote you . . ."

"I heard you're the best." Miss Molly's head tossed. "Best conjure-women always from Barbados, I've heard that, I'll pay. . . ."

For a few moments Elizabeth sits mute. In just a moment this will stop. In just a moment. She watches her cousin's hands move over the bedclothes. Come back, come back. Elizabeth takes the wandering hands in hers. The blue eyes seem to clear, to focus on Elizabeth's face. The brittle fingers squeeze hers. Miss Molly shifts nearer, sighs, takes a breath. "In gold," she whispers confidentially. "I'll pay in gold, pay what you ask. *Spinster,* they're starting to say it, oh God, my God. . . ."

The words stretch out and flatten into a wail, a wail that fills the room like smoke.

"*Giselle!*" Elizabeth calls in fear, and the maid is there, her thin face taut, dark eyes sad.

"I know," she says. "I thought when she saw you—I thought she might . . ." Giselle shakes her head.

"But she looks . . . everything looks . . ."

"She left instructions. For everything. She feared this, it happened this way with her mother. . . . She feared so much she'd disgust, be pitied. . . ."

Giselle's hands are guiding Elizabeth from the bed, across the Turkey carpet. For a moment, coming toward her, are all the afternoons Elizabeth has spent in this room, rustling, whispering, unbearably sweet. Then Miss Molly laughs from the bed: the laugh of a child, the laugh of a madwoman, and Elizabeth runs from the room, from the house.

Back at John Street, Mary's house is quiet. A note on the mantel reads: *Back at six.* Elizabeth drops it, climbs the stairs. The steps jerk under her feet. Gray light shatters in squares around her. The banister pulls away from her hand. She opens the door to Wright's study. It sprawls in chaos, so unlike her father's private room: a clutter of papers litters the desk, the medical bag is tossed on a chair. She pulls it open, stretching its mouth like a stubborn animal's jaws.

Her fingers pass over the cold steel forceps and over the flasks, their cork stoppers rough to the touch. She holds them up to the window, scanning the labels: valerian, foxglove . . . *laudanum*, there. Closing the bag, she takes the drug back to her room. She sits on the bed and turns the bottle in her hand, watching it flash in the late afternoon light. Slowly she eases the cork from the bottle's neck. She sniffs it: a bitter smell rises up to her. It won't be easy to get this down, she'll need water. She'll have to draw some from the pump, fetch it in, have it beside her. No. Something wrong about that. About doing it here. They won't be gone long enough, they'll find her. And Wright, of all people, might know what to do. And if he couldn't . . . No. She couldn't do that to Mary. She would have to do it somewhere else, somewhere she wouldn't be discovered. The churchyard—she'd go to the churchyard. Wrapped in her cloak on a bench there, the drug blooming within her, she would look for all the world like another sack woman huddled up for the night.

The plan glitters on the dim air of the back bedroom. Her mind feels stiff, her eyes burn, dry. The silence of the house seems a sign. If God chose to prevent this, He would have by now. And surely, surely He wouldn't condemn her for this; not someone driven by misery, no choices left.

She takes her light summer cloak from the wardrobe and puts it on. She takes off her bonnet; it might give her away. She goes to the mirror. Her face in the glass is very white, almost livid; her dark eyes, dilated, blaze out at her. She has never quite seen that face before. Her mind has slowed. She stares at herself as if she is underwater, her reflection floating on a murky surface. What more now? Something else she must do. A note—should she leave a note? She tries to think what she should say. There is a rushing in her ears, her mind gathers words and spills them. Her sister's face seems to slide in front of hers in the mirror. It does not frown, does not rebuke. In mild distress, it simply waits. Oh, Mary, sorry, but you won't miss me for long. In the mirror Mary's face is displaced by their father's: elegant, aloof, unmoved. She looks for regret in his eyes, for guilt. She sees only faint distaste. Faster now the faces slide, shift, blur: uncles, aunts, cousins, servants—all impassive, unimpressed, untouched by grief or surprise. *A difficult child,* they whisper, *always was.* And now she sees Miss Molly's face, separate from the others, lingering: the fine high cheek-bones, the knife of a nose. The face, framed by a pillow as it was today, looks wise and keen as always. But something whirls through Elizabeth now, breaking through the crust of her mind, and "Cheat!" she spits, "Cheat!" Her voice spins from her, higher, louder, *"CheatCheatCheat,"* and she is shouting it, screaming it, shooting the word at that face like a stone; her palms strike the dresser, the mirror shakes before her. Suddenly the face there shifts to Mag's, smudged and sharp-eyed, alternating with her own—Mag's face watching, floating beside her, coming with her to that bench un-der the yew tree. But no: not that bench—too close, too known, won't do. The north side of the churchyard, Mag points, that's best; in the back, on the north, by the wall—that's where you'll end up anyway. Apart, over there, on the cold north side: that's were the suicides go, the felons, the ungraced. If you do this, that's where you'll lie. Even in death: apart, cast off, no family plot, no neighborhood of kindred stones—remember: that's what will be. Mag's eyes are keen on her now, and now Elizabeth feels a wind of a voice gusting through her, rising, rising, "No!" Louder now, *"No!"* she says to the mirror, to Mag, and with a shuddering spin she sweeps mirror and bottle off the dresser. Shaking, she looks at them as they lie unbroken on the rug—the mirror suddenly plain glass again, lying in its frame, the bottle rolling like a child's toy.

Elizabeth stands there gasping, weeping at last. She stands there a long while—how long, she doesn't know. At last she picks up the mirror, sets it back in place; picks up the bottle, returns it to its bag. She walks, stumbling, back to her room and lies on the bed, her tears wetting the pillow, filling her her mouth with the taste of salt. She can't stop them, won't try, and she is weeping that way even as she drifts, dream-less, into sleep.

Time had jumped.

The window was dark.

She was awake again; her sister was there. Mary's face

hung in the dimness above the bed, pale, moonlike, concerned. If Wright had found his bag disturbed, she didn't say; maybe it was just this tear-soaked sleeping that worried her. Elizabeth's limbs ached, her eyes felt swollen; she sat up stiffly, as if after some unremembered fall. Mary's face flowed around her like water: really must get you up, really mustn't leave you so much alone, party tonight, a world of good, what better way—dancing, diversion, must come.

Elizabeth allowed herself to be led to the washstand. She smelled chamomile tea; saw an amber circle of it in a saucer, two folded handkerchiefs alongside—the remedy for puffy eyes. It was so simple to Mary: chamomile for the weeps, dancing for the spirits. It wouldn't help; Elizabeth could have told her that. It would accomplish nothing, change nothing—but it was easier not to protest. Her head was pounding. Her stomach was queasy. She dreaded any inquiries, explanations. And deeper than that, just now, she dreaded being alone.

All the while Mary was lacing her gown and smoothing her hair, Elizabeth was still traveling back, passing over fields of air from where she had been that afternoon. Once this numbness quit her, she knew, she would feel shame. But now she was only dazed, on the road back, and in this daze she entered the carriage, breathed night air, gave her hand to the footman, and walked toward the spill of light from another open door.

The chamber beyond was a blur of silks and candlelight. To Elizabeth, standing on the threshold, it had the delusionary shimmer of an image seen in fever. On the edge of the room she stood as if on the edge of sleep, floating, dispassionate. As if from afar, she watched powder fog a gentleman's bobbing wig; she watched a fat woman in pink satin dancing by like a great glazed ham. A cluster of young people stood across the room; their laughter, like chips of falling crystal, showered toward her. At the group's center, a small redheaded young man crouched on the floor, one arm dangling, his face contorted in an apelike grin. He was held on a length of twine by a tall companion, a tall black-haired man, also young, scraping away at a violin. The redhead held out his hat; the violinist sang. "The cow jumped over the moo-oo-oon," his voice laughed, "showing her *ankles* in short pantaloons." The mimicry was good; Elizabeth recognized its inspiration, the street singer at Nassau and Wall. The laughter rose as each verse revealed more and more beneath the short pantaloons; the singer, feeling Elizabeth's gaze, glanced at her. She realized she was the only one who wasn't smiling. She turned away.

Across the room another face sprang into clarity: not the face of a guest, but a butler, a man who had worked for Miss Molly. Gentle, aging, with flat feet and tufts of gray hair in his ears, his Dutch name had unraveled in her mind simply to Van. She watched his pigtail reflected in the mirrors, drifting past the candelabra. She saw him across the table, its stemmed glasses lifting gemlike wedges of green liqueur. As the fiddling ended and the spinet began, she moved toward him, moving through a smell of pomade and perfume and sweat, feeling all around her the press of bodies and faintly, beneath her, the rap of dancing feet on the floor. At last Van's face was close, poised above a tray of cherry tarts. She called his name. He looked up, and just as he did, his tray was swept from his hands. The tall musician, his violin tucked under his arm, presented it to Elizabeth with a flourish.

"William Magee Seton." He bowed.

Elizabeth stared.

"No appetite, I see." He handed the tray back to the butler and steered Elizabeth to a corner. "Now," he said. "You weren't laughing at our masquerade. I hope you'll say why—tell me, I can bear it—was it too broad? Not broad enough?"

"Neither one, sir." She heard her voice as if it were someone else's, hitting those notes of social banter she had learned early, by imitation, repetition. It was easy; she didn't even have to think. "It was rather too deep, sir, for a simple female brain like mine."

His eyes glimmered at her. "I'd doubt that." Brown eyes, she noticed. "Not simple—just solemn this evening, I'd guess."

"Forgive me." Her voice clicked along in pattern. "I've been . . . ill. They say music's a tonic. . . . though not for me."

"We didn't work a cure? . . . I'm sorry, I hope the malady was nothing grave."

The word gave her a darkly humorous poke.

"It was, for a time."

"My sympathy. A malady of which humor, may I ask?"

"None of the humors, sir. It was . . . the heart."

"Someone has broken your heart, then?"

She saw Miss Molly's face on the pillows. "Yes."

And suddenly tired by the effort of maintaining this exchange, she made an apologetic half-curtsy and slipped away. She sensed his eyes following her; she sensed them later as she wandered about donning and doffing her courteous mask, her charming mask, as needed. She felt his gaze later still as she left the party, feeling not much cheered and very much exhausted.

She undressed in the dark, not lighting the candles, not looking at the mirror, not thinking at all. A breeze came through the window, smelling of rain. The house was hushed. As she fell asleep Elizabeth saw a great company of silken ladies and gentlemen rustling toward the moon, dancing over it in a many-hued hoop. She saw Miss Molly among them, and her father, but she saw them with the detachment she had felt at the party. And leading them on, dancing them across in perfect time, she saw, was the laughing violin.

5

The pearls. Not the pearls. The petticoat with the lace, the undershift to match—dress cushions tucked into the bosom, he'll never know. The stays, tight, tighter. Perfume on the curls. An extra ringlet here, and here. The perriot, it needs a pin; the latest color, "London Smoke." The pearls. Or not?

She was whispering to herself, she was dressing as she whispered. It steadied her hands and made them deft, the words curling like the ribbons she pinned on. They were going to supper, they were going somewhere after that; he'd said to bring her dancing slippers, he'd put them in his pockets. She had to smile, thinking of the slim pink slippers riding inside his coat.

At the window, standing flat against the wall, she could see the street without being seen. She had learned to do this, these past few months. She liked to see him first. She saw him now, as he turned into the street. As usual she felt an odd little lift, as if something within her were suddenly placed on a higher, better-lit shelf. As usual, she tried to ignore it. She tried to watch him with that first evening's aloofness—this tall young man with the athlete's stride, his shoe buckles and coat buttons catching the light from the oil lamps by the doors. He was no dandy but he was no bumpkin, this banker's son, himself a clerk of discount at the Bank of New York. This evening he wore a white silk waistcoat embroidered with flowers; in his pocket, she knew, was a gold snuffbox, and in his hand was a nosegay from Thoburn's in Liberty Street. Whenever he brought a nosegay he had a way of presenting it; had a way of turning his leg in a bow, bending over her hand. He was worldly, six years older, a grown man of twenty-three. He sometimes spoke of his schooling in England, his recent tour of Europe for his business education. He had been to the theater in London, the opera in Milan. She wondered briefly if, as part of his seasoning, he had also been to these cities' brothels—what had made her think of that? His polish, that was it; his experience. There was little awkward about him. She had noticed only that when he was kept waiting, he became a pacer, a nervous whistler, a rearranger of coat pockets; that was all. Sometimes his eyes gazed through the webbing of words and bows; eyes that were clear and guileless, as they'd been the evening she'd met him.

They had met on other evenings after that, at other parties, other houses. Mary had been firm about Elizabeth going out; Elizabeth had not resisted. At these houses the same sedan chairs would appear in the dusk; the same patterns would form on the hardwood floors, the same faces reflected the mirrors. William Seton always arrived late, always walked. He was always there, dancing, flirting, often playing his violin. There were rumors about him. He was courting Mary Hoffman. He was courting Abby Brickler. He was wooing this one, that one, another, all three.

There began to be rumors about Elizabeth as well. There began to be callers at her sister's house, notes under the door, flowers on the knocker. Elizabeth had surprised herself. Gradually, grudgingly, she had gone to the parties, mostly in hope of pleasing her sister—and in dread of questions about that bad afternoon. Gradually, grudgingly, she had to admit, the parties had kept her mind from turning backward, or inward, at all. On the dance floors, by the punch bowls, a part of her still stood outside, sad-eyed, observant—but now it observed this new self too, this pink-cheeked stranger. She had stood for so long on edges, she knew how to read the tides of a room, the rhythms of advance and retreat. Flirtation came oddly easy to her. She pinned up new gowns, she walked through new dances in the midnight stillness of her room, and the gowns and the dances seemed to ease her. She did not think of that day in the churchyard, the twilight in the mirror. She did not think so often of Miss Molly or French convents. She still tried to say her prayers at bedtime, but after a dance it was difficult: her mind would dart like a trapped songbird around the room.

She had watched herself, amazed, one night a month before—the night of her bravest stroke. She had dared it partly to entrance William Seton, partly to amuse herself: for the lark of it, as boys climb higher and more intricate trees. She had decided to attempt The Swoon.

She had never swooned before, actually or feigned. She knew a few things about swooning nonetheless. If done in a certain manner, extended in duration, the swoon was an excellent way out of a dull evening. If done in briefer, less intensive form, it became a maneuver, revealing who would rush first to one's side. Moreover, the astute swooner could closely observe the gentleman who did, while lying limp and alert, slowly raising one's lids. She had seen it done, she had seen its effect. She had to try it herself.

She had chosen her moment. She was facing William Seton across the stately pattern of a minuet. The spinet chuckled. The candles winked. The last thing she saw was a pineapple in a passing servant's hand. She let her eyelids fall, her knees bend. Sinking, she felt the thrill of a high diver beginning a descent. The next sensation she expected to feel was her skirt enveloping her. But before she could touch cool silk or cold floor, she felt his arms, surprisingly strong and immediate and close; then the rough brush of his cheek as he carried her—sped her, it seemed—from the room. His solidity, his nearness, was startling. There was a smell of shaving soap and tobacco and starched shirtfront. His breathing touched her skin. And then he was stopping, leaning, lowering himself onto something—a chair? a step? Maddening not to be able to see. He shifted her against his shoulder, her legs across his lap. His hand rummaged in her reticule. By a sudden odor on the air, she knew he had found her flagon of hartshorn. Moments later, its bitter brown smell under her nose, she knew it was safe to stir in his arms.

She let her eyes open, saw the backstairs they were perched on. She saw his face—wide-eyed, grave, intense, as if she had fallen into his arms from a great height or a fast carriage. She felt a needling of guilt. She was looking so fragile and feeling so strong.

"My God," he said. "You just dropped."

"*Did* I?"

"Better now?"

"Oh much . . . I scared you?"

"Not at all." He capped the hartshorn. "But if I ever swoon, I'll expect you to do the same for me."

"A fair exchange."

"And give me salts."

"The entire treatment."

"I'll hold you to it."

"My solemn word." She raised her hand.

"I can't risk swooning away from you, then." His face above her was playful and earnest by turns.

"In that case," she said, "you'll have to stay near."

"I'll see to it." His eyes were serious again. "You really did scare me, you know."

He had seen to it.

After that, whenever there was a dance or a party or no party at all, he had called for her at her sister's house. They had gone to the exhibition near the coffee houses of Dr. King's curiosities, which included tigers and lizards, and to the exhibition at the Colles House, which included a solar microscope that magnified to thirty feet. They had gone to the concerts at the Lutheran Church and to the waxworks near Crane's Wharf, and to the John Street Theater to see *Darby's Return*, credited with having made President Washington laugh in public. Even though the Washingtons, and the capital, had moved to Philadelphia, the city was still gay and so was Elizabeth, moving out into its currents.

She looked forward to these times in this city with this man. She feared she looked forward to them too much. She feared that he, like everyone else she'd ever cared about, would suddenly, simply disappear. Thinking of this now, she felt her shoulders shift, her face change. It was again a sad-eyed face, a hungry face. Below she heard a line of pacing footsteps, the high thin sound of whistling. She pinched her cheeks. She put on the pearls. She took her slippers and went down to Willy.

Almost as soon as they went out the door, they were caught up in the crush around the nearby theater—the shoving confusion of coaches and chairs, orange sellers and ticket buyers and pickpockets; the crowd abruptly pressed her against him. "Not going to faint again, are you?" he said into her hair. "Certainly not," she murmured, eyes down. She was aware that his lips brushed the nape of her neck; she was aware that an artificial ringlet might come off in his mouth. A bubble of laughter rose inside her, laughter he felt rather than heard, laughing himself just to join her as they inched their way through the crowd.

She knew where they were going now. Not to supper; not quite yet. They were going three blocks over and two blocks down—going to pass, as always, the violinmaker's shop. She understood his need to be so often outside this shop; she understood by watching him. Before its window he would stand rapt, stilled, his eyes larger, darker, as hers would be looking at mountains or stars. Shyly, once, he had taken her inside. The proprietor had been out; the low-beamed room was quiet, dim, firelit—to Willy, she saw, a kind of sorcerer's cave. He moved about, in wonder and at ease, wood shavings crunching under his shoes; his head grazed the lutes and violins hanging like ripe fruit from the ceiling. He held a span of planed sprucewood to his ear, tapping it: the board made a humming note.

"A-flat," he said, his face alight. "He carves the soundboards till they make a C-sharp." He ran his finger over the outline on the wood. "He listens while he's carving, checks with the tuning fork, you can hear it get closer, go up the scale. . . ."

His voice trailed off; he looked at her. For a moment he turned away, coughing. She waited, hoping this wouldn't be one of the bad spells. He looked at her again; she saw he hadn't stopped because of the cough. It was as though he were appraising her as he hadn't before, testing her and the air of the room before he spoke again. He looked tentative, vulnerable, unsure—she felt for him a sudden rush of warmth. He saw it, felt it; he bent and took his own violin from its case. He had done this so many times at parties; she had seen him play it so many public nights. But now he did not tune it, did not touch the strings. He held it out to her.

"From Italy, Cremona, I bought it there." His voice was low. "A Stradivarius, from his studio—only one in New York, far as I know. I never tell people, protect it like a child." He tipped the violin so she could see the label inside it. His fingers touched the strings then, making them peep like new chicks. "Thought I'd be a violinmaker once, a luthier. Wanted that so bad, thought about it all the time."

"Not anymore?"

He touched the violin again, turned a peg. "Oldest son," he said after a while. "I never could have been 'just' a craftsman."

She remembered how he'd looked there in the shop, touching the strings, that ache in his eyes; she had, at that moment, felt closer to him than she had to anyone. She had felt like that, and he had looked like that, another time —the time he'd taken her home to the house on Stone Street; the time when no one was home.

They had gone to find a book he had wanted to lend her. The book was never found and Elizabeth suspected that he, for some reason, simply wanted to take her there alone. His parents had been out, his brothers and sisters had scattered for the day. The only sound in the house had been the tick of a tall case clock in the hall and, from backstairs, the faint hum of the servants at tea. She remembered how he had loped through this house that had awed her—even she, a doctor's daughter, used to fine houses herself.

But this was the house of the cashier of the Bank of New York, intimate of Hamilton, Jay, Talleyrand. This was a house that opened around them like an elaborate cake: a blur of creamy walls, intricately scrolled and paneled; a profusion of gilt-edged mirrors and carved fireplaces, their mantels blooming with marble flowers. She had felt diminished by its halls, its carvings, all the way back to the study belonging to Willy's father.

She had paused in the doorway, but Willy's voice had led her inside. His father liked to have the family in here, he said; he had played as a child under the desk. That was Papa, there, that portrait, reddish hair—Scottish stock, his people served the Stuarts before going to Yorkshire in England. "Papa, you'd like him—he's my tightest friend. Come on . . ." He waved her farther in.

The vast estate desk, its top flung up, amazed her—it was a butler's desk, a housekeeper's desk: not a banker's. Now it was happily cluttered with papers, one pile weighted with a child's wooden top, another with a porcelain hawk from the row of birds on the mantel. However grand the leather-bound books, however imposing the ivory chess table, it was impossible to feel awed in the presence of this blowsy, good-natured piece of furniture.

Willy had stopped at the chessboard. For a few moments there was silence. Then his hand moved a king; he smiled. "My brother and I, we keep a game going. He likes to play . . . just for the playing. Not me—I like to win."

He came around the table fast, as if invigorated, and sat behind the desk. She could not make sense of the impression that despite the tipped-back chair, the loose-limbed pose, he wasn't comfortable there. Maybe it was the tilt of his head, the set of his jaw. Maybe it was the way he kept tossing his father's silver notarial seal from hand to hand. But maybe she was just used to seeing him in ballrooms, nothing more than that.

His eyes followed hers to a series of oval frames on the opposite wall: silhouettes of himself and his brothers and sisters, eleven of them; he ticked off their names: Sammy, there, Charlotte, Ned, Bec, yours truly, that one's James.

"James, you've met him at the dances, he's the one I beat at chess. We started gaming at school—at Richmond, near London, God, I loved it there. Sometimes, you know, when I'm falling asleep I still see it, the cricket field, that green—I wake up wishing I was back . . ." His voice had quickened. "All I thought of then—before music, before ladies—was cricket. I was out playing all the time, all weather, led the team—still have my bat, don't laugh. That sound, the way the bat cracks"—his hand made a quick smack on the desk—

"and you're off, you're running, fast, so fast, that field just flies. . . ." His arms spread as if to wing him from the chair.

"You and James, you still play?"

There was a pause.

"James does. Not me."

"Too old?" she teased. "Too dignified?"

He shook his head. His chair creaked in the stillness.

"My fifth year in school"—he spoke slower—"I couldn't run so fast. Chest complaint . . . it was starting then, cutting into my wind. My last year . . . I didn't play at all. Could have. Wouldn't. Not if I couldn't be good." His chair creaked again; the silver seal flashed in the light. "Spent a lot of time with the music master that year. That's when I learned about the violin."

For a while they sat silent in the dim room, listening to the rumble of wheels outside. Willy's face, half-turned toward the blinds, was closed, unreadable. Neither of them had spoken again about what was cutting into his wind; what he referred to only as the "Seton complaint." Once more she had felt a rush of warmth for him; a desire to touch his face. Then he had clacked the chair legs down on the floor.

"I hereby decree"—he stamped the blotter with the silver seal—"it's time to go dancing."

Now, moving away from the violinmaker's window, he was speaking of dancing again: did she want to go, or perhaps not; there was someplace else he'd like to take her.

They were moving down the street again. She could feel the pressure of his fingers under her elbow, she could feel the warmth of his hand. From somewhere a clock was chiming; their heels clicked in rhythm with its strokes.

"I was thinking . . ." There was a hesitation in his voice. They turned a corner into a lane, his thought trailing on the air; before he could complete it they saw, directly in their path, a woman's body. The woman was sprawled facedown on the pavement, her hands flung out before her. Her head seemed to emerge from a layering of shawls and skirts, one over the other; her bonnet, mud-spattered, was knocked askew. Elizabeth dropped on her knees beside her. The woman raised a gin-flushed face—a face not Mag's, as Elizabeth had feared. Muttering, cursing at them, the sack woman stumbled away and Willy jerked Elizabeth back to her feet.

"How could you touch her?"

"How could you not?" Her eyes snapped at his.

"She could have robbed you—"

"She could have been dead."

"Dead drunk." His voice was harsh.

"You would have just stepped over her."

"Don't preach at me, Eliza."

"I'm not, I thought I knew her, she—"

"You would have wrecked our time, our night—"

"I said I thought I knew her."

"—for some crazed drunk you thought you knew."

A space had opened between them, like a sudden crack in the sidewalk. For a moment they stared at each other, then looked away. Elizabeth studied her hands. She was angry that he'd held her back, but more than that, she feared she'd angered him. He'd think her a fool. He'd think her a prig. He'd scorn her, he'd leave her—he'd drop her. Of all the feelings that passed through her as she stood there, smoothing her sleeves, the strongest was the longing, still, to please.

"You think I'm selfish." He threw it across the paving.

Eyes down, she shook her head.

"You do." His words were wooden. "You don't realize. I was going to tell you something. Tonight."

He did not look at her; his voice stamped the words out, stiff and flat. "I'm going away. Another voyage. Italy. I wanted you to know."

Her eyes remained on the tops of her shoes, edging out from the hem of her gown. He was letting her go, easing her down. She would concentrate on her shoes, her hem; she'd try not to feel this. Black shoes, gray hem. This was what she'd known would happen. Gray gown, black shoes. This was what always happened. The pearls, the careful curls: they made no difference. It was happening again, it would always happen. Her dancing slippers were in his pockets. She didn't want to go dancing now. What she wanted was to get out of this lane and out of these hopeful clothes. She wanted to get as far away from him as possible and she wanted to do that as fast as she could. She reached across what seemed a fence of air and pulled her slippers from his pockets. Then she turned and walked to the corner, veering sharply left. He was still standing in the shadows. At no time did she meet his eyes.

She walked; she went on walking. The streets were streamlike shapes before her. The footsteps around her seemed far off. She walked to the gate of St. Paul's and stopped beside it, afraid to sit in the churchyard at night; unable to think where else she'd rather be. She stood by the gate, her fingers curled around its bars. She didn't know how long it was, she only knew that her fingers grew stiff. Her eyes were hot and needled with tears. For a while they only picked out blurs: the curve of the gravestones, the form of a man edging up beside her. She turned to go. The man reached out, put a hand on her arm.

Clumsy, fumbling, Willy took her face in his hands. She saw him smudged through tears; to her shame, her cheeks were wet, her handkerchief absent. He touched his to her eyes.

"What I meant . . ." His words came fast now. "I said it wrong, I wanted to say . . . I wanted us to be promised. Before I went. I told my father. But I was afraid to ask you." He looked at her, his voice lower now. "And I was afraid of that woman."

She touched his face; she felt its male roughness, surprising, real, endearing. Promised. She touched his hair, fine hair, pin-straight, falling in his eyes. Promised. She touched the ruffles on his shirt, felt the rise and fall of his chest beneath them. "Promised," she said, into his shirt. "I want that too."

He lifted her chin. His fingers were light and warm against her neck. He leaned to her, his cheek scratching hers, his hand moving down her spine, and he kissed her light and he kissed her deep, and it seemed a long time before they moved away from the gate. It seemed a long time before she smoothed her hair and smoothed her gown and got into the hack he hailed—the hack that would take them to his family's house; they were going to tell them now.

Around them the city sped, jingling, harness bells and carters' gongs and vendors' tunes studding the dark. The evening stretched ahead of her now like a dark line in her hands, leading her in one direction: to the house on Stone Street where Willy's family stood suspended on the night air in one glaring cluster. They were expecting her; they'd hoped she'd come. The streets unrolled before them; the house rose up ahead, enormous, larger than it had been before. Willy paid the driver. He lifted her down. She felt cold, too cold. Her shyness had come over her again like an old smock. She moved within it toward the door, her mouth empty of words. She imagined the family waiting for her in the hall, sharp silhouettes turned against her. They would watch her, they would judge her. They would see in her the laudanum, the laboratory, the back bedrooms: all. They would see in her the perennial poor relation, they would set her on their rim, it would happen again. She looked at that grand gabled front door. She knew she could not walk through it. She looked at Willy and saw him looking at her.

In an instant he was leading her around to the back of the house, through the servants' gate. This way, he said, leading her toward the back door. This way she could catch sight of them first, before all eyes turned to her. This way, this way—he led her along.

They went in and up narrow stairs, into a smell of allspice and cloves. The warmth of the kitchen curved around them, and from the pantry door Elizabeth looked out.

She saw them, saw them in the mirror: a vast gilt-edged mirror reflecting the drawing room and the family within it. There was a swirl of velvet, a foam of lace, the glint of earrings and stickpins as they assembled there. Candle flames dipped from sconces and sideboards and the chinking chandelier; light swam in the punch bowl and shone from the brass newel post on the stair. Elizabeth took a step forward, out of the kitchen's aromas and into a smoother smell of wax and wine. She heard the family saying her name—"Do you think Elizabeth likes sweets?" . . . "Do you think she'll like *us*?" This last from a sister near her age, a girl with Willy's dark eyes. Touched, Elizabeth stepped from the doorway.

There was a moment's hush. Then they were beside her,

drawing her into the room, murmuring welcome, pressing a glass of wine punch upon her. She stood by the table, eyes suddenly misted, feeling the closeness of them, taking her in without question, without one appraising glance—for Willy's sake, once and for all. His father took her hand in his, this tall banker, his freckled face homely and kind; the warmth in his eyes lifted her out of the rest of her shyness. She began to explain, to apologize for taking them by surprise.

He smiled her words away. "Guests come through the front," he told her. "Family comes through the back."

He raised his glass to her. She heard the rustle of sleeves as every glass was raised in suit.

"If it's not presumptuous," he said, "and from what my son has said, it's not: To Elizabeth—welcome to the family."

6

You see them, these young women, trembling before you at their weddings, looking so young and thrilled and scared, you wonder if they'll make it through their vows—flowers, veil, everything trembling, trembling.

You see them a year or two later, standing before you for the first child's baptism. Trembling less. Still thrilled. And young, still looking so young. Events like these don't seem to age the women much; don't "grow them up," as my grandmother used to say. Not in my experience, anyway. Some dignity is conferred, of course, a title, a ring; but as for growing them up—that takes something harder later on.

So it seems to have been with Elizabeth Bayley—a girl of nineteen wed to William Magee Seton by the Right Reverend Provoost on a winter's evening in her sister's home; a girl of twenty coming before him again on a spring morning in Trinity Church for her first baby's baptism. A girl still thrilled. Still tremulous.

Dearly beloved, ye have brought this child here . . . She stands at the font, framed by the arch of the window behind her, and by the family fanning out around her, holding her like a brooch at its center. *Sanctify this Water to the mystical washing away of sin.* She stands framed by the large and generous clan now hers by marriage—eleven Seton sisters and brothers, their grinning father and moist-eyed mother, for whom the baby is named Anna Maria. *We receive this child into the congregation of Christ's flock.* She stands framed not only by these but, holding the baby, godmother Rebecca Seton, already a deep friend, and beside Rebecca, Dr. Bayley. It is the sight of them all around her, even more than her new motherhood, that makes Elizabeth's lips tremble as she listens to the minister: *Grant you be strengthened with might;* it is the sight of all of them afterward, over white cake and red wine, that makes her eyes fill all over again.

They are ranged about the oval mahogany dining table, all its leaves in place, sitting amid fruit and silver and ribboned gifts, watching Willy's father raise his glass in another toast. He lifts his hand through the cigar smoke that is just beginning to haze the air. In other homes the women would now be expected to leave, but that custom is frowned upon here; the cheers and chatter go on among all. Elizabeth looks at her father-in-law, wishing to invent some witty toast for him. Without a clever word to pin it firm, she fears her voice might falter. Nothing clever comes. Once again, this homely, stocky, ginger-haired man has moved her beyond words—she who had feared walking through his door.

How many times had she walked through it since that evening? Dozens, hundreds: her father-in-law had opened his home to them, their first few months of marriage, until they could find their own. How many times had she walked through that door, with parcels, packages, parasol, and heard that voice call from the study, "Lizzie, come take a cup wi' me." His words still curled around a Yorkshire burr. His talk still cupped the tales of his youth: ghosts and witches who walked the north country's crags. His ghosts were always helpful, his witches always wise, their magic white. He would lean back in his big chair, his eyes kindling with a story; his face, fleshy and freckled as a hound's belly, would shine at her. "Now, one house, it ha' a gude spirit in it—a spirit tha' li' the fires and li' the lamps each night," he'd say, his accent rolling broader as he talked. She had come to look forward to that voice, its call—and it often came, he was often there. He had resigned his bank for a boyhood dream, founding his own firm, and with Willy as his assistant, he had become an importer of marbles and wines, raisins and silks. He liked to think of his sober ships, he said, on the Mediterranean. He said he could smell the sun in the raisins. He preferred his study to his counting house, unperturbed as his smaller children raced and crowed around his desk; often Elizabeth had heard Willy's violin in there as well. Sometimes the study filled with agents, shippers, clients, with talk and blue smoke—her father-in-law's voice would be firm then, terse, and utterly clean of Yorkshire. But often in the late afternoons he was alone; "And I like a woman's company," he'd tell her, offering a chair. "What's in the box, Lizzie, new hat?—show me then, try it on, ah, *feathers* are back for spring, are they?"

She had ceased to wonder at his fondness, his goodness. He was a bighearted man whom everyone loved; she felt as nourished by his presence as by a bowl of barley broth. Once he had shown her a sheaf of letters from his schoolboy days, homesick letters to his own father; once he had pressed into her hand a locket worn by his mother in childbed. Elizabeth had put this locket on when her pains began, and now, as her father-in-law finishes his toast, she feels the locket under her dress, cool against her skin. She feels the room circling out from it, from her, from the baby sleeping against her shoulder. She looks for the edges of this family, for that boundary line where she had always sat before, and cannot find it—it is out of sight, she is too far away from it now.

". . . and another letter, just arrived," her father-in-law is saying, standing at the head of the table. "If I might read it aloud—from the Filicchis, in Italy, my friends."

More wine gurgles into glasses. The baby stirs. Beneath the table Willy's smallest sisters crawl, giggling into hems, rapping on shoetops. Crumbs of christening cake trail like sand across the shining table, suddenly bisected by a spinning red top. Wine spills, laughter ripples.

Her father-in-law shouts into the rising chaos, " 'Blessings! Blessings! Blessings!'—that's all it says, this page, writ big as my fist . . . ah, here, next page 'To your grandchild, who must be in the world by now, and to your William and his wife: a long and happy life.' "

Beside her at the table Willy winks and, under the table, touches her knee. He has watched the misting of her eyes all day; he has sensed her drifting. Now he wants her to come back, wants to feel her solid in the room beside him. She knows he is starting to want the quiet of their narrow Wall Street house; he spends so much time here, closeted with his father on business—it delights him to have his own home. It's not just the fashionable address that pleases him, she knows, not just the pride of ownership. It's the privacy, so novel as to seem almost enticing, exotic, illicit.

They both remember how unprivate the Stone Street house had seemed on their wedding night; how still, how silent, how close its rooms had pressed against theirs. She remembers walking through its stillness to the dressing screen in their bedroom. She remembers standing there, cringing at the loudness of her every move. She hadn't known that a stocking, unrolled down a leg, could make that liplike sucking sound. She hadn't noticed that a petticoat, drawn down the hips, could make that series of whispered screams. Her buttons seemed to pop like corks. Her stays groaned, uninhibited, as she unlaced them. Beyond the screen she could hear Willy shrugging out of his shirt. She heard a longer jingling slither: that had to be his breeches sliding off. Beyond their room, she felt the house circling them like a band of big-eyed wedding guests, listening, invisible and alert. And beyond its stillness, deepening it, she'd heard the wind outside, a high wind off the river, tossing the trees. A shutter banged. She'd jumped, turning, her nightgown held to her chest. Willy had appeared at the edge of the screen, a blanket around him, his chest and shoulders bare above it.

"Eliza—come look."

"What?"

"Out the window."

"Willy!"

He'd drawn her under the blanket with him, leading her to the window. Passing the nightstand, he'd blown out the candle—and then she'd been able to see what he had seen. Streaking down the wintry sky was lightning, sharp and white, like quick rips in black paper—moments later followed by the drumming of thunder. They'd stood there awkwardly, watching the rain start to slant against the panes. She'd seen

the windowsill and the draperies and his shoulder spring
suddenly into brightness. She'd heard the storm crack and
roar; the house no longer seemed so still, so breathlessly
listening. Willy's skin was against hers, the warmth of him,
the length of him solid and naked beside her. The storm
went on crashing about the house, prankish and alive,
tugging the shutters and tweaking the roof, and through its
noise he'd carried her to bed, and through its flashes they'd
pressed and held, and whatever moaned through the house
that night, it could be said, was only the wind.

*Man that is born of woman hath but a short time to live,
and is full of misery.* Sun glinted on the spade. The shoetops
ranged around the grave were dusty. The black hems
clustered, overlapping. *He cometh up and is cut down like a
flower.* Every pew had been filled. The churchyard streamed
with black bonnets, black hats, bending as the bells began.
O Lord, who for our sins art justly displeased . . . Elizabeth's throat was too tight for tears. She looked at Willy.
His face was composed, stern, white, his chin thrust out.
He had been a brick, everyone said so. *Thou knowest the
secrets of our hearts.* The spade was extended to him, blade
up; a clod of earth was offered upon it. He took the clod,
turned it in his hand, let it fall on the coffin. The spade
passed on. *The corruptible bodies of those who sleep* . . .
The spade passed to her. The clod of earth felt dry in her
fingers. For an instant she could not seem to let it go, let
it fall. And then it was in the air. The spade was passing
on. *Accept our prayers on behalf* . . . No sound now but
the thudding earth. Thudding earth, and in the hawthorn
trees, the shrilling of cicadas. *Thy death didst take away
the sting.* The spade was still. They would start moving,
walking soon, it was almost over. *With the Father and the
Holy Ghost.* They would go back to the house. They would
shake all those black-gloved hands. They would talk, they
would thank, they would praise. And tonight they would
lie awake . . . *world without end, Amen.*
    In the house on Stone Street, as always on a family
occasion, there was wine, there was cake, there was careful
service and courteous conversation. From the parlor, Eliza-

beth found herself glancing toward the study door, still too stunned to cry. Surely, surely he would come bounding out soon, welcoming the guests as always; surely she would hear another of his toasts. As she watched, the study door opened slowly, not much more than ajar, and she saw Willy slipping out. Without glancing about him, he moved down the hall away from the parlor, going down the back stairs. She had seen his face. She knew he was taking a shortcut outside. Excusing herself, she went after him.

Moving through the streets, she could not catch up with him; eight months gone with this third child, she felt slower and bigger than she had with the others. She was able, however, to keep him in sight until he turned at Trinity Church. Breathless, her hand pressed to the small of her back, she scanned the churchyard for him. She was prepared to find him at his father's grave; she was not prepared for the sight of him crouched beside it, his violin in his hands.

She drew near, touching his arm; he looked up at her, his face streaked with dirt and tears. Awkwardly she lowered herself onto her knees and took his hands.

"I wanted . . . to play something for him," he said after a while. "I can't. I keep . . . I keep thinking of this time, this one time . . . this time when I was small, I fell out his study window into a flowerbed. It was . . . it was all spaded up for planting, I sank in . . . it terrified me, I screamed. And Papa . . ." His voice broke on the word like a wheel on a rock. "Papa, he just came and picked me up and he . . . he . . . lay down in the flowerbed himself . . . laughing, laughing. . . ." He broke off, eyes wet again; a fit of coughing took him. "Shameful," he said, swiping at the tears.

"Everyone's said how strong you've been, a brick, an absolute brick—not shameful."

"They don't know how I . . . I feel so so angry—what kind of way was that to die? A fall, fall on the street— is that enough to start a death? A fall like a child, a skid, a slip, is that a death for *my father*? No one expected—I never thought—Fifty-one, he was only fifty-one, my father, Eliza, a *fall*."

"I know, I never thought he'd really die. I never told him . . ."

"It came so fast, none of us told him what we felt . . . And he never told me. . . . Eliza, he never told me a thousand things, business, papers, clients, bills . . . he was so damned good at it all, he never needed help. Never gave me much to do, did it all himself. Now I don't know. . . . Now there's so much."

He reached out and pressed his hands to her face, urgently, as if to warm them; then slowly he moved them down and pressed them to her belly.

"We'll have to move," he said heavily. "Have to move back to Stone Street."

"Willy, *no*." It came out unguarded.

"Seven children still there, the business all in that study, my mother ill—What else can I do? They'll need me, they'll want . . . I can't be what he was, Eliza, *Christ* I wish I could."

"No one could be, no one expects it."

"Oh, yes they do—somewhere inside they do. The children, the partners, the merchants, all of them, God, it's just too fast. . . ."

She held him against her, feeling his wet face on the bodice of her gown; feeling at the same time the baby kick within her. She smoothed back his hair, her hands shaking, wishing strength into him, into them both.

"I wish . . ." he began, stopped. "I wish I could just . . . play some music for him . . . here, like this. . . ."

"Then do, he'd have liked it."

"No . . ." He glanced around. "Someone might come. And I can hear them now—'Young Seton's gone mad.' *He* never cared what people said. I do."

She left him there, alone with the grave, as he wanted. There were children to feed, letters to write. Already she felt chores pressing in upon her. But for a moment she stood there, unable to move, to walk forward. For the first time since her marriage she felt unsafe; almost as unsafe as she'd felt that night of the Doctors' riot.

~

Julia, dear friend, it's such a blow. Poor Willy, his attach-
ment was so great, this loss is . . .

Her quill scratched to a stop. Her friend's face came before
her, just as it always looked on afternoons of tea, of talk; a
fine-boned face, gentle, inquiring. A blot of ink was forming
on the paper. The face sighed, growing impatient. Elizabeth
sighed in turn. She had again lost the thread of the sentence.
At this hour, the house asleep, she had hoped to finish this
letter; she had hoped it might concentrate her mind.

. . . most severe. It is five days now since the funeral,
and . . .

I still can't shake it from my mind. Mustn't say that,
mustn't admit. Still hear the minister. Still see Willy facedown. Scared me. Shook me. Want to tell Papa Seton.
Strange. Listening for him. Looking for him. Still. Five days.

. . . think we shall have to move from here back to
Stone Street after the baby comes. . . .

And how I fear it coming. Baby kicking now, always
kicking late at night. Belly making little jumps through
gown. Belly so big, must stretch to reach desk. Pain in back
all the time, grinding. But that's nothing, nothing really.
Commonplace. Don't know what's wrong. Fancies, foolishness. Mustn't fear. Mustn't admit.

. . . due in July, we move this fall, and I cannot help but
feel some trepidation, I . . .

Can't go on in this vein. Must sound plucky, brave. Keep
thoughts clear. Much to do. Packing, all those chests. Children's clothes outgrown, not a stitch put into new layette.
Mammy Huler, she'll help, no better help you ever did see,
but still I . . . Stop. Just stop.

All will turn out for the best. It will be a change, of
course, for I have come to cherish having our own . . .

. . . dear small house, breaks my heart to think of going.
After all the homeless years, my own home—the world, and
heaven too! How long it took us to get the parlor paint
just this shade of green. Never be another green just this
green. The piano. The hearth. I look at them—tears. Tears!
Keep walking, room to room, looking, looking. Banister
where Anna rode—sailed. Worn place, bedroom floor, chip
on wall where Billy fell. All over house, precious spots, stains.

My precious children stick to me like little burs, nor can I write one word without some sweet interruption. . . .

And how it tries my patience sometimes. Will they remember it here? Remember Willy dancing around this parlor, playing "Rosy, Dimpled Boy," "Carmignol," and "Pauvre Madelon," one after another, no breaks, fast as he could—me at the piano, children hanging on my skirts, singing, all of us—laughing, laughing. Keep remembering, too, our Widows' Aid Society, ladies in a circle here, tea, afternoon sun. Coziness. Won't be the same, bigger room.

I have learnt to commune with my own heart and try to govern it by reflection . . .

. . . but still cannot, not always. Willy's health. Not mending, scares me so. Now this family to head. Five of us. Twelve of them, dear God. And the business, I just don't know . . .

He keeps me employed assisting him to copy and arrange his papers, for now he has no other confidant . . .

. . . and how he needs one. Me—don't know enough. Can't help enough. Feel so unequal to this. So does he.

I never view the setting sun or take a solitary walk but melancholy tries to seize me; and if I did not fly to my little treasures and make them call Papa and kiss me a thousand times, I should quite forget myself. . . .

Enough of that. Sounds too maudlin. Try not to think dark. Must not. Only tired. Only worried. Try not to think. Plucky and brave. Must. Shall. But oh, Julia . . .

There is not an hour in my life in which I do not want either the advice or soothing of a friend. Your E.

She looked at the letter; considered tearing it up, starting again. No blots this time, nothing but courageous sentiments. Too weary, she sanded it, creased it, sealed it. Beyond the window a shadow moved. She waited to hear the voice of the town watch—it would be near eleven now, the hall clock would soon be striking. Eleven o'clock and a mild June ni-ight. She listened. No voice came. There was no one beyond the window now. More fancies, more foolishness. Around her the house slept on, securely pocketed within the darkness. If she stood at the top of the stairs she would hear the steady breathing of her children. She would hear the pulse of the clock. She rose, shaking her head at herself. She turned and saw the shadow again; tall, vague, a man's form outside. She took a step. It was gone. She stood very still. There was a rap at the door. In fear, in fierce protectiveness, she wrenched open the door. Her father stood there before her.

"I know it's late," he said as she said, "What on earth . . . ?"

"Someone ill?"

"No." He shook his head. "No one ill."

There was a pause.

"Would you like to come in?"

"Thank you, yes."

"Everyone's asleep."

"I thought so, my apologies."

They sat opposite each other, she on a hard chair, he on a soft one. They had sat opposite each other before, the past few years; they had spoken in the company of others but not alone. She had not sought that, nor had he. She knew he was not always living at the house on King Street now, knew there was some trouble there. She had not wanted to discuss it. She had withdrawn herself from him like a hand from a tight sleeve; it had been arduous, too arduous to risk doing again. He had been correct, she had been polite. He had stood at the fonts, the feasts, the graves, and she had stood across from him, a sea of air between.

"How are you, then?" She heard the brittleness of her voice.

"I'm well, and you?"

"Very well, thanks."

"And Willy—been a brick, hasn't he."

"A brick, he has been, yes."

"And the children?"

"Well."

There was a pause.

"A glass of wine?"

"No," he said. "Don't trouble, please."

She rose and poured the wine anyway, handing him his glass and sipping hers before she resumed her seat. His shirtfront gleamed white as salt across from her. His hair, unpowdered, beginning to gray, still fell in perfect layers. The planes of his face, faintly lined now, still looked crafted, carved. It was the eyes that seemed different. The fine dark eyes showed pain.

"My stepmother, how does she do?"

"Not quite certain." Her father twisted the stem of his glass. "Haven't seen her in some months, you see."

"I see."

"We have, in fact, parted. Nothing official. Nothing public. But. There it is. Didn't want you to hear it elsewhere."

"Of course." Elizabeth studied her wineglass.

"I'd meant . . . to come much earlier."

"Yes, the children are up till eight."

"I meant. Long before."

Elizabeth drained her glass.

"I meant. Elizabeth . . ." His eyes seemed to grow even darker. His chin, for an instant, appeared to tremble. "I've walked past this house. Often. At night. Wanting to come in. To talk."

"You know you're always welcome here."

"I meant. Like this. With you. Alone." He set his glass, untouched, on the table. "I know I haven't. Done that enough. Perhaps I haven't. Done that at all."

Elizabeth said nothing.

"I know . . ." He shifted in his chair. Abruptly his mouth twisted. "I've been alone more of late, you see. And I've thought . . ."

Elizabeth saw that her glass was shaking in her hand.

"I've thought about those years I never . . . At the time, so busy, you see. So impassioned. Still am, still am. But not so . . . so anchored, you see. I suppose."

Her glass shook. Her chair shook. The room was too warm.

"You see, I wanted to tell you. Tell you that. Tell you I realize—"

Her wineglass flew out of her hand, shattering against the table. She was on her feet, still shaking.

"You realize. You say you *realize*?" Her words were slicing in from somewhere else, skidding down all the bad years. "All the back bedrooms, the moving, never belonging, you *realize*? You come in here now—now that you don't have the old home. You come in here now, now it's convenient for you. You come in here and say you *realize*. Do you realize it's past the time you could have made it right?"

She stopped, hearing her voice in the room: a whip of a voice. She saw her father bend his head—a posture so unlike him she thought he might be ill. And then she saw the tears on his face. That immaculate face. Those long clever fingers, pressed to his eyes.

"I am . . ." His words were thick. ". . . so very sorry."

She sat down unsteadily.

"I wish . . ." he said. "I wish I could have seen it then. I wish I could have. All that time—how I resented that household. The children, how they irritated me. The demands. The crying, the noise." The irony flickered back into his voice. "*I*—I had things on my mind. *I*—I couldn't be disturbed. But now. She's kept the children from me now, you see. And. It's come to me. Late, rather late. Can't say why. Now I seem to want it. Very much. Family, demands. Even the noise." For a while he sat silent. "Elizabeth. I long for that time past. That time neither of us had. I lost it too."

He stood. He put his handkerchief away.

"I . . . ought to go," he said. "I'm tiring you too much. But . . . perhaps . . . with your permission . . . I might . . . I hope to . . . come again."

He waited a moment. He turned toward the door.

"Yes," she said then, as if the word had been stunned from her.

Over his shoulder he looked at her. Over his shoulder there came a smile, hopeful; grateful. Very gently he shut the door behind him.

Elizabeth went to the pantry and got the broom. I will not feel this, she thought, will not. She moved about the room as a visitor would, stiff, formal, slow, sweeping up glass, banking the fire. She began to put out the candles. She paused to straighten his chair. And then, in the half-dark, she felt within her something ease, unlock. She knelt on the floor, unwieldly and big, her face against his chair's brocade, and let the tears come down.

Her contractions began three weeks later as she spooned

breakfast porridge from the kettle. She stood breathless at the table, gripping the spoon. For an instant the kettle faded before her. Then she felt her water break, soaking her skirts, hitting the floor. She heard Anna laugh, loud and high, a fear-tinged laugh. A chair scraped back. Willy's hands steadied her, lifted her. Another pain grabbed hold, harder, longer. From his arms she saw the hall slide past. This pain was not like the others, not like any she had had before; she knew that right away.

She lay in bed and jolted along on the pain; it was like a bone-rattling ride on a bad wagon. The midwife was coming, Willy said. Her sister was coming for the children. Once the children were gone, she knew she could let herself scream. Hurry, Mary. Her back was breaking. Mustn't scare the children . . . hurry, Mary . . . can't wait. The pain was a sharp-edged square within her; her voice broke from her, sharp-edged too, and strange. Willy's hands grasped hers. Easy, Liza, he was saying, easy now. His voice seemed far away, coming from across the room, across the street. His hands were solid, warm. She held to them, strong sweet hands; hands that had stroked her breasts, fingered the violin. Afraid of crushing them, she pulled her hands away.

The room lurched around her. Dresser jumping, night-stand, rug. Mirror leaping, pitcher, bowl. New hands reaching past the jagged, jerking walls: old hands, gnarled as a hickory cane; midwife's hands. Hands lifting her gown, briskly pushing knees apart; one hand on her belly, one between her legs. Five fingers open, the midwife said; breathe, lovey, breathe. For a moment the pain let go, the room fell still. Elizabeth gulped air, sucked ice, felt the pillowcase sticking to her neck. Oilcloth spread beneath her now. Willy—where? Cool wet weight of something on her head. Then pain. Pain stronger, sharper than before. The midwife's hands touching the pain, prodding the pain. A breech, the old voice said; a breech is what.

Again the room rocked, and then a smell blew through it: an acrid smell, pungent. Laudanum, the old voice said; just a whiff. Oh God, oh no. She tried to fight it, strained against it; could not fight it, had to let it pull her down.

Darkness fell upon her like a hood thrown over her head.

Lift it up, she called, let me out. Did the porridge burn? So much to do, the breakfast, the packing, the layette not finished. She saw, passing her on the patterned dark, the half-done gowns and caps she had stitched, the stitches coming loose. She saw cups and kettles and bowls scattering, disordered, on the black wind. Her daughter's braids, knotted, tangled, blew across her face. There was hair to brush, half a dozen shirts to ruffle. All the things she had never finished blew back at her now, everything she had been unable to tie up neatly, stitch together, save. Miss Molly's silken skirts rustled past, and Mag's layered shawls. Miss Molly had died; she knew that. Mag had not died, where was she? Her father-in-law's waistcoat brushed her face, satin, smooth. She had wanted to tell him something—if only she could remember what it was. Where was her mother? Her mother, her sister, she did not see them here. The laudanum was carrying her further down now, sinking her in a new dark— a dark that rippled around her in circles, in whirlpools, closing over her head like a lake.

Bitter lake, black lake. Waters awash with bones; bones and weeds in her hair, rank wetness in her mouth. Deeper: eyeless dying fish. Deeper now, deeper still: a wrecked and battered ship, chilling the waters and making her weep— great sad lovely splintered ship. She felt its cracked keel skim her spine. She saw its cargo, golden ropes and silver strings, streaming from its shattered hull. Gasping, thrashing, freezing cold, she swam and saw some figures floating near, arms wide, facedown—saw Willy, white and strange, saw Anna, saw the baby being born, and into the water she screamed—screamed that ship away into the dark.

Hands were reaching, pulling her now; pulling her back onto the bed, back into the room—deft long-fingered hands. "Good Christ," a voice above her swore. "Forceps, *now.*" Her eyes opened. She saw her father's face below her, saw it between her parted knees, saw it through the arching pain. Pain sharp as glass thrust within her, strained against her. "Oh Papa Papa," she screamed.

"Hold on, Bet." His eyes were grim and kind. "Push, now."

The pain was a blow that sent her spinning off again beyond the room, this time a different way, down a hall of milky dawning light. Light trembled and lengthened before her, drawing her on. The hall was filled with thin mild air and set with doors and doors and doors; somehow she knew they would open onto other halls of even brighter, sweeter light. She would stay here, she decided, she would float here; this was good. The hall branched around her like a sunlit tree, and down its many turnings she saw another ship, its sails filled with wind, its masts bright as flame. As soon as she saw it, she longed to go toward it, and as soon as she saw it, it sailed farther off. Not yet, not now, someone said, and reluctantly she obeyed. Slowly, slowly she turned and let herself float back.

The pain had stopped.

A scissors flashed.

She listened for that first high wail, but no wail came.

She turned her head and saw the baby in her father's hands: the baby, blue and still, her father's mouth to his. Sweating, rumpled, crouching on the floor, her father was breathing down the baby's throat, pausing, gasping, blowing again.

She tried to watch, to will them strength; in spite of herself, her eyes closed. She drifted into a perfect void, neither light nor dark. And then she felt a hand on hers. She clasped his hand and heard the baby cry.

7

"C. C as in . . . ?"

Elizabeth waited.

"Can't hear you, children. C as in . . . ?"

"Cat." A thin chorus of small voices.

"Everyone this time. D. D as in . . . ?" Discourage, she thought. Danger, dismay. "Let me hear it. D as in . . . ?"

"Dog!"

"Good. Now, E, E as in . . . *egg*, F as in . . . ?"

Failure, fear. "Louder, children." Drown me out.

She was standing in the parlor of the Stone Street house, leading a class of five: her two oldest, Anna and Bill, and Willy's two youngest sisters. The childern sat chanting before her, dangling their legs from parlor chairs and clutching their long-necked hornbooks—these they held like trowels and gazed into like mirrors, studying the ABC's printed there; the smooth horns were sticky from sucked fingers and worn at the edges where they had been chewed.

It was the only way to manage, this makeshift dame school she had devised. Every weekday she led these lessons, even as she grew big with another child; every weekday from ten to three, these two uncertain years, the little class was islanded within the sprawling household. Four of Willy's brothers and sisters were in boarding school—that was all he could afford, he was overextended as it was. Elizabeth could hear his voice now, through the study door; a door he always kept open, in his father's style.

". . . this shipment, absolutely the *finest* quality marble you could *possibly* . . ."

Willy's words were coming too fast, his voice too tight. He badly needed orders, and the need glared from his voice. He badly needed this order, this customer; this brocaded merchant, reeking of snuff and wig powder, had been one of his father's best.

". . . wholesale, sir, even *with* shipping costs and duties, I can offer you a *far* lower total figure. . . ."

His voice strained harder. With an effort, Elizabeth brought her mind back to the class.

". . . now, S. S as in . . . ?"

"Soup!"

"Sad," her son added suddenly, looking up at her face.

From the study, a cough. From the hall the comforting *whisk-whisk* of a broom, Rebecca's voice. The sound of it was warming. Bec was more than a sister-in-law, closer than a friend; she was an indispensable part of this home.

Standing there, Elizabeth could feel the household turning smoothly around her. From the pantry came the orderly chink of china and silver; from the kitchen, the thick sweet smell of rice pudding reaching a boil. Drawers opened, cupboards shut. Elizabeth knew which ones; she knew what was in them. Plates gently thudded onto the dining-room table. She knew how many. She knew there were clean shirts in the wardrobes and new cheese in the larder and fresh leaves of tea in the canister on the third shelf. Knowing these things pleased her. Listening to the house, knowing its crannies, connecting its corners, she felt somehow rich. It helped to counteract other troubles, other shadows. She remembered that first dim house of her childhood emanating, it seemed, from her white-gowned mother. Now she knew she could stand centered in this house and feel it radiating out from her own skirts. The feeling was fairly new; she hadn't had it in the Wall Street house, she wasn't practiced enough then. Here, to her surprise, she felt herself to be mistress, most days. But here, to her sorrow, the more control she gained of her sphere, the less Willy seemed to have of his. And the less money there seemed to be, not just for sweets, meat, and tea, but for everything.

"Now the sums." She looked at her class. "Say them with me, begin. . . . Two plus two is *four* . . . four plus four is . . ." Four more places to set tomorrow, Julia coming, other friends, Dué, Sad; good to have them at table but think of the marketing bills. . . . "Six plus six is . . . *twelve*. . . ." Twelve children, with Willy's family, six adults with her father there—and again the fishmonger would shake his head at the unpaid account. And the baker. And the chandler, the brewer, all of them. And Willy in there nearly begging for this order. Don't beg him, darling. We need it, God knows. But don't beg.

"I need a reciter now . . . Lord's Prayer, whose turn, Anna? . . . Good, go ahead."

In the study the merchant's voice muttered as Anna's rose.

"Our Father which art in heaven . . ."

Elizabeth wished she could hear what the merchant was saying.

"Thy kingdom come . . ."

She wished the brewer could be paid.

"Give us this day our daily bread . . ."

She wished the baker could be paid.

"Forgive us our debts . . ."

She wished the order could be signed.

"As we forgive our debtors . . ."

She heard the merchant offer his regrets.

". . . deliver us from evil . . ."

She heard him rustle down the hall, out the door.

"For thine is the kingdom . . ."

In the study a ledger slammed shut; coughing began.

"World without end, Amen."

Elizabeth steadied her voice and disbanded the class for its noontide break. Freed, the children ran screaming down the hall toward the back door, hearing their grandfather's voice there. Mama meant constraint just now; Grandpapa meant marzipan and painted kites. And Papa—somehow that study didn't draw these children as it had once drawn him.

She kept herself from going in to Willy—she knew he wouldn't want her there now. She knew how he'd be sitting; sitting in a kind of crouch above that big open desk, flicking the silver seal he'd kept as a talisman. He would wait. He would compose his face. He would not speak of this latest defeat. Nor would she. For an instant she longed to run with her children to her father's knee. Instead she walked into the dining room and surveyed the table set for dinner, still, serene. She adjusted the fold of a napkin, the slant of a fork. The serenity of the room could not seem to reach her. A fork fell through her fingers; a napkin fluttered from her hand. Elizabeth turned, her steps quickening. She knew where she was going. She was going backstairs—backstairs to the servants' hall.

She had no business to do, nothing to oversee there just now. All was prepared, dinner would soon be served; the low-beamed whitewashed room drew her nonetheless. In her father-in-law's day there were eight servants here; now there were only three, unpaid for months, save for their room and board. She saw them coming now, the cook from the kitchen, the others from upstairs and down—coming, hurrying, always at noon, for their prayers. Just as the clock began to chime, they bent their heads over the wooden table here, their rosary beads in their fingers: Patrick, the ancient butler, his salt-white hair falling across his folded hands; Jenny, the cook, her broad red face lifted, eyes closed; Maura, the maid, young and pretty, pumpkin-haired, one hand over her eyes.

They sat within a scent of furniture polish and fennel, beneath fragrant bunches of hanging herbs. The table spread before them, wearing its plain white cloth. Around them the high-windowed light gathered into a rounded shape, and from them came a quietness, a calm that pulled Elizabeth nearly every day. She did not know their prayers. She did not understand the Gaelic they often spoke among themselves. Irish, Catholic, immigrants, they sometimes still seemed foreign to her. Here it didn't matter. Here, at this hour, she knew she was welcomed. Here, at their table, without grasping how, she always gained a measure of peace. The small wooden clock on their mantel ticked softly, *full of grace*. Whispers, only, in the room, *blessed art thou*. Fingers clicking down the beads, well-deep quiet, *blessed is the fruit*. Sun like syrup on the table, on her lap, *and at the hour of our death.* They crossed themselves, one slowly, one briskly, one with a fluttering sweep, and the room regained its normal shape. It filled with the scrape of chairs, the talk of roasts and linen, and Elizabeth surfaced, blinking, back up to the choppy-watered afternoon.

There was blood on the napkin. There was blood on the towel. There was blood on the fine silk handkerchiefs monogrammed WMS. She hadn't seen the blood till then. Till then she hadn't done the wash.

That autumn, at noon, only two heads bent with Elizabeth's in the servants' hall. Maura had found a better position—no one could blame her. The cook had more than she could do as it was, and so, with Rebecca's help, Elizabeth had hauled the dirty clothes out into the sunny yard, stoking the fire under the caldron of water. It was October, a time of year that had always seemed to her crisp with beginnings, air apple-tart, spiced with the remembered smell of new books. The look of the late-afternoon sun burning through the red of a maple had lifted something within her; something too wary now to be completely cheered, but hopeful nonetheless. The feeling of working outdoors had pleased her as well—until she had started sorting the linen and seen over and over, threadlike and clotlike and one pear-shaped stain, the blood coming with Willy's deep cough.

She had known.

Of course she had known.

She had known but not seen, and seeing was different.

There had always been that cough, that chest complaint —but for years the cough had been mild enough. There had been the occasional spells of fever, weakness—but they had been occasional enough, brief enough. "The Seton complaint," Willy always called it—it ran in the very best families, he'd say, and laugh. "The Seton complaint": they had never called it by its right name. She had sometimes worried; he had always dismissed her fears. And he had seemed so strong so long, his stride still an athlete's, his dancing till lately the envy of all. It was only in the last two years that his cough had taken on that tearing sound. It seemed only at Stone Street that her father listened sharply when Willy's spells came on. You couldn't watch him coughing; he'd leave the room. You couldn't catch his gasping; he'd turn away. And now, she saw, he'd hidden his handkerchiefs, hidden his towels, turned over his pillow, and let the maid be the only one to know.

Before her in the caldron the water rolled to a boil, releasing a fine veil of steam. The bunched white linens swam in leisurely circles, sleek as dunked swans, as Rebecca prodded them with a stick. Elizabeth stood unmoving, her stick in her hand, her eyes arrested by a swirling string of red on the water.

"Eliza . . . ?" her sister-in-law asked.

"Nothing, Bec." Elizabeth oared her stick into the water. "Just dreaming. Where's the soap?"

She could not speak of this. Not to anyone. Especially not to Rebecca. Her sister-in-law, she knew, also had the beginnings of "the Seton complaint."

"Eliza . . ." Rebecca nodded at the water. "I saw, I know." She looked at Elizabeth, her heart-shaped face faintly misted with steam. It was a face people liked to take in their hands; so delicate, so fey and finely boned, it seemed to ask to be cupped. Willowy, wand-waisted, with ink-dark hair and skin like candlelit porcelain, Bec looked almost breakable. "Careful," people were always saying to her. "Watch your step; bundle up." But her eyes, at twenty, had a gaze that was calm and wise, as if some seasoned elder glanced from behind that quicksilver mask.

"I know it's worse," Bec said now. "But I know it can get better again—I know how it is with me. Odd sickness, up and down, almost like a moody friend. 'My friend'—I call it that, sometimes, to myself. For years I hated to say flat out what it really is: consumption."

Involuntarily Elizabeth winced. "My family's always dropped their voices on that word—even Papa, even him."

"People do," Bec said drily. "But it's not always doom, you know. Some things make it better—some things don't."

"The work, the worrying, that's made Willy worse, I know it. But what can I do—that can't be changed."

Rebecca wiped her hands on her apron, eyes on the water. "You know, Eliza, sometimes I look at Willy and I think he . . . he drew all his strength from Papa. I think, you know, he's maybe one of those people who gets everything from outside themselves. Your father, now, his strength's mostly from inside, I think. But not Willy's. And he's . . . he's so alone with the business troubles."

Elizabeth jabbed at the wash. "Alone . . . he's not alone. I copy all his letters, I do everything I can, help him whenever he asks, I—"

"He doesn't ask much, does he?"

"Not much, no," Elizabeth snapped. "He doesn't complain. And I don't like to intrude, interfere, I shouldn't, that's all, it's not my place." She glanced sharply at her sister-in-law; Rebecca's eyes, frank and stubborn and loving, were upon her. "Don't you be so quick to judge me, Bec."

"Oh, please, I don't mean to. But, Eliza . . . is it just that you don't want to intrude? Look: I love you, love Willy— and I can't help thinking, thinking you're both just saving each other's faces, avoiding . . . avoiding—"

"Ridiculous, how can you say that, why would we—"

"Because you're afraid."

"*Nonsense.*" Elizabeth's voice rose. She yanked her stick from the wash. "I'd go to him now if I thought it would help. If I thought you could manage this laundry alone."

"I can."

"Well, then. Do."

And Elizabeth, shamed, fuming, stricken, stalked off, stabbing at the ground with her stick. Bec was right, she thought, turning into the street, tossing the stick away. She was right and I hated to hear it, couldn't admit it. Avoid, avoid—of course. And of course—I am afraid.

She was afraid as she kept walking, down one street and over two; it wasn't far. In a few minutes she was at the Seton, Maitland counting house on Mill Street, opened by her father-in-law just six years before.

There was no reply to her knock. She rapped on the door again, then pushed it open and went in. For a moment or two she couldn't see anything at all, her eyes blinded by the brightness outside. Gradually she began to make out forms in the dimness; it seemed to her no one was there.

No stock clerk in the ware hall, no lamps lit, no sign of Willy in the small office to one side. The hall itself was a big drafty barn of a place filled with casks and chests, its windows mostly shuttered. There was a smell of rancid water; there was a faint skitter of mice. Before Elizabeth, like rows of ornate tombstones, was a shipment of marble chimneypieces; they gleamed dully white in the filtered light, intricate and finely wrought. Months before, at a supper party, Willy had met an architect who had spoken of these. Everyone, he'd said, *everyone* in prospering New York was wanting hand-carved marble mantels from Italy. They would be the rage, they would be *la mode*, the architect knew this for a fact. He had purchased two himself, after the shipment had arrived. He and his son and his wigmaker had been the only customers.

"Willy," Elizabeth said now and heard no reply. "Willy," she said again, feeling some dread take hold of her. "Willy!"

He came toward her then, threading his way among the marble. She realized he had been sitting there in the dark amid the mantels, ashamed to reveal himself. For a moment his face was angry, embarrassed; then it was only pained. As he came nearer his eyes glimmered at her, glad to see her after all. He put his hands on her shoulders.

"I'm sorry . . ." she began.

He gave her half a wry smile. "You must've known I had to talk to you."

"I didn't. Bec did."

"Bec didn't know what I have to say." He sat on a crate; for a few moments he delayed, running his hand through his hair. "They've stopped payment in London," he said at last, not looking at her. "Hamburg too. All our accounts. My receipts—sent back to me, all my receipts. Not only that . . ." He flexed his fingers as if about to throw a long ball. "We lost a ship. Near Brittany, she was loaded. Wines, the one thing that was selling. The French, they're to blame. The French, their pirates . . . the bastards." He paused a long while, rubbing his knuckles over his mouth. Elizabeth, sitting beside him on the solid crate, felt the sensation she'd once had as a child, falling out of a tree. She put her hand on his to quiet it; to quiet herself.

Willy began to talk again, faster now, his words skidding into one another. "We'll have to bring my sisters back from school, have to let Jen and Patrick go, have to put off some payments, manage till something comes in, just till. Something will, of course it will, no question. Sent agents to London, clear it up—Stone, Ogden, good men, good men. And till it's cleared, no one must know, understand, *no one*."

"But, Willy . . . maybe you should ask for help, get a loan, I don't know—"

"No loans." His voice was sharp. "Loans look bad—look scared. I've had offers, two last spring, one from the Filicchis, I told them no. Papa never took a loan, not in his life, proud of that."

"But that was . . . then. Times were . . . different."

"That's not what you mean."

"It is, I—"

"You mean I'm not my father, say it." His eyes moved to her from the chimneypieces. "Say it. Go on. I say it myself every day. Know what else I say? Do you?" His voice was rough. "I say, 'Dammit, Papa, what do you want me to do?' I say, 'Papa, what would *you* do, tell me, dammit— why didn't you tell me before?' " His hands clenched; his voice rose, echoing in the room. "I say, 'Dammit, Papa, dammit to hell, I *just wanted to make violins.*' "

She sat there feeling him tremble beside her; she knew she was trembling herself. She could not let that show. She concentrated on the chimneypieces, she counted them; she tried not to lose count as he went on.

"Every night," he was saying, "I keep thinking of Richmond, school, the cricket field. Every night I see it again. Playing. Running. I was good. I was so good. One time, I remember, this big boy came up to me just before a game. Wanted to start a fight, hurt me, get me put out. Some lord's son. Taunting me, shouting. I broke his nose. I put *him* out of the game. Liza, I just keep thinking of that."

They sat there together till what little light there was had waned, the one unshuttered window gone blue. In the Stone Street house it would be candlelighting time, suppertime; bedtime for the children soon after that. She had to go back; he couldn't bear to. In the end she had to leave him there in the counting house, his posture oddly formal, sitting amid the marble—that graceful sculptured marble, flowering with vines and roses, turned out like girls in white dresses still hoping to be asked to dance. As she went out the door she heard him cough. She realized she'd not even asked the questions she'd come with, hadn't said anything of what she'd meant to say.

What comfort had she been? What consolation? She had been stunned, she had been silent. Later, ideas and plans would come to her, she knew; in times of trouble her mind gradually gathered a force unmustered otherwise. But now, when he'd needed her, she had been mute, she had been stone, sitting beside him like those damnable chimneypieces. She felt a sudden disgust with herself, and then a choking unreasonable anger—at herself for having failed; at Willy for having failed; at her father-in-law for having died; and then at everyone she'd ever loved who had ever failed her, ever died.

She walked fast, as if leaning into a strong wind, and before she could stop them, tears began to wet her face. She wiped at them with her sleeve; she couldn't go home this way—a fine way to prepare the family for bad news. She needed a little time before going home. She needed to go where she'd gone before, this year, more and more often, alone. She was already moving toward it: the arching door of St. Paul's Chapel.

Trinity was the Setons' church; there her children had been christened, her father-in-law eulogized. There she went on Sundays with Rebecca, the only other churchgoer in the family, and there she came betweentimes, by herself, just to sit. But sometimes when she felt most troubled, she walked past Trinity to St. Paul's—and sometimes, as now, the need to be there was visceral.

The church was unlit, dimmed by the dusk, as empty as it had been that night of Washington's arrival when she had come, lost long ago. Emptier: now she saw no vagrant sleepers. She slid into a pew, head pounding, and pulled the kneeler toward her. The heels of her hands, pressed against her eyes, made pinwheels of light on the dark. At times like these her prayers were never neatly worded, never narrated or listed at all: they were pure inarticulate feeling. She saw in her mind Miss Molly's straight spine at the prie-dieu that long-ago day of the fire; she saw the bent heads of the servants at the table in the house on Stone Street. She thought of the calm she had seen in the eyes of Quaker market women, the peace she had heard in the hymns of Methodist neighbors—she thought of all the wells of comfort she could draw upon. Again Miss Molly came into her mind: Miss Molly standing here in this church, writing a prayer for her in the open book by the door. The book was still there; how many prayers it had held, how many pages turned since then, she could not guess. Elizabeth rose from her knees and went to the book, lighting the candle in the sconce beside it and dipping the quill in the ink.

Please, oh please . . .

She crossed that out. He wouldn't want that where anyone could see, could infer, could deduce there was trouble.

Please, that W.S.'s health mends soon.

She crossed that out as well. He wouldn't want that written either.

Please, oh please . . .

Again her quill struck through the words. *Please, oh please* —she sounded like one of her own children, wheedling, whining. She stood still for a moment, watching the candlelight flare on the page. All around her she could feel the building arching, curving into the night, holding her within its quiet.

Dear God, she wrote at last. *May my family be safe.* She paused; there was something else. *May we remain in Thy care.* The quill hesitated, then dipped and lifted once more. *May I not be homeless again,* she wrote, and blew out the light.

8

. . . One pair candlesticks, silver.
One pair candlesticks, pewter.
One mantel clock, marble, gilded.
One pair andirons, ornamented, brass.
This completes inventory of parlor. . . .

She glanced away from the list in her hand. No reason for it to look strange; she had copied it out herself. A copy for Mr. Kitlett, a copy for her. Efficiently done on the day before Christmas, her own paper, her own ink. No reason for it to look strange at all.

Absurd for it to swim this way before her eyes. She thought she'd come to terms with this months before; this had been expected, she had been fully prepared. She just hadn't thought about this moment, was all. She hadn't quite thought out how it would be, actually checking the list with what was left in the house; she hadn't quite thought out how this moment would be, leaving the house for good.

These past few months she had made herself think only of items, objects—candlesticks and clocks and sheets, counting them, classifying them, listing them in short expressionless phrases for the bankruptcy commission. She had told herself how safe this inventory made them. With this list in the hands of Garrett Kitlett, no overeager creditor could rush through the door, carrying off what he chose. Garrett Kitlett had told her this himself, pressing the balls of his fingers together and gazing at her from rheumy eyes. He was a rumpled dome-bellied man, gravy on his shirt, snags in his hose. "Not a pot, not a plate," he had said, bringing his slack-jawed face close to hers. His disrepair had made her think, not of the bankruptcy commission he represented, but of the way her family might soon look themselves. No. They would not look that way. She would make certain, no matter what. They would not look that way and she would not look directly at Garrett Kitlett. She would not look directly at anything to do with this—no lingering gazes, no sentimental stares, no mooning whatsoever. She would keep her mind on items, objects, lists.

This was how she had got through the fall since that evening with Willy in the counting house. This was how she had got through that last Christmas in the Stone Street house. She had completed the inventory and roasted the goose her father had brought them. She had hung boxwood from the parlor arch as always; as always, she had stirred the fire, lit the candles, mixed wassail—and she had watched from the window for sheriffs, agents, repossessors, anyone who might challenge the writ and seek to carry off their goods.

How festive the family had looked by the fire that Christmas afternoon. How regular, how normal. Within the room, yet beyond the room, she had stood at her post by the window, watching them: watching the usual commotion, the usual fusses. There was the blaze of the hearth behind them, fire leaping like an eager hound; andirons, candlesticks gleaming. There was the usual gathering around the gifts—two great barrelfuls of gifts, carried in the night before by Dr. Bayley. She remembered how he had sat amid the children on the hearth rug, this returned prodigal, this spare and elegant Father Christmas, silver-haired, pearl-buttoned, with a bright red wooden horse in his hands. And little Dick, the baby saved by him and named for him, tottering across the rug, hands stretched out toward the horse, tumbling down, looking up to gauge if he should cry or not —then off again toward the horse, giggling suddenly, secretly to himself. Anna, small and delicate in the firelight, gazing into the face of a china doll. And Billy, small and stocky and, even at four, so like her father-in-law. The eleven Seton brothers and sisters, clamoring and laughing and clowning about—and the one whose absence she felt in her chest: Willy. An hour before they had gathered there, he had banged shut the wardrobe in their bedroom and said he was going out. There was a wassail party at the Jays', there was a reception at the Livingstons', he was going. He was going in his embroidered waistcoat, he was going in his silver buckles. He was going to keep up appearances, someone had to; he was going to have some merriment, some relief, would she deny him that? For a moment they had stood and glared at each other over the bed. The silence had tightened. Then he had grabbed up his keys and slammed out. It was only after he had gone that she realized what he had grabbed up with them: the larger, longer key to the counting house. It was due to be returned, and he was going to return it now. She understood then. He had postponed this for weeks. This was the only way he could do it.

One chessboard, with pieces, ivory.
One desk, estate style, cherry.
One desk chair, cherry. . . .
She brought her mind back from Christmas, back to the study in the Stone Street house, where she stood now. She was listening to her children racketing about the empty house—its rooms seemed newly large, nothing there for elbows and boots and waving arms to break. The carters would soon be here. The remaining furniture waited by the gate outside: a jumble of bedsteads and upended chairs she could see from the window—all that was left after the bankruptcy auction. Again, again, she wondered if it had to happen; her mind searched the issue as if it were an old coat, its pockets and linings holding answers, reasons that would be to her liking. There was no such answer. There had been no other way, once payment had been stopped, once the ship had been lost, once the bills had been seen. No use going over it and over it, no use at all. She forced herself to set her mind ahead, to think of the new house.

Number 8 State Street: how she dreaded it. She knew the children dreaded it as well. Not a bad house, she had told them; told herself. Quite a nice house, she had said, three stories, brick, roomy enough. What a view of the water they'd have, what a view of the ships, the Battery, the park and Promenade. Never mind that they had never lived in a neighborhood like that before. Never mind the lodging house right next door, the refreshment stand a few doors down. It wasn't really that. Well, being honest, it wasn't only that. It was leaving Stone Street—leaving this house— that made her throat constrict.

She looked at the place where her father-in-law's great desk had been. It had left a large H-shaped mark on the floor, like some huge-petaled flower pale against the darker hardwood boards. A crate sat behind it where the chair had been. She looked at the oval on the walls where the framed silhouettes had hung; she looked at the long rectangular outlines from the bookcases. *Lizzie, come take a cup wi' me.* Tears filled her eyes. Dear proud grand old room. How long it seemed since she'd sat listening to him; seven years now. How young she had been, trembling there on the brink of this room, this heart of the house where she had, for the first time ever, felt truly at home.

Her children appeared in the doorway now: Dickie held to Anna's hand; Billy leaned against his sister, thumb in mouth. Their eyes, large and grave, were fixed upon her, catching the unguarded sadness on her face. Behind them, Willy's youngest sisters, Harriet and Cecilia, drew close— a pyramid of big-eyed children, suddenly subdued.

"Almost time," she told them, striving for brightness, hearing instead a voice frayed and torn.

"Papa . . . ?" Anna asked.

"Papa's at the *new* house." In fact she didn't know where Willy was—out walking somewhere was all he'd said. "Papa's helping to get it all *ready*."

The children heard the forced cheer in her words. They shifted closer together as if for warmth, and silently, stonily, Anna began to cry; then noisily, with great gulping sobs, Billy started. Tears glimmered in Cecilia's eyes, and to her horror, Elizabeth felt them again in her own. Good glory, she thought, look at us, just look.

She stood there for a moment wishing Willy were there; wishing she did not have to face this scene at all. Her eyes went once more to the marks on the floor of that grand old desk. *Come, Lizzie, come on back to me.* She seated herself on the crate there, drawing the children to her. *Now, one house, it ha' a gude spirit. . . .* She cleared her throat and the children pressed closer. She could feel their soft expectant breathing, she could feel their fingers twisting in her skirts. She blinked to clear her eyes. Beside her she could almost see her father-in-law once more—that freckled homely radiant face, the way he'd lean into a story.

"Your grandpa told me this. I'll tell you while we're waiting . . ." she began. Again she wished that Willy were here. Her voice was trembling, not only with sadness, but with anger.

"This is a story about . . . a family that had to move from their old house to a new house . . . far, far away."

The story didn't sound the same in her mouth. Resentment was coming out in her voice, she could hear it.

"The family didn't want to move . . . and they hated leaving their luck behind. Their luck's name was Tom Cockle —he'd taken care of them for years and years. No one ever saw him . . . but everyone knew he was there. . . ."

Her eyes strayed to the window, hoping to see Willy there. Of course he wouldn't appear. He was not unlike Tom Cockle these days—she hardly saw him: she tasted the bitterness in that thought. He had grown so distant, so remote throughout these last bad months. And she? She had answered his silences with her own.

". . . and they all cried, leaving the old house and telling Tom Cockle good-bye. And the mother, she wondered how she'd manage in the new house . . . she knew it would be big . . . and empty . . . and drafty . . . and cold. It would need a lot of hands to take care of it. Worst of all, it would be new . . . new and very strange. . . ."

For a moment all the back bedrooms of her childhood came before her again, all the strangeness, the sickness in the stomach. For a moment she blamed Willy for making her feel it again—unreasonable of her, she knew. She felt it even so. The children looked up at her. She took a breath, went on.

"The new house would need twenty servants . . . and they hadn't got one. It would need a spirit like Tom Cockle to light the fires . . . to fill the larders . . . and sweep . . . and cook . . . and warm everyone's hearts. Back home, all they'd had to do, you see, was call out for Tom Cockle and tell him what was needed. . . ." Elizabeth looked down on the children's heads, trying again to steady her voice. Maybe in the new house she and Willy would talk again. Maybe in the new house this space between them would close.

"Well, the mother hid her tears. And as they all drove through the night to the new house, she made some plans. She made plans for a fire. And for a kettle of porridge. Bad enough to come through the dark to a cold empty house . . . worse still with nothing to eat."

The children leaned against her as if under an umbrella, sheltered by the story from invisible rain. The room seemed to gather around them, holding them close one last time, its air alive and dancing with flecks of dust.

"Well, then, they came up the road . . . and they saw the house in the dark of the night." Elizabeth's voice lifted. "And then one of the children called out, 'There it is, there's the house—and it's got lights in it!' And so there were. It was their new empty house indeed. But there was a fire in the hearth. There was food in the kitchen. There were lights to welcome them in—Tom Cockle had got there ahead of them."

9

Families in trouble—they have a certain look. A certain
tightness to the shoulders; a certain strain around the eyes.
I've seen it in this plush cathedral parish. I've seen it in my
own family, since my sister's death. The shoulders: that's
always the tip-off.

Families like that, it's mostly the woman who comes looking for help. Mostly the wife who first appears in the rectory
parlor, who first starts coming to early Mass. I talked with a
woman like that today, a fashionable matron from this
fashionable suburb: well-dressed, discreet; a little apologetic.
She needed to talk, she said; needed someplace to come to.
There was something about her, something a little disarrayed,
a little worn—made me think of Elizabeth Seton. The intensity, the eyes. Made me think how she must have been,
that summer, 1801, after the bankruptcy, the move. How
she must have looked in the new house. Trying to anchor
that family. Beginning to turn to her father again, and to
the new curate at Trinity Episcopal. Turning to them, but
turning inward, more and more, as well.

I can see her sitting there on the steps of Number 8 State
Street that evening in June, watching the couples drift along
the Promenade. The trees in Battery Park, fuller now than
the month before when she moved in, are not yet massy.
Above them, through the slow-falling dusk, Elizabeth can
still see the tangle of spars and rigging in the harbor. The
breeze smells faintly of fish, and of nutmeg: the cargo of

a ship, just docked, from the Indies. Rumbling by, their outlines softened by the changing light, are a crested carriage and an undertaker's wagon, then a sedan chair drawn by a liveried slave. On the air laughter and violin music are floating; music not from her own house, but from Columbia Gardens, the refreshment establishment up the street. From its door there is a yellow spill of light, and from its bright, garish interior Mr. Corré has just come, his striped apron flapping, to bring her children free ice cream. She hears them slurping delightedly behind her now on the steps; she feels both grateful for the treat and ashamed to be beholden for it. She nudges the shame from her mind. This is easy to do just now, easier than usual—easy to shift her entire attention back to the man standing by the steps, talking with her and Rebecca. His face, boyish and owlish and kind, is tipped toward Elizabeth. The light from the lantern in his hand reflects off his thick spectacles and catches in the cowlick standing straight up from the middle of his head. Passing by, you wouldn't think this is a clergyman, a curate: the Reverend Henry Hobart, already gaining a reputation as the light, the voice, the silver tongue of Trinity Church. No older than Elizabeth, no more than twenty-six, he looks vulnerable, almost naive here in the street: he shines forth only from the pulpit. The women love him; they mother him, root for him, feel proud of him— and Elizabeth feels closer to him than most. It has been this way since he found her sitting in a back pew one evening when, the church empty, the hour late, he had come in to practice a sermon. He had asked her, stammering, if she would listen, comment perhaps. She had suddenly begun to cry. What he had said, she could not precisely remember; only that he had spoken ordinary, homely words. He had come to call on the Setons, he had come often. Elizabeth and Rebecca look forward to the Sundays when he preaches; they cannot stop talking about him.

"Of course we have but one Comforter, this is what we must never, never lose sight of for a moment."

"Of course . . . it *is* easy to lose sight of, between churning the butter and, you know, the diapers. . . ."

Their voices hang on the dark above the music, above the sound of fingers being licked.

". . . Running a house—sometimes I think it must be as hard, *harder* than running a parish."

"But we must *always* remember our Divine Friend, mustn't we, behind it all. This is what I try to get across now, even in regular conversations, but people, they're so *heedless*."

The children shift uneasily on the steps. The pressing pious voice is not the curate's; it is their mother's, ringing with the zeal of one who has newly found a clerical friendship; God knows, I've heard that tone myself.

"Mrs. Seton . . ." Hobart hesitates, his hands fiddling clumsily with the lantern. "How can I, uh, put this . . . it's just that perhaps you might, uh, be a bit less direct. . . . People, you know, have a tendency to, uh, dislike being preached at . . . not to say you're exactly doing that, but . . . you see?"

Elizabeth flushes. Of course that's what she's been doing; it scalds her, but he's right. That's what she's been doing with Willy, with friends, to no avail. Mr. Hobart is unerringly perceptive, and ducking her head, she tells him so. There is a silence as the darkness deepens around them. In the silence they are unable to avoid noticing the smudge pot before the house a few doors down, its shutters drawn against the balmy evening. They are unable to avoid noticing another undertaker's wagon passing in the street. They say nothing of this, almost out of superstition. They turn their eyes to other things: the lights of Columbia Gardens, the lantern in the rigging of a ship. They know they have seen signs of the summer's beginning, and with it, the dreaded time of contagion as well. The signs are still few, small, possibly even misread. But they make everyone, even the children, think of the sickness too frightening to mention: yellow fever.

Reverend Hobart clears his throat and bids them good night. Above her in the house, Elizabeth hears Willy tuning his violin. She wonders if this time he'll really play; she watches Hobart's retreating back. Tomorrow her father will come to fetch her and the children to Staten Island for the summer: she doesn't know if she feels saddened or relieved. The little ones catch things so fast, it's best for them to be out of the city—but she'll miss her Sundays at Trinity; she'll miss Willy, and Rebecca, who will stay to keep house for him. Maybe they shouldn't go. Maybe they should all stay in one house, especially now. Her temples have begun to throb; her children tug at her skirts, wanting more ice cream.

"Up, up now, out of the night air."

Within the house the baby cries, Willy's tuning breaks off.

"Come, hurry, bedtime, prayers . . ."

"Aw, *Mama* . . ."

The smudge pot glows in the dark down the street.

"Up, up—tomorrow, Grandpapa, Staten Island."

From the house on Staten Island she could see the house on State Street. Across the bay at night, she saw its lights and thought of Willy with Rebecca there. Keeping watch on it made her feel less guilty about being on the island; and now that she'd got used to being there, loving it.

Days had passed. Weeks had passed, she had lost count of them. She could not, if suddenly asked, tell you with certainty what month it was, even what year. This morning, starting a letter, she had caught herself dating it 1797. Odd thing to do, she had thought, staring at the numbers for an instant before scratching them out. Odd; but not so odd. 1797 was the year before her father-in-law's death, before there was any hint of loss, trouble, failure. They had spent the summer that year at Cragdon, she remembered, the Seton country home out in Bloomingdale. The house had been crowded, too noisy, but thinking back on it now, that summer seemed serene and enchanted, caught forever in the amber glow of its best afternoons. And here on Staten Island this summer, Elizabeth felt that she was somehow back in similar, protected time.

Here on Staten Island there was air clean enough to drink, air that smelled of salt and grass and something else she could not name, some freshness she associated with early mornings and clean wash. Here there were meadows blowing with cattails and lady's slipper, pillowed neatly with haystacks—she could see her children running a ring around one now, *round we go, friend or foe, one two three four freeze.* Here there were honeysuckle and strawberries and a broad piazza for walking, and most of all there was her father, morning and evening, breakfast and supper and candlelighting time. She met him every day at the double white fences he had had put up before they'd come: one fence around her father's house and land, and another fence around the first, to keep them perfectly clear of the Quarantine Station.

"Children," she called while she thought of it.

"*—five six seven eight—*"

"Mind the fences, remember now."

The Quarantine Station was the only thing here that did not remind her of peaceable summers, blessed times. It was far enough so they couldn't smell it, couldn't see it very clearly. In fact she did not have to look that way at all—but she did, and didn't know why. Morbid curiosity, she thought.

Beyond her white pickets and the station's split rails, the immigrants crowded off the ships, most of them ailing, some of them dying, all of them reeling from steerage passage in reeking holds. Many of them, she knew, were Irish; how many times she had thought of her noontides backstairs at Stone Street, watching them. She had watched men and women falling to their knees, kissing the ground; she had seen, catching the light, the rosary beads in their fingers. Even the ones who were ill knelt and crossed themselves, gathering American soil in their hands—even the ones who fell forward and did not rise again. In the daylight she had watched them, huddled jumbled groups of shawls and caps and skirts, and in the dark she had seen their lights: lights from the tents pitched in the yard of the convalescent house, lights from the convalescent house itself—lights from every shelter but one, the dead house. Once she had seen a woman watching her, a woman about her age, with a fringed shawl pinned around her dark hair, an infant in her arms. The woman's face was the color of tallow, with pouches the color of figs beneath her eyes. She had stared at Elizabeth over the fence, over the top of her baby's head, and Elizabeth had stared back, over her fence, over the head of her baby. For three days, whenever she had gone to the gate to wait for her father, the woman was there, staring; the second and third days, she was sitting, not standing, her chin resting on a rail. The first two days, Elizabeth had thought she'd heard a crooning kind of song rise from her; the third day, silence. It was a long time, that last day, before Elizabeth realized the woman wasn't moving, that the staring sick eyes were not blinking. It was only when the woman's baby cried for five and ten and then fifteen minutes that she knew the woman was dead. Elizabeth had opened the gate, she had taken a step toward the station, and then her father's hand was on her arm. He would see to the baby; she must not, he had told her; he had led her away in tears. After that she had not looked in that direction so often. She had looked toward the bay, she had looked toward the haystacks and meadows; she had watched her children play.

"Look to the *east*, look to the *west*," they chanted now, their voices stern and sweet on the air, "look for the one that hides the *best* . . . one . . . two . . . saw you, Billy, you moved . . ."

She would look to the east, not the west. She knew her father was there, doing whatever could be done. He was almost always at the station, sometimes twelve, fourteen hours a day. She had watched him too, his tall spare figure moving among the blankets and shawls. They would grab at his breeches, they would clutch at his shirt, they would make way for him. They would watch for him at their fence, just as she watched for him at hers. She had seen him with his sleeves rolled up, his shirt plastered to him as he'd walk up the path to the pump, then disappear inside the little shack where he'd change his "pesthole clothes," he said. She worried for him every day, but after so many summers around the immigrants, he seemed fast to fevers. Only in that way did he still seem faintly supernatural to her. Odd, she thought, as he came up the path to the pump now— when she was a child he had awed her so, that legend in a ruffled shirt; he had really been just a bright young surgeon then. Now he no longer awed her, this man in the sweat-soaked waistcoat, and now he truly had awesome credentials.

"Grandpapa . . . *Grand*papa!"

"Stay back, dearies, I'm coming."

Coming to wash at the pump was, she smiled to think, the first professor of anatomy at Columbia, its second professor of surgery. Coming to change his clothes in that shack was the author of the celebrated piece on yellow fever in *The Monitor*. Coming up the path to kiss her was the organizer of the New York Dispensary for the Poor, and running toward her children, arms wide, was the health officer of the Port of New York, the first to hold that title. The chandlers and the soap boilers, stung by his edicts, sometimes petitioned to have him removed; he could not be removed, all the same. He dined with the famous in Albany, this man on his knees in the meadow grass here. He knew whose portrait in the Capitol got the most attention, he knew people of influence—but that wasn't why he could not be removed. He was brilliant, he was dedicated, people still said: this man with the children climbing all over him. "But I don't care for what they say now," he had told her, surprising himself, "now that I've been domesticated."

"Observe, gentlemen, milady."

A puppet bloomed suddenly on his hand, its pointed hat bobbing.

"Observe—aha—he knows your names."

The dry ironic voice crowed.

"Anna Maria . . . Billy . . ."

The long clever fingers danced the puppet.

". . . and Dick, named for someone I know well . . ."

He turned, stood, moved toward Elizabeth.

"Kit, and my favorite, Lady Bet."

The puppet ignored her misted eyes.

"Come on," it called. "I want my supper."

"Thank you, God, for all this stuff."

Dickie looked around the table, thumb in mouth, mumbling his contribution to the suppertime grace. There was blackfish and chicken pie spread before them, new bread and a dolphin cheese and a punch bowl of strawberries sent by a neighbor. The candles dipped and danced in the breeze; the curtains blew in and out the window in a gentle rhythm as Billy took his turn.

"Thank you, God, for supper and . . . for the haystack out by the fence in the clover field . . . the *biggest* one, I tagged it first, it's *mine* now . . . *not* Anna's. . . ."

Elizabeth, at the foot of the table, suppressed a smile. Glancing over her clasped hands, she saw her father, at the table's head, doing the same. The flickering light fell over her son's eager face and over her daughter's, chin thrust out, primed to rebut.

"Thank *you*, God, for this supper . . . and for Thy bounty," Anna said, immediately outdoing her brother with two clerical words. "And for *all* the haystacks in the clover field *except* that little puny one by the fence that I didn't want *anyway*. . . ."

From the head of the table, Dr. Bayley suddenly chuckled out loud, and the children, amused that their grandfather had laughed during prayers, burst into giggles.

"I'm not a religious man"—Dr. Bayley glanced at Elizabeth—"as someone at this table likes to point out . . . but I think I can finish this grace by saying *I'm* thankful . . . for this evening, for you all . . . and for this food, of course, let's make a start on it now, Amen."

There was the usual suppertime commotion: the usual amount of potatoes in the hair, peas in the ears, forks dropped, and milk spilled. Through it all Elizabeth found herself still trying to compose some form of grace, some thanks, some praise. Returning to the house, mid-meal, taking Dickie back in from the privy, she saw how the dining room hung on the dark, its candlelit space framing that gemlike mountain of berries, those bobbing heads—all safe and, despite the noise that burst from the window, somehow serene. A sense of well-being came over Elizabeth, strong as wine; her hand tightened on her son's. Almost immediately she felt a needling of guilt, and turned, from habit, to glance across the bay at the State Street house.

It was dark, as she knew it would be just now; Rebecca visiting friends, Willy in Baltimore to see about reestablishing there. He would be out here this weekend to report on that—another weekend too brief, him too weary to enjoy it, nothing but worries to talk of. She always felt faintly disappointed and resentful on Sunday nights. But these weekday evenings, fleeting though they were—they more than compensated for the rest.

That evening after the children were in bed, Elizabeth sat with her father in the spare whitewashed parlor and listened to the breeze in the clover outside. They sat in peaceable silence for a time, he working one of the word puzzles he relished, she with the newest baby on her shoulder: the baby named Catherine for the first wife he had loved, the mother she had lost. Of all his grandchildren, Kit was his favorite—she soon displaced his puzzle, receiving sips of chocolate from his cup.

" 'Papa,' " he murmured to the baby. "Say 'Papa.' " He glanced over at Elizabeth. "Must seem odd to you still, Bet—seeing me like this."

"I love seeing you like this."

"Odd, nonetheless, must be—sometimes it even seems odd to me. I mean, after so many years the other way. . . . I've hoped, one of these evenings, some explanation would occur to me."

"No need, Papa. Not anymore."

"*I* need to explain this change. If only to myself. I don't, quite. It's not just that I grew older. *Not* just that I was lonely after the . . . separation. *Not* that my work had ceased to absorb me, not that atall. I don't know, Bet. A strange thing, in the midst of life—a busy life—to feel that kind of longing. Actual yearning: never felt it before. And for me to yearn for family life—*me*—well, it knocked me flat at first, I can tell you."

He jiggled the baby, giving her another taste of chocolate on his finger.

"I suppose," he said, "it's like this fascination with yellow fever; it just *grew*. It pulled me, drew me, that was all. Now the practice I used to have—it seem so dull. And these people here . . ." He jerked his head toward the station. "How much they teach me. A far sight more than that class of young wise-asses at the college."

Elizabeth smiled, and, grabbing for the doctor's spectacles, Kit gave a sudden cackle.

"Ah, you're both laughing at the old man, heartless of you. . . . Well, you know, Bet, I *am* an odd bird. Perfectly happy not to be married. Some people think me quite a scandal. Good! I love to think on the oddity of my life—what would be affliction to someone else only amuses me. But being a part of your family . . . now, that I take quite seriously. And to say what it means, I wanted . . ." He looked at Elizabeth, helpless for a moment, mouth tight, eyes wet.

"Well. Enough of *this*." Expertly he burped the baby. "Mawkish, maudlin, don't know what's come over me. Play for me, Bet, no use sitting quiet as a couple of Quakers."

She sat at his piano, her skirts crackling and whispering around her on the bench, and he stood beside her, Kit still in his arms. Elizabeth picked out a ballad, then another, and his voice joined hers. "Something *brighter* next," he said, "something cheerful, one of those damn rebel songs, can't beat them for cheer." She began to pick out "Yankee Doodle," letting his voice rise alone; an energetic baritone, strong and true, taking the song and flying it through the room.

" 'Yankee Doodle, keep it up, Yankee Doodle Dan-*dee* . . .' "

His face shone in the candlelight, an arm swinging as if he were on a march. Under his voice her fingers galloped, and from the tail of her eye she saw the cook in the doorway, watching, smiling. " '. . . and with the girls be ha-an-*dee*.' "

All that night the song ran in her head, even as she drifted toward sleep and into it; even as she waked around four to calm a whimper from the boys' room. On her way back to bed she heard her father downstairs, heard the door shut behind him, and from the window she saw his lantern on the path. A large cloud bank had arisen over the bay and was spreading toward New York; now and then there was a flash of lightning. As she watched him going down the dock, rowing out to a ship, she hoped it wouldn't storm. Above Long Island the sky was clear, spangled with stars; the thunder sounded far away. She could see her father's lantern passing the shrouds of the vessel, disappearing within it. The cloud bank began to shift away, leaving the sky bright. She yawned and went back to bed, "Yankee Doodle" still racketing around in her mind; she dreamed of soldiers with macaroni in their hats.

At breakfast, she remembered, her father was silent, but that was his custom, most mornings. He soon went off again on his way to the station—it was only when she rose from the table that she saw him through the window. She stopped, suddenly numbed, a napkin still in her hand. Her father was sitting on a log on the dock, his head in his hands. His shoulders quivered. His feet made small confused shufflings on the boards. When she reached him, he looked at her for a moment as if he didn't know her, and he looked that way till she'd got him indoors.

"It's nothing, nothing," he said, and she echoed, "Nothing, nothing, of course."

"My legs, they just gave way," he said in a voice that trembled.

"It's nothing," she said, and "Nothing," he echoed her, "Of course, nothing at all."

It was only after he'd been put to bed that his eyes cleared, his voice steadied. He reached for Elizabeth's hand as she sat beside him, and in his best bedside manner, began to speak of himself and his "case." The voice was calm, matter-of-fact, detached: the patient, a fifty-seven-year-old male, had a middling constitution. He had been exposed to yellow fever for years. He had always before taken care not to go into enclosed, unventilated areas of contagion, until last night, when, finding a large group of immigrants transferred off a ship and confined in such an area against his instructions, he went in among them. Instantly he experienced pain in the head and in the bowels. Subsequently he experienced weakness, vomiting, and the start of delirium: symptoms of yellow fever which, judging by the severity of exposure and his age, would be fatal.

"Why, Papa, why?" Her voice rose in a wail, a child's voice again. "Why did you go in there, knowing that, why?"

"The patient," he said dryly, "is a hot-tempered individual. And the patient was angry."

"Papa . . ." Her voice trailed off. For a moment she just sat there, not looking at him. Then she smoothed her skirts. She wiped her face. She arranged for cool drinks and clean basins to be fetched to her father's room. She arranged for the children to go visiting. She sent notes to her sister, her stepmother, her husband. And then she went back, for as long as it might be, to her father's bedside.

A line of moonlight moved across the bed. He retched into the basin she held. His chin, unshaven, scraped her hand. His sweat wet her bodice as she held his head. His face looked different now: aged, hollowed, the color of old cheese. She hadn't noticed before the pouches under the eyes, the loose flesh at the throat. She wiped his lips, leaned his head back on the pillow. His eyes remained on her. "Catherine," he said, and then a woman's name she didn't recognize. She set the basin down and walked to the window. She could hold his head, breathe his vomit, she could sit up with him night after night, but she couldn't bear his deliriums. There were things about him she didn't want to know. And there were pictures she didn't want to see again. She didn't want to see in her mind Miss Molly as she'd been that last time; she did not want to see that hot still desperate afternoon.

How many nights was it now? The fourth, the fifth? She couldn't remember. How hard he fought; of course he would. Maybe he'd mend, maybe still. *Please,* she breathed at the window, recognizing her oldest, simplest prayer of desperation, *oh please.* Whenever he was lucid, she felt strong. Whenever he was delirious, she felt like a child: frightened, alone; the way it had been when she'd wake in the dark with the candle gone out and the world gone away and her cries gone unanswered. Not only a frightened child, an angry one as well, raging inwardly that it had to be taken, this time with him; that it had to be so short. She had thought he would outlive half the family; he was the healer, after all. In some dim cranny of her mind, she'd thought if anything happened to Willy, at least she'd have this: this place, this peace, this man watching over them. Maybe he'd mend. Maybe, after all.

Now he was on his hands and knees on the mattress, as if that way he could somehow find ease. She touched his back; it arched in pain. Outside on the water a ship's bell clanged. She didn't catch the hour, knew it was late. The house was hushed, but then, it was always hushed now, daytime as well. The dining room had filled with flowers; and with strawberries—every neighbor seemed to have sent them. She'd ordered them to be given away—they reminded her too much of that last happy supper. Maybe he'd mend. He'd looked so strong, singing at the piano. She could hear him still. He'd looked so strong, his light so clear, going abroad that damnable pestilent ship, oh Papa.

The retching began again. "Oh, Christ, Christ," he gasped. Oh, Lord, Lord, she said inside her head. Help me hold on. She held water to his lips, a spoonful of honey to ease his throat. How he had given Kit sips of his chocolate, how strong he'd looked then. Again he retched, clutching her. She heard a seam open under her arm. This man who had once seemed too perfect, too remote for sleep, this man had soaked her with his sweat, his vomit. She loved him much more now. He leaned against her, breathing hard, his eyes clearing once more. "Lady Bet," he said. Her eyes filled. "Papa . . . ?" He was too exhausted to say any more. He had predicted this. Before his last delirium he had told her "all the horrors are coming." He had listed them, described them, calmly as before. He had warned her to take rest the moment he sank into heavy sleeps.

Wiping her hands, she left the room for a pillow, a blanket, and stopped a moment at Kit's cradle. She had scarcely seen this child except to nurse her, these bad sick days; the only child left in the house. She had missed the feel of Kit against her shoulder. With the baby bundled in her arms, Elizabeth went out on the piazza. Too tired to sleep, she paced up and down. Maybe he'd mend. His face came before her, half-bearded now, white. What if he didn't mend? A shutter banged, the breeze ruffled the grass. What if he didn't mend and Willy didn't mend? She walked faster, shivering. What if and what if . . . oh Lord, what? Across the water the bell clanged again, urgent, ugly, loud. Oh, Lord, if this is a sin forgive me, but please . . . she shifted the baby in her arms. Take this child instead of him. Let me have him for longer than this.

Shaking, she went back in the house and laid the baby in the cradle. She returned, still shaking, to her father's room. The line of moonlight had shifted, just a faint silver thread on the rug. Her father lay quietly, sleeping still. She sat beside him, smoothing the sheet. His breathing seemed to crowd the room, as the sound of crickets had crowded the parlor all these summer nights. He opened his eyes. They seemed clear. She felt a stir of hope. He took her hand. He looked at her; he looked at her with love. "Papa," she said. His breathing rattled in his throat. "Papa, stay." His fingers loosened on hers; a bluish cast came over his face. *"Papa."* His rattled breathing ceased.

She wanted to bury him on the island, but they couldn't carry him across it—transport was forbidden, since he'd died of the fever. Still, she was stubborn; she wanted to bury him beside her mother at St. Andrew's Church. At last his boatman, Darby, took the coffin on a barge and carried him by water near enough. Elizabeth, with Willy and her sister in a carriage, met him at the wharf and rode behind the coffin up the steep road. Two carriages of mourners followed; Elizabeth noticed the second Mrs. Bayley and her children weren't there.

On the way back to the house, an axle broke. Elizabeth stood and watched them fix it, her eyes dry, her face still. She had not cried, she had not trembled, wavered once. Willy was watching her, waiting for her to break. She would not break, she would not cry. She would pack up the four extra plates and the five white night shifts, she would put away the brushes and go back on the boat. She would not feel this. Not just yet. This grief would have to be wrested from her, wrested like an aching tooth from a stubborn jaw. It would hurt at the parting and it would take a strong hand, for bitterness had locked her jaw, frozen her tears, and set her soul, hard as diamonds and as cold, blazing, raging, against this loss.

In the city it was hard to forget; the fever was everywhere. White rags were hung from the knockers of afflicted houses. Mattresses were burned in the streets. Smudge pots smoked on doorsteps. Coffins rumbled by on carts, rattling the windows of the State Street house in the mornings and the evenings and during noontide dinner. Windows were shuttered, doors barred. Housewives glanced uneasily at the lettuces and loaves in their market baskets. The parks emptied, businesses closed; some did not reopen. Moist heat hung over the city, and with it a stench of burnt bedding and pinewood coffins and rotting human flesh. The gravediggers, the only men in the city's taverns, could not keep up with the demand.

At bedtime in the house on State Street, the children tugged at Elizabeth's gown.

"Will it come here?" they asked every night, their pillowed faces tilted toward her. "Will it get us?"

"No," she said, and the children heard the flatness in her voice and were frightened by it.

"Mama . . . ?"

"What."

"Two doors down, there's a white rag out."

"Go to sleep now."

"Mama, Mr. Corré, he's got it too, we *heard*."

"Get back in bed."

"What makes it come?"

"No one knows."

"Grandpa knew."

"Not exactly."

"Grandpa said—"

"Go to sleep."

"Will we die like Grandpa?"

"This minute—back in bed."

"Mam*aaa* . . ."

As she went about her household tasks, her temples hurt. Her teeth hurt. The roots of her hair hurt. Her face looked pained, she knew, and bitter. She waked within the bitterness, as within a shell; she moved through the day within it. She still could not cry, could not mourn. All she could do was rail inwardly against the death, unmaking it each morning in her mind. She hadn't had him long enough, she shouted silently to the coffee grounds and the dishwater; not long enough, not fair.

The children began to cling to Willy for comfort instead of her, crawling over him as he lay on his chaise, writing endless letters. His grandfather sent money; Willy sent back painstaking accounts of expenses. His hopes for a Baltimore business had faded; now he sent letters to Philadelphia, Boston, even London and Livorno in Italy. Elizabeth had seen the letters he left where she would find them, letters from his father's friends the Filicchis: *regain your health here in our sunshine, get refinanced, let us help.* . . . She had seen the hopeful look on Willy's face; she had thrown the letters into a drawer. She would not let these people make her hope. Better not to hope. Safer, less painful. She would not make that mistake again. Willy still hoped; it pained him all the time. Elizabeth could hear his quill and his cough as she folded linens and scraped plates. The sound of both made her head hurt more. He would touch her hair as he passed her; he kept the children out of her way. He seemed to know the sound of them made her head hurt too. At dinner she sat between her throbbing temples as if between two pillars, reliable in their way, and ladled cabbage stew, viewing her family as if from some distance. As soon as possible after supper, she went to bed. Her sleep, deep and thick, was the only thing she regularly looked forward to. In her dreams she often saw her father, young again, dressed for a party: she saw with great clarity the ruffles on his shirt, the green embroidery twist around the buttonholes of his waistcoat. There was always music in this dream, and she and her father would dance, slowly, formally, not touching, their hands separated by a thin slice of air. In the mornings she could never remember the steps or the music and her temples would pound as she rose from the bed.

Of course she could not go to church. Senseless to go out among sickness if she didn't have to. Senseless; useless. In fact she did not choose to go. She didn't feel the need for

Mr. Hobart's sermons now, for the arch of the church over her; didn't feel the need, the want. She had praised, she had prayed—her father had been taken anyway. Now she only felt the need to stay away from church, as from a friend who had abruptly, irrevocably betrayed her. To such a friend she would have nothing more to say; she would only want to withdraw. And so she did withdraw, as much as she could, from Mr. Hobart's condolence calls and from Rebecca, on Sundays. Her sister-in-law did still feel the need for church and, defying Willy's pleas, went off in her bonnet through the stricken city to Trinity.

The evening before Sacrament Sunday, the one service a month that offered Holy Communion, Rebecca appeared in Elizabeth's bedroom. Willy was downstairs with the children; Elizabeth was in her nightdress, unpinning her hair. In the mirror she saw Rebecca hesitating in the doorway.

"Sorry to disturb you, Eliza . . ."

Elizabeth said nothing; she dropped a hairpin in the dish on the dresser.

"It's just that . . . tomorrow's Sacrament Sunday."

Elizabeth pulled another pin from her hair.

"I wondered," said Rebecca. "I wondered if you'd come with me."

Elizabeth dropped the pin in the dish.

"Remember our pact?" Rebecca's voice strove for lightness. For a moment her face in the mirror looked hopeful and pinched and big-eyed, like a child come before a stern mother. "Our pact, you know, to go together and—"

" 'Keep to ourselves, retreat afterward to our rooms in prayer, no matter what, without fail,' I know, I know," Elizabeth repeated, hearing the words with distaste. She had phrased them herself, but now they only reminded her of adolescent bargains made in tree houses. "Well," she said, not looking up. "Go without me."

"Are you sure?"

"Bec. There's an epidemic, remember?"

"Mr. Hobart just buried a man who'd been in all summer."

"I just buried a man who'd been out all summer."

"That's it, isn't it, Eliza—your father, not the fever."

A pattering of pins, quick angry clinks.

"Eliza, I wish you'd come with me."

A tortoiseshell comb fell to the floor.

"I wish you'd talk to me."

Elizabeth's brush whipped her hair.

"Eliza . . . I *miss* you."

In the mirror, Elizabeth saw Rebecca's eyes fill with tears as she ran from the room.

The next morning, wearing her bonnet, Elizabeth caught up with Bec at the door. Her sister-in-law, eyes brightening, pressed her hands but did not force an embrace—Elizabeth still looked so stiff. Upstairs, there had been words with Willy about this, the whole household had heard. Madness to go out, he'd said, voice rising. Madness, didn't she care what became of her, of them all?

Now Elizabeth followed Bec out the door, that question unanswered. The two of them moved, arm in arm, into the silent street, handkerchiefs held to their noses. The stench was almost overpowering. A yellowish haze hung over chimneys and gables; heat shimmered before them on the motionless air. They passed no one but a boy struggling to hoist a coffin onto a cart; they saw little movement besides the leap of flames from feather ticks piled on every corner. Elizabeth wondered if she were venturing through this for Bec's sake or her own; perhaps she was only wooing the fever, flirting it into taking her as she had once flirted boys into asking her to dance.

As Trinity's spire rose before them, sending a slim shadow onto the Broad Way, Bec's steps hastened. Elizabeth's seemed to drag. As they went through the churchyard, she began to feel unaccountably weak in the knees, and as they neared the vestibule, she knew she would faint if she walked through the door. "Go on," she hissed at Bec, who was looking at her, white-faced. "I'll come in a minute." She gave Bec a little push, unable to explain. "*Please*, just go *on.*"

She turned and made her way off toward the hawthorn trees, leaning against one, closing her eyes. For a few minutes she heard steps on the path; once or twice they seemed to move toward her, then swiftly away. Everyone would leave her alone, she knew. Leaning there like that, she likely looked to have the fever. And that, she knew, was not what ailed her at all. After a while the footsteps ceased, and through the church doors, open in the heat, she heard the organ swell into the chords of the opening hymn. She would not go in. She would just stay here. Stay here, eyes closed, wait for Bec.

The smell of fresh-turned earth came to her. Fresh-turned earth and flowers. All those recent graves. Her father-in-law's grave was in this churchyard. For a moment the thought of him made her eyes sting; then that bitter lock within her clicked and the stinging stopped.

"Before the hills in order stood . . . or earth received her frame . . ." Someone in the churchyard was singing along with the hymn. Elizabeth felt eyes upon her, though she'd heard no steps for some moments on the path. There was an odd *clink-clink* she couldn't quite place. She opened her eyes.

"From everlasting you are God," sang Mag, her voice thin but true. In her shawls and skirts and strings of spoons, she seemed a glittering, sun-struck apparition there in the churchyard just beyond Elizabeth's tree. *"To endless years the sa-a-ame,"* her voice lifted; her eyes scanned some pages torn from a hymnal. Unaware of being watched, she sang the hymn softly through, then stuffed the pages into her sack. Her body swayed with the final chords; waves of heat made her shimmer before Elizabeth's eyes.

"The Lord be with you . . ." The minister's voice carried out-of-doors.

"And with thy spirit," Mag made the response.

She stood, head bowed in the sun, shimmering still. Elizabeth could see in that full light that Mag's face had changed: there were lines at mouth and eyes now, and the eyes themselves were different—deeper, tired, grieved.

"Let us pray. . . ."

Mag knelt on the ground, facing the church, and bent her head into her hands. A lock of hair fell forward over her fingers. Everything else about her was wholly still. She knelt as if she were transfixed, and Elizabeth stood as if transfixed herself, watching. She watched as Mag knelt for the Confession, and as Mag stood for the Doxology and the Creed; she watched the pageantry of motions made with

shawl and skirt and hands, the rising and bending and swaying of Mag through the prayers, an oddly lovely dance. At
the Collect Mag fumbled in her sack, bringing into the light
a series of bright treasures: pins and thimbles, coins and
keys and a small nickel-plated snuffbox. "*O God, who on
the mount didst reveal to chosen witnesses . . .*" Mag
touched her things with a finger, studying them; at last she
chose the snuffbox. She took it in her hand and touched it one
more time. Then, holding it out before her, she walked to the
front steps of the church. She laid the snuffbox down and
backed away.

Mag stood hesitating then, as if torn between the service
and something else that was nearer. She shifted from one foot
to the other; then she moved, slowly and deliberately, toward
a fresh grave. Carefully, gently, she reached out and touched
its mounded earth. She murmured something, shook her
head. And then she knelt beside the grave, her hands patting
the spaded dirt, her face beginning to stream with tears.

"Now, there . . . now, there," she murmured. Her fingers
brushed the grave with a gesture that arched, curved; a
gesture at once tender and deft. Elizabeth recognized it: the
gesture one uses to smooth a child's hair. The grave was
small, narrow: the grave of a child. Mag's tears fell upon its
earth. Elizabeth felt her own eyes fill. She blinked her eyes.
They filled again. She blew her nose, compressed her lips.
The tears slid, hot, down her face. Mag blurred; the church
blurred. She felt pushing up from deep within a sound, a
sob, a cry that hurt and jerked and tore to get out. Elizabeth
turned her face to the tree and wept. The weeping seemed
to sweep her along with a power of its own, taking her beyond church and churchyard, even beyond the borders of
herself; beyond sensations of gown, heat, bonnet, stays. She
wept for the father she'd not have again, she wept for the
mother long gone. She wept for her husband, wept for herself, she wept for the loss of their home. She wept for the
woman who'd died on the island, she wept for the child who
was Mag's. She wept for her sins, for her offer of Kit, for
all the days soured and spoiled, and then she wept just because it kept coming, it kept keening through her like hard
cleansing rain.

When at last she looked up, Mag was gone. The church-yard was flung before her again in all its ordinary shapes, its bleached and sun-struck colors. The organ was swelling again with the closing hymn, *All glory laud and honor to thee, Redeemer King.* Elizabeth wiped her face, blew her nose. *To whom the little children*—she straightened her bonnet, wiped her eyes again—*made sweet hosannas ring.* She saw Rebecca appear on the steps; then for a few minutes she was lost in the crush around the minister. When at last Bec reached her, Elizabeth was putting her handkerchief away.

"Eliza, what happened?"

"I don't really know."

"You're all right?"

"Yes, Bec . . . sorry."

"You do look a sight." Rebecca smiled. "Look what I found—no one seems to know whose it is."

Mag's snuffbox gleamed from her palm.

That evening Elizabeth sat in the dark of her bedroom, turning the snuffbox in her hand. Outside she could hear a breeze sending a whisper through the leaves. The house was quiet, the children in bed. Willy would be coming up soon.

She rose and went to the drawer where she'd thrown those two letters; the letters from Italy. She spread them out on her lap, listening to the crinkle of their paper. *Your health . . . our sunshine . . .* She folded them, creased them, unfolded them again. *Let us help . . .* She saw Willy's face, wishful, hopeful; she saw her father's face bathed in sweat. The letters brushed, winglike, against her fingers. Her father's face was falling away from her now, fading. It was Willy's face that remained before her, hopeful, longing, lit with plans. She heard his step below as he moved about, putting out the lamps; she heard his step on the stair. A moment later he was silhouetted in her doorway.

"Willy," she said. "I've been reading these . . . letters, the Filicchis' letters."

"In the dark?"

"In a way."

"You don't have to read them."

He came closer. She reached up, touched his face.

"Why'd you keep them, then?"

"I don't know . . . in case . . . in hope . . ."

"In hope I'd read them?"

He nodded; in the dark she heard him smile. "I had this idea," he said. "This idea we'd burn them to celebrate a . . . decision."

She let the letters float on her lap. She took Willy's face in her hands. In the dimness she could see only the line of his profile, the shape of his head, but she could see him as he'd looked below her window years before, and how he'd looked pillowed beside her a thousand nights since. She wanted to say she was sorry. She wanted to say she'd been wrong. She wanted to say she had somehow come past the pain of her father's death. Her feelings for Willy seemed to fill the dark room, sea-deep and strong. Speechless, she sat there and pressed his face between her palms. She could not say any of these things at all.

And because she could not, she stood and laid the letters in the washbowl, and struck a match, and in the washbowl she touched the match to the letters. She had read them. She would talk of going now. She would talk, she would plan; she would let him see, in the flame rising from the bowl's cold curve, some light of hope. And she would feel it with him.

Part Two

10

The hematologist is speaking of remissions.

He sits before us here in the basement of the Cathedral of Mary Our Queen, a small neat man with a small neat voice, crimping the edge of his papers.

". . . the drug aminopterin was used and did induce remission in the child Ann O'Neill. . . ."

The doctor is immaculate, precise. We priests—ten of us around this table—we look disheveled, sound imprecise.

". . . but remission, by definition, is only temporary. . . ."

Papers rustle. Aluminum chairs squeak. The room is close, cluttered with the leftovers of other meetings. Plastic nativity figures spill from a box. Potluck supper memos pile up by the door. An alb on a wire hanger dangles from the blackboard. Hardly the atmosphere of the Spanish Inquisition.

I glance again at the Vatican's interrogatory. Twenty questions. Sounds like a television game show. Twenty questions in Latin, in English. *Interrogatur testis . . . the witness may be asked if he is moved by motives such as fear, love, hate.* . . . I go down the list. *Ex officio*, I ask if a permanent remission has ever been recorded.

"Not that I know of." The doctor pauses. "Not in lymphoid leukemia."

Now I must ask, in that case, if this is a miracle. I'd like to ask instead if he'd mind if I smoked.

"Bear in mind," I say, feeling absurd, like a medieval throwback addressing modern man, "bear in mind that a favor is not a miracle. A favor can be explained by physical laws. A miracle cannot. Bearing this in mind . . . is this case a miracle?"

The doctor clears his throat and looks at his coffee cup. "I . . . don't know if it's a . . . *miracle.*"

His bald head sweats. He has trouble with that word. No more so than I.

"Could you say an extended remission came about through natural laws, physical laws?"

Another pause. "We are speaking of a form of cancer in which death is inexorable." The doctor hesitates, sips coffee. "You would have to say . . . in this case something was different. You would have to say . . . its behavior was . . . remarkable . . . unique. . . ."

"What makes it unique?"

"The continued state of the girl's health—ten years now."

"And that state is . . . ?"

"Good. All symptoms disappeared. They haven't recurred. No pathological traces. The bone-marrow test shows no abnormality. She has a perfectly normal differential."

"Could you," I ask, "could you, then, in fact, consider this not a remission—but a cure?"

Another pause.

Another sip.

"You would have to say . . . this case has defied the normal course of events. You would . . . have to say . . . if cure were possible . . . In retrospect, I'd say . . . yes, this was a cure."

In one hand I have a cheeseburger, in the other a bone scan. The meeting is over, the tribunal has scattered. Above this room the cathedral is quiet, becalmed between Saturday weddings and confessions.

Interrogatur testis . . .

There are papers to straighten; papers to look at again.

The witness may be asked if he is moved by any human motives . . .

The meeting room is cooler now, more comfortable.

Such as fear, love, hate . . .

Fear. The doctor's discomfort had to do with fear, I think.

So does mine. We want to believe in comprehensible laws, he and I—proven predictable laws. Miracles are not predictable. Miracles are not comprehensible. That disturbs him; that disturbs me. Only once in my life did I want to believe in miracles. Only once did I pray for one: the night my sister was dying. Fool that I was.

My mind has gone off track, turned inward, backward. I get up, go into the men's room, splash water on my face. In the mirror I look older, drawn. Not the way I picture myself. I go out quickly, letting the door slam. For a moment I think of climbing the stairs to the sanctuary above. I can see my fingers tightening on the banister. I can't go up there. I can say Mass for others; I can't pray alone anymore. Whenever I try, my sister's face crowds my mind and my anger at the Church, at myself—it chokes me. I return to the basement and pick up the papers on the table. Gradually I feel my mind shift; it crawls back into the task at hand.

Before me is the log of Mrs. Seton's Italian sojourn. It may present some answers to this case. It may pose new questions. Take her growing attraction to faith, for example. So far, it could be construed as escapism—a psychological substitute for loss. And how many times, in religion, have we been taught that this is the wrong motivation? How many of us, as novices, were warned that the Church is not a refuge—that we must run toward God out of desire, not fear?

Or am I wrong?

I wish I could summon her, sit her in one of these aluminum chairs, hand her a paper coffee cup and put the interrogatory to her.

Name? *Elizabeth Bayley Seton.*

Place and date of birth? *New York, August 28, 1774.*

Religion? *Roman Catholic; born Anglican.*

That's what I'd like to talk to her about now, *ex officio:* her conversion. All the rest hangs on that.

And, short of another miracle, only these papers will tell me what I want to know.

Or don't want to know.

Depending.

11

Everyone said they were crazy to do it.

The perils of shipwreck, the danger of pirates, the six weeks at sea, that alone; the war with Morocco, the threats to our frigates, the children, the risk, and for what? Everyone said it, the scheme was a mad one—they listened, went on with their plans. The money was raised, the children arranged for, the sailing date chosen and fixed. Again they were scolded, again they were warned; I'm sure from the start they held firm.

I'm sure that they felt they were starting afresh. They felt it in the first week of the voyage and in the sixth, felt it on the decks of the *Shepherdess* and below them; felt it in the ocean air, saw it in the wide ocean skies. In this air he improved, she rested, they dreamed, and under those skies they felt brave. They knew they were taking one last glinting chance—a chance at health and good fortune once more—and they felt the hopeful daring of chance-takers.

For the first time in nine years there was no house to run, no babies to nurse. The newest one was with her sister, the middle three children with Rebecca; only Anna, the oldest, was there on board ship. For the first time in years Elizabeth and Willy had time to themselves, and would have more. They would dance in Italy, he said; for the first time in years they would dance. She had packed her old pink slippers in hope.

They watched the sun rise and set and they sensed Italy nearing, floating toward them on the mists, the counted days, the thousand thousand waves. They talked of what they would see together, where they would go. He recalled Livorno from a decade before, with the gleam of his younger self upon it, boundless, buoyant, brash. She imagined Livorno with the shine of a Promised Land upon it—and so it looked to her over the ship's rail in the late-afternoon light, that November day it appeared at last. There, beyond the web of rigging from the port, were the tiled roofs, the stucco walls, and the cypress, the pine. There was the hill of Montenero rising above, and there were angelus bells ringing on the warm, brilliant air.

There was wine and a toast that night on the ship; next morning there was a boat of musicians to starboard, playing on trumpets and accordions, "Hail, Columbia." Immediately after this boat came another; Elizabeth recognized the figure in its bow—the tall slender frame, the blowing dark hair of her half-brother Carleton. She had not known him well at home, remembering him best as a boy sliding down a banister—but there he looked so much more familiar than anyone else; so much like her father, too, for a moment. Carleton was working in Livorno, she knew; she had written him about their arrival and now he was there, doubtless with a welcome from the Filicchis. She ran to the rail, calling his name.

Carleton pulled back.

Carleton wasn't smiling.

It was only then that she saw the guard behind him; the guard with the bayonet who said sharply, in English, "Don't touch." Swiftly, through a handkerchief, it was explained: the *Shepherdess*, bringing news of New York's 1803 yellow-fever epidemic, lacked a bill of health itself. It would have to be put out in the roads, and Willy, suspect because of his illness, would have to be put into quarantine with his family. They would be taken immediately to the *lazzaretto*. They would be there for thirty days.

They had letters of introduction, she told the guard.

It makes no difference, signora, he said.

They had no yellow fever, she told the guard.

It makes no difference, signora, he said.

After that, everything happened quickly. A boat with fourteen oars appeared, trailing another. In this trailer Elizabeth, with Willy and Anna, was rowed from the harbor and down the coast. She remembered little of the trip except Anna's trembling, Willy's total silence. She watched the backs of the oarsmen; she sat as if struck. At this moment they should have been driving past cypress groves, through the chiming of bells. They should have been feeling it begin, the new time, the healing. They should not be going to this place named, after all, for a dead man; they should not be going to a quarantine station—they, Dr. Richard Bayley's nearest kin.

They reached a canal with chains across its mouth. The boat paused. A bell, high and shrill, rang from somewhere; then another. The chains were let down. They were rowed between walls two stories high, cracked orange stucco walls that seemed to sweat and lean. The oarsmen shouted; the boat drew up to a stone landing. Another bell, shrill as the first. A series of bells, a series of guards. One final bell, and then a short swaggering figure appeared, his belly straining his waistcoat, his nose clifflike, eyes bright. There was gold braid on his sleeves, a plume in his hat; the guards made way for him. On the end of a long stick, a letter was passed from boat to landing. A letter from their ship, Elizabeth guessed, because it was handled with such dread—the plumed man set it smoking before he would read it, still hanging from the stick.

"*Avanti*," he called then, nodding to them. The instant they moved, the guards drew back, one pointing with his bayonet the way to go in.

They walked down the narrow stone landing and were for a moment waved toward a fence; through it, for a moment, they saw Mary Filicchi's fine-boned worried face. Elizabeth caught an impression of blue bonnet, pale skin, freckles.

"Mary!" Willy pressed his hands to the fence.

She gave them a murmur of welcome, of regret; nothing could be done. They were prodded on.

A door opened before them, a hall snaked ahead. Steep

stone steps rose at its end, twenty steps: Elizabeth counted, listening to Willy breathe harder with each one. At the top: a door marked with a large six. Beyond the door, a room with high ceilings, brick floor, bare walls. The room was cold and very damp; no fireplace could be seen. A single window was cut in the wall, double-grated with iron, its shutters notched with marks of counted days. The roaring of the sea seemed to fill the place, a roaring so constant it could not be ignored. Three mattresses were tossed in after them. Three eggs, bread, wine, were slid toward them in a basket by an old bent man. He crabbed away, crossing himself, and the door was bolted behind them.

Thirty days to go. Milk and matin bells in the morning. Damp clothes, sharp cold, sea beating on rocks. A weightless feeling, time arrested, stunned into perpetual present.

Elizabeth goes to weep in the little closet where the chamber pot is, emerges with eyes dried, hair combed, smile set. They pretend. They act as if. They won't yet disbelieve. Willy winks at her, his teeth rattling: one of his chills has come on. He has not had these chills since the voyage began. This takes him by surprise; he tries to joke. The mattress rustles with his shaking, his eyes for an instant show fear. He mentions again the opera in Florence, the famous tenor Davide; he goes on shivering. Elizabeth sits beside his mattress, rubs his hands. The floor is cold. The coughing begins. Elizabeth lies down beside him, holding him, trying to warm him, and Anna, coming out of the closet, sees her parents like that and bursts into tears. Anna cannot pretend.

Twenty-eight days to go. *This is the day the Lord hath made; let us be glad and rejoice in it.* This time, Elizabeth thinks, I will be strong. Will not give way, will not withdraw. No more hysterics, no more going numb. *We bless you from the house of the Lord.* She will read her prayer book. She will try to see this as a useful time. She will try to see this as a time to rest; a part of some Divine plan.

Today the dampness in the cell is heavier, her bones ache with it. But today there is warm milk fetched in by Louis, a servant sent by the Filicchis. He is an aged reed of a man with ashen hair and pale blue eyes and knotty veins in arms and neck. He looks at them: the pallid man shivering on the mattress, the woman gripping her prayerbook, the child huddled with them. He lifts his hands to the ceiling, to heaven, to *la Madonna, ai-ai.* He rushes off to speak to the captain of the *lazzaretto.*

The Lord is God and He has given us light, Elizabeth reads, tracing the words with her finger. Willy needs the jellies and syrups he had on shipboard to ease his cough. There are none here, the cough sounds ragged, *join in the procession with leafy boughs.* Turning, she sees Anna jumping a rope she has taken off one of the big trunks. Good, my darling—look at you: Anna, so thin-faced, dark-eyed, big-eyed still at eight, leaping in her foam of petticoats. One potato, two potato, three potato, four. *My Lord, my God,* five potato, six potato, seven potato more, *I give thanks to you.*

A knock, a key's rasp, the bolt shoots back. There is the captain of the *lazzaretto,* the dome-bellied man with the plumes and gold braid. For a moment they stare at him as if he is flooded in radiant light: for a moment they imagine him calling *avanti,* there's been a mistake, *avanti,* go, you're free.

He sweeps off his hat, showing elaborately curled gray hair, and beckons Elizabeth toward him.

"I tell you something, signora," he says. "I had a wife, I loved her—how I loved her. She gave me a daughter—and died, signora, she died." He looks pointedly at Willy, sighs hugely, and proudly adds a fragment of French. "*Que voulez-vous,* signor, when God calls—*que voulez-vous?*"

He produces a pen, takes their names. Willy lies back. There is some indefinable sign of defeat, of letting go in the way he leans his head; she sees it, cannot stop it.

"*Grazie, signor, signora, buon giorno.*"

The door shuts behind the captain.

Let us lift up our hearts. Outside, a sunset the color of apricots. *We lift them up to the Lord.* Orange light on the bricks of the floor, a ladder of light shaped by the window's bars. Anna sleeps, tears on her face, curled in a circle like a cat. Her thumb is in her mouth, she hasn't done that in years. Willy sleeps, blood on his lip, head back, hand extended as if reaching for something. Elizabeth takes his hand. *Let us give thanks to the Lord, God of all creation.* The Book of Common Prayer is solid on her lap. The words hang, solid, on the damp air. They are palpable to her, dimensional; she can almost touch them. She feels their edges, their outlines in her mouth. *The Lord be with you.* Hold on, hold on.

Twenty-one days to go. Elizabeth is jumping rope. It warms her. It does more: the sound of the rope against the bricks of the floor carries her beyond the *lazzaretto*, across the ocean, and back to a childhood swatch of noon-lit grass —sun on the grass, on her own jumping shoes, on the windows of the house with the safe red door; the sunlight scented with Miss Molly's perfume. . . .

Elizabeth is warmer now, from the jumping; from the remembering.

Now Anna snatches the rope, throws herself into its arc with a lunge, a splash of skirts, as if she has jumped at a run into a pond. This is unlike her—this quiet girl who from her earliest years has preferred to sit dreaming. She is a deep and narrow well of a child; you can't usually tell what she is thinking. Hold her chin in your hands, in a certain light, and she looks old, woman-faced, formal and sometimes wise. Catch her with the wrong word, a sharp look, and her eyes fill with tears. Catch her with a warm word, a strong hug, and she gives you a sunburst smile; she remembers things like that. Never a runner, a pummeler, a screamer, she used to worry them with her preference for staring out windows. But now she is rough as her brothers, pounding the floor, shouting the rhymes, "*Lon*-don bridge is *fall*-ing down, *fall*-ing down . . ."

Elizabeth watches her. *Come hug me, Anna.* Nothing so healing as the cheek of a child laid against yours, pillowed there, nothing quite like that. Especially, somehow, this child—this first one. Elizabeth remembers feeling frightened on the ship one night in a storm; not wanting to wake Willy, she had knelt on the tilting floor, prayerbook in hand, unable to calm herself till she heard Anna's voice. "'Come hither, all ye weary souls," the child had said, imitating her mother's prayers, and Elizabeth had crawled into bed with Anna, unsure, as she fell asleep, who was comforting whom.

Now Louis is cooking over three clay pots filled with charcoal, he is stirring and whistling under his breath and the rich brown smell of soup is filling the cell. There are chunks of beef in the crock, wine and leeks, there are curls of pasta shaped like shells. Their simmering sounds like low congenial laughter.

The soup. The rope. Two good things today. Three: the stiff bouquet of jasmine and pinks the Filicchis sent. And, of course, the bed: Willy looks quite elegant in it, she thinks; this marvel of a bed the *lazzaretto*'s captain ordered in, dismantled to get through the door, reassembled before their eyes with carved posts and canopy and bright red curtains—it sits in the stark cell like some flounced lady on a charity call. Propped up against its bolsters, Willy smiles, makes a face, plays an imaginary violin in comic-opera style. "Ah-ah, signora," he mimics the captain perfectly. "*Que voulez-vous*, eh?" His laughter does not catch on a cough just now; an hour before, he brought up a quantity of matter from his lungs and seems better.

Maybe all the voyage's benefits haven't been lost after all.

Maybe there will be more afternoons like this.

Maybe they will leap from one good afternoon to another as Anna does from rhyme to rhyme, and come to the end of them, whole.

Sixteen days to go. Six in the evening—noon back home. Here the bells tell her the time each quarter-hour and at least once an hour she calculates the time there. What time is it, what are they doing now—it's a game that never palls.

Outside the cell there is a high gale. Wind throws spray against the window. Willy tosses and coughs. There have been no more good afternoons; there have been afternoons so damp she smells mildew on her sleeves and it's hard to pray. But even when it's hard to pray, it's easy to think of what time it is there, what they're doing now.

Now the children are sitting down to dinner, sitting with Rebecca in a house that isn't theirs. Of course it's a house they know; the house of friends, the Maitlands' house. Of course they know Rebecca, love Rebecca, of course. Elizabeth thinks of waving good-bye to the children from the ship, the three of them, Billy and Dick and Kit, all dressed up and standing at the Battery; Elizabeth had waved with a red handkerchief so they could see it. They had seen; they had started to cry—she'd seen that too. She quickly turned her thoughts to the baby: the baby with her sister Mary and Wright. Elizabeth wishes the baby, named for Rebecca, were with her here. If she were nursing now, she would feel better. It was comfort, always, to feel that pleasant tug at her breast. She imagines the way the baby sometimes screws up her face at the approach of a spoon. Just fourteen months old, she is newly weaned. Maybe weaned too soon. Maybe not eating at all. Such thoughts. Stop this.

Here in the cell the light is gone. The candles look feeble. The crash of the sea sounds like thunder and there is a strong smell from the night closet. Elizabeth watches the beads of moisture on the bricks by her prayerbook. Louis will have to put out the little fire pots, the smoke is hurting Willy's chest. She rises, wanting to sigh; wanting to scream. If only the wind would stop for one hour. If only she could have a bath. She gestures to Louis, tries to explain. He understands, carries out the pots, and the instant he does, Anna stamps her foot.

"*Mama*, it's *cold*."

"Papa's cough—"

"Papa, *Papa*—what about *me*!"

She throws a cup against the wall; it smashes. Mother and daughter stare at each other, then break from the stare as from a window. Their backs turn sharply, like slammed doors. Can't expect her to be good all the time, Elizabeth tells herself. Not here, not after all these days. Her eyes go to the shutters, to the notches others have left there. She will not do that, will not leave marks here like a criminal. She will not write Rebecca that she is thinking about it. It is important to sound brave for Rebecca: Rebecca will be reading her words to the children. She must use words to cheer, to edify—only that. She will tell Rebecca how Anna enjoys the rag-baby sent by the Filicchis. She will say how she, Elizabeth, takes up this cross, kisses it too. She will say she finds this present opportunity a treasure, a time to think. And then she will put down her pen and give Willy two opium pills and a clean handkerchief.

What time is it there and what are they doing now? She can see the house on State Street in the afternoon sun: the house rented, furniture distributed, the precious private things locked away. It lifts her spirit just a little, thinking of her pretty oak dresser in Mary's house, her piano and writing desk at the Hobarts'.

If Mr. Hobart were here now, how she would be lightened. A picture of him comes to her. He is sitting there. His legs are crossed. His face, to her surprise, puckers with prissy distaste at the room's smell. He takes off his glasses and polishes them, his little fingers lifted as if pouring tea. He is discoursing about original sin. Personal sin. Her sin. "We offend God *every day*, no matter what we do, how we try," the image says, and holds its nose. Elizabeth feels suddenly more depressed than before. She lets the image fade.

Another bell, the quarter-hour. What time is it there and what are they doing now? . . .

Fifteen days to go. The doctor is there, sent for at dawn. Willy cannot breathe, he rambles in a high fever; it breaks just before the doctor arrives. Tutilli is the doctor's name; a name that makes her think, absurdly, of candy. The doctor examines Willy, looks at them both for a long while without speaking. Then he tells them he's not the man they want; they want someone who ministers to souls. He waits a moment longer, then goes out.

She and Willy are silent, each fearing to weaken the other. Of course they had known this for some time. She had seen it in the eyes of friends, in the eyes of Wright Post. She had told herself she really mustn't hope, the consumption was so far along. But she *had* hoped. And he had improved. And whatever she had told herself, no one else had told her otherwise until just now. Just now she feels slapped, shocked; silenced.

At last Willy rises, the blanket around him, and creeps to the fire. Its smoke is contained now by curtains; it gives a feeble warmth. He sits on a stool and she sits on a stool and still they say nothing. Behind them, the door opens again. The *lazzaretto's* captain sweeps off his hat in his usual style, breaking their silence.

"The bed, still nice?"

They nod mutely.

"In that bed I have seen such sufferings . . ." The captain shakes his head. "There lay an American, begging for a knife to end his struggle, there a Frenchman shot himself, dying in agony . . . now you, *que voulez-vous*, signor, eh?" He stays a moment longer, listening to the operatic echo of his words; then, satisfied with his effect, he sweeps out.

Slowly, unsteadily, Willy moves back to the bed, leaning on Elizabeth. She remembers how his hand used to feel under her elbow, strong and somehow sexual, suggestive of more. She has a sudden image of him in his embroidered waistcoat, swinging into the street below her window. The long athletic stride. The cocky grace. The hat in his hand slapping his thigh. Willy dancing. Willy with his violin. Willy carrying her that time she feigned the swoon. And now she is half-carrying him.

"Rebecca has the keys," he says after a while. "You know where all the papers are. It's all in order—what there is," he adds, bitter.

"Maybe—" she cuts him off.

"No," he cuts her off.

"There's always the chance—"

"Not always. Not here." He takes her finger and runs it through the film of dampness on the walls.

She looks at him: the hollowed face, the bearded chin, the frame so thin, so thin. His eyes, on hers, have the startled brightness of fever; his lips are cracked, dry.

"The keys," she says. Her voice shakes. "The keys, Rebecca . . . the papers, I know. . . . The children . . ."

"Just tell them . . . " He stops. "Tell them I stayed in

Italy. No, tell them I went to sleep . . . No, they'll be afraid to go to bed then. . . ." His lips tremble. "Tell Billy, he'll make the most sense of it, tell him . . . I didn't want to. Didn't plan it like this . . . not saying good-bye, I . . ." He stops again, his eyes full. "Tell him when he holds the cricket bat, he just has to . . ." He wipes his eyes. "Damn. *Damn.*"

She touches his face, unable to speak.

"There's money in the teapot," he says into the silence. "I just remembered, maybe ten dollars. And somewhere else . . . I can't quite . . . Oh, God, Liza, I don't . . . want to go. . . ."

"But, Willy, Willy, to be out of this pain, think of that, to be out of it, free . . ."

"Not like this. Leaving you here. Leaving you, leaving them—with nothing. Nothing but a handful of coins in a *damn teapot.*"

"We'll be at State Street, same as ever, we'll be fine . . . and you . . . Shall I tell you what Mr. Hobart says? When you wake in the new world, he says, you'll find nothing, *nothing* can tempt you to return to this."

He coughs, resting his head on her shoulder; his fingers move through her hair.

"I'd go in your stead," she whispers into his neck. "Oh, yes I would, too." She hears the fierceness in her voice. "If only I could make you see, the way it seems to me, dying."

"But you have this faith now."

"I couldn't stand this if I didn't, it . . . it hushes me, I can't explain it. . . ."

"*You* hush me, Liza . . . Liza. . . ."

She holds him. She hushes him. The wind shakes the room. Spray hits the windowpanes like hurled sand. There are no more words she can think of to say.

December 19: All the days gone.

Elizabeth ties the jump rope back around the biggest chest. The captain unbolts the door.

Two men cross their hands to form a seat, and on it Willy is carried out of the *lazzaretto* and out to the Filicchis' waiting coach. Temporary rooms are engaged in Pisa; the coach starts away. Elizabeth, holding Willy with one arm, Anna with the other, sees nothing but sun on the cypresses, mud on the road.

The next week is a jumble—chaos beautifully furnished and housed. Their lodgings at Signora de Tot's house are opulent, selected by the Filicchis with comfort in mind. Elizabeth watches Willy shiver against green brocaded walls now; his bloody sputum stains the finest linen sheets. It is such a sudden contrast with the *lazzaretto*, Elizabeth feels vaguely as if she has entered the set of some dazzling opera; she wonders if it will vanish in the night. The nights are the worst, but one day Willy is better, talking to Carleton, telling an intricate political joke about President Jefferson. Christmas Day is good as well: Willy follows the service Elizabeth reads, he takes a little wine. He speaks calmly, even serenely, of the children, of dying, of going to God— he pleases her by saying she's given him faith after all.

That night she falls asleep easily, listening as always to his breathing, but losing track of it somewhere in the dark. And from the dark, that morning around four, she hears him shouting, "We won, we won!"

She is awake at once and groping her way to his bed. There is something about the joy in his voice—she feels a surge of hope that somehow, somehow his will has miraculously triumphed over his disease. She fumbles, lighting the candle, and again he shouts it: "Eliza, Eliza, we won!" His face is pasty in the light; his eyes are lit with fever. "The lottery," he says, "the grand prize. The ticket, I bought it, it was in your name—the London Lottery, Liza, the grand prize, thank God, we won."

His fingers jerk her sleeve, his eyes are wandering. She feels an inner sinking. Stupid of her, stupid to feel hope now. She holds a cup of water to his lips. He strikes it from her; the metal cup rolls across the floor. "Why do you do it, why?" He slaps her hands away. "Let me *go*, water keeps me—want to go, get me *out*, let me *go*."

The hem of her gown is wet with spilled water. She feels it against her ankles; she feels his head blaze beneath her hand. All at once he grasps her hand, kisses it. "Eliza," he says in a low, confidential voice. "Wonderful news, darling, my brother—he's just shown me the receipts. The bills, they're paid, every one of them, I'm cleared."

She picks up the cup, pours more water. She sees her hand is shaking. She sees, for a moment, her father in his sickbed. It comes to her that Willy is actually dying—not next week, next month, but now; arranging his mind so he can go.

She holds the water to his lips again.

"A toast," he says. "So good to be home again."

Home. In her knees she feels a sudden numbness. Her ears ring. She isn't home. The fact bears down upon her as it hasn't before. For almost seven weeks the American ship had been their home; for four weeks the *lazzaretto* had come to seem familiar. For seven weeks and four weeks Willy has been with her. Even ailing, his presence has been there; now that presence has slipped away. Now she is standing knee-deep in darkness in a house she doesn't know. She doesn't know the names of the other sleepers in this house, or the linen in its cupboards, or the crocks that fill its larder. She doesn't know the names of the streets that cross under this window or the words of the language that could tell her. At other deathbeds she had at least known certain facts. She had known what was for supper and what was in the wardrobes, and knowing these things had steadied her in small, crucial ways.

Willy is pulling at her hands now, he is raising himself in the bed. "You said you'd come with me, you promised." His voice rises, he pulls harder. "Prom-ised." His cracked lips can hardly form the *m* at the word's center.

"I came with you." She wipes his face. "To Italy, here we are."

Here we are. She wishes she hadn't promised, wishes they hadn't come. She had favored it too much, it was her fault. Maybe if they hadn't come he would have lived. She knows better than that, but thinks it just the same. Italy: she hates it suddenly, deeply. She sees its map in her mind, that blasted boot she stared at for months, planning this journey. She sees the map shredding in her hands.

"Italy," she says again, flat. "Livorno." She throws that word like a stone at the floor.

He jerks his head from side to side. "You promised, Liza, you said." His voice is the voice of a small boy pleading to play outside. She holds him back from getting up; he leans his head into her arms and cries. "Want to, want to, please, pleease . . . pleeease. . . ."

The words, lengthened and sinewy, seem to coil around the room. As it gets light he says them still, and all the next day he says them, moans them, croons them; all that day and that next evening the sound of them are in his ears.

By that evening the strange city, the strange country, have receded: not real, not now. Even Anna, beyond the room with Carleton—even she seems dim, distant. This room is the world. Its language is Willy's voice and the prayers she keeps running in her head.

After midnight his voice stops trying to press itself into words and forms instead a low settled sobbing. His head in her lap, she rocks back and forth, making a series of low soft sounds. He is no longer a man, he has become a child—but however she mothers him, she can't quiet him. It scares her, this strange migration from husband to infant—scares her, confuses her, and still she clucks and croons to him, not knowing what else to do.

He looks up at her, a cough shaking him and bringing blood to his lips. His eyes change, become his own. For a moment his hand smooths her hair. Then another cough takes him and the pain carries him off again; soon after that, the wailing begins.

"My darling-dar-ling . . . Jesus Lord Lord . . . Billy Kit darlings Dick . . . my Liza Liza Lord Lord Lord . . ."

She holds him, she sings to him, she doses him—nothing seems to soothe him. She begins to fear she can't bear it; she begins to fear they'll be put out of the lodging house. Fear has made her mind very clear; it has made everything in the room very sharp—each edge, each plane, even the buttons on her shoes by the chair. She looks at the shoes. She goes to the trunk, takes her dancing slippers from it. She holds the slippers so he can see, holds them out to him. His fingers wind themselves in the ribbons, his voice sinks lower. When it rises again she rises as well and puts the slippers on. His eyes follow her, follow her hands. She stands and curtsies to him. His face relaxes, the wailing stops. She sways and steps and circles through a minuet, its stately patterns stilling the room. Bow and step and sweep; her arms up, his hand keeping time. The room begins to fill with morning light. His face is calm. His eyes are fixed on her and on the intricate steps of the dance at a quarter past seven when he dies.

12

For those of us in the helping professions, there seems to be a new approach to "crisis counseling." In the past year I have been invited to six Grief Seminars. I have recently been a guest at a Grief Workshop. I recall the words "sharing" and "caring" were constantly used. I recall the group leader yelling "Emote!" I have a terrible feeling this is the start of some tidal trend.

But maybe we do need the help. Death is a crisis few of us handle flawlessly. Every priest is sometimes daunted by hysterical mourners, rendered helpless himself by the face of frantic grief. I'm certainly no exception. I tend to prefer the sort of control which leads eventually to ulcerative colitis. I've had my own problems with mourning; I have them still. And I must admit I'd dread facing Elizabeth Seton after her husband's burial, after the Protestant chaplain's final *Amen*. Personally, I'd dread it because it would remind me of my sister. Professionally, I'd dread it for another reason. Before workshops, before seminars, priests have always known that it's after the funeral that the very worst time comes.

I can see her in the Filicchis' house early that January, that cold new year; I can see her in the room that had been Willy's a dozen years before:

Elizabeth sitting on the floor in front of the open armoire, her back to the neatly folded clothes, her handkerchief bunched at her mouth, a pillow to her face. She was trying to cry without being heard, she was trying to muffle a storm of crying that would not stop. The pillow smelled of soap and feathers. Lace-edged and lemon-shaped, it seemed insubstantial against this onslaught. Around her the mansion squatted, substantial as a hill, and yet she felt there was no rug, no boards beneath her; she felt herself dropping through floor after floor with nothing to catch her. She sensed herself turning back into a child, a lost child, and for the first time in years she remembered all the strange houses, the strange back bedrooms of her childhood—and here I am once more, she thought. A wave of nausea came over her. She'd been so calm at first. She didn't know what had snapped her.

She had laid Willy out herself.

Under law, burial had to be within twenty-four hours. No one else would touch the body till it was in the charnel house; it was still believed that Willy had died of yellow fever. And so she had laid him out, her mind clear and her hands steady. She had tied a towel at her waist and set a basin of water on the bedside table. She had kept the curtains drawn. In the candlelight she had shaved him. She hadn't cried then, hadn't trembled. The candlelight had shone from the razor, flickered on her hands; her hands had looked deft, quick. Still calm, she had laid towels on the bed and rolled him onto them. His body was not quite cold, he hadn't yet stiffened. He had grown so thin, he was light and easy to turn; she could lift him if need be. She had eased off his nightshirt and rubbed the soapy rag over his chest, watching the dark hairs curl in the water. She could see his ribs plainly; she had counted them for distraction. She had noted, coolly, dispassionately, the faint reddened line left at his waist by the drawers he insisted on wearing to bed. She had concentrated on that; on the sound of sloshing water, on the cake of yellow soap, on the prayers she clicked through her mind—and it was done. The man who came up with the coffin marveled at her composure.

But now, thinking of it again, she choked and retched. She wished she could wash him again, feeling it this time.

She remembered his hands, that first night in the Stone Street house, his hands showing her how to touch him. She couldn't believe she wouldn't touch him another time. She could still talk to him, no matter where he was. But not touch him, be touched—she doubled over the pillow on the floor.

Below her in the house she heard the discreet steps of servants, a clock chiming four. Willy had heard that clock. He had told her about it, he had talked so much about this house. They had quarreled over that: Why, she'd snapped, why must he keep talking about Italy, Italy—had he been in love with some girl there? She heard her voice the way it had been then: high, sharp. She heard her voice every time it had sounded like that over the years. The times she was impatient. The times she was shrill; the times she'd lost her temper. The times she was absent, preoccupied, not listening. Times she could not say sorry for now, make right. Those times, Willy . . . She keened his name into the pillow; then found she was spitting into it, screaming in a whisper. Her fists hit the pillow with a suddenness that startled her. Alone, alone, you left me alone. The one fear I had, the nightmare, you knew it—you said all those nights you'd never leave me alone.

Face streaming, she went to the trunk and lifted out the dancing slippers again. They trembled in her hands—she hurled them against the wall. She heard the twin thuds, she didn't care now. Everyone always left, everyone she loved, always. She crouched on the floor, kicking the pillow away, throwing another after it. Everyone, everyone. She saw her tears staining the rug.

The doorknob turned. The door eased open, Anna was there. She had heard something crash, she began, then broke off, frightened. She stared at her mother: hair wild, eyes swollen, nightgown awry, down on her hands and knees on the floor. Anna began to cry. Oh, Anna, Elizabeth thought. Not everyone. Everyone hasn't left after all. She opened her arms to her daughter and Anna came, and for a long time they sat rocking, crying, holding each other close, there on the rug by the big armoire.

~

Downstairs in the parlor, Antonio Filicchi was lifting a donkey in one hand, a glass of liqueur in the other. Elizabeth and Anna saw him from the doorway, pausing there. The donkey, from the Nativity crib in the window, was porcelain; Antonio was waving it in such agitation at his wife, the liqueur spilled from his glass.

"No no no," he was saying. "It's wrong, wrong, *think*."

"I *am* thinking," said Amabilia, kneeling beside him with two shepherds in her hands. She leaned over the box before her and began to wrap the figurines in paper. "She really must go, it's the only answer."

In the hall Elizabeth drew back; Anna's hand tightened on hers.

"It's best." Amabilia took the donkey from her husband. "I've thought of little else today—Mary, you agree with me, don't you?"

There was a rustle, a tinkle of bracelets; Mary Cowper Filicchi came forward, holding an ox and an angel in her hands. "You're aaabsolutely right, there's no doubt," she said in her flat Boston accents. Mary, the wife of Antonio's brother Filippo, was the only American in the family; English was always spoken in her presence.

"It will upset her, *devastate* her." Antonio lifted one of the wise men out of the crib. "Think of her state of mind, it's as fragile as . . . *this*." He held the small king out on his palm. Its face was not unlike his, Elizabeth thought, and with reason; the Nativity scene had been commissioned by the family, and the artist had put his patrons' features on the figurines. Like this beardless king, Antonio had a narrow elegant face, a long arching nose and high ascetic cheekbones. Short, wiry, with hair the color of chocolate, he moved with the alert grace of an aristocrat and gestured with the jabby energy of a lawyer. He was both: in Rome he had earned a doctorate in civil and canon law. He had been a Church lawyer and a diplomat before joining Filippo in business.

Filippo's voice, sober and formal, carried across the room now. "No need to prosecute this case, Tonio, I line up with you—she shouldn't go." He brought another king to the box and handed it to Amabilia. "The ugly one," he said of the king, and of himself, and Amabilia clucked at him. At forty, the eldest by a year, Filippo was a tall thickset man, moon-faced, with a flat porcine nose and small perpetually red-rimmed eyes. His gestures lacked his brother's quickness but he was the family linguist, fluent in five languages. It was he who had been befriended by the elder William Seton on a trip to America; it was he who had been made consul general at Livorno by George Washington. And it was there he had returned, a dozen years earlier, with an American bride and an American friend—the young William Magee Seton.

"We must remember William," Filippo was saying now. "This is what he would have wanted—Mary, *cara*, surely you know that."

"Filippo, *caro*, you're entirely wrong—"

"Please, please." Antonio held up his hand, and in it, the figure of Joseph. "It's very simple. Just imagine. This terrible scene: a man dying slowly, his true love at his side. He tries to tell her how he loves her—he falls to the floor in mortal agony. She kneels over him, weeping piteously. He rises again, staggering about the room, ranting, crazed with pain—he falls for the last time, struggling to speak, and dies with his head on her lap, *poverino*. Believe me, I have seen this opera, you have not. It reduces the audience to tears every time—think, *think* what it would do to our Elisabetta."

From the doorway, Elizabeth began to laugh, half from relief, and the family was around her then, drawing her into the room, settling her in a chair, talking at once:

"We were worried . . ."

". . . planning an outing."

". . . take you somewhere . . ."

"Somewhere cheering."

"*Firenze* . . ."

"The opera . . ."

"The right opera, *cara*. . . ."

Amabilia, seeing Anna hanging back in the doorway, beckoned her in and laid in her hands the Madonna and Child figurines. "The most important ones—can you wrap them for me, Anina?"

Elizabeth's eyes welled up again, watching, and Amabilia took her hand. A pretty rounded woman, her dark hair frilling at her forehead, she smiled and tapped her cheek. "You see, if you look at the Madonna's face from the right, *ecco,* she resembles me quite well—ah, but then you look at her from the left, she resembles my sister-in-law. The poor artist, two women to flatter with just one figurine, what was he to do, here, *dolce,* take my handkerchief."

"Oh, *dear.*" Elizabeth blew her nose. "I'm weepy as I was right after each baby. I'm sorry, I just—"

"No need, no need." Antonio winked at her. "It makes us all sad to put away the *Natale* crib, after Epiphany everything seems so bleak for a while. And so, we were thinking . . ."

"Before you go home . . ." said Amabilia.

"A little diversion," said Mary.

"*Firenze,*" said Filippo in his resonant voice. "Florence— the opera, the sights, the art—they would cheer your heart."

"I really . . ." Elizabeth shook her head. "My children, really, I should go home."

"Ah." Antonio drew his mouth down in mock despair. "Then you'll have no use for our Christmas gift to you." He drew out a box wrapped in deep crimson paper; it matched the rich rug in the room. "We couldn't give it to you on the day itself . . . considering how things stood . . . but we meant it for you and for your William, open it, *per favore,* open it."

Elizabeth, surprised, disarmed, pulled off the paper and opened the lid of a small blue box. Inside was a pair of delicate black opera glasses.

For a moment they blurred before her eyes; she swallowed, unable to speak. Oh, Willy. How you would like these. How good your friends are to me.

"They're beautiful, beautiful, I don't know what to say."

"Say you'll stay—a week, a month—let us try to cheer you, say."

The opera, Willy. The opera, the Uffizi, we were going to go.

"He so wanted to hear Davide sing. . . ." She blinked her eyes to clear her sight. "Well . . . a fortnight, then. . . ."

"Brava!"

Firenze, Willy. Be there, a little, with me.

Afterward, when she saw it in her sleep—and she saw it in her sleep for some time——Florence appeared to her as one vast riverside house under one vast orange-tiled roof, topped by the cathedral's dome and ribboned with narrow hall-like streets. She moved through it, dazed, from opera to museum, piazza to palace, as if from room to room, shepherded by Amabilia. She saw it through a constant mist, not from the river but from her eyes, and at no time did it seem entirely real.

She felt herself to be a guest in this expanded house, listening to its bells and shouts and rush of language, looking politely at all it showed her. As a guest she wanted to be good; she wanted to like all she heard and saw. But she had been unable to like the opera—it seemed to her an evening of incomprehensible ranting, nothing more. She had been unable to enjoy the Museum of Physical and Natural History, the Specola—each exhibit made her think of her father. She had been unable to enjoy the Ponte Vecchio: on the boxy toylike bridge of shops, she had seen, not the shops, but couples: couples walking, touching, pausing, buying rings and charms and tokens from the gold- and silversmiths there. The Boboli Gardens, with their sloping lawns and boxwood hedges, had reminded her so much of the New York parks, she had pretended to doze on a bench to keep herself from weeping. Even the glories of the Uffizi Gallery had not cleared her eyes; even for Willy's sake. Few rooms in this mansion of a city had held her as she had expected; only one had drawn her back for another, solitary visit. She sat there now, this second time, feeling a little foolish. This place had nothing to do with Willy.

She had at first been drawn to the building across the piazza: its blue and white majolica medallions, each showing a different baby in a different attitude—they had charmed her, made her smile. This was a foundling home, Amabilia had told her, the Hospital of the Innocents. This square was the Piazza Annunziata, and there, across the way, was the church it was named for, Santissima Annunziata. They had gone in.

As Elizabeth passed through a curtain by the door, her eyes were struck by the sight of hundreds of people kneeling at once. In the taper-lit dimness they appeared softened, indistinct, as if afloat just above the floor, misted in incense. The small clerestory windows, darkened with green silk, gave everything a faint underwater cast, pierced by the points of a hundred small candle flames. For an instant it seemed to her so strange as to be enchanted. It looked like no church she had ever seen before. Then the organ had begun to play, its tones familiar. From somewhere down the aisle a baby cried. A woman at the end of the last row had looked up, smiled, moved over. Forgetting Amabilia and Anna, forgetting herself, Elizabeth had taken the place made for her and, to her great embarrassment, put her head in her hands and wept. It had been so long since she had been inside a church. It had been so long since she had felt this sense of shelter. Her soul had been so scalded she hadn't even realized how much she'd missed this.

The rhythms of the Mass calmed her; by the time it was over she had regained her control, blowing her nose and whispering an apology. Amabilia had patted her arm, shown her the frescoes, and they had gone out again into the thin winter sunlight. Elizabeth had not thought, at the time, that she would return.

But here she was once again, sitting in the center of the nave, sitting alone, not entirely sure why. She had admired the Church of San Lorenzo and the Medici Chapels, but she had felt this sense of release nowhere else.

Around her now the air was still spiced with lingering incense. Banks of candles bloomed with light like white-stemmed flowers. Echoes drifted past her like shadows, and with them, the firmer sound of a scrub brush on stone. The high rounded space bent over her, flickering, sighing, bringing her the smell of roses and wax and wood. Before her, to the right of the door, was the Virgin of the Annunciation: an ancient fresco of Mary, learning from the Angel that she would be the Mother of God. The fresco was sheltered in a houselike shrine, hung with gold and silver lamps, glinting and glimmering and faintly tinkling; it looked dressed up, decked out, celebrational in a way she didn't associate with worship. People knelt around it and throughout the church, praying with a lack of self-consciousness that startled her. She had never realized there were churches open and filled, all day long, every day of the week. She had never realized there were churches that looked this way —gold petaling the ceiling, trimming the altar, rimming the arches; a place at once like a palace and a mine: dark and rich and mysteriously joyous.

She thought of the churches at home: Trinity's simple chancel, St. Paul's spare lines. Pastor Hobart's voice came back to her, amused and scornful as it had been before she'd sailed, warning her of the Italian churches' beauty. Sumptuous, he had called them. Seductive. And laughed.

Well. He was right. Of course.

How predictable of her to be dazzled.

Something darkened within her. She rose and began to walk toward the door. She was dazzled, she was a fool. Maybe she was worse than that. A half-hidden fear edged toward her like a pickpocket. Maybe she was being punished for foolishness, wickedness; for sins she could not even see. Why else was her life so filled with losses? Mr. Hobart, she knew, would say that she was being chastened. Miss Molly's old Reformed prayerbooks had said the same, though Miss Molly herself had not.

Elizabeth passed the shrine, her cloak drifting against an elderly lady in a veiled bonnet who knelt there. Something about the line of her back, the flounce of her skirt, the tilt to her head made Elizabeth look at her again. This had happened all over Florence: she had thought she'd seen her father in the Specola, Willy on the Ponte Vecchio—now she was seeing Miss Molly at this shrine. The lady looked up; her face was indistinct behind her veil. Her ringed hand lit a candle, paused; held out the taper. Elizabeth took it, feeling uneasy, and stood with it burning in her fingers. She looked at the candles. She thought of this church's Cloister of Vows; the life-size wax effigies people used to leave there, for prayers. The thought made Elizabeth wince. Votive effigies, votive candles—were they so different? Were they anything but superstitions? Pastor Hobart would say not. Pastor Hobart would say . . . dazzled. Foolish. Bewitched. She shouldn't have come here. She dropped the taper in the box of sand and walked quickly out the door.

The sunlight outside felt warm on her shoulders. The sudden profusion of orange-tiled roofs, the washing on poles, the smells of garlic and coffee and leather seemed good to her. It seemed good to hear the sound of a broom, to see a round woman in a striped apron sweeping the doorstep of a house on the corner.

"*Scusi, signora,*" the woman said, speaking in a rush and gesturing toward the ladder between them. Elizabeth, understanding the gestures, held the ladder steady and the woman climbed up, her arms filled with roses from a bucket by the door. Roses in winter, Elizabeth thought; they must cost a fortune. Above her on the house's corner, she saw a small niche with a ceramic statue of Madonna and Child. All over the city, on almost every corner, she had noticed these small shrines. The woman set her roses in pots before the figures and, panting, climbed down. "*Grazie, grazie, signora,*" she said, wiping her hands on her apron and holding out a flower; her eyes lit on Elizabeth's black mourning dress for the first time. The woman drew her hand back. "*Condoglianze, condoglianze,*" she said, shaking her head, and Elizabeth turned away. As always when she forgot the pain for a moment, it returned stronger than before. It struck her again: she was a widow, in widow's weeds; no flowers for her. She was a still-young woman in black amid all these old women in black. All over the street she saw them, suddenly, as the bells rang the hour. She walked faster, head down, and turned into the doorway of her lodging house.

Even as she was fitting the key into the door, she could hear Anna crying, and as soon as she was through the door the child was clinging to her. "Papa, Papa . . ." she wept. I really must get her home, Elizabeth thought. If it was this way with Anna, how would it be with the others—the others, who had heard the news only by letter? She must get home. At least she could be a widow on a street she knew. She must tell the Filicchis as soon as she returned to Livorno.

~

~ 144 ~

". . . and so you can understand how . . . anxious I feel . . ."

She turned her wineglass in her hand, looking at them.

". . . and why I can't delay anymore. . . ."

Elizabeth looked down. Everything she said sounded somehow ungrateful. She was sitting with the Filicchis at a table under a grape arbor on Montenero, a few yards from its ancient church. The weather had broken unseasonably warm as she'd returned from Florence; the family had packed a basket with pastries and taken Elizabeth up the mountain for the sunshine.

"And for the church," Antonio had said several times as they rode the mules up the mountain trail. In the sanctuary of Our Lady of Montenero, there was a miracle-working image of the Virgin; it would be a moving sight to a visitor, he felt certain. Elizabeth had said nothing, embarrassed. Amabilia must have told them all how she had wept in the church in Florence; she would not lose control like that here. She had stood politely in the doorway to the sanctuary, her view partly obscured by a pair of black-veiled nuns. To her sun-blinded eyes, the place had mainly seemed dark, difficult to make out. She had glanced around a room off the nave, another Gallery of Vows. Its walls were lined with drawings of shipwrecks, sickbeds, accidents—mute appeals to the Madonna of Montenero. Elizabeth had again heard Pastor Hobart's voice pointing out superstitious practices. She had nodded politely once more and turned away.

"How did you find the church?" Antonio was asking now. There was an insistence to his voice she found disconcerting.

"Interesting." She tried to be mannerly.

"Aside from the art, I mean."

"Tonio." Amabilia shook her head at her husband.

"I mean, did you find it moving?" Antonio pressed.

"Tonio."

"I only ask, *piccina*, because . . ."

"Because you heard I kept breaking down in churches all over Florence?" Elizabeth half-smiled.

"We heard you were taking comfort in the churches—no wrong in that." Filippo tossed a stone down the mountain and watched it sail across the umbrella pines. "To knock, to inquire . . . to seek comfort, this is good. This is a beginning."

Elizabeth set down her wineglass. "A beginning?"

"If you wish it to be . . . of course."

"To knock, to inquire . . ." She saw that they had misunderstood her. She took a breath. ". . . to change my faith, you mean—oh, no, Filippo. I'm sorry, I wasn't thinking of that. I could never think of that. I don't know what I was really feeling there in Florence . . . just homesick, I guess. Please . . . I've worried you so much as it is. Don't worry yourselves about my soul too."

Amabilia flashed the men a look and sliced cake with quick little chops. Antonio flushed and looked at his brother.

"I too am sorry," Filippo said, awkward, formal. "I never would have spoken if I'd thought . . . We never would impose ourselves on you, Elisabetta. We only thought to help."

"And this isn't helping, look at her face." Antonio stood and lifted a folded napkin from the basket. "Look at Amabilia's face, for that matter, look at all of us. In this sunshine! If you'll pardon my choice of words, it's a sin, nothing less—*ecco*, look here."

He opened the napkin with a magician's flourish, and the smell of fresh-baked aniseed cakes rose from it, mingling with the mountain's scent of pine and thyme. Talk at the table resumed, talk of food and flavorings and childhood treats. Elizabeth felt herself relax again. She smiled at Amabilia, who was fervently describing the best filling for sweet *cannoli*; she glanced away from the medal glinting at Amabilia's neck. Images of Mother and Child only reminded her of her own children now. She looked out over the port of Livorno, the sea spreading before her in the sun. In less than a week she would be sailing. In less than seven she would be lifting her children high, so high, in her arms again.

In six days, Montenero was a shadow in the rain-needled dark, Livorno a blur of lights off the *Shepherdess*'s stern. Elizabeth stood for a moment on the afterdeck, her cloak pulled over her head, then went back down to her cabin. Everyone else seemed to be below; a feeling of calm lay over the ship. The rigging creaked. A cow lowed. She had seen it led aboard earlier by a seaman calling, "*Latte per mattina*" —morning milk. She had seen Captain O'Brien bending over his kitchen garden planted in the jolly boat, alongside a store of greengroceries. He remembered her, this big cliff-faced Irishman. He had given her the best cabin in the star-board quarter. Everything was arranged for her comfort, he said.

The cabin, as she entered it, was still. Anna had gone to bed, queasy, but had left the lamps burning. Clustered in brackets, they warmed the walls with a serene light. The pitcher and bowl glowed from their fitted niches in the wooden washstand. Elizabeth sat on the bench with the drawers built into it. Earlier she had filled those drawers with necessaries; when she packed them up again, the ship would be nearing New York. She glanced at the sleeping child, the small rag rug, the bottle of red wine from the Filicchis. She hated to open a whole bottle just for herself; she took some water from the cask instead. On the voyage out, the water had been bitter; they had had to flavor it with peppermint oil. Now the water was good—an omen, she hoped. If she could only keep her eyes off the bed. As required by the ship, she and Willy had supplied it them-selves. This would be the first time she'd sleep in it alone.

She took out her sewing basket, threaded the needle, began to mend her other black skirt. She was wearing out the blacks, these days. Against the side of the ship there was a dull thudding of higher seas. The wind rose, whistling, and the cabin tilted slightly. Thank God she didn't get sea-sick. Her needle flashed; Anna tossed but did not wake. There was a sudden hard shower of spray against the window, then another. She pushed the needle through the cloth with her thimble, and as she did, there was a sudden slamming jolt. The floor sloped up like a steep-pitched roof—there was a splintering crash; it sounded like matches snap-ping. Elizabeth saw the water bloom from her cup, felt the drawers spring open against her legs. She saw the needle and the thread and the black skirt fly out of her hands. As she tried to stand, the lamps went out; she slid across the cabin, grabbing at air. A pillow struck her face. Abruptly she felt bedding beneath her. For an instant she lay still; gingerly she moved her hands. The thimble was still on her finger.

From the darkness Anna was crying. Shaking, calling her

name, Elizabeth groped for her, found her, bundled her and the bedclothes into her arms. The floor shifted; not quite so steep now. Above them there was the sound of running feet, muffled shouts; the ship did not seem to be moving. Before they could right themselves or find a light, the door of the cabin was thrown open.

"Hurt, anyone hurt?" The first mate's face was lit by the lantern in his hand.

"No, what—?"

"Storm," he said, flatly laconic. A stringy man with a gaunt thin-lipped face, he raised the lantern to look at them. "Collision," he added grudgingly. "Back to port now, repairs." .

He saw Elizabeth's arms tighten around the child; he saw her trembling. "You the widow? This your girl?" He peered at Anna. "She sick?"

"Just seasick. It was my husband—"

"You bring her on this way? . . . Look here."

The lantern, as he lifted it again, threw shadows on the walls and light on Anna's flushed face. The mate reached out and drew the quilt away from her; a rash ran down her jaw and neck. Elizabeth had not touched her except through the bedclothes; now she laid her hand against Anna's cheek. The child's skin blazed.

"Sorry, ma'am—have to put you off in port."

". . . please, the captain—he knows me, ask him, he—"

"Captain won't say different, ma'am." He lowered the lantern, turned away. "Won't want us quarantined at Barcelona—let go my arm, ma'am, no disrespect meant." His voice was kind. "Easy, now, just take yourself in hand."

She could not take herself in hand.

Not on the ship on the way back to port; not in port awaiting the Filicchis. She shook, she talked. She talked too much; to Anna, to herself, to the captain, who shook his head.

She could not take herself in hand in the carriage or in the house, even with Amabilia's help. She especially could not take herself in hand in the Filicchis' house, in the room where Anna was put to bed. She could sit there, she could watch there. But she could not stop shaking, could not stop fumbling, could not stop her mind's stunned chatter, especially after the doctor had said those bad words: scarlet fever.

On a chair she sat and stared. Her muscles quivered. It was too much, too much. The child was flushed, the child was delirious. Tossing inside herself, Elizabeth felt almost delirious as well.

Anna Maria, Anna Maria. Why didn't you tell me you felt sick? Why didn't I see that rash? Measles, why couldn't it be measles instead? When you had the measles I watched you like this. When you were a baby—those words you hate—I watched you like this too. Constantly. I sat, I stood. I hovered. New baby, first baby, you seemed so terribly fragile. I thought you might stop breathing. I thought you might die if I left you alone. Sometimes I'd turn you over, just to feel you in my arms. I never watched the others quite as much as you.

Anna, Anna Maria. You didn't say you were sick, I know, because you wanted to go home. Wasn't that it? So often now I can't read your thoughts. When you were two I could always read them. Even when you were five, six. Almost always. Once, I remember, you surprised me—you came clomping down the stairs in my shoes. My shoes, my ball gown too. The pink one, three of you would have fit inside it, you looked as if you were dragging draperies behind you. How I laughed, seeing you—you fluttered my fan at me. I was surprised you'd do that, somehow. Playacting hadn't seemed to appeal to you. Later, when you got sick that time, the measles, you asked to have the fan in bed with you. I wish I could give it to you now.

Anna Anna Anna. Are you trying to go to your papa? Are you tired of grieving for him too? I know, I know. But please: don't go. Not now, please God, not here. I couldn't bear that. Anna, I never told you—why don't we think of these things?—I never told you the first child's somehow special. I never told you how long your lashes look when you're asleep. Anna! Listen. Your papa doesn't need you now. And oh Anna, I do, I do.

Delirious chatter.

Fumbling hands.

She couldn't control it, she didn't know how.

She spilled water on the rug and on the bed; she knocked over a chair, she paced. She could not pray clearly, she could not sleep. She threw up what she ate. The Filicchis seemed to move about at a distance, blurred. The child on the bed appeared to dwindle, then grow alarmingly large. The room was too cold, chilling her through; then it was too hot and her skin felt taut and glazed. She saw specks like snow falling over the quilt. On the third day of Anna's illness, the floor of her room seemed to shake. Elizabeth told no one, fearing to admit it to herself. On the fourth day Amabilia, distinguishing shock from illness, sent again for the doctor, and on the fifth day Elizabeth was put to bed with scarlet fever herself.

In the room next to Anna's, she lay on her back. She watched the cream ceiling, the green silk walls. She could not seem to shut her eyes. Willy had lain here in this bed—how many years ago was it now? He had lain here and heard violin music in his head. Willy was in Pisa now, not here, in the ground. She'd have to buy a plot for Anna there. She'd have to do that soon. So many in the ground. She was only twenty-nine, she had so many in the ground. Too many; she had to know why. The ceiling gazed down on her, not telling. The walls, vibrating, did not know. Inside, she burned and blazed: the fever would tell her if she listened close. The fever was taking her through the ceiling, through the orange-tiled roof of the house. The fever was taking her where she would find out.

She lay on the fever, flat out, eyes wide. The wind shrieked past her, fast dirty air. She climbed astride it, flying past the port, the *lazzaretto*—she clamped the wind between her legs and rode. Below her: greenish sun, black sea. Along the shore, houses: stained, shuttered, dark. One of these was hers. The one with the stones in the garden, the one with the tombs in the yard. The house trembled, its walls shedding swiftly like skin. Its roof trembled next, peeling off, and so stripped, the house showed its bones to the sun—black bones: with the floors, they collapsed, rotted through.

So you see, said the wind.

"I see, I deserve it," she wept.

Amabilia took her face in cool hands. "No, *dolce*, no."

Elizabeth blew out of her hands, back out onto the long dirty wind. She watched the trees bend in it. She was bent with them. She had thought to ride this wind, but it dragged behind her now; it scourged her and broke her back. Her skin unspooled from her limbs; the wind flayed her of muscle, of sinew, it flayed her down to her black hollow bones and flung her away in disgust.

Now you know, said the wind.

"Now I know," she cried, "I'm being punished—but please, enough."

God says when it's enough, said the wind, Not you.

"O Mama Mama Mama," Elizabeth cried.

Amabilia's cool hands touched her hair.

In the air there were always bells and the bells rang her dreams in and rang her dreams out. The bells seemed to be in the room with her, with the murmured voices also there, but the bells spoke louder than the voices and the voices in her head spoke loudest of all. Even as her skin began to cool, the echoes seemed clearer than the bells; clearer than the soup held toward her on a spoon; nearer than the sound of any voice—until the day Antonio's voice, repeating her name so urgently, so commandingly, cut through to her at last.

"Elizabetta."

She could hear his voice but she didn't care.

"Elizabetta."

She didn't care enough to move her lips.

"Elizabetta!"

She didn't want her name to pull her back.

"Elizabetta Bayley Seton!"

As if from a long distance she looked at him.

Antonio's face hung above the bed, intent, concerned, canny.

"And so," he said, sitting back in his chair. "I understand

from Amabilia that you are not recovering as you should."

Elizabeth's eyes slid back to the ceiling; the effort to keep them on Antonio was too great.

"I am given to understand that the fever is gone, the attack is finished, and still you do not improve."

She watched the ceiling, feeling herself starting to float away from his voice.

"Elisabetta!" The voice suddenly roared. Her eyes came back to Antonio. Quietly then, his voice went on. "I have heard of cases where patients refuse to heal—is this the case here?"

She did not search for the strength to speak.

"I understand," he said, "that you believe you are being punished. I understand, moreover, that you believe you deserve this—is that so?"

Elizabeth did not answer.

"*Elisabetta.*" Antonio brought his face close to hers.

"Why else . . ." Her voice came out weak and thin. "These terrible things, so many . . . why else . . . ?"

"Ah. You think you are afflicted, is that so?"

Elizabeth glanced at him with a flicker of impatience.

"You think you are suffering, is that so?"

"How can you ask . . ."

"A lawyer always asks."

She flashed him an indignant look.

"Good." He smiled and leaned back in his chair, pressing the balls of his fingers together. "Now. You believe that suffering means punishment, is that so?"

"Antonio . . . please . . . I don't know, I . . ."

"You believe that a person who suffers, suffers greatly, is being punished by God, Elisabetta—is that so?"

She wanted to drift away from his voice, but his eyes held her. After a moment she nodded.

"Ah. Now. I can tell you about a man in this town who lived a good life—an exemplary life—beloved by all. And last year his wife died, his house burned down. Was he, would you say, being punished?"

"I suppose . . . maybe, maybe you saw his goodness . . . but God saw something you couldn't."

"Ah. I see. Now I can tell you about another man, he

lived in another town. He too lived a good life—a life of service and kindness. But his friends turned against him. His enemies condemned him. He was humiliated, tormented, put to death young."

"I told you . . . same thing, he must have done something, and God saw. . . ."

"I am talking here of God's son. We both know the story." Elizabeth flashed Antonio another look.

"I used to practice law for the Jesuits in Rome." He smiled briefly; then his face grew serious again. "You see, your belief does not, as they say, hold water. It is full of holes, in fact! Many good people suffer. Many bad people do not suffer at all. Suffering, punishment—these are not necessarily related." He smiled again. "Except perhaps where the justice is human, in courts of law."

"Then why . . . I don't understand . . . why . . ." Tears started in her eyes.

"Elisabetta . . ." Antonio's voice softened. "I am no priest, no sage. I do not know many things. But I have seen things, observed people, working out in the world. And I have never seen any sign that people are punished by God."

"But my pastor . . . the prayerbooks, my cousin's . . . punishment, always . . ."

"But think. . . . Can you really believe that a God who became human—a God with such empathy—can you really believe this God would punish as you say? . . . I wish I could tell you why some people suffer so much. Why you have suffered so. Sometimes, we're told, it's a grace, a refining process. . . . This I don't know. Sometimes, it seems to me, we simply suffer just as we eat, we breathe—it comes with the human condition, perhaps. But the suffering, it does not come from God, I don't believe—this God who suffered with us . . . died for us. Think of that, Elisabetta . . . perhaps you will feel some comfort in it—so I hope. . . . And now, I think you have suffered with a liquid diet long enough as well. A fortnight of soup—now, there, that is suffering indeed." He rose and opened the door, calling into the hallway, "Amabilia—sermon's over, we're ready now."

There was a clinking sound beyond the door, and then a table jerked into the room, carried by two of the servants—

a table flapping with white linen, tinkling with china and crystal. As Elizabeth watched, amazed, the table was set down by the bed. Chairs were fetched. Covered dishes were arranged. A cork popped.

"We thought you needed a lively evening." Antonio lit the three-branched candelabrum.

"A little supper for four," Amabilia said from the door. "Can you guess who your partner is for the evening? We didn't want to tell you till the doctor said absolutely yes, no danger. . . ."

Amabilia beckoned. Anna appeared in the doorway. Nightgowned, thinner, still pale, she took a step into the room, another—then ran the rest of the way to her mother. And Elizabeth, wrapping Anna to her like a robe, watched the wine and the pasta and Livorno's best veal swim before her eyes.

In a bright blue wrapper, in a soft blue shawl, Elizabeth sat in the empty dining room of Antonio's house. She was watching the light come in, thin and bright, and she was watching Amabilia, pen in hand, planning the day's menus. Keys jingled at Amabilia's waist. Clocks chimed from the hall and from upstairs; a bell pealed from down the street. Spread across the end of the mahogany table with a marketing list, a list of repairs to be made, a recipe book, a prayerbook, paper, inkpot, and an amethyst earring.

"Beef, very thin, pounded just so . . . you could eat that, you think?" Amabilia rubbed her earlobe and smiled at Elizabeth.

"Of course, don't trouble, please."

"No trouble . . . the spinach, creamed; the *cannoli* I make myself . . . tonight we eat 'fat,' tomorrow: Ash Wednesday. *Dolce*, your appetite, the way it is, will suit our Lenten menus. For Antonio, though, fasting pinches . . ." She clipped her earring back on and winced. ". . . like this."

"I remember Ash Wednesday at home . . ." Elizabeth half-smiled. "Sitting in church, saying the prayers about penance and fasting—full of buckwheat pancakes and coffee."

"Don't worry, we won't starve you—you sit here while I take this to the cook."

Elizabeth nodded. The smallest effort tired her; just staying downstairs seemed a mighty feat. The doctor, however, had advised her to start moving about, while Anna's prescription still called for rest. And so Elizabeth, childlike and wan and docile herself, allowed Amabilia to shepherd her through the days. For the first time in her adult life, Elizabeth had nothing to do: not a single duty to perform, not a single person to tend to. Her only task, Amabilia said, was to get well, a task which still left her largely indifferent. The hours rose up before her, vast, formless expanses, and without Amabilia she knew she would sink down, give up, get lost. But Amabilia, her keys and earrings chinking, kneaded the days and gave them shape. Elizabeth could feel the morning rise around her like bread in an oven, fragrant and finite.

At seven in the morning, Amabilia was coming back from Mass at St. Caterina's, her cheeks flushed from walking; Elizabeth could see her from the bedroom window above the breakfast tray. By eight the children were dispatched to school and governess, and Elizabeth was with Amabilia by the study fire, listening to her pen, watching her keep up a voluminous correspondence. Throughout the morning, Elizabeth followed Amabilia as she supervised the household, moving from kitchen to laundry to springhouse; Elizabeth found herself listening for the sound of Amabilia's keys. And throughout the day, six times a day, Amabilia would lay down pen or spoon or smock and open her prayerbook. Elizabeth watched her in the tiny chapel off the study; watched the straight back, the calm face. Amabilia was the only person she had ever seen who smiled as she prayed; her dark silks whispering, earrings aglitter, kneeling before the Virgin's porcelain figure, she looked like a woman in conversation with a beloved neighbor.

The afternoons were harder; then Amabilia went out in the carriage, visiting the hospital, visiting friends. Though she always looked in on Elizabeth when she returned, her time after that was spent in her children's rooms. It was then that Elizabeth felt a subtle sense of danger, a desire to sag into sleep and illness again. It was then that all the days coming toward her seemed steep, too hard to climb. It was then that she needed markers to lead her through that wasteland of time: the striking of clocks, the arrival of tea, and at five o'clock the appearance of La Signora. La Signora: so Elizabeth called her; she did not know her name. She was an aged woman, tiny, birdlike, always in black, who came every day at five to the small public shrine across the street. The shrine, like a birdbath, held an image of Madonna and Child; the mother in blue, the baby in gold. La Signora brought to the shrine a token each day—some days a bit of evergreen, some days a ribbon, some days a flower, a piece of fruit. She would sweep out the shrine and pray before it, then gather her skirts and walk slowly off, her hands in her shawl. Elizabeth imagined she was an outcast penanced for some shameful sin, or a mother mourning the death of sons; she was, Elizabeth found her more reliable than the hall clock for signaling the afternoon's end.

Even now she felt those long hours crouching behind the morning; she felt them even as Amabilia came back in the room, dusting flour from her hands, smelling faintly of licorice.

"Forgive me, forgive me—the *cannoli* were stubborn, not right. All that beautiful ricotta! I had to throw it out and start again, some days I do everything backwards—and twice." Amabilia glanced at her. "Ah-ah, that look—you're wilting, I can see it."

"It's just . . . I feel like such a burden, you have so much to do . . . and I can't imagine you doing anything backwards."

"Pah! I run my house, you've done the same—and you will again."

Elizabeth said nothing.

"You don't believe me—yes, but you will."

Amabilia, she wanted to say, I'm afraid of the afternoons.

"And then I'll come visit your house in New York. . . ."

Amabilia, she wanted to say, I'm afraid to think ahead.

". . . I'll sit and let you wait on me."

"Amabilia," she whispered, "I'm afraid."

For a moment there was silence in the wide sunny room. Amabilia put her head to one side and looked at the table. "Yes," she said then. "So it is after sorrow like this . . . I know." She looked up, her eyes direct, hands still. "I tell

you something . . . this I never tell. You think everything's
so easy for me, no struggles. I struggle, Elisabetta. I struggle.
Not a struggle like yours. But . . . my own. I grew up, you
see, in a big fine house . . . but my father, my mother, there
was such hate between them, it filled up this big house. And
I felt it always. And the one person . . . the only person
I had . . . I loved . . . it was my brother. We were always
together . . . all the time we were growing up, he was there,
he was my nearest friend. But then when he was eighteen,
he left the house. He didn't say where he was going, he
didn't say good-bye. Even to me. And he didn't come back.
We heard he went to sea, we heard he went to France
. . . we heard many things. I never saw him again. And I
tell you, Elisabetta, I felt that loss so sharp, so sharp, to the
quick of my soul." Amabilia's eyes filled; for a moment she
was silent. "For some time after he left," she went on then,
"for some time I was afraid of everything. Going out, waking
up. Going to bed again. I . . . don't know why it was. I
thought . . . I felt . . . that I would die without him there.
And so . . . and so, *cara*, I know something of what you
feel. I don't just pity . . . I know. . . ."

They sat in silence for a while, the warmed silence of
friends.

"And then," Elizabeth said, "you turned to your faith? Is
that how you managed?"

"Oh, no." Amabilia rose, smiling. "That was always
there, I was educated by the nuns, you see. Ursalines. I was
saying the Little Office when I was fourteen. Well . . . I tire
you, all this talk of troubles, this isn't the medicine you need.
Tell me, what frightens you this minute?"

". . . it sounds so . . . Amabilia, the afternoons."

"And what do you do, afternoons?"

"I watch Anna sleep. I . . . watch this woman, outside at
the shrine."

"Oh, yes, Signora Bertelli."

"You know her? *She* must be troubled, she comes every
day."

"Troubled?" Amabilia began to laugh. "Signora Bertelli
was the envy of Antonio's mother. She was beautiful, rich.
She married one of the finest men in town, who never took a

mistress. She raised healthy children, traveled, gardened—gardens still. She still has her health, her husband, her house. . . . Tonio's mother, till she died, wrestled her brains to find something wrong with her."

"Oh." Elizabeth felt faintly disappointed. "I thought she came to the shrine, you know, every day, I . . . thought it must be sorrow. Or penance."

"Perhaps . . . somewhere inside." Amabilia paused, thoughtful. "Still . . . I doubt it. She's a merry soul, it's her nature. Laughing, always laughing at market. I think she comes for Mary's joy. And, I think, for her own."

As Elizabeth grew stronger, the household grew quieter, drawing inward; the rhythms of Lent drifted over it like a hushing fall of snow. Meals were not taken in the mornings. Menus were left to the cook, and for more and more of the day Amabilia was in the chapel. Elizabeth was welcome to sit with her there as long as she liked, but the doctor had urged her to increase her stamina and get out in the air. Once Anna was able to venture out as well, they went together, slowly, slowly, to the end of the street; the next day a little farther, the next a little farther still. Leaning on each other, moving with the tread of elderly ladies on stony ground, they walked and watched the light flash on the Mediterranean. It still looked ominous to them both, impassable; still, Elizabeth remembered how it was spread, silvery, when she'd seen it from Montenero. And so, the last week in March, she and Anna rode the mules up the winding mountain road again.

Where the road broadened near the top of the mountain, Elizabeth found the wooden table where she had sat with the Filicchis before. It seemed long ago to her now. The groom took the mules, and she and Anna sat watching the wind stir the cypresses and oaks and umbrella pines. Here and there a tiled roof showed orange among the green, and far below, the sea lay like a vast shining floor, no longer menacing from that height. Amabilia had packed them a basket of cheese and oranges; cheese from Florence, oranges from Naples, she had said. They spread a cloth, unpacked the basket—then packed it up again. Their appetites were still too delicate for Amabilia's treats. For a while they just sat there looking at the sea, listening to the wind. Then, hearing music, they rose and followed it up the steps and across the piazza to the doors of the church.

The Shrine of Madonna della Grazia was old, medieval, flanked by the faded stucco of monastery walls. As Elizabeth and Anna approached it, they saw a group of people leaving the church: perhaps a dozen, brightly and carefully dressed, talking with a priest in white chasuble and stole. Behind them the sanctuary crouched, small and dark, like a sorcerer's cave. The group made way for them, standing aside; Elizabeth and Anna, feeling their eyes, moved past them into the church.

Elizabeth paused inside the door, unable at first to see much with her sun-dazed eyes. Then she began to make out a white form, cloudlike before the altar—a girl in a white gown and veil. A bride, she knew, was a rarity in Lent; this wedding, just finished, must have had a special dispensation. Elizabeth looked again at the girl, motionless, kneeling. A soft sound came from her: "*Mama, Mama . . .*" Then she rose, genuflected, rustled up the aisle and out the door. As Elizabeth moved toward the altar herself, she saw that the girl had left her bouquet by the rail—white roses, no doubt brought up at expense from the South. A shame—the girl must have completely forgotten it; she must have been troubled, young, lingering like that after her own wedding, crying for her mother. Elizabeth picked up the bouquet and hurried with it from the church—the bridal party was gone. Feeling slightly foolish, still holding the flowers, she returned and took a seat beside Anna. An acolyte was moving slowly about the altar, putting out the candles. The sanctuary grew darker; its seats and floor seemed to sink away. To Elizabeth it became even more like a cave than before: a magical cave banked with flowers, glittering with jewels. By the light of its small high windows, she could see the marble altar, the gold of its rail, and like a blaze of sun, the gold radiating from the panel above the tabernacle. Two candles were left lit near it, and the panel shimmered above them: a painting of a blond woman, robed in blue, a baby on her lap. The figures were crowned with gold and hung with pearls, jeweled medallions, golden hearts—but for all their splendor, the child's fingers curled like any baby's, around the top of his mother's dress, and her hands cupped him securely.

The light flickered before Elizabeth's eyes. Anna leaned, dozing, against her shoulder. Footsteps crunched down the aisle and an old man knelt in the row ahead, his beads swinging from his fingers. A scent of flowers, a sensation of warmth came over Elizabeth; silence, well-deep, rose around her, save for the faint clicking of the beads. She sat there as she sat with Amabilia, early mornings in the chapel: sleepy, childlike, contented, oblivious for a time of anything beyond this rounded darkness. How long she sat there, she wasn't sure, but then she became aware of someone moving softly across the sanctuary again. The light grew; the candles were relit. She heard the chink of pattens and cruets as the sacristan readied the altar for Mass. He paused a moment, genuflecting before the tabernacle and the Madonna, on the spot where the bouquet had lain. Elizabeth, shifting it in her hands, realized that the girl had not forgotten it. She saw whom it had been left for and for whom the girl had been calling. I ought to put this back, Elizabeth thought, but the church was filling, the priest was entering; Mass had begun.

"*In nomine Patris, et Filii, et Spiritus Sancti.*" Her eyes moved over the altar cloth, its border of lace; the border of lace at the priest's wrists. "*Introibo ad altare Dei . . .*" Before her a man already on his knees; beside her a man taking a seat: an Englishman, by his dress and manner, he smiled at her. "*Dominus vobiscum . . .*" The priest's voice floated out to her, singing, calling. The Englishman's voice nudged her, social, sarcastic: "Quaint, isn't it?" She avoided his eyes. She watched instead the old man's face, in profile to her right: seamed, sagging, intent, his voice lifting, "*Et cum spiritu tuo.*" There was a snicker in the Englishman's voice now, in her ear: "Really quite a show, don't you think?"

There was a shine from the basin held for the priest, a shine from ciborium, cruets, chalice. *Seductive splendor of their churches.* The acolyte's face, round, ripe-cheeked; the

Madonna's face, serene, above. *She comes, I think, for Mary's joy.* Candles tall as lilies, pale lit stalks; centered among them, the crucifix. *Can you really believe this God would punish as you say?* A lamp shaped like a boat, a woman carved within it, lighting a wick; marble hazed with incense, incense rising with her thoughts. More incense now, people rising around her. "*Jubilate Deo, omnis terra.*" The priest's arms open wide, purple chasuble in folds like wings. *To knock, to inquire, this is good.* A flash of the censer in the light; the sound of people shifting onto their knees. "*Miserere nobis . . . miserere nobis . . . dona nobis pacem . . .*" Glowing chalice, glowing cruet, the sound of wine being poured; tears at the corners of the old man's eyes. "*Ecce Agnus Dei*": Behold the Lamb of God. A bell rang, a silver thread of sound. The hush deepened. Into the hush the bread and wine were raised; no longer bread, no longer wine. Into the hush all heads were bent. And into the hush suddenly came the Englishman's voice, scornful, audible, harsh: "Quite primitive, really—this is what they call their 'Real Presence.' "

Elizabeth looked at him: the neat mustache, knotted cravat, the mocking smile. She looked at the bent heads around them, the clear-eyed Madonna and the wet-eyed old man, and the chalice held above them all. Suddenly, silently defiant, her eyes on the Englishman, Elizabeth lowered herself to her knees. His face changed; she eclipsed it with her hands, covering her eyes. In the darkness behind her fingers she felt a tremor of rage. He had wanted to be her ally; the very thought shamed her.

"*Oremus . . .*" The Real Presence. The bread and wine changed, she knew the doctrine: but how? Christ was present on the altar now, Christ's body and blood; Christ came among them every Mass—but how could that be? A hundred other questions swam through her mind, a hundred other things she didn't know. She wanted to know. She wanted to ask. The importance of knowing grew larger within her, a well of comfort she must taste. She would admit this to herself, here and now. She would knock, she would inquire. And perhaps that would be all.

"*Ite, Missa est.*"

"*Deo Gratias.*"

As the Mass ended, she lifted her head, sat back on her chair. The Englishman was gone. Anna was beside her, watching her face. People were filing out. Across the altar the sacristan moved again with a long candle snuffer. Elizabeth rose and walked to the rail. She laid the bride's bouquet on the steps where it had lain before. She hesitated. Somehow that didn't seem enough; there was something more she wanted to do. For a moment she stood there, uncertain as to what it was. Then she reached inside the basket hanging from her arm. She set down on the altar a cheese from Florence, an orange from Naples, and bent her knee. Then she turned, feeling oddly warmed, and walked with Anna out into the sunny piazza.

13

*C*onverts! my novice-master used to roar. Converts, they're the worst: the strictest, the most holier-than-thou, the most attached to form, rules, ritual. And pre-converts, taking instruction—he had even less mercy on them, especially a certain kind: the ones he'd say, who just want their hearts to go pitty-pat.

I've learned a thing or two since I was a novice. I've come to reject a good deal of that novice-master's teachings. But I'm still not sure he was altogether wrong on that point. Not altogether right either, mind you. But I've known those types myself: the ones who tend to be attracted to the Church out of sheer romanticism. The ones who tend to fall in love with the incense, the vestments. The ones who tend to see religion as theater, religion as magic, religion as cure.

I'm wondering if Mrs. Seton saw it that way. I'm wondering if her attraction to the Church didn't begin that way, in Italy and on the ship home, encouraged by her chivalrous escort, Antonio Filicchi. Maybe if I'm overly suspicious—after all, like Antonio, I'm a lawyer. But even with that taken into consideration, I'm just not certain that her conversion wasn't based primarily on her bereavement, and on her arrival home to yet another deathbed—Rebecca Seton's.

Consider her conversing with Rebecca, the two of them in the corner bedroom of Elizabeth's new house on Moore

Street: an unfashionable street a half-mile out of town; an unfashionable little house, the lower floor rented out to boarders; a small corner room, but clean-swept and sunny —cat on the rocker, daisies on the dresser, the window aflutter with curtains. A spare white room, it was tucked around the women like a freshly sheeted bed. It was colored only by Elizabeth's words and by a wide expanse of apricot silk between them, which they hemmed as they talked, their needles working toward each other.

". . . if you could have seen it, Bec . . . the way the altar would just . . . *float* in the incense. Amabilia said the incense stood for the presense of the Holy Ghost . . . oh Bec, if you could have seen. . . ."

"I can see it, listening." Bec smoothed the silk and looked up. "You feel it so much—that makes it seem close."

"At first, you know, I couldn't admit it to myself, even feeling it that strong. Now I . . . I've told a few people, my sister, some friends, not Mr. Hobart, not yet. . . . No one takes it seriously, Bec, but you."

"But have you told them about it the way you've told me?"

Elizabeth stopped to thread her needle. "No . . . not exactly. . . . I'm almost afraid to."

"Then don't." Rebecca laid her needle down. "Let it be private, like our retreats."

"But I want to, all the same. Now that the children are settled, the household's going along . . . I mean, wouldn't it be devious not to? After all. Mary's husband's paying my rent, he and my godmother, Mrs. Startin—don't they have the right to know?"

"To know you're thinking of converting?"

"Am I?"

"Eliza, yes—don't you see that?—and *no*, they haven't the right, not to my mind. Don't have the right to stop the rent, either, if they don't approve."

"It sounds so good, Bec—you taking my part. You may be the only one. . . ."

"I know you, Eliza." Rebecca looked up. "You want to tell them so they'll give you their blessing—that's it, you know, that's what's in your mind."

"No—of course it's not."

"But it is. I *know* you. And, Eliza, you'd best see now—you likely won't get that blessing."

"But surely they'll understand, they'll . . ."

"I just think you should keep it in mind."

"You can remind me."

"I can't."

"Bec! You said you felt as drawn to this as I, you—"

"I was. I am. But there's something else you'd best see now, Eliza—you'll be going through this without me."

"Don't talk like that, of course I won't." Elizabeth stitched rapidly, head down, voice fast. "We're hemming this for you, you'll wear it soon—you chose it, after all, said you wanted something bright, something like a flame, you did—oh Bec."

Across the silk Rebecca reached out to cover Elizabeth's hand.

How thin Rebecca was; how thin her hand felt. How like Willy's her dark eyes were—except that hers were calm, not frenzied: they held Elizabeth, they quieted her now.

"Eliza, I wanted this color, this silk, because I want this to be my . . . laying-out dress. I *want* to go all bright, like a flame. I want to *go*, understand that. I've wanted to for years—how I've feared hanging on and on like Willy."

"Bec—"

"No, let me say it. I see it very plain."

"You see everything very plain, you always have, I used to hate you for that."

"That's what comes of being sickly—you have so much time to watch. But, Eliza, I have to tell you this. I'm glad to go for another reason. I know I'd need to come with you into this new faith, this new church—it sounds as if I looked for this, somehow, in all those Sacrament Sundays. But to tell you the truth, I wouldn't be able to fight for it—no, I wouldn't. You may have to do that, poor Eliza, and I'll just get to . . . rest. Rest in this lovely, lovely silk dress."

The yards of apricot skirting shimmered in the light. Elizabeth's needle paused above it for a moment. Then she looked at Rebecca and pushed the needle through the hem. She understood from her sister-in-law's face that she wasn't to cry. She wasn't to contradict. She wasn't to make much of this, now or afterward, and she would try. She would sail Bec off in her flame-bright dress and she wouldn't think too much about it till she was gone. And till Bec was gone she wouldn't think too much about church, about faith; about fighting. After her fractured childhood, her scattered family, there was nothing she feared more than shattering family peace again. The thought of it shook her more than the thought of Bec's death. She would not think of it now; not yet. She would finish this hem. She would lay in those sleeves. She would find a way to buy a bit of lace for the neck. And she would remember, for as long as she could, sitting with Rebecca in the very center of this afternoon, the apricot silk shining between them with all the words they couldn't say.

They were tolling the bells for Alexander Hamilton when Elizabeth next walked the half-mile into town. Hamilton had died in a duel the night before; Rebecca had died in her bed four days before, and to Elizabeth's mind the bells rang for her.

From the corner, from the street, from the steps, and at last from the edge of the door, Elizabeth looked at St. Peter's Church. Since Bec's death she had been wanting to come here, to stand on the fringe of the Catholics going in to Mass. This was the only Roman Catholic church in the city; it had stood there on Barclay Street for less than twenty years. She had never been this close before. *St. Peter's*, she had said to herself, throughout Bec's dying and laying out and burial; *St. Peters, St. Peter's*. Although she had seen it from a distance before, Elizabeth had seen it in her mind these past few days as its glorious namesake—domed and golden and hushed within, even more beautiful than the Montenero shrine, than the Annunziata; even more healing to be near.

But from the corner, the street, the steps, she saw what she had always seen: a small run-down building with a tired roof, chapped walls, and a lean spire, topped not with a weathercock but a cross. And now between the ker-

chiefed heads, the shawl-covered heads, the rough bare
heads, between the threadbare shoulders and the sweat-
stained backs, she saw an interior that did not draw her.
She saw walls marked by water seepage, a floor muddy and
unswept. The windows were clear, some of the panes cracked;
the altar was laid with a plain cotton cloth and was bare,
except for a wooden crucifix and a small painting above.
The paint on the Stations of the Cross was peeling. The
light looked gray as scrubwater. There was a smell, under
the incense, of mildew and mice. Elizabeth hesitated at the
door, a wilting sensation within her. *Your people shall be
my people,* Rebecca had whispered to her, *your God my God.*
But these people moving about here, finding seats—they
were not people either one had ever called hers. They stared
at Elizabeth now, her presence as strange to them as theirs
to her. A woman who worked as a maid for her sister saw
her, hesitated, then dropped her a little curtsy from the
aisle. The man who did the groundwork for her godmother
bobbed his head from his seat. Many of them, she realized
with a jolt, were indeed the servants of people she knew;
many were immigrants newly arrived, having passed, no
doubt, through the quarantine station on Staten Island. She
was growing uncomfortable under their eyes: curious eyes,
suspicious eyes. Odd how she could go into churches in a
foreign country and feel instantly at ease, as if she belonged
—and here in her own city's church she felt as if she did
not belong at all. She knew she could not pray, feeling this
way; she knew she could not forget herself and let her
thoughts rise as they should. Ashamed, confused, she
turned away from the door and walked down the steps.

She could see, from the next street, the familiar steeple of
St. Paul's, and rising beyond it farther down the Broad Way,
the spire of Trinity. She moved toward it, not intending to,
her steps simply taking her that way, until she stood once
again in its churchyard—lush and green now in July, and
as neighborly as a close friend's yard. How could she leave
this, after all? She thought of all the Setons lying near; she
thought of Rebecca. But Rebecca had said she might seek
elsewhere, if she'd lived; she had said it with conviction,

not politeness. Elizabeth sighed and went up the path to the church's door.

What would Willy say? she thought, as she still thought so many times a day. What would Papa think? Perhaps toward the end, Willy would have understood. But for most of his life, he and her father would have shared a question: why did it matter so much? No one in their families had been racked by religious conflict; no one in their families had been religious at all, except Miss Molly. And what would she think? Elizabeth wasn't sure.

She stood in the doorway of Trinity, letting her eyes move over the Gothic windows, the altar and rail—everything simple, polished, elegant. Something was missing, though. She could not quite define it, but something was different from before; something, she felt sure, had been taken away since she'd been gone. For a moment her mind floated to Italy, to the altar at Montenero, then back again to where she was. Nothing had been changed here, she saw then. The change was in her eye, her spirit. She sighed again and as she did, she heard footsteps behind her.

"I only sigh like that when I've written a h-h-hopeless sermon," said Henry Hobart.

His spectacles glimmered in the filtered sunlight; a lock of hair fell across his forehead. As always, he brushed it back with his fingers—as always, it feel across his forehead once again. His face, turned toward hers, was as scrubbed and earnest as ever, though not quite as boyish as it used to be. And his eyes, those large nearsighted eyes, were kind.

"Can I help?" he said simply.

Tears stung her eyes; she blinked them away.

"I-I've a sponge cake in my study," he said. "Someone left it there, don't know who. May-maybe you can help identify it?"

She nodded, mute, and followed him through the church and down a path to his calm desk and sane walls. She sat in a straight-backed chair and took a sensible serving of sherry and cake. The study was small, shaded, cool. Here, she knew, everything would clarify. She told him about Italy, told him about the churches and the Filicchis and the pull of their faith; he did not say he'd told her so. He did not smile or rise his brows. He listened. He let her finish. And then he leaned toward her, his eyes still kind, his face still earnest.

"You were in grief," he said, simply, again. "So much grief, so, *so* much loss. . . . I grieve, I do, for you. Grief like that . . . it d-d-distracts the mind . . . you reach here, grope there . . . you flail about for relief, it's natural . . . it will pass. . . ."

For a few moments there was only the sound of a bee at the windowpane.

"It hasn't," Elizabeth said then, thickly. "It hasn't passed."

"You're still in grief. Be . . . be patient, it will."

"No," she said, her voice small. "I don't think so."

Hobart pushed his glasses back and looked at her again. "You'd consider, you mean, leaving your church, your . . . your family's church, that's what you mean?"

She nodded, eyes down.

"The church you were baptized in . . . and your children? The church Willy . . . Rebecca . . . your father . . . were buried in?"

She nodded again, still unable to look up. "I've thought of little else since I've come home."

He sat back in his chair, regarding her for a while. "The Roman Church is . . . very beautiful, isn't it?"

"Sometimes." She thought of St. Peter's on Barclay Street.

"But th-that isn't all that pulls you, surely?"

"No . . ." Surely not.

"What else, then?"

"I think it's . . . it seems there's . . . comfort, such comfort there . . . Mary, the saints . . . the Presence, you know, the actual Presence of God, God in Christ, right there, the bread and wine changing, actually changing . . . so hard to explain, these things, it's just . . . to think of God there, right there, on the altar, carried to the sick, I . . ."

"Ah, yes, 'transubstantiation,' interesting notion, bread and wine turned Godhead entirely, yes . . . a theological muddle akin to polytheism, really. It presents us with as many gods as there are altars, as many gods as there is consecrated bread. A primitive notion. We've come beyond that now, you see." His eyes shone, his face shone; his stammer was gone. She saw in him the man who rose in the pulpit on Sundays, the man whose preaching drew crowds. "And yes, the cult of Mary—Mary as an almost separate Godhead, a fourth Person, almost, of the Trinity—very comforting, yes. But totally unscriptural, you see. This idea of God's mother interceding for us, as if we can't pray to God directly. ·. . ." He shook his head. "Elizabeth, my dear Elizabeth, when you examine each of these doctrines in clear light, you'll see what they really are."

She felt his eyes on her. She watched the piece of cake on her plate, the sherry in her glass. She couldn't debate these points with him; she lacked the knowledge, she lacked the will. Her mind, she knew, would never gladly leap to challenges like these. Antonio's would, Rebecca's would have —for her, she would always rather conciliate. What she wanted most of all just now was to agree with Hobart, to feel at peace with him; with herself.

In the silence he had risen and was pulling books from his shelves. This would help, he was saying, and this, and this, this too. And she was taking the books, she was thanking him and saying good-bye, she was walking from the church feeling heavier than before. She was walking as quickly as she could for home, wanting this hour over with; this day over with. She was not intending to stop in St. Peter's again.

And yet she was climbing its steps. She was climbing its steps with her Protestant books and her Calvinist doubts and her deepening grief for Rebecca. Rebecca would understand. Rebecca would understand that beyond doctrine, something else sat quietly, solidly, undeniably real: something purely in the range of feeling. Rebecca would understand that this church was still shabby and strange; even shabbier, stranger, now that it was empty. She would understand why that mattered. The only thing of beauty was the painting of the Crucifixion over the altar, and Elizabeth sat looking at it, the books balanced on her lap. "Oh, Bec," she whispered aloud. "Help me. You know how much I hate a fight."

~

By autumn she thought she'd be decided, but by autumn she wasn't decided at all. By September the children had whooping cough and she had constant headaches and a pile of books on the parlor floor: books from Antonio next to books from Hobart, the Manning beside the Newton. And one October night, she thought that if she couldn't put them all out of her sight, she would go mad.

Outside, the air was still and sharp and crystalline. The house, in this new cold, seemed suddenly fragile: eggshell walls which might spontaneously shatter. It seemed more fragile after dark; it seemed most fragile late at night. In five minutes the clock would chime two. Elizabeth wished the chiming could sail above her sleeping brain, and three o'clock, and four the same. But every night was like this now. Every night she sat, shawl over gown, knees to chest, waiting out the darkness. Every night she crouched like this by the banked parlor fire and swore tomorrow night she'd sleep. For a while she had used this time to study her books; now she could only sit there, watching them, her mind too paralyzed to read or put them away.

From the street below came the echoing uneven step of a drunk lurching home. From the bedroom a child gave one of those odd yelping coughs she'd heard all week. It occurred to her that she was the only adult in the house now. She was its only guardian for the first time. Rebecca's death, coupled with Willy's, made her feel more acutely alone. She felt their absence in the parlor, in the kitchen, in her bed. She felt the absence of them, and of her father, in the crouching darkness around the house—and in a sense of darkness within herself. As always when she felt this way, her mind began to visualize the center aisle of her church. But now it stopped, confused, unsure of which church to picture.

All praise to thee, my God, this night. The hymns of her childhood unspooled in her brain; how could she go where they were not? They were a part of her language, her interior vocabulary; how could she never sing them again? *Keep me, O keep me, King of Kings, beneath thine own almighty wings.* Even without meaning to, she was comforting herself with those words. Set against them, the words of the Mass were dense, impermeable, still foreign. *Gratias agimus tibi propter magnam gloriam tuam*, she summoned up, her mind stumbling over the Latin. O may my soul on thee repose. *Suscipe deprecationem nostram*. And with sweet sleep my eyelids close. . . .

Indeed.

"Willy," she said aloud. She said this many nights, just to hear the name; she feared forgetting. Many nights she let herself imagine he was still in the house.

Another muffled cough; a child shifting in bed.

Willy: whooping cough, only that. No, really, they're fine. And so much bigger, hard to believe. Anna's nine now, Billy will be eight next month, he still looks so like your father. Dickie, he was six this summer, and tall as Billy, going to be a big man, I think. Kit, she's four; Bec, our baby, she's not such a baby anymore, two years old and talking, talking like a magpie. How I wish you could see them—but you can, I believe that. How I wish they could see *you*. Sometimes . . . sometimes they still have nightmares. Nightmares about the time we were away; all except Bec, who doesn't remember. And Anna—she has hers about the *lazzaretto*. Willy, the three middle ones, they wake up crying, thinking we're gone forever . . . thinking they were bad, that's why we left. It cuts me clear through. I remember so clearly, so clearly, feeling that way when I was a child—it's still with me, that feeling, it always will be. And I gave them that pain too. Oh, I know, I know, we had to go, we had to try . . . but I feel, sometimes, so guilty. And alone.

When I felt alone before, I'd pray. Now . . . prayer, it just confuses me. These books here: just looking at them makes my throat feel tight. Wish I could explain to you why. Wish I knew why it matters, this much, *this* much. Mr. Hobart, he's exasperated with me now. Has left me to my own judgment. Antonio—traveling, business—he writes, sends books. Filippo—his last letter from Livorno, it made me weep: "You act as if you thought God was not to be obeyed without the consent of your friends." So harsh. But truer than I'd like to admit. Friends . . . some are keeping their distance. I'm afraid of losing them, it's true, I feel so alone as it is. . . .

Oh, Willy, I don't know. Am I just looking for something because you're gone? I thought so at first; now I'm not so sure. If that was all of it, I think I would have given up by now. There are easier things to cling to. Like the old faith. Like Mr. Hobart. How I wish I could please him—can't seem to.

Picked up Amabilia's St. Bernard last night, read his prayer for the Virgin to be our mother. It stilled me somehow. Imagine God having a mother—being curled inside her before birth, like our own babies. The thought of God that humble—well, it amazes me, touches me, I never thought of it that way before. And, Willy, you know how I've always missed my own mother. Well, now it seems I've always had one after all. Some nights I cry myself to sleep on her heart—I'll admit it to you and no one else. Mr. Hobart would scorn me for that, believe me. I'll admit something else to you—only you. In Livorno, one evening, I was standing at the window and . . . I saw a procession, it was passing in the street . . . priests, children, they were carrying the Blessed Sacrament in a monstrance, all gold— Willy, I found myself on my knees. I can't explain that; even to myself.

I think of these things . . . I think of you. The Setons. And the Bayleys. If I took this step, I'd be separated from you—from them—wouldn't I? Maybe I'm wrong. Maybe I'm a coward. I fear so much being an outcast. Being lonely. I'm still not quite used to being a widow instead of a wife. I've had to let my membership in the Widow's Aid Society go . . . how I miss those afternoons with the ladies, I do. It occurs to me, I'm now a candidate for aid from my own club.

If only I could decide this. Willy, Willy, if only I could just *go to sleep*. I guess I've always needed to draw my strength from outside . . . from God. But now—whose God? Look: these books. The Manning. The Newton. The choice: plainly set forth. Advise me. Counsel me. Your soul to mine. Husband to wife. Tell me, decide me—please, now.

She waited, kneeling in the silence of the room. There was a soft stirring behind her; an almost imperceptible step, a sigh.

"Mama, what are you *doing?*" Anna said from the doorway.

Elizabeth jumped, a book in each hand. "Debating," she said. "Studying."

"Both books? At once?"

"It's not easy."

"What do they say?"

"This one . . . this one says all non-Catholics go to hell."

"Really?"

"And this one says . . . all Catholics go to the bottomless pit."

"Mama! Which one do we go to?"

"Oh, Anna, I don't even know that much."

By Christmas she thought she'd be decided and by Christmas she wasn't decided; after Christmas she was even less decided than before. The season itself had silently pulled her down, reminding her the *lazzaretto* this time last year. *This time last year*: she said it to herself every day, those last days of December, and she said it to herself on Christmas Day, at her sister's table, over the goose and stuffing.

There were twelve at table that day: Mary, Wright, and their children; Elizabeth's children and her godmother Startin; and Willy's youngest sisters, Cecilia and Harriet, fawnlike girls in their teens now, graceful and big-eyed. There were chestnuts in the stuffing and plums in the pudding, wassail in the punch bowl and toys underfoot— all the things that told Elizabeth that this was Christmas, kin, home. There was even the usual desultory discussion, over the pudding's remains, as to whether Christmas evensong would be attended. This discussion was a family tradition as much as anything else—some years they mustered for the service; other years, lulled by the wassail and the food, they simply talked about it till the bells had finished ringing. The only difference this year was the tension at the table; unspoken, almost imperceptible, yet present as a silent guest.

"The suspense is killing," Mary said as the bells began to peal. "Are we or aren't we?"

She smiled, and a crease appeared under her chin. Mary had grown heavier these last few years; always square and solid, her face was rounder now. With each new baby she seemed to soften, losing the clear angles of her profile and rib cage. Her dark hair still rose cleanly off her high brow, her brown eyes were still matter-of-fact, but there was something prim about her mouth, something fussy about her hands that hadn't been there before.

She glanced at her husband now, and Wright Post raised his hands in mock helplessness. "Damned if I know . . . let's have another glass of wine while we think it over." He lifted the carafe and bent forward, his frame still trim, face still lean, though his hair had begun to thin. Elizabeth could remember how fervently she had hated him when he'd been courting Mary, how pompous she'd thought him then. Now she felt only gratitude for the help he'd been giving her, and a genuine liking for this rumpled doctor, sitting loose and easy at the head of the table. "We emphatically do not want"—he tipped the bottle—"to do anything rash."

"Well, Wright." Sarah Startin passed him her glass. "If you can't decide, and if Mary can't either . . . far be it for me . . ." She raised an eyebrow, raised her glass. Mrs. Startin's gestures were always understated. Her hair, her gowns, her hats were always in the simplest taste. "Simply expensive," Willy used to say. She was a grand lady, a massive lady, seemingly upholstered in good black silk. And yet, at sixty-five, she still retained a coyness from her girlhood, a sly flirtatiousness which showed, like lace below a hem, only after a third glass of wine. Now, lifting her eyes from her fourth glass, she inclined her sleek white head toward Elizabeth.

"Eliza, perhaps *you* can decide for us," she said, her voice arch and sweet. "Although I can't help but wonder . . . which church *would* you lead us to?"

There was a sudden stillness at the table. This was a subject much too dangerous for mealtimes; it was a subject this family did not discuss, like adultery and money, within the hearing of children or servants.

"I think," Elizabeth said, "evensong would be fine."

"Oh?" Mrs. Startin took another sip of wine. "Not the little Roman church?"

"Is this the time . . . ?" Elizabeth cast a look of appeal at her sister, but Mary glanced away.

"I'd like to know the answer myself," Mary said quietly, after a moment.

Elizabeth looked at Wright, but he did not meet her eyes.

"I have . . . been going to St. Peter's," she said finally. "Not . . . as a communicant . . . yet. As a . . ." She trailed off.

"Interested observer?" Wright supplied.

"Not . . . exactly."

"The people you stayed with in Italy, they were papists, I hear." Mrs. Startin threw her another glance. "Well, my dear, of course you know they always try to win converts, don't you? They believe they get extra grace in heaven for each soul they bring in, it's a well-known fact, oh yes. Our laundress, you remember Bridget, she told me all about that."

"The Filicchis were very kind to me after Willy . . ." Her voice trembled around the rage at its center. "The Filicchis are good people . . . good friends . . . you mistake them, I think."

Another silence, deeper than the first. A spoon clinked as Mary laid it down.

"Eliza," she blurted out suddenly. "Do you mean to go on with this, do you? It's not just today, evensong. It's just that . . . Eliza, I feel as if I don't know you anymore. I've been to that church, St. Peter's, I went last week. They had a musical program, I went—yes, Wright, I went, I went to see if I could understand, I wanted . . . Eliza, I wanted to understand you. And I don't, I just couldn't. That miserable little place, it smelled bad, it's not even clean. They were just finishing a . . . a Mass when I came in, pushing, shoving, people spitting on the floor, the floor of their own *church*. I mean, the disrespect, and not just that. All those statues—like idols, it's true, like pagan shrines. All of it ruled by some corrupt foreign prince in a gold palace—oh, Eliza, to think this is what draws you, where you spend your time now—I don't understand it, I don't know you anymore at all."

Elizabeth looked at her sister. For an instant she saw Mary as she'd looked long before, sitting on the stairs saying *don't be scared*; Mary with her in all the back bedrooms— this strong sister she had always wanted to please. And was now displeasing. In another moment, she feared, her eyes would fill.

"My dear," Mrs. Startin said. "Think what it would mean to be of the Roman church, just think. A despised church— a church made up of people so unlike ourselves. You'd always feel so alien there. Oh, I know, there is a smattering of people like you—but only a smattering."

Elizabeth felt the tears subside, her face grow hot. A thin flame of anger rose in her again. She still said nothing.

"Don't think it doesn't matter—class." Mrs. Startin's eyes were cold now, not at all tipsy. "We're so swift to embrace those lofty egalitarian principles now, aren't we— Mr. Jefferson's rhetoric, so very fashionable." She gave Elizabeth a deadly accurate look. "Don't you be thinking I'm just an old snob. We're always more comfortable with people like us, it's always been true. And those people at St. Peter's are not like you, Elizabeth. You were fortunate to be born as you were, and you'll need that good fortune now. Haven't you enough strikes against you—husbandless, pennyless? Can you really think of adding the stigma of Romanism—not just to yourself but to your children? My dear. It simply isn't *practical*."

Elizabeth folded her napkin with two killing creases and looked at her godmother. "Practical? Is that really a question when it comes to faith?" Her voice was high and much too fast. "But if it were—*if it were*, if this faith helps me to go on, to take care of my children—then, yes, it's practical as salt. But, Godmother . . ." Elizabeth heard the fury rising, pushing her words; she could not stop it. "This is no sewing circle. No social club. This faith, this . . . feeling I have—it has nothing to do with those other people who go to St. Peter's, *nothing*, do you understand? This has to do with my beliefs, my self, with *me*, not them, *me*."

There was silence again. Elizabeth heard the shrillness of her voice hang in the room. She saw the children's wide scared eyes.

"My dear . . ." Mrs. Startin's voice was thin and clear. "You lack control. But no matter how you carry on, no matter how you protest . . ." She cocked an eyebrow at Elizabeth. "No matter what, you'll always be an Anglican. There's no getting away from who you are. And it *is* who you are, my dear. There's no changing birthright."

"Ridiculous, religion's faith—never birthright, it's—"

"Eliza, please." Wright Post's voice cut in. "I tend to side with you on one point—this isn't the time for such a discussion. But. It *is* begun. And I'd be a hypocrite if I didn't tell you this. . . . This is the way it will be for you, do this thing—if you convert. You'll come into town, go in a shop, see someone you know. Someone you're glad to see, perhaps someone you like a good deal. And that person will turn away from you. You'll go to borrow money, rent a house, seek work perhaps. And you'll be turned away, shown out. You'll seek friends for yourself, your children—you'll seek them among people you've always known and you'll find none. Your children will feel this coldness too, don't think otherwise, Eliza. You'll have your new faith of course. But if it's no more than a crutch, it will wear out soon enough. So think what you do, think—and I know you'll find the right way."

Elizabeth felt herself rising from her chair. She heard her skirts whispering around her. She saw her hands reaching for her children, pulling them to their feet. She saw herself as if she were another person, this livid taut-faced woman in the dining-room mirror, and as if her voice were someone else's she heard it speak, harsh and hurt.

"Merry Christmas to all," she said, and herded her children out the door before her.

By January Elizabeth felt she was drowning. She tried to get a message to Father O'Brien at St. Peter's; there was no reply. Father O'Brien seemed distant. Antonio, traveling in Massachusetts, seemed distant. Amabilia seemed distant, and Italy itself, floating on the borders of her mind, seemed so remote and fastastical now as to be a delusion. Transformed by a continuing snowfall, the city looked fantastical as well, trapping her inside with her thoughts—thoughts which seemed more real than the whitened world beyond the Moore Street house.

She watched the snow. Her head pounded. She tried to calm the restless children. Her head seemed to vibrate with their noise. The snow thinned. Before her eyes were sparks of bright sharp pain. She snapped at the children, she listened for shovels below in the street. The scrape of the shovels clanged in her head: tomorrow was Sunday, the roads would be clear. She would not be spared the choice, as she had hoped: which church this week, which church. The ache in her head reached into her neck, her shoulders. She tried to think of Amabilia's face. She saw her sister's face instead. She tried to think of Antonio's voice. She heard instead Wright Post's. She walked that night through the sleeping house—she walked, she thought, two miles. The safe furniture skidded past her, pocked and rippled by the pain in her head.

At dawn the sky reddened. For a moment the snow-covered ground turned the color of watermelon. Kneeling on the kitchen floor, she bent her head over the washbowl and vomited. I can't see the way, she thought, gasping above the bowl. I can't see the way. And until You show me the way, she prayed, the way You want me to walk, I will trudge on in the path I was born in. That's all I can do.

She wiped her mouth. She washed her face. And, leaving the children with the woman downstairs, she went out in her cloak to St. Paul's.

Tramping in late, she found a seat near the back. The walls of the church were still pink, the ceiling still blue. The Ten Commandments still rose behind the altar, and except for new crystal chandeliers, the church looked just as it did when she had first knelt there with Miss Molly. She tried to fix her mind on Miss Molly, on the comfort she had found with her here. She could not bring the images to mind. She heard the bishop offering the congregation general absolution. She did not feel absolved. The minister preached, the choir sang; she could not seem to follow the words.

She rose to receive Communion; she felt heavy and dulled as she approached the rail. She could see the chalice in the minister's hands, moving down the kneeling row, moving toward her. "The Blood of Christ," the voice said, over and over, "to be spiritually taken and received." Only spiritually. Not the Presence itself, replacing the wine, the bread. And for her that wasn't enough. Not anymore. Not now. No matter how she wanted it to be. She rose from the rail and, shaking, walked out of the church.

She walked down the steps and down the street and into the next street, and still she shook. St. Peter's was between Masses. There was an echoing and a shuffling and a damp murmuration within. Elizabeth took a seat, again near the back. Candles, crucifix, and Christmas crèche, still on display, blurred before her eyes. She jumped as a bundle of rags stirred in the pew ahead. Elizabeth looked down on a woman's huddled form. Petaled in tattered skirts and ragged shawls, strung with pots and spoons, glittering up from the dimness, was Mag. Her head was bent, her face was taut, rapt, gentled by the low light and by something she held nested in her layered lap. Elizabeth saw her through a screen of dust motes, saw her shimmer there in the pew; saw her rough-knuckled hands move over the thing she held: the figure of the Christ Child from the crèche. Elizabeth looked and looked again, jolted. She's stolen it, she thought— holding it to comfort herself. Mag leaned over the figure; a low crooning came from her. Elizabeth saw that Mag, as if it were real, was trying to comfort the baby. Rising slowly, still crooning, Mag moved down the aisle and carefully replaced the figure in the manger. Elizabeth, rising swiftly, repelled, moved up the aisle and out the door before Mass could begin.

When she arrived at home, Elizabeth could not bear the touch of her children or the sound of their voices. She could not say the blessing over the food at the dinner table. In silence she lifted the plate of chicken pie and took the serving spoon in her hand. Steam rose as she broke the crust. She felt the sense of unreality she had felt, fevered, in Livorno. *The suffering does not come from God.* She held a plate, spooned out chicken, carrots, peas. She ladled gravy, she filled another plate. *A God with such empathy.* She could still see Antonio's face, fatherly, concerned. She could see her father's face, concerned, bemused, in the whitewashed kitchen on Staten Island. *A strange thing, in the midst of life, a busy life, to feel that kind of longing.* Gravy spilled on the tablecloth; her spoon clashed against the crock. *Actual yearning, never felt it before.* She filled plates for the children, none for herself, she couldn't eat. She thought of Mag cradling the Christ Child—she thought of how she'd fled that sight, left the church. She passed the milk and realized why. She had wanted to do that herself. It was true: she wanted God to be that close, that immediate. *We've come past that,* Mr. Hobart would say. Nonetheless. She wanted God to be that present, on the altar, in the bread, the wine. She wanted Him near as a friend, taken within body and soul, carried to houses and bedsides in the Host. *This is what they call their "Real Presence."* She stared at her empty plate. Not simply did she want this. This was what she believed. *If it's no more than a crutch . . .* At first it was. Not now. Not just to cling to. No more than Mag was clinging to the Infant. She passed the breadbasket and wiped a chin. She had been afraid of feeling this way. Just as she had been afraid of taking that taper in the church in Florence. She had feared candles, effigies, symbols of Christ's nearness; she had feared them and been drawn to them. She had been drawn by the incense, the flames, the gold—and drawn past them. She saw that now. And now she saw she could do without the shining altars, the elegant naves. She saw she could do without fellowship, community, even that. But she could not do without that sense of God's presence, as immediate and near as the chicken pot pie on this table.

She saw it plain: she saw she had decided at last. Not in church, as she had expected. Not on her knees, not face-down in the road like St. Paul. She had decided at supper, amid the chink of forks and spilling milk. She looked around at her children. Yes. It was right. For her; for them. She felt it now.

Tomorrow she would go back to St. Peter's. She would go back to that shabby, hopeful, compelling little church and find Father O'Brien. She would make arrangements. There would be the Profession of Faith, the First Confession, First Communion—all the mechanics of conversion. Conversion: Antonio had told her the Latin: *convertere*, to turn about. Tomorrow she would begin the steps toward the ceremonies, the solemnities. But here at the supper table, her turnabout, she knew, had truly occurred.

Thank You, she said silently. *Thank You.*

She looked at the bread, the cup before her.

She wiped her eyes.

She filled her plate with chicken pot pie.

That evening, after the children were asleep, Elizabeth took her cloak and went out. She had no destination in mind; she was simply so filled with sudden energy she could not stay indoors. For months she had been tired; for months her step had been heavied, slowed. Now the force of her decision seemed to have freed her stride, the swing of her arms—she had a sensation of speed as she moved into the street. She walked past a house where the people always stared at her, unsmiling; a house she'd been in the habit of avoiding. She walked past a house guarded by a black dog who always snarled; a dog she'd been in the habit of avoiding. She walked past pumps and wells and fences she had seen so many times—but not quite at this pace; not quite in this way.

She had felt like this before, she remembered, perhaps twice in her life: lying in childbed, immediately after the birth of her first baby . . . And as a child herself, lying in that long-ago clearing on the sun-soaked moss, laughing in her sleep. She was laughing now, she realized; laughing softly out into the darkness, into the house lamps and streetlamps and carriage lamps going by. It foamed from her, this feeling of relief and strength and joyousness, and the more she felt it, the larger it grew. It was there as she returned to her house and found the ladder to the roof; it was there as she climbed, her head filled with *Alleluias*, to offer up, like a bird on a chimney, her laughter to God.

14

The knocking on the door was louder now.

Elizabeth, sleeping soundly, had at first fitted it into a passing dream. Her eyes opened; the rapping continued. It must be three in the morning, she thought. Three in the morning and cold outside. Alarming as the noise was, she delayed another instant in her bed's warm depths before rising, finding a shawl and a candle and going through the chilly house to the front door.

As soon as she had unlatched it the knob turned and Cecilia rushed into the hall. Her face, rosy from the cold, looked troubled and exhilarated at once.

"No one's died, don't worry, Eliza," she said, breathless.

"Glad to hear it," Elizabeth said dryly and shut the door.

Cecilia followed her uncertainly down the hall; she hadn't yet been to this house, Elizabeth remembered. This was her third house in the past year, the year since her conversion; it was hard to keep track of who had visited which. There had been the house attached to the school where she'd briefly taught; there had been Mary's house where she'd stayed when the school failed; now there was this new house where she boarded schoolboys for St. Mark's School next door. Above their heads she and Cecilia heard a board creak. Behind them, angled in a doorframe, was a blur of white nightshirts. "Go back to bed, nothing's wrong," Elizabeth told the boys, and moved into the parlor, where, kneeling at the hearth, she stirred the banked fire.

From the wing chair, Cecilia was already talking, rapidly,

urgently—apologizing for the urgency, the lateness of the hour. Tall, dark, quick-moving, and big-eyed, she reminded Elizabeth not of Willy, not of Rebecca, but of herself a dozen years before. There was a luminous, nervous intensity about the girl; something deeply sensitive in her manner, sharply perceptive in her gaze. She had more fire than her brother, less wisdom than her sister, and yet there was something steady about her underneath it all. She sat there, her cheeks pinked and her eyes lit, like a girl on the verge of an elopement. She had run away from her brother James's house, she was saying, she had gone to her sister Charlotte's; she had run from her as well. She was running, not for the sake of a man—though they'd thought so at first—but for the sake of faith.

"Faith?" Elizabeth's voice was sharp.

"*Your* faith. Oh, Eliza, please support me in this—it means everything. I've watched you this past year, I've come and stood in St. Peter's, watched the Masses—"

"Cecilia!"

"Please, please don't think I was spying—Eliza, it's just that there was this change in you, marked, so marked, I couldn't help noticing. This way you are now, I don't know what to call it—not just peaceful, not just calm—even before Willy got so ill, I can't remember you being this way, not ever. It made me wonder, made me . . . want to see what it was you'd done. So I started to read. And I started to go, just quietly, to St. Peter's. I stood in the back. I watched . . . I watched when you were confirmed, Eliza, I was there, I saw Bishop Carroll, saw how kind he looked . . . and other times, I saw . . . oh, Eliza, I saw I belonged there, I feel it so strong."

Elizabeth watched her sister-in-law's face. She wished that Antonio Filicchi had not gone back to Livorno; she wished that it wasn't three in the morning. "Think, Celia," she said quietly. "Think what you're saying."

"I have thought. I know it seems sudden, but it's been almost a year. I *know* how rebellious it sounds—like running off with the wrong boy and throwing it in everyone's face.

Except . . ." She hesitated. "That *is* how it feels. Like . . . being in love. I mean . . . oh, I know, that sounds daft."

"No." Elizabeth brushed the hair from Cecilia's eyes. "That sounds true. That's how it is with me."

"Still?"

"Still. More so."

"You understand, I knew you would, but James—he won't hear of it, and Charlotte, she's worse. Eliza, they say . . . they say you . . ."

"They say I've . . . corrupted you?"

Cecilia nodded.

"Seduced you into this, no doubt, as well?"

Cecilia nodded again. "They looked in my drawers, my dresser—they found that little prayerbook you gave me when I was sick, they think—"

"I can imagine what they think."

"And they say . . . Eliza, they say they'll see you punished for this. Charlotte's husband, he says he'll see you're made to leave New York, he says he can do it. Don't laugh, he *is* an assemblyman, he says—"

"Well, deportation's better than some fates, like . . . oh, say, burning at the stake." Elizabeth had to smile. "No, darling, don't look that way. I'm not important enough for a vote in the legislature. But, Celia . . ." Elizabeth's face grew serious again. "I still have to ask you to think again. Don't you remember that Christmas dinner, my family . . . ?"

"They've stood by you, even so, haven't they?"

"Yes, but things are strained and—"

"Your friends too, Julia, Dué, Sad—they all held firm."

"But, Celia, *listen*. Remember my teaching post, that little school—that wasn't so long ago. How I'd counted on it. Do you know why it failed? Because people wouldn't trust their children with a Catholic teacher—no one said so straight out, but it's true, that's why. Now, I have to admit, most of the things I feared, the things Wright said, they haven't happened. But still, I can't teach for a living anymore, and there's only one reason. . . ."

"Well, of course, I do realize—"

"You don't realize," Elizabeth said dryly. "Neither did I.

You can't, not till it happens to you. But, Celia. If you promise to think about this quietly, *quietly* . . . and if you still feel this way in a few days . . . I'll take you to see Father Hurley. He's new, he's . . ." Elizabeth was nearly knocked off her feet by Cecilia's embrace. "Not to convert, necessarily, understand. To talk, to ask questions. I'm not the best guide for this, a priest is. Celia. I can't help trembling for you, a little."

And for myself, she added silently.

That was a Tuesday, Elizabeth remembered afterward. Cecilia made her profession of faith on a Friday. And by the following Monday morning, two weeks before Christmas, even the butcher knew. Elizabeth could tell by his glance and, more important, his refusal to sell her a leg of lamb and a pound of bacon. "All out," he said, first thing in the morning, and turned to another customer.

The tea man knew. Elizabeth could tell by his silence and his refusal to sell her two pounds of Darjeeling and an ounce of cloves. "All out," he said, and bent over his ledger.

The baker knew, and the stationer, and the women marketing in their shops. The tradesmen said, "All out"; the women looked away. In the street a friend of Mary's did not say "Good morning"; across the street Mrs. Startin's bonnet nodded left and right and suddenly froze as Elizabeth passed by. Amanda Stockton, Kit's playmate, knew: Elizabeth found her daughter crying by the house with two hoops in her hands.

"Never mind," she said, and picked Kit up. "Never mind," she said again, and thought: it's starting.

It's starting, she thought as she went in the house, as she looked at the cupboards, at her daughter's tear-streaked face. Never mind. There were Catholic butchers, tea men, bakers. Never mind. There were other friends. There was Christmas coming, boarders to feed, a thousand things to do. Best do them, then, best do them now. She had this work, this house; this was still certain. St. Mark's, an Episcopal school, could not be shut down, and its owner, Mr. Harris, had told her he didn't mind Catholics. This house, with its dim safe halls, its elderly parlor, its rows of rooms and creaking beds, its boyish smell of sweat and ale and books upstairs— this would still be hers. She would set the long table for dinner. She would sweep out the downstairs hall. She would take her basket and market again and she would tell herself, every step: *Never mind, never mind.*

By the next week she was setting two less places at the table; two of her boarders had left. Three of her children were jeered on the street; one morning she woke to find trash on her steps. This happened to other Catholics, she knew, from time to time. It had never happened to her before and it was hard to keep saying *Never mind.* She stopped saying it, stopped thinking it by the end of that week when Mrs. Startin came to call.

Her godmother was in the parlor when Elizabeth came down with a broom in her hand, her hair in a kerchief. With the kerchief she felt at an immediate disadvantage, and felt this even after she had taken it off. Mrs. Startin was sitting in the chair Cecilia had sat in, that breathless night of her arrival. Thinking of that, Elizabeth felt for Cecilia a flash of love and a flash of resentment—both eclipsed by her dread of her godmother. Mrs. Startin would not take tea. She would not take off her gloves or take her eyes off Elizabeth. For a few moments she sat in silence, the purple of her cloak and bonnet shimmering in the dusty afternoon light.

"It wasn't enough for you," she said at last. "Your own folly wasn't enough."

Elizabeth said nothing. She could hear her godmother's heavy breathing.

"It was bad enough," Mrs. Startin went on. "Bad enough, the course you took for yourself, your children. But I will say this: you used discretion. And we used discretion. And now you have broken that discretion, you have gone beyond boundaries I can tolerate. Mr. Hobart has warned our congregation against you. What you have done—it's a disgrace."

"Cecilia's conscience is no one's affair, it's—"

"Cecilia," Mrs. Startin's voice scorched the name onto the air. "Cecilia is a changeable young girl. She does not

yet know her heart. You . . . took . . . advantage . . . of
. . . that." Her voice trembled. "You took advantage, Elizabeth, you seduced this young girl."

"I did nothing of the kind, I—"

"You seduced her from her faith. From her family. You
. . . tampered with someone . . . not your charge, your
responsibility, you . . ." A vein throbbed in Mrs. Startin's
temple; her face filled with blood. "You've done more than
start gossip . . . don't think me so petty I mind only that.
You have taken . . . a . . . beautiful . . . young . . . girl
. . . a girl with no parents . . . and made it impossible for
her to ever have a husband. You have stoned her road . . .
and Harriet's, her sister. . . . Poor Harriet now wants to
convert as well."

"I've had no influence on Harriet, I—"

"Eliza. There is nothing you can say. You have . . . bewitched two fine girls. And you . . . you have wounded me,
Eliza." Mrs. Startin's eyes were wet; she rose unsteadily. "I
have come to tell you that. And to tell you that I have this
morning altered my will. I had meant to take care of you.
I had wanted to do that. And that pleasure, too, you have
denied me."

For a moment the room seemed to swell with the sound
of her breathing. Then, her face still filled with blood, Mrs.
Startin walked slowly from the parlor, her kunckles white
on the walking stick in her hand.

At the door, she turned and looked at Elizabeth.

"Don't call on me," she said. "Don't attempt to see me.
And don't . . . don't say any of your prayers for me . . .
I don't want your pious words."

"I am thinking," Elizabeth said, "of some extremely impious words."

"You people may think what you like, say what you like
. . . *do* what you like . . . isn't that true? . . . and simply
confess it afterward?"

Mrs. Startin turned with a sweep of skirts and Elizabeth
stood listening to her halting steps in the long dark hall.

~

"Father, I wanted to hit her."

"You speak figuratively, of course. . . ."

"Physically strike her—nothing less."

The kneeler in the confessional was hard; the cushion was thin and worn and Elizabeth could feel the wood beneath it in her kneecaps. She could hear the vague shufflings and murmurings in the church beyond; the sound had become familiar. She liked the confessional, liked its dim secretive attic smell, its sheltering walls and listening grille. And she liked Father Hurley, the young Irish priest whose profile floated now behind it.

"But you didn't strike her," he said now. "You fought the impulse. You didn't utter those . . . impious words?"

In the darkness she thought she heard him smile.

"Not out of goodness, Father. Because that would have given her more gossip, more pleasure. I feel so . . . angry, Father, angry."

"Perhaps you're being too hard on yourself . . ."

"But feeling it so strong . . ."

"You're not a saint."

"God knows."

On the other side of the grille she heard a rustle, and then, almost imperceptibly, a chuckle. Father Hurley had been her spiritual adviser for some months now; he knew her voice, knew who she was. She knew how his blunt features creased in a smile; she knew his thoughtfulness. After a moment she went on, saving the hardest for last.

"Father . . . I was wondering . . . wondering if I should leave New York. My children . . . this hurts them, they're feeling it so deep. And the boardinghouse . . . three more gone. If I can't find work here, I just don't know . . . My friends the Filicchis, their letters keep saying I should move . . . they think I'd do better in a city with more Catholics. That probably means Canada, Montreal maybe . . . I don't know, New York's my home, my family, they're all here. . . ."

"But your first thought was right—the children. They'd thrive in Montreal. And you—you could find work, maybe teach . . ."

"Sometimes I want that . . . sometimes I just long to be part of some community, maybe a lay teacher with a convent. . . . Sometimes I just feel scared of any more changes. The thought of leaving the country again . . ."

"Maybe you wouldn't have to. I'm thinking Baltimore may be another place. I could write to Father Dubourg there, he'll be in New York soon too. And Bishop Carroll, it would be easy enough to do."

"But, Father, just listening to you, I see I . . . No, I couldn't leave. I still need this . . . home to hold on to, even though I have the Church now, even so . . . I still need New York, I wouldn't feel safe, somehow, away from it."

"And that's just what you may not be here. Safe. I'm wishing we could be, all of us. But this hatred, for Catholics, it's rising again, who knows why." Hurley sighed behind the grille. "Back home in Ireland, there was so much hating. Fighting. It never stirred me like my brothers. I hoped when I came here there'd be peace. Well, now. Isn't that always the way of it? God seems to take from us what we want to cling to the hardest."

"Yes, but . . . I've had so much removed, and this, this is something I couldn't . . ."

"Elizabeth: in the end it's not up to you . . . or me."

Elizabeth sighed. "I guess . . . I'd hoped somehow, when I converted . . . I hoped everything would finally be quiet, calm . . ."

"And safe? Peaceful?"

"What's *wrong* with safety . . . peace?"

"Nothing in the least. But sometimes—it seems to me—we grow more, somehow, from strife."

Elizabeth sighed again.

"It's Christmas," Hurley said quietly. "At least, Elizabeth, there is this little time for peace—can you not take this time? Can you not allow yourself to enjoy it, celebrate it, and simply trust in God for a few days? Now, there's a penance made for your soul, I think: a hard one, too."

He was right, she knew. Her mind kept nudging the problem as she made her Act of Contrition, as she received absolution, as she stepped out again into the hushed church. A line of kerchiefed women waited beside the box. The silence streaming from them and from the empty nave was calming, sweet. The church looked peaceful to Elizabeth as she walked through it to the door, and the city in the dusk looked peaceful as well; the streets were empty, it was Christmas Eve. She remembered that afterward—that devious sense of peace as she returned with Cecilia and her children that evening for midnight Mass.

St. Peter's was filled and bright, except for the crèche left dim by the altar rail. Still shabby, the church now looked to Elizabeth like the face of a dear and homely friend; familiar, lit from within, its features seemed different. Tonight, amid its crowds and candles, Elizabeth smiled. Clustered in a pew with her children, she took Cecilia's hand. This was their first Christmas here, so different from the one before. Elizabeth knelt, her eyes on the painting of the Crucifixion over the altar; Cecilia's hand stayed in hers.

Behind them the processional started, the acolytes with the candles and the cross—it always moved her, watching them move down the aisle. The cross tonight was a triumphant Christ, His arms spread as if in joy, His head crowned with gold, not thorns. Behind it, two priests, vested in white and swinging bronze censers, began to fill the church with soft spiced smoke. Last of all came Father Hurley in a long white cope, and cradled in the folds of the cope, lifted higher and higher as he moved down the aisle, the figure of the Christ Child, its hands outstretched. He laid the Child in the manger, in the crèche; he lit the candles around it—six candles, a dozen candles, twenty, thirty, fifty. The crèche glowed, the crèche blazed; it blurred in Elizabeth's sight. "*Hodie Christus natus est.*"

It was during the Sanctus that Elizabeth first heard the sounds outside: a constant shuffling noise, like the scrape of many boots. It made a low, deep undertone beneath the priest's voice; it was nothing, she told herself. It was during Communion that the shouting began, the first yelped calls: "*Papist-trash-Papist-dirt,*" then louder, stronger, "*Cannibals-cannibals!*" Father Hurley's hand paused as Elizabeth knelt at the rail; for an instant he seemed to tremble above her. Then his hand dipped into the ceborium; his fingers raised the wafer.

"*Corpus Domini nostri Jesu Christi . . .*"

"Amen."

And outside, faster now, "*CannibalsCannibalsCannibals.*"

A stir went through the church. Communion finished, Mass was ending, the howling went on. It was during the final blessing that the rocks cracked through a window near the altar. There was a sudden splintering crash. Father Hurley, arms raised, cope spread, flinched. In the front row a man fell forward, blood spurting from his scalp. Anna screamed; screams answered hers, men were suddenly in the aisles.

"*Ite, Missa est,*" Father Hurley said, his voice blurred by the noise. "*Ite, Missa est,*" he repeated, louder, and Elizabeth heard the fear in his voice.

"*Deo Gratias,*" came the faint response.

Father Hurley motioned for quiet, for calm; there was a sudden ominous hush outside. The recessional began to form. The cross was raised, the candles lifted. The acolytes moved slowly down the aisle like boys stepping deeper and deeper into chilling water. Elizabeth watched them near the doors of the church. She saw them stand aside; she saw Father Hurley facing the doors, hesitating there. The white cope seemed to hover around him. His hair, reddish and springy, stood out around his head. For a moment his hand raked it; for a moment more he waited. Then he pulled off the cope. He pulled off the white chasuble and alb. He motioned again. The acolytes moved through the church, putting out the candles. In the darkness Elizabeth heard the door open, and in his black cassock, Father Hurley slipped outside.

Elizabeth closed her eyes. She felt her children trembling against her. She heard rising around them a dense scared chattering. She saw, behind her lids, the mob around her father's laboratory again; she fought the urge to run as she'd run then. She felt again that sense of something lost, wrecked, gone from her forever. Her children pressed against her; she rocked them, hoping they wouldn't feel her trembling as well.

She did not know how long it was they huddled there. Time seemed to skid and skip its common beats. The whispering around her grew, became a lowing of fear, and then someone was touching her sleeve. She opened her eyes and saw the face of Father Hurley. He was crouching in the aisle beside her, his face lit by the taper in his hand.

"Elizabeth," he whispered. "I need your help. The mob's still there—but Mayor Clinton, he's come. And the constables, there are enough of them now, I think. We want to be taking the women, the children out first. Not just for safety. The men in here, they're looking to fight, we can't have that. I asked the women to start out—they won't move. Too scared, God knows they should be. Elizabeth. It's hard to ask this. But you—everyone knows you here. If you would get up, start, walk out—if you could do that, I know the others would come after. . . ."

Elizabeth looked at him. She looked at her children. I can't do this, she thought. Her knees felt numb; sweat had begun on her palms.

"Elizabeth. I'm sorry—sorry to ask." Hurley's face was waxen in the candlelight. She looked at his eyes, large, gray, wide. He was as frightened as she was, she saw.

"The constables guarantee safety," he said. "But me, I can't guarantee it. . . ."

Elizabeth looked at him again. She heard herself sigh, that deep sharp sigh she had made in the confessional. They both heard it; they both smiled.

She stood up and stepped into the aisle. Drawing her children after her, she followed the priest toward the door. She felt the safe floor threading away behind her. She saw the faces flare up, fall away, as Hurley's candle passed them. For the first time she saw there were fragments of glass on her sleeve. She saw the doors flash up before her. For a moment she stood looking at them, unable to move. She did not want to open them. She did not want to leave this church, this city, this safety. She wanted only to close her eyes and stay. Down the aisle she heard footsteps. She felt people moving behind her. She put her hand on the door. She pushed the door and slowly swung it open. Beyond her a mass of faces stared, hostile and curious, in the torchlight. Behind her now there was a gentle press of shoulders, shawls. I don't want to, she thought as she moved forward.

With her children holding on to her cloak, she walked out the door and down the steps and through the crowd, walking faster and stiff-kneed and increasingly grateful, into the chill dark morning.

Part Three

15

*N*ormally, *I'm told,* an unembalmed body, buried in average soil, will in twenty-five years deteriorate to skeleton. Normally.

Incorruption of mortal remains is not normal: a sign of sanctity, in the eyes of the Church, when it occurs. Incorruption of Elizabeth Seton's mortal remains was hoped for, a hundred and fifteen years ago, when her grave was first opened.

I am standing where they stood then, in Emmitsburg, Maryland, this mountain town, this country town, here in this little cemetery where they brought the coffin up. I am here as an advance man, as it were, scouting the location. I am here to report on logistics for an official exhumation sometime next year—"canonical recognition of the grave," as we say in the Saint Biz. A formality. A solemnization. A verification that eleven feet below, encased in mahogany and copper and cloth, do in fact repose the bones belonging to the venerable Elizabeth Bayley Seton, the candidate in question.

No signs are hoped for, this time. Eyewitness reports of the first exhumation exist; I've seen them. The coffin, when raised, was found to be partially decomposed. The contents, when examined, were found to be dust, skeleton, rosary beads, and earth. These were placed in a new casket and reburied there—under that mortuary chapel a few feet away. Tiny, Gothic, with miniature spires and gingerbread trim, it looks like a gnome's house in a storybook. I fidget before it, pat my pockets for a cigarette; refrain.

An ordinary grave, really. Nothing miraculous about it. Except, perhaps, the cures effected through one small bone removed from that first coffin.

Perhaps.

Rome may or may not approve our findings. Rome has already rejected another Seton cure, in another city, involving the very same relics. Hardly an exact science, this business. And this business will go on. It takes four miracles to make a saint.

Beyond the graveyard now, blowing and scudding on the paths, I see the black habits and white coifs of nuns: her nuns, her Sisters of Charity. This wind—it will send me home soon. Emmitsburg is high in the Catoctins, near the Pennsylvania border; near Gettysburg, Camp David. The place still looks rural to me. To her it was wilderness. It took me ninety minutes to drive here from Baltimore. It took her, by wagon, four days.

Here she founded her order, the first American sisterhood. Here she founded her school, the prototype of Catholic elementary education. Here is where she became Mother Seton—and here is where I lose track of her entirely. Here she vanishes behind those firsts, those facts; she disappears behind her title, turns into a Holy Card given out at a spelling bee.

How did she get here—to this mountain, this grave, this height of location and position? On the face of it, she got to Emmitsburg via Baltimore. And she got to Baltimore, not via Divine summons, but via human invitation: from the Founding Fathers of the American Church, who saw a place for her in their plan.

Consider the facts.

She wished to join a Catholic community, perhaps a convent, perhaps as a lay teacher, perhaps in Montreal. She sought advice from Hurley, from Dubourg when he visited; from Bishop Cheverus of Boston, from Bishop Carroll of Baltimore. The churchmen were interested. Mrs. Seton was an intriguing case. Mrs. Seton was a prominent convert. In a nation of few Catholics, especially of her stock and social position, Mrs. Seton stood out. Letters were exchanged. Counsel was proffered. Mrs. Seton was steered to Baltimore instead of Montreal, was given a house there and, still as a layperson, the germ of a school to organize. And so it began.

Convert; nun; foundress . . . saint?

I still can't make that declension with ease—though I admit I'm satisfied now about her conversion; perhaps I had misjudged her there. Even so. There are hundreds of good converts, gifted converts, holy converts—who still are not material for the religious life, let alone sainthood.

I've heard the chancery gossip. I've heard that Rome wants to present American Catholics with a native saint in time for our Bicentenniel—that's only fifteen years away. In the Vatican there's intense lobbying for the Seton cause; some even say her status as "venerable"—the first public step toward canonization—was rushed through for Eisenhower's visit to Rome in 1959.

Not surprising, of course.

Not at all surprising that politics figured in Mrs. Seton's time as well, in her own rise. Not surprising, not disturbing; not to me. In fact, I like her better now, tracing that rise. There's a shine to her, a bravery I didn't see before.

But is it enough?

How do you measure shine?

I've come up here, advance work aside, to find out.

There is the stone house where she lived. There is the white log house where she died. This is the place she called her mountain, her valley—this may be the closest I can get to who she became. I can trace back the course from the grave, trace back the steps that brought her here: the steps that led to her vocation. Perhaps if I can see the leap from convert to nun, the leap from nun to foundress will reveal itself.

Thinking about her vocation makes me think of my own— a subject I have repeatedly pushed away these last two months. Standing at her grave makes me think of that other grave: my sister's, filled in eight weeks ago today. That grave in that strange cemetery: not ours. No funeral

Mass: not for my sister. Bright hard sunlight, high wind. Me, mumbling a few prayers; my words blowing back in my face.

Damn—I think of that and I want to explode like a fast car against a wall: I want to pull off my collar, pull out of this assignment and out of my vows.

What keeps me?

Not much. Not much more, I think, than the habit of completing what I start; handing in assignments, finishing everything on my plate. That, and fear: fear of leaving, beginning again somewhere else. I'd rather think of Elizabeth Seton's vocational struggles than my own—my God, I'd rather think of anyone's—and I will, and now.

I know that people discover religious vocations in different ways. A few hear voices out in the fields. A few find themselves facedown in the road. A precious few. That's how it's supposed to happen for saints; we tend to expect that. I suppose I expected Elizabeth Seton to find her vocation in the time-honored mystical manner. But here again, the lady seems so human, so much like the rest of us. I find no evidence that she heard the call in an exalted state, a golden glow. And I do find evidence, I think, that she began to hear it in a coach, on an errand, on the Baltimore–Washington road, while thinking rather worldly thoughts about her traveling companion.

"You see," he was saying, "you must *want* the thrust—really want it. If not, it won't feel right, won't be the proper climax. Look, it's this way: feint, feint, parry, thrust. . . . Without the whole body behind it, it glances off—or misses entirely."

Samuel Sutherland Cooper was fencing with an invisible *épee* in the narrow confines of the Washington coach. Elizabeth, across from him, could not look away. His voice was low and secret and compelling; his hands, moving in accompaniment, were long-fingered and strong.

It was just the day before, arriving in Baltimore, that she'd met him: this heir to a Philadelphia fortune, this prominent new Catholic whose conversion had made, as the French priests said, "a big noise." He was visiting Baltimore with

Father Hurley; Hurley himself had introduced Cooper to her. Now the two men were escorting her to Georgetown Academy, where her sons had been studying these past two years. It had seemed best to start their education there, but now they could continue nearer to the family in Baltimore; Elizabeth was coming to fetch them today. Scarcely transplanted, hardly moved in, she was grateful for Cooper's concern and friendship. She was especially grateful at this moment, on this journey, with Father Hurley stricken with migraine on the floor of the coach, huddled under his cloak and generally incapacitated.

"I hate to admit it," Mr. Cooper was saying, "I was fencing when I realized I had to convert, *fencing*. Not praying. Embarrasses me to talk about it."

They had been talking since they'd left Baltimore that morning, unable to stop, finding a mesh of words and thoughts that drew them closer. He knew all the people she knew in New York; she knew of all the people he knew in Philadelphia. His mother had bought hats from her milliner; her husband had had coats made by his tailor. He knew the scenery of her life and she his: its theaters and suppers, its corniced walls and gabled doors—but most of all they knew one another's struggles to convert, knew intuitively, because their struggles had been so much the same.

"I'd thought about it so long," he was telling her, "agonized as you did, up nights, pacing around . . ."

". . . headaches, dreams . . ."

"Awful, yes. . . ."

"Wondering why it mattered so much . . ."

"Exactly. And my proper Protestant family—you can imagine what they had to say. . . ."

"I can tell you *verbatim*."

"You could, I know." He nodded. "Well, for a time I gave way, gave up the whole idea. And then, suddenly one morning, *fencing*—of all things—I saw I had to do it. Saw I couldn't just . . . jab at it all my life. Saw I wanted to . . . throw my whole self behind it, I knew that then, listening to that blamed fencing master shouting at me about thrust."

He laughed, his face candled from within, his words soaring and darting with his hands. He was an exceptionally tall man, over six feet, and angular. He seemed to branch from his seat like a great tree, a knee protruding here, an elbow there. His nose was high-bridged in a narrow face; his cheekbones too were high and his eyes extraordinary—deep-set, intent, a pale pearl-like blue. Strands of fair hair, falling across his forehead, were combed back with quick fingers; his hands were seldom still. Like slender birds they swooped and dived about the coach, alighting now and then upon his elegant clothes: dove-gray coat, salt-white shirt, monogrammed watch on a chain of braided gold.

She had been watching him; he had been watching her. They had been speaking of the Church, of prayers, of psalms, of priests who had helped them—and they had been speaking of things that had nothing to do with prayers or priests at all.

She had found herself speaking of her fondness for dancing; he had found himself speaking of a fondness for clams. She had found herself speaking of sadness in summer, in the worst of the heat; he had found himself speaking of sadness in early mornings, in the last of the dark. She had found herself speaking of small fears: of mice, of snakes; he had confided a terror of heights. They had spoken of these things and looked away, then looked at each other again, in surprise, in delight, hearing the click and fit of their minds. They had turned to smaller, safer talk: his lodging house on Charles, her new house on Paca. They did not mention, though he knew, that she was here to stay and teach school. They did not mention, though she knew, that he was here but not necessarily to stay; to see about entering St. Mary's Seminary. They talked only of what could be shared, of what could include them both— that was how she wanted it, she saw; she saw that was how he wanted it too.

When they stopped for noon dinner, they were talking still. Hurley, ashen-faced, remained huddled in his cloak on the coach box; weakly he waved them on. They walked across the innyard together. Under her elbow, she felt his hand. He called her by her given name, then broke off. Eliza, call me Eliza, she nodded at him. Sam, he said: I'm Sam.

Sam: she was walking toward the stoop-shouldered inn with this man; with Sam. She was remembering how it was to walk with a man; to feel paired, linked, bracketed with a man. She was walking in pace with his stride. She was watching her hem brush his shoes. She was watching herself: a dark-eyed black-bonneted woman; a woman with a certain animation, a certain shine—a certain color in the face that hadn't been there the day before. She saw herself, a small woman, fit with this tall man. She sensed his arm by hers, his shoulder above her, his quick downward glance, his eyes. They passed through a narrow door; they moved together down a narrow hall. For a moment, to their sun-glazed eyes, the hall seemed impenetrably dark. They stumbled on the sloping floor; his hand skimmed hers, they laughed. She was remembering how it was to laugh with a man; to be in the dark with a man, alone.

They emerged into the bright-windowed taproom, into light slivered and scattered across wooden tables, and into a warm rich smell of stewing meat. They were seated by a smiling red-faced woman who bobbed her cap at them, mistaking them for husband and wife. They laughed again; they did not correct her.

Around them the crowded room rumbled and chuckled and drifted with smoke. They were served lamb stew and brown bread—ordinary food, an ordinary room; and yet to them, food more delicately sauced, a room more cheerfully lit than any they had ever noticed before.

And am I a goose? Elizabeth thought, watching him over bowls of raisin-studded rice pudding. Am I an idiot, enjoying being seen as a wife again: his wife? I'd forgotten. Forgotten how it was. She watched steam rise from the pudding, smelling of cinnamon. I'd forgotten, she thought, how sweet it feels.

"Cinnamon," he was saying. "It reminds me."

She watched the spoon in his hand.

"Reminds me of a cook we had, I was five, six . . . she'd make rice pudding every Saturday . . ."

His hand was tanned, veined, strong; his finger ran slowly, thoughtfully around the rim of his bowl. She imagined his hand touching her face.

". . . only child, spent so much time alone . . ."

She imagined his hand lifting the chalice, the Host, at Mass.

"Never felt lonely in that kitchen, though, not once. . . ."

She imagined his hand passing pudding to her children.

"She used to give me raisins . . ." His finger dipped into the pudding, gently prodding a raisin up and offering it to her. ". . . Like this."

"Cinnamon," she said, taking the raisin, tasting it. "Rice pudding, too, I remember."

He was thirty-nine, she knew; she was thirty-four. He had never married; she wondered why not, knowing he was wondering why she had, and whom.

His hand moved to his napkin, then his watch.

"Well," he said.

"Well," she echoed.

For a moment they just sat there, watching and not watching each other, wanting and not wanting to say more. Above them they could feel the presence of quiet rooms, curtained alcoves, deep beds. They folded their napkins, pushed them through the pewter rings. They paid the bill. And then they walked down the narrow hall again, out to the waiting priest and the waiting sons and the insistent sun-soaked road. But in the coach she tasted cinnamon still, and on the way she tasted cinnamon, and at the academy she tasted cinnamon, standing before the Academy's two brick buildings, watching her boys: her boys in their blue school uniforms with the red waistcoats and the large yellow buttons—her boys walking with Sam by the locust trees. And how fine they looked with him, their eyes raised to his, and how fatherly he looked with them, his head bent to theirs. How fine, how right, and yet, at the same time, for some reason: how wrong.

That night, asleep in her Baltimore house, she saw his hands again. They hovered again at the rim of a bowl; they lifted the bowl, and the bowl became a cup, a chalice raised for consecration at Mass. His back was to her, the chalice lifted before the altar. He turned suddenly, sensing her presence— above his vestments she saw, not his face, but her own. She woke breathless, heart drumming, in the back bedroom of the Paca Street house.

For a moment she wasn't sure where she was; then she saw the dim outlines of the sleeping alcove around her. This house was built in the French style, with recesses and folding windows—she remembered now. In bed with her, sleeping still, was six-year-old Bec, her youngest; the child had felt too strange in the new house to sleep upstairs with the others. Elizabeth sensed her children's nearness now, just above her head—they made the house feel less new, less strange to her. She sat up; the dream she'd just had was filtering back to her. Disturbing. As if it couldn't follow her from the room, she rose, moving quietly down the hall. She opened the door to the front room on this floor, giving onto the street. Designed as a bedchamber with another sleeping alcove, this was to be the schoolroom. Tomorrow they would paint it. Next week they would furnish it. Soon she would teach in it, her voice setting words in orderly rows across its walls, slate, desks. This was what she had come here to do; she still wondered if she'd be able to. Her experience seemed so limited, so scant. Her mind seemed so disordered. What was that dream about? Never mind, never mind, she told herself—better not to know. Tomorrow she would feel better. Tomorrow with the smell of paint, the sound of voices, the clang and slam of daylit things, she would stop these strange imaginings. It was only the new house; it was only the new city, the new school. "Go to sleep, Betsy Bayley," she muttered, and went back to bed, pressing her face against her sleeping daughter's hair.

But the next day in the schoolroom, amid the smell of paint and the sound of voices, she still felt as she had the night before. She moved. She talked. She laughed. She tried to make it not so—tried to submerge herself in the chaos rippling knee-deep around her. Around her were five children, two priests, eight paintbrushes, four buckets, one ladder, three cats; underfoot were canvas and rags, two of the children, and all of the cats. Painting the molding on the door, small brushes in their hands, were Anna, thirteen now, and Kit, eight. Their dark heads bent together. Their strokes were slow and neat. Elizabeth was amused by Kit's serious face, her sturdiness so like her Aunt Mary's—and Elizabeth was startled, as always lately, by the loveliness, the sudden womanliness of Anna.

Across the room from their sisters, the boys larked and splashed: Bill up on the ladder, paint in his hair, paint dripping from his brush, hallooing across at his brother. At twelve, Bill's voice was starting to crack and warble; his freckled face looked less like her father-in-law's and more like his own. But he was still not as tall as his ten-year-old brother, Richard, who had shot up alarmingly, outgrowing two sets of clothes this year. "Daddy Dick," Bill was calling him, because of his height, and Dick, dark eyes snapping, sent a shower of paint back. He was a thick-necked brawny boy, dangerously handsome already and given to eccentric bursts of charm—ducking down, he scooped his smallest sister off the floor, wielding her like a live paintbrush against the ceiling while Bec shrieked with laughter.

Just beyond, on his knees, thinning the biscuit-colored paint, was Father Babade. His white head bent over the bucket; a marmalade cat rubbed against his sleeve. He was smiling, Elizabeth was grateful to see; he made a small circle of serenity within the frantic splattered air. Of all the priests she had known, Elizabeth already left closest to him. His poetic French-crisped speech had touched her in welcome, and in the confessional, and she knew she would seek him out again. Like many of the priests here at St. Mary's College and Seminary, he had fled the Revolution in France and taken refuge with this Baltimore enclave of Sulpician priests. Like Father Dubourg beside him, he had kissed America's ground as an immigrant less than fifteen years before. Reedy and elegant, enveloped in a white smock, he might have been taken for a portraitist there, not a priest —and Dubourg, she thought, might be a courtier in a portrait. He had a long sensitive face, a thin Gallic nose, and alert, shifting eyes; his sinewy frame was covered with a denim apron. There was a moodiness to him, but kindness too, a low firm voice that managed her boys. There was also, Elizabeth thought, something not quite at ease about him; even the cats noticed and kept their distance. He seemed constantly to be watching Father Babade, comparing words and brush strokes with him; and this younger man, she sensed, was not entirely comfortable with her, a woman. To cover his discomfort, she suspected, he had started them all singing, lining out the words of a Negro spiritual for them. Before he'd become president of St. Mary's, Elizabeth remembered, his special mission had been to Baltimore's blacks.

"Oh you can't get to heaven . . ." His voice was strong and tonal; unmusical all the same.

"OH YOU CAN'T GET TO HEAVEN . . ." Her children's raucous chorus answered it.

"In a rocking chair. . . ."

She tried to join in the singing; her voice was small. She tried to concentrate on her painting; her brush was dry.

"Cause the Lord don't want . . ."

She watched Father Babade raise his brush as if in blessing to the wall. Again her dream image floated before her: the chalice, the hands.

"NO LAZYBONES THERE . . ."

She had missed a stanza. The smell of paint and dust was making her head ache. "Lazybones: *here,*" she said, pointing to herself and murmuring an apology. She left the room, left the house, and in the garden gasped fresh air—she could not get her breath; it scared her.

She walked away from the house. Perched on the edge of the seminary grounds, surrounded by orchards, it seemed farther from town than a half-mile. She could see the back of the chapel and the little garden behind it: hardly big enough to plant cabbages in, the garden held a small knoll representing Calvary. Its path wasn't much wider than a sheep track, its cedars just shrubs—its tininess gave it a fairy-tale look she liked. She started to walk up the path, then turned guiltily back toward the house. A figure was moving beyond the house, she saw; a white shirt flashed among the trees of the nearer orchard. She knew the slope of those shoulders, the shape of that head. It was Mr. Cooper; it was Sam. She stood watching him some moments. She watched and felt her headache tighten like a hat brim. What disturbed her was not a temptation to go to him; it was her lack of it.

She moved around to the front of the chapel. It was new,

just dedicated the day she'd arrived. There was still some brick dust on its steps; the niches in its squared facade were empty of statues. She loved this chapel, this bit of Gothic gingerbread—this little *bijou* of a thing, Father Babade called it. She had thought, that first day, she would never feel troubled living behind it. Here she was, at last where she chose to be: in this peaceable city, this Catholic community, within moments of vespers, benediction, the angelus bells. Here she was, with a post, a paying job, a school for her children—and here she was still feeling troubled. It wasn't right to be so. It wasn't right at all.

It would be right to feel settled. It would be right to feel rooted. It would be right, too, to feel drawn to Samuel Cooper. If he didn't lean toward the semonary, it would be right to think of marrying him. She knew this. She knew she should want this. She should pair off again; she should find someone to help raise her children. And she had been drawn to Sam. She was still drawn to him. But something else was in the way.

She pulled open the chapel door. No one was inside. A single lamp burned before the altar. Light filtered dimly through crimson curtains at the windows. The silence was well-deep—the silence she had found in the church on Montenero. She stepped into the aisle. Maybe she would be married here; maybe in this chapel, as a bride, she would end her worries for her children. She tried to see that: tried to see herself moving down the aisle with flowers in her hands, her hair. She could not see it. She tried to see Sam waiting for her by the altar with Father Babade. She could not see them. She could only see the altar's white cloth and across it, the ripple of crimson light.

Something rubbed against her legs. The marmalade cat had followed her. After a moment, tail high, it trotted down the aisle and slipped through the altar rail. She moved through the low gate after it, glad to be distracted. The cat curled against the altar, arching its back just out of reach; she sat by the altar, watching it, her gaze held by its wide yellow eyes. It edged closer, came purring against her as she knelt down. Elizabeth did not move to go. She would, just for a moment, stay. She would, just for a moment, pretend that this was where she was supposed to be. Just till her headache went away.

She closed her eyes, feeling the faint vibration of the purring cat; feeling the curve of the church around her. Gradually, as she entered deeper into prayer, she lost her sense of cat and even church—there was only a wordless sense of connection. Sometimes it happened this way, sometimes not. Whenever it did, she would find herself startled by the sense of her surroundings once again. They began to come back to her now: the cat, still purring; the church, still quiet; and the feeling that she was no longer alone. Someone else had come in. With her head in her hands, she couldn't see who was beside her, but she sensed him. There was a gentleness there, a peacefulness: Father Babade, she thought, not Sam. Father Babade, sensing her trouble, coming to help pray her through. With this presence beside her, she picked up the thread of her own prayer; now she found it forming words. She found herself asking to stay here, to stay always, promised to this peace; she found herself startled by this prayer—so startled her head snapped up, she opened her eyes. She glanced beside her. No one was there. No one had been.

All at once she heard laughter in the church: her own. Presences, promises—what was she imagining, some sort of religious vocation? The thought set off another wave of laughter. Herself, a nun: a mother of five? Herself, habited: a scapular on this body that had bred, borne, nursed? And who would have her? She wasn't even sure if there were convents in this country yet—certainly there were none in Baltimore. The only nun she had ever seen outside Italy was a waxworks figure in a New York museum: a stiff curiosity children pointed at and giggled "witch." The memory tapped her laughter again.

And look at me, she thought. A fine candidate for a convent. Ducking out of a chore. Sitting against this altar. Paint in my hair. Cat on my lap. Laughing, laughing.

She rose to go, the cat in her arms. As she opened the door, the darkness hurt her eyes. The garden was quiet, the orchard was empty. As she walked up the stairs of her house, she heard the last snatches of "Roll, Jordan, Roll," the crash of a bucket, the shriek of a child—and a shrilling of "Mama Mama Mama."

Of course.

That was who she was.

She could never get away from that, never be anything else. Her headache, eased in church, tightened again as she walked back through the schoolroom door.

16

To add 2/3 + 3/8 . . . find common denominator.
Which makes it . . . 16/24 plus . . . 9/24.
Bad at this, hate this, let's see . . .
16/24 plus 9/24 equals . . . 25/24?
Right?
No, wait—1 and 1/24.
I think.
Why didn't I learn this twenty-five years ago?

Elizabeth was muttering to herself in the empty school-room on the second floor of the Paca Street house. This hot July of 1808, these weeks since she'd arrived, she had spent late afternoons this way—bent over her slate, forcing herself to practice one of the subjects she'd have to teach her grammer-school pupils: arithmetic. It was torment; she had to trick herself into it. As a child learning verses to recite, she had been promised an apple, a chocolate, a marzipan rose if she could get so far. As an adult stuffing her head with fractions, she promised herself what had become for her a treat, a sweet, a prize: a quarter-hour alone in chapel. How chapel had come to equal marzipan she could only explain to Father Babade; he was intuitive, he understood. It was the silence, she'd say, it was the peace. . . . And she would trail off, he would smile. They both knew it was more than that. The feeling she had laughed off by the altar was now too strong for words.

For a month she had been living, it seemed to her, with

the chapel as neighbor, attuned to its rhythms like the rhythms of a friend. It wakened when she did, its bells ringing first at five-thirty; it seemed to move and lean through the day with her, its doors opening, closing, its organ groaning in practice; its bells rang again at the slope of the day, one-forty-five, and near the day's close, a quarter to eight. She was within its walls twice a day at least, with her pupils at six in the morning and six-thirty at night, and more often if she could be. She had never lived so close to a church before; she wondered how she had managed without. Even while she was teaching her pitifully small class—only two pupils as yet—she was aware of the chapel, of the life of the seminary turning around her. This classroom was the reason she was here, she knew: her purpose, outlined for her by Father Dubourg, was to provide young ladies with a Catholic education—but sometimes now her purpose simply seemed to be within sound of those bells.

Fifteen minutes more.

3/4 divided by 2/3.

Two hours more and it would be time for benediction. Across the black smudged slate she could see it unwinding through the garden, the procession of white-robed priests and seminarians, the Blessed Sacrament in the monstrance aloft above them. Their chanting would rise to her back porch, it would fill the rooms of her little brick house. She would move her lips with the words, she would follow the seminarians with her eyes. She wished she could be among them. Sam Cooper was among them; he had decided at last.

She remembered the afternoon he had come to tell her, not long ago. She had been in the kitchen, her hands in a bucket of soapy water, washing dishes while Delia, the cook, was ill. Elizabeth had been hot, she had been damp, she had been harassed—exactly as she had not wanted to be when she saw Sam's tall frame in the doorway.

He had sat on a kitchen stool and told her his decision, his voice lifting as it had in the coach. And under its lift, its intensity, she had heard something else in his voice as well—some small undertone of regret.

"At *my* age," he was saying. "Almost forty—twice as old as the others, most of them."

"They'll start calling you 'Father' before you're ordained."
Elizabeth kept her eyes on the dishwater and tried to banter.

Sam laughed. "I've been closing accounts," he said, "almost as if I'm about to leave this world altogether."

"And in a way you are." She felt a distinct spearing of
envy; she scrubbed the blackened bottom of a pot. "I'm
happy for you, Sam," she said above the whisk of the brush.

"It's such a relief, knowing, deciding," he said slowly,
after a while. "I don't feel . . . ten feet off the ground, the
way I did when I converted. I guess this is more like . . . a
marriage. Less like . . . falling in love."

For some moments the only sound in the kitchen was the
slosh of water in the bucket. She could not speak. He could
not speak. The clink and splash of the dishes seemed to fill
the air between them. Again she felt a twist of envy—not
disappointment as she had expected. The envy felt worse.
The envy was strong. It was so easy for him: a man. It was
so much harder for her. A plate slipped through her fingers,
shattering on the floor. In silence he fetched the broom; in
silence they swept up the crockery. She wiped her hands on
her apron, gave her hand to him and wished him well. He
pressed her hand; he was gone.

And now she was watching him in the white-robed procession through the garden. She was longing, she knew, not
for him, but to be where he was. She shook her head. There
seemed no solution to this constant wistfulness. Each afternoon she found herself waiting for benediction, counting
time to it as if the day divided there, as if each hour tended
toward that procession, that white-robed streak that shone
and sang and shot the evening through with splendor.

Twelve minutes more.

4/7 minus 1/5.

She had been meaning to speak of this envy to someone:
to Father Dubourg, her director, to whom she should go; to
Father Babade, whom she would go more easily. Someone.
Next week. The week after; next month. She would put it
off. She would keep intending to tell someone—just as she
intended to tell someone about the shortness of breath, the
pains in the chest. It had begun soon after this move; she'd
thought at first it was the paint. Every time they saw her

gasping at the top of the stairs, her children fluttered around her in fear—it reminded them too much of Willy. And every time they fluttered, she laughed: it couldn't be that, "the Seton complaint," she told them. The Bayleys never had it, and besides, it couldn't be heaven's plan to orphan them now. She believed that. She knew that, felt that, trusted that. Next week she'd tell someone about the pains.

Twenty-five percent of forty-six.

Ten minutes more.

Abruptly now the afternoon quiet fragmented around her. The knife grinder was calling at the front door, a peddler at the back; Dick was pounding up the stairs, Bec down them. From the kitchen below there was a crash, from the bedrooms above a shriek—and all the voices from doors and stairs, kitchen and street, below and above, were calling "Mrs. Seton," "Mama," "Mother," "Madam." Elizabeth sighed, seeing the prospect of chapel dwindling. The slate still in her hand, she ran upstairs and down till the knives were sharpened and the peddler paid; till Dick was scolded and Bec was soothed and the greens brought in from the garden for supper—till Elizabeth stood in the schoolroom again, leaning on a desk, gasping for air. She groped for the door, shutting it behind her. She didn't want to see frightened eyes on her again. She was for the firt time frightened herself. Small points of light danced before her eyes. Her breathing made a jagged pattern in her ears. For a moment she saw the *lazzaretto* again. For a moment her head seemed to float slowly toward the ceiling. Gradually each breath lengthened, lightened. The pain was still there, but not so sharp. The fear was still there, knife-sharp. Elizabeth put down the slate, walked to the door. Perhaps she should tell someone after all, and now; not next week, next month. Just so she could stop feeling so afraid, afraid for the children. If she didn't go now, she wouldn't do it, she knew herself that well. She walked back to her bedroom, tied on her bonnet. She moved down the stairs like a child sneaking out. It felt suddenly important to go, not to stop. In a few moments she was across the garden, down the walk, and knocking at Father Babade's door.

There was a sound of tools, a clink, a soft small crash; the door opened and Bishop Carroll, not Father Babade, stood before Elizabeth. For a moment she didn't recognize him. He was covered with a large earth-stained denim apron; he had a trowel in one hand, a flowerpot in the other. Then she did recognize him, all at once, and in spite of herself, almost as reflex, she felt herself begin to curtsy. He smiled at her, ignoring her bob, waving her in with the trowel, and quickly shutting the door.

"Father Babade's silver jubilee . . ." He waved at the window box, half-filled with clay pots. "There's nothing he loves more than flowers. I meant to surprise him. And then when you knocked, I thought . . ." He made a quick lateral movement with the trowel before his throat. Elizabeth, startled, charmed, laughed aloud. "Daisies." He nodded toward the box. "Too many yellow ones, not enough white—you think?"

"I think . . ." Amazed, she trailed off. "Lovely."

She was amazed at him, standing there in a smudged shirt and apron, his white hair fluffing out around his head like a dandelion in seed. She had seen him often from a distance, seldom close to, except when he had confirmed her in New York and spoken to her about her children. They had corresponded—he had praised her courage. If he only knew what I'm really like, she had thought then; she thought it again now. She began to wish she hadn't come. Here she was, standing just across a blue rag rug from one of the greatest men in the country: Maryland aristocrat, cousin of a signer of the Declaration of Independence, friend of Washington, Franklin, Jefferson—the country's most famous Catholic. She had taught her pupils to recite his accomplishments, and they unreeled now in her head: architect of the Church in America, first bishop, founder of Georgetown, writer, thinker, defender of the faith . . . and here she was, catching him in an apron, his hands dirty, his face smeared, to talk about shortness of breath. She really ought to leave.

"Sit down, sit down," he said. His light eyes were alert, gentle, shrewd. A heavyset man, seventy-three now, his face retained a boyish roundness, his cheeks applelike and ruddy.

His voice had gone reedy, though, the voice of an old man telling tales by the fire. He leaned toward her, sensing her hesitation.

"But you came to see Father Babade, of course—and he's gone till tomorrow." He scrabbled around on the desk for a scrap of paper, a quill. "You might leave him a note . . . ?"

"No, no, it's not that important." She felt an inward sagging; he saw it, sensed it.

"Something I can help with?"

"It's just that . . ." Behind his head she saw the oak trees in the slanting light of late afternoon. She looked from them to him; she wanted so much to speak. She felt all the afternoons of her life pressing against her, pushing her forward, sending her into this moment. "It's just that . . . something's happening inside me, something I don't . . . I can't, I'm afraid, that is, to talk about. . . ."

Carroll's eyes stayed on her, attentive, discerning. In the distance she could hear the seminarians gathering for benediction; a white surplice drifted past the window.

"I'm . . . it's hard to say . . ." To her horror, she felt tears run down her cheeks. "Every time I see them . . . the procession, the seminarians . . . I want to be . . . with them, one of them. I think about it all the time, almost . . . I'm sorry." This wasn't what she had come to talk about at all; she didn't know why these words were falling into the room.

"You feel you have a vocation—is that what you're saying?" His face was serious, his eyes kind.

"I don't know. . . . I can't, how can I?"

He leaned back. Carefully, as if trying to make them fit, he pressed the balls of his fingers together and studied them. "When I entered the seminary . . . a thousand years ago . . . it had to be abroad, you know, there were no seminaries here. I'd already been in school in Flanders, St. Omer's, when I went to the Jesuits in Watten. I was certainly used to being away—but suddenly I felt very far from home, I felt . . . not so sure why I was there. And I came to my novice master, I talked to him. I talked . . . about other things. The food. The dampness, I remember the dampness seemed to be worrying me. And my health, I seemed obsessed with my—"

"Oh *no*," she interrupted involuntarily. "That's what I'd come to see Father Babade about."

Carroll nodded. "My novice master told me something that struck me, at the time, as strange." He smiled, remembering. For a moment, across his aging face came the incredulous look of the boy he had been. "He told me that finding a religious vocation was like running away to sea. And I remember thinking, *What?* Brawling sailors, scholarly Jesuits: nothing seemed more opposite to me. But it was the same sort of attraction, he said. That pull. That draw. You can't explain it, can't express it. But you have to leave what you know and go to it. And from that time on your home is a place where human beings generally don't live. A place that isn't firm. That shifts, moves with currents you can't see. You think you've chosen the sea. But of course the sea has chosen you. And in the beginning, you can be queasy." Carroll looked at her. "Perhaps you're just feeling a little green?"

"But I can't . . . *can't* have a religious vocation." She studied her hands. "My children, my *children*." She heard her voice rising on the word. "I've thought about this, I've . . . tried to think very coolly. There's no order I could join—I know there are Carmelites from France in Maryland now, in Port Tobacco, I know there are Visitation nuns at Georgetown. But they're cloistered, I couldn't go into their convents with five children. It's useless, this thinking, I know it—an exercise in vanity, the whole idea, I'm sure."

Carroll looked at her some moments without speaking. His eyes narrowed, his face seemed to withdraw from her in thought. She could see in him the prelate he was, the bishop who sat within this affable gardener. His gaze took on a depth of judgment absent before.

"I'm not so sure," he said then. "Not so sure as you. You know, Elizabeth, I've thought about you since your conversion—that great struggle. I confirmed you. And I felt, when you came here, that you would do more. I felt that, not mystically, but because that's what I hoped. It was my wish, you know, that you move here, not Montreal. It was my wish that you start that little school."

"And I know that I sound so ungrateful—I should be content with that."

"Should you? *I'm* not content with it."

For a moment she felt a sense of failure so chilling she could not speak. Only two pupils scheduled so far. Of course it wasn't satisfactory.

"I mean," he said, "you could be doing more. We need . . ." He ran his hand over his face and sighed. "We need so many things. The difficulty in finding people, gifted people, it's tremendous, I can't begin to explain. . . . Priests, the priesthood alone, it's so very slow in growing. A native clergy, it's what we need, it's what we can't seem to develop fast enough. French priests, German priests, Irish—some fight, some make their parishes rebel against the whole church. And against me, the bishop. I've been take to court by them more than once, it'll happen again. . . ." He smiled briefly. His face was abstracted, he seemed to be speaking more to himself than her. "We need our own institutions. American orders. American schools. It overwhelms me, thinking of it. Thinking how short my own time's grown too. When I was thirty, thirty-five, the years ahead still seemed infinite, infinite. . . ." His voice trailed off. For a moment she could hear birds singing in the trees outside. The light was fading. Carroll's face had blurred. He looked no longer like a gardener, a prelate, a sage. He looked simply tired; old. "Of course, things are better now," he went on, still as if to himself. "Twenty-five years ago we had only twenty-four priests, half of them circuit riders—twenty-four priests in the entire country, imagine. Now: maybe fifty. And two colleges, a seminary . . . not much, not nearly enough, but better. You know, when I was born, priests were forbidden to baptize in Maryland. We were taxed doubly, couldn't hold office—almost all those laws are gone now. Of course there's no law to repeal bigotry. You know, I can still remember the verses they'd chant at us, even us, families like mine: '*Abhor, that arrant whore of Rome/ And all her blasphemies . . .*'"

"'*And drink not of her cursed cup/ Obey not her decrees,*'" Elizabeth finished for him. "I know. I was one of the children who chanted that."

Carroll laughed suddenly, hugely; the weary look left his face. "And for your penance, you've been given a calling." He chuckled again. "And *I've* been given a variety of ideas. Elizabeth, for some time I've wanted to see an American order of nuns. The Carmelites, the Visitation sisters, the Ursulines—they've all been transplanted here from Europe. We need our own sisters. But again, I've been stopped by something simple, so simple: that lack of people to do it. There are still so few of us. And still so many of us who are immigrants, uneducated, struggling just to eat. So many women who might lead a new sisterhood—they can't, for the simplest reason: they're married. So of course you caught my attention. And watching you has held my attention. I've thought of you perhaps with a teaching order, educating girls. . . . I haven't spoken because I've learned it's best to let people come to me. It would have been wrong . . . yes, very wrong to put this idea in your head if you didn't first feel that sense of vocation. But now you do feel it . . . now you've come. . . ."

Elizabeth sat very still. Questions formed in her mind and scrambled, evaporated. At last they coalesced into two words.

"My *children?*"

"We could find a way to accommodate them. We could make a plan for them if we were to start a foundation, an actual order."

"But myself . . ." she said after a while. "No experience . . . no . . . anything. . . ."

"I'd say that's excessive humility," he said, and smiled. "You've run a household of twenty, a boardinghouse of thirty. I'd be amazed if any young order began that big. You've been teaching children too, Elizabeth, and for some time. You've been thinking your children disqualify you— actually they qualify you more than you realize. And you have done extraordinary things in your personal life—Father Hurley, Father Babade, they've told me." He laughed again at the utter disbelief on her face. "Even so," he said, his voice lower, more serious. "Even so, I wouldn't ask if it weren't for something else. Something no one has told me about, something I've noticed myself. I've seen you at Communion . . . do you always smile . . . and weep?"

She felt herself flushing to her scalp, her ears. "I . . . feel it . . . so much."

Carroll looked at her a moment, then shook his head. "I've never felt what you seem able to feel. I envy that, I'll admit it. You look like . . . a sun shower at the altar rail. Some of us quite naturally are pillars of faith. Rocks of faith. Bastions of faith. Few of us are . . . lit wicks. That's something people can't learn in seminary—but that's something people can see a long way off. I've seen people be sober with God. It's rare you see someone laugh with God—rare as a mule with wings, as my grandmother used to say. Well." He stood, taking up his trowel again. "Consider it, if you would, Elizabeth. If you decide against it, of course you may remain here. And I should tell you this, as well: we've no money to found an order just now. No money, and no land to found it on. Perhaps it will come, though frankly I can't see where from. Perhaps it won't take shape. . . . I only wanted . . ." To her surprise, a sad look, a shy look came over his face. "There are so many things I haven't done," he said after a while. "So many plans still in my desk drawers. I only wanted . . . to dream this one out loud with you." Briskly then, he stuck the trowel in his pocket, dusted his hands together, glanced at her. Seeing her still sitting there numbed, he made a patter of talk to take them from the room.

"I ought to use Father Babade's office more often. Mine's not so quiet. Yesterday a drunken sailor stumbled right in, said he was informed by some revelation that all his sins were forgiven . . . without any penitential works on his side. The same revelation informed him he would write a great book, which I must read . . . and so must you. . . ."

Carroll steered her outside and told her good evening. She stood there on the path alone some moments, startled to find that dusk had fallen, benediction was over, and the tightness in her chest had eased.

"It started in chapel. I felt this . . . I don't know. We saw each other, well, we watched each other, what's wrong with that? I'm in love, Mama—I've done nothing wrong, *nothing*, you *can't* say I have."

Anna's back was turned, her shoulders taut; she stared out the window of Elizabeth's bedroom, she stared and spoke in jabs and did not move. She was telling her mother about her romance; a secret romance, hidden for months, marked by secretly exchanged gifts and notes—scandalous behavior, if not first graced by betrothal.

"You kept it from me." Elizabeth's voice was sharp now. "But you wrote every detail to your friends in New York. I had to find out from gossip. Gossip—through the mail."

Anna's face, still half-turned, began to run with tears. Elizabeth thought of their closeness in Livorno in the *lazzaretto*. She looked at her daughter's face now, wet but still defiant; there was no closeness now.

"This young man—"

"He has a *name*."

"I'm aware of his name. Charles. Charles Du Pavillon." Elizabeth scissored it out, angry at how beautiful it sounded. "I'm also aware of his age. He's at least twenty. And you, may I remind you, you're only fourteen."

"So what."

"Anna!"

"I said we've done nothing wrong."

"You don't know him—"

"Yes I do, he's finishing at the college, he's Creole, he's from the islands, he's the handsomest of—"

"I don't care what he looks like. I don't care who he is, where he's from. You're too young, he's too old—you've both been devious, improper—"

"Improper, *me*? You're the one, Mama, talking about being a nun—after Papa, after *us*, *that's* improper."

"How you're talking to me, I—"

"This is the first time *you've* talked to me in months, Mama, *months*."

"That's not true."

"It *is*. You've been too busy talking to Father This, Father That . . . talking about nuns, nuns, nuns. And money, money, that's all you *think* about, you're not thinking about *me*— you've gotten too *holy*, too—"

Elizabeth raised her hand to slap her daughter's face. Anna flinched from her; she'd never flinched before. Elizabeth lowered her hand. Oh, Lord, she thought. I'm proposed to be the mother of many daughters now. And I can't even manage my own.

For several moments there was silence in the room. Elizabeth could hear Anna's sniffles, then a series of small choked sobs; then deeper sobs, racking painful sobs crowding up from what seemed the depths of Anna's soul. Elizabeth felt her anger wane; she felt a sense of shame begin. Maybe it was true, what Anna said. Maybe in some way it was true. She put her hands on Anna's shoulders. Slowly Anna turned, then, ducked her face against Elizabeth's neck. "Mama, I thought you didn't care for me anymore—thought you didn't care what I did. . . ."

Elizabeth smoothed her hair, hair that felt fine and fragile under her hand. Holding Anna, rocking Anna, she felt tears beginning in her own eyes. *I thought you didn't care for me.* That had been her own cry once. My God, she wanted to cry out now: How can I mother her, mother the rest—and mother nuns, how, I don't see how.

An hour later on her way to market, her thoughts cast the same words ahead of her on the leaf-strewn streets. It was autumn: the maple trees were showering red; the narrow brick houses stood in sharp relief against the hard bright sky. Elizabeth wasn't seeing houses, leaves. Her mind was full of faces.

Anna's face.

Pupils' faces: seven of them now. The children's faces: Bec, Kit, Bill, Dick—all at once, crowding close.

Five children, seven pupils. Five and seven are twelve; five-twelfths and seven-twelfths do not necessarily add up. Fractions, fractions, I'm crazy to think I can make this balance.

Camden Market rose before her on Howard's Hill; she could hear its noise before she reached it, the voices, the horses, the hawkers' shouts. She was coming here this Saturday, basket on her arm, not because she had to—Delia, who cooked for her, often marketed. Elizabeth wanted to come. Now and then she wanted to have touch with the realities of flounder, butter, cheese. Especially when she was troubled, stocking a cupboard still calmed her. And when she was troubled, especially in certain ways, she was always calmed by talking with Madame Fournier, who lived on the way to the market. Madame, Father Dubourg's sister, was a quick, kind woman with flinty eyes, a sharp-angled face, and a tart manner which was deceptive. On Saturdays when Elizabeth passed by, Madame would lean up against her doorway, her bony frame like a ladder in black silk, and invite the younger woman inside. Once inside, over the teapot, Madame's eyes were less flinty, her tartness gone. A giver of small gifts, of candies, roses, embroidery thread, she sang French songs in a low grave voice and also listened carefully; she gave sound advice as well. Elizabeth found herself looking forward to these visits, found herself telling Madame what she could not confide in the priests. And today she found herself walking faster toward the slim brick row house, anxious to tell her about Anna. The house was three doors away when Elizabeth saw, with an inner sinking, that the door was closed, the windows shuttered; Madame must be away for the day. Elizabeth's steps slowed. Of course they had no definite appointment. But she had wanted so much to talk to another woman. She had needed so much the sound of another woman's voice. Absurdly, an image of Miss Molly came before her. Abruptly, Elizabeth felt like a needy child. She moved on toward the market, eyes down, feeling somehow smaller, weighted, frail.

The market's noise dropped around her, descending tentlike, as if from some other, busier place. Elizabeth walked slowly through it, past the hawkers, the stalls, the carts, the smells of fish and crabs and crab-boil, seaweed and thick bay mud. Chickens flapped in her face; faces again crowded her mind.

Anna's face: close, wet, familiar.

Elizabeth selected a chicken.

Cecilia O'Conway's face, the young woman from Philadelphia who'd written of becoming a nun: a misty face, distant, unknown.

Elizabeth selected a side of bacon.

Other faces, mistier, blurred: other women writing to her, dreaming of joining a sisterhood that did not yet exist.

Elizabeth selected measures of flour, coffee, sugar.

Five children, seven students, two hopeful nuns, three, four—five dollars and sixty cents, ma'am. Elizabeth reached for her purse.

As she did, she felt eyes upon her. Moving out through the stalls, she felt them still. Someone was following her, moving through the market with her. She glanced back. Children, maybe twelve, thirteen years old. Instinctively she held her purse tighter. They weren't marketing, they were simply following her. She moved faster; they did too. She glanced back again—saw they were not ragmuffins, beggars; saw they meant no harm. Carefully dressed, faces scrubbed, two Negro girls, three white, they kept a respectful distance. Timidly she smiled at them. Their faces lit. They were looking at her, she saw, as if she were something bright that had crossed their afternoon. They were looking at her as if to drink her in.

She moved beyond the market, back up the street, sensing them still behind her, sensing their thoughts flowing toward her. They had heard. They knew about the talk of a sisterhood. They knew, if it formed, she would be Mother. Perhaps they dreamed, as she had in the churchyard long before, of a place to come to: a place entirely different, a life entirely different from what they knew now. She knew that longing. She knew how it felt, left unanswered; knew the feeling of being an oddity for having it. These children were not the only one who would want to follow her: she realized this for the first time. Beyond this market, this street, there were other girls waiting; girls who fell in love this other way, who perhaps despaired as she had. And beyond those girls, there were children: children who also needed a place, a path, as badly as she had. She had looked to the Church as mother —she had not thought of mothering others within it. She had come out today to be mothered—she had not thought of others needing her for mothering: others beyond her own children, far beyond. She, stepchild, half-orphan, had only looked to be found. She had not known she would be asked to do the finding.

Elizabeth glanced back again. The girls had fallen behind, blending with the market-day crowd. She felt an odd sense of disappointment. Somehow she'd hoped to speak with them, tell them something, some good news. But there was no good news, she knew; not yet. The order still lay unformed, unfinished—might never form, never be financed. And in that moment Elizabeth realized she cared if that happened; cared more than she had ever realized, ever expected.

As soon as she got home, she set her basket down in the kitchen and, bonnet still on, hand still smelling of feathers and horehound, went alone to the chapel. All that evening, at benediction, at supper, at bedtime, she saw the faces of those girls. And next morning as she knelt after Communion, their faces were still in her mind.

Elizabeth looked through her fingers at the altar; she pressed her fingers to her eyes. Behind her eyes the market girls blurred, faded, merged into one face: the face of Mag, bending to count her shiny things, her spoons. As Elizabeth watched, her face blurred too, dissolving, becoming the face of the *signora* who came every day to the shrine in Livorno; she offered to Our Lady a bright silver spoon. But the *signora* too was fading, changing, and Elizabeth saw the face at the shrine was now Antonio Filicchi's, his kind, canny eyes turned toward her, the spoon in his hand. *Ask. Ask Antonio.* Perhaps the Filicchis had the means to help found this order; they would surely have the desire. But now Antonio's face was fading. Gradually Father Hurley's took its place, rounded, young, and ashen as it had been on the way to Georgetown; only for an instant did she see it before it shifted shape, shimmering, elongating into the face of Samuel Sutherland Cooper. Above his seminarian's surplice, his light eyes looked at her; eyes waiting, inquiring. *Ask him. Ask Sam.* She waited. The face remained before her, watching her so intently she became uncomfortable, opened her eyes—and then it was gone, the face, all faces, and she could not again find the thread of her prayers. She became aware of the ache of her knees on the prie-dieu; the slight pain in her head between her eyes. She rose, genuflected, and walked out into the day, the garden. Samuel Sutherland Cooper was walking ahead of her, some distance away. Head down, moving quickly, he turned into a doorway, disappeared. In her mind there was a click, almost audible. Her own step hesitated. Crazy, she thought; he'll think I'm crazed. And still she kept walking, hastening again, till she had reached the doorway of Father Dubourg's office.

"Father," she said before he had asked her to sit down. "Father, we should ask Mr. Cooper for help—for money, for the order, I'm sure he'd help us, don't think I'm presumptuous, please."

Dubourg looked at her, his head at a quizzical tilt, his lean frame shifting in his chair. "Mr. Cooper—what makes you think so?"

He shifted again. Her pace, her intensity, were wrong for him; she knew that, could not help it, went on. "Just a . . . feeling, a . . . strong one."

"Have you spoken with him about this?"

"No, it just came to me in chapel, it was . . . almost like hearing a voice, it was that clear, that . . ." She broke off, watching Dubourg's face change. She could hear him thinking her a hysterical female. She wished she had gone to Father Babade, wished Babade could be her director—wished she had not come at all.

"A voice." Dubourg let the words hang in the air.

Elizabeth said nothing.

"A voice," he said again. "Well." He rocked his chair back on two legs, his eyes looking down his sharp nose. "*Tiens*," he said, almost to himself. "Mrs. Seton, if this . . . 'voice' . . . was truly heard, if this . . . 'voice' . . . was not merely your imagination, I trust Mr. Cooper will come to me himself." He smiled. "Wouldn't you say? *Alors*, if you'll forgive me . . ." He riffled the papers on his desk. Elizabeth rose to go, her face burning.

Her face was hot throughout the morning, throughout the day, in class, in conversation; in her bedroom after supper as she took down her hair, in the hall downstairs as she answered, brush in hand, a late knock at her door. The heat in her face leapt higher as she saw Dubourg on her stoop. She hesitated at the door, additionally mortified by her dressing gown, the braid down her back. But Father Dubourg ignored how she looked—or didn't see how she looked at all. He moved quickly into the hall, pushing the door wide and forgetting to shut it behind him.

"Have you talked with Mr. Cooper today?" he asked so fast the sentence seemed compressed into one long word.

"Mr. Cooper, no, has something happened?"

"Nothing of our conversation, nothing?"

"Nothing, no. What—?"

"Mr. Cooper has just been to see me—to offer ten thousand dollars toward the founding of an order of nuns." Dubourg's eyes were still dilated; he shook his head. "We'll see, we'll see, he may turn out to lack these funds, though from what I've heard of his family . . ." Dubourg broke off, shook his head again. "He had another pronouncement to make. . . . Says he knows where this order will locate, where the land is right for it. . . . Do you know?"

"Not here? Not Baltimore?"

"No, no—nothing so simple. He's chosen some village about eighteen leagues from here, and from there, he says, *enfin* the order will grow. As if he could know!"

Elizabeth smiled, thinking of how Sam could look, transported by an idea.

"So he says, so he says." Dubourg lifted his hands. "I suppose the land is cheap there, I suppose he reasons there's a boys' school there already, Mount St. Mary's—but maybe not. This is a man who does not always reason, he gets 'feelings.' He has 'a feeling' about it, he says, this mountain place, this wilderness—he calls it Emmitsburg."

Emmitsburg: she was saying the word to herself and to others several times a day now; every time it conjured up for her a different scene—a peaceful village; a threatening forest; gentle hills, stark mountains; Indians, wolves; grazing cows. She could picture the place in all these guises, but she could not yet put herself into the picture; could not yet see herself or a small band of women against these backdrops in her mind. *Emmitsburg*: everyone here was saying it now, referring to this place none of them had seen except for Cooper, Father Nagot, the Sulpician superior, and Father Dubourg, who would act as the new sisterhood's director.

The acreage had been purchased, and a stone farmhouse. A handful of women had gathered; vows had been :aken. The children's arrangements had been made: they would all come. Now all that remained to be done was to put on the habit and pack the trunks. In three weeks, on the Feast of St. Aloysius, they would leave.

On Elizabeth's bed was the new habit, the black dress, black bonnet, black shoulder cape. The material lay in careful folds, the sleeves spread wide across the white quilt on the high thick mattress. She sat on the floor before it in her night-gown, watching the black skirt sharpen in the first of the morning light. She had been up all night. She didn't know why she had not slept, why she had watched instead; she hadn't intended to. These clothes were hardly different from the widow's dress she'd worn for nearly six years. Even so. Laid out on the bed, it seemed to repose like another self: the self she had aspired to for so long now—longer than she had realized, till this vigil, this night. This was the self she had glimpsed around corners, in crowds, in solitude; in Livorno, New York, even in New Rochelle. They weren't sudden, these vows she had made on Lady Day; she had been groping for those words, those promises, she saw, long before she had made the others.

Were any of the other women sitting up like this? Perhaps to them this step was unimportant—simply new clothes to wear; clothes smelling faintly of dye. She wondered if she would indeed come to know how they thought, these women: these four who would come with her, the handful who would come later that summer. She went over their names, their faces in her mind: Cecilia O'Conway, Mary Ann Butler, and Maria Murphy from Philadelphia, Susan Clossy from New York; the Thompson sisters, waiting in Emmits-burg; perhaps two more women from here in Baltimore; best of all her beloved sister-in-law Cecilia Seton. "Best of all": she must not think that, not anymore. She must have no favorites, no attachments, no preferences. She must be Mother now; not sister-in-law, not friend. And again, as it grew lighter, she doubted her ability to do it.

She rose and walked through the quiet house, up the stairs

to where her children slept. She knew, before she saw them, that Bill would be sprawled out facedown; that Kit would be curled in a ball. How much she knew about these natural children; how little she knew about her spiritual ones. Maybe she was only meant to be a mother after all—not Reverend Mother, Mother Superior. And she was not even a superior mother, not in any sense, to these sleeping boys and girls. She knew that; she knew it well. Her sons mastered her now. Their time at Georgetown and St. Mary's had done little to discipline them, as she'd hoped. Elizabeth could not manage them; the priests could not manage them. And now she would be taking them to yet another boarding school, Mount St. Mary's in Emmitsburg: another school run by priests—fathers her boys would not accept, would not be fathered by. It worried her, worried her deeply. It worried her to move them once again—to this new school, this new town; to tie them irrevocably to a community of women. With these sons she felt a sense of helplessness she did not feel with Kit, with Bec; even with Anna. Still, the boys were young, just eleven and thirteen. Perhaps in Emmitsburg they would ripen. Perhaps—how she hoped for it—one of them might somehow discover a religious vocation there. Already they sensed this wish, she knew; already, of course, they were quick to scorn it. But there was still time. She could not let go of that hope yet.

Elizabeth reached out and touched Bill's hair. In his sleep he squirmed away. She moved on to Dick's bed—he'd grown so tall his legs hung over the end. She pulled the sheet over his feet; he kicked it off. Elizabeth sighed. Did other women feel so useless around their sons? She stood in the shadowed bedroom, feeling something dim within herself. Abruptly an image came into her mind: an image that had come over and over this past week. It was a picture she had seen in a book of Bible stories, illustrated for children. A picture of a man with a long beard and a long knife; a man trussing up his small son with rope—Abraham, preparing to sacrifice Isaac. She had seen this image each night as she was falling asleep. She had seen it as she looked at her boys across the supper table. She had, each time, dismissed it. Too ridiculous. Too dramatic. Too wrong. Now she stood listening to her sons' even breathing and she could not make it fade.

She walked back down the stairs, pausing in the doorway to the schoolroom. Just a year ago, the boys had been helping her paint it; the boys and the priests. Father Babade's face flickered before her, gentle, Gallic, kind. After a moment it was replaced in her mind by Carroll's: tired, wise, patrician, old. For an instant what she saw in her mind was a man with a knife and the archbishop's face—then the image of Abraham vanished completely. *Few of us are lit wicks.* She walked slowly down the hall, back to her room. *Something people can't learn.* She heard the orange cat padding softly behind her. *Something people can see.* She opened the bedroom door. The cat moved, purring, through her legs and into the room.

Elizabeth looked at the habit on the bed. She remembered getting dressed for her wedding. She remembered all those times she had looked out the window, dressing for Willy: the pearls, not the pearls. She felt the same dread, the same excitement now, though this was certainly the simplest of Clothings: no ceremony, as other orders had—no bridal gown changed for the habit; no ring, no veil, no new name. And yet, she knew, this morning, this quiet Clothing, marked a place in her life. She reached out, touched the beads of the rosary she would wear at her waist. The beads were large, the cross engraved *Caritas Christi urget nos,* "The charity of Christ urges us on." It was St. Vincent de Paul's motto, given to his Daughters of Charity; her order's rule would be based on theirs. A silver ring attached to the cross was engraved *Cor unum—anima una,* "One heart— one soul." Again she wondered if she could promise this— one heart, one soul dedicated to this life, to God. She wondered if she wouldn't always be divided: the vocation, the children; the sisters, the children; the prayers, the office, the children, the children. Again she felt an inner sinking, a sense of smallness coming over her. She smoothed the habit; she heard the others stirring in the house. Soon they would be dressing too—putting on, in the private morning shadows, this same black dress, this same leather belt. The stirring grew louder; there was a faint murmur of voices, a pattering of steps. She could not delay the moment, hold the morning back.

Below her in the street a peddler called, children ran and whooped: "Look out, Robbie—ready or not . . ." Their voices floated up to her. *"Here I come."* Listening, Elizabeth smiled.

She let her nightgown fall around her ankles.

She pulled the habit over her head. The material felt cool and smooth against her skin. She buckled on the belt; she heard the rosary clink. She took a step toward the window. Her skirt rustled. She was aware of herself moving within these clothes, aware again of how she'd felt on her wedding day years before; how her gown had rustled around her then as she'd walked, thrilled and scared and joyous, toward her groom. And now, alone, crossing this quiet room, she felt it again—the thrill, the fear; but the joy was stronger, sweeter, more searing, than any she had ever known.

17

$O_{K.}$ Let me get this straight.

She gets to Baltimore; she hears a voice in chapel. She gets funded, through some mystical coincidence, by Cooper. And presto—she gets this germinal sisterhood to lead into the mountains, into the sunset.

Not the most normal scenario.

Not the way things happen in real life.

Not usually.

No wonder she felt unequal to the task. She was unseasoned, inexperienced; a Catholic for only four years. Imagine her résumé. Housewife, albeit for a large family. Boardinghouse mistress, briefly. Teacher, briefly, mostly in her own home. In fact she was a gamble, a risk, and on some level she knew it.

It amazes me to think of her America—an America so lacking in Catholics, so lacking in Catholic leaders. Growing up in Baltimore, this century, I was surrounded by monsignors, mother superiors, mother generals, father confessors. Hard to imagine an America with only fifty priests. Hard to imagaine an America without one native priesthood, one native sisterhood. Only three Catholic colleges. No sanctioned primary schools. No hospitals, orphanages. Only four dioceses, just created; one archdiocese.

Looking over these notes, these figures, this Emmitsburg experiment seems even more of a gamble to me. Mrs. Seton wasn't just a pioneer in religion; she was a pioneer, period.

She walked toward those mountains behind a canvas-covered wagon. She moved onto unsettled land. She lived for a month in a log house; then, when it was ready, in a stone farmhouse—a four-room house for fifteen people. Community life: it's always an adjustment, I know that well. But I shudder to think of making that adjustment at such close quarters. Few of us ever have to do that, thank God. Few of us have ever had to start religious life in the wilderness, washing clothes in a creek, drinking water from a spring, sleeping piled together on the floor.

And none of us has had to start from scratch.

That must have been the greatest hardship of all.

I must say, I have to hand it to her. She was doing something pretty tough. Something I'm not sure I'd choose to join her in—let alone take her place. I'm not sure I'd like to be settling that land, raising that community. Inventing each step as it was taken. Each hour. Each day.

If I were to walk about four hundred yards from this grave to those trees, to where the water shimmers through the leaves and Toms Creek runs over flat broad stones, and if I were to walk back over the years, stepping from one to the other like stones in this creek, I would come upon an afternoon in August 1809—an afternoon of sun, of warmth, of dragonflies. And I would come upon a small company of women kneeling there in the afternoon's center; kneeling not over prie-dieux but over tubs; not in prayer but exertion.

The nuns are doing the wash.

Eleven women kneel there, dressed identically in black, shod in black, bonneted in black, their faces framed by crimped white borders. Scattered on the grass, they look to an outsider like a little band of widows out for a picnic. This grass is not yet used to the print of their knees; these trees are not yet used to the sound of their voices—they've only just set up housekeeping here in St. Joseph's Valley, here in the small stone farmhouse some yards away. They are not yet entirely used to the sound of one another's voices— they've only been together like this a little over a month. There are still odd pockets of silence, quick clashes of words now and then. There are still some curious looks, searching looks, sidelong looks as they call one another "sister." In their sleep at night, crowded together on the floor of the farmhouse, they still sometimes dream they are following a wagon down a dusty road, watching the road wind higher into the mountains; some nights they wake in the country stillness and wonder where they are. Then they remember the valley; they remember St. Mary's Mountain and the boys' school there, like a brother in the wilderness. They remember the little town and the presence, all around them, of the others— these women shifting and sighing in their sleep, trying together to become sisters, schoolmarms, brides of Christ. They came in two groups: the newest, led by Sister Rose, in July; the first, in June, led by Mother.

Mother. They all call her that. Not Mother Elizabeth, not Mother Seton. Just Mother. That word is in the air more than any other, spoken in low tones and eager phrases and caroled in the high light voices of the children playing amid them. "Mother . . . Mother. . . ." They all glance at her more than one another: there isn't one who doesn't care what Mother thinks.

Elizabeth is the smallest of them all, dark-eyed and delicate-looking at thirty-five, birdlike in her movements. She sits and reads aloud; she looks up from the page and watches the women. And there isn't one whose thoughts she doesn't wonder at. She is so new; they are so new. Already there has been trouble, upheaval; already they have been shaken. Elizabeth wonders if some of them doubt now if this little company can endure. She wonders herself.

"*If you seek, O Christian soul, to attain to the highest pitch of evangelical perfection . . .*" She reads aloud, she glances around.

These two: she knows them. Their thoughts are loyal, perhaps the only ones she can accurately read. Cecilia and Harriet, her sisters-in-law: their presence is a comfort. Cecilia, ill with consumption and thin, lying in the grass, Harriet healthy and strong-limbed, wringing out sheets—the dark one, the fair one; the clever one, the beauty; two girls so dissimilar they seem to have grown in different gardens. But both here, both smiling at Elizabeth, giving her strength.

"*. . . it is requisite in order to succeed in a design the most* *sublime that can be expressed or imagined, that you be first acquainted with the true nature and perfection of spirituality. . . ."*

This one here: this strong country girl leaning over that tub, sleeves rolled up, hands and elbows red, nose sunburned —she is, perhaps, thinking of leeks and potatoes. Elizabeth turns a page and watches her between the words.

Plainspoken, hearty, rough, and kind, Emmitsburg-born Sister Sally is *procuratrix*, the community's link with the town, going out into it for them with her market basket, opening accounts with the butcher, the baker. Elizabeth appointed her with a flicker of hesitation: Sally is lacking in education and the title *procuratrix* elevates her over others who have more. Still, no one else is better suited to this office; Sally and her sister Ellen bring ties to the village that are crucial to them all. And you never know, Elizabeth reminds herself. Sally might not be thinking of leeks and potatoes at all. Elizabeth wished she knew; wished she had some clue to her, some key. And not only to her. To them all.

"When you look up to the sun, reflect that your soul, when adorned with the sanctifying grace, is incomparably more bright and beautiful than all the firmament together. . . ."

That one there, her mouth set tight, hands wringing out black stockings as if to punish them—Sister Maria, stern, unsmiling, she looks middle-aged in her twenties; yet she has a strong contemplative gift. And those two, spreading clothes out on the sunny grass—Sister Cecilia O'Conway, Sister Susan: they smile, they work at their task with just the right dutifulness, their faces relaxed. But perhaps those faces mask discontent, despair, wishes that they'd never come. Elizabeth worries that they are trying too hard, holding up in their minds the image of an ideal nun, just as she used to hold an image of an ideal wife. She watches as they bend and lean toward the spread of black dresses, like dancers bowing to their shadows: Cecilia O'Conway, thin and freckled, her gestures direct, quick; Susan, plump, sweet-faced, her lips and hands given to trembling, her eyes asking for approval. Are they in love with the idea of being nuns—or in love with the Lord? Eizabeth wishes she could trust herself to know.

"If the beauty of creatures should charm you, imagine you

see the Fiend concealed under those bewitching appearances,
endeavoring to sting you and destroy the life of your soul. . . ."

Splashing in the creek, skirts hoisted, are Kit and Bec and Anna. Their laughter ripples above the nuns, above the washtubs; laughter now piping, now shrill: children's laughter, fierce and innocent by turns. Loud laughter, to Elizabeth, louder to her than anyone else. They're only nine and seven, these younger two, surely they're allowed to laugh—elfinlooking Bec, her giggle is a reedy trill; sturdier, steadier, black-haired Kit, her voice is a low warble. Actually Anna is making most of the noise. On Anna the playfulness is less seemly: Anna at fourteen splashing, hooting, hoisting her skirts a little too high, a little too sensuously—making it known to her mother she'd rather be in Baltimore near Charles du Pavillon. As it is, she can only wait for letters here and hope. And splash. And rock the washtubs just a little.

Elizabeth winces, listening. She looks to see if anyone else is wincing with her. She fears that the children will intrude on the nuns, interfere with mental prayer. And at the same time she fears the nuns will intrude on the children, squelch them, still them, like a perpetual tea party with a group of maiden aunts. These children have never been so long in the presence of so many adults—and all but one of these women has never had children.

"When you hear the warbling of birds, think of Paradise,
where the praises of God are sung without ceasing. . . ."

Elizabeth watches her now, the only other widow in the group: Sister Rose, Rose Landry White. She is startlingly pretty, even with her cap and bonnet hiding auburn hair Elizabeth saw once, being dried by the fire, after everyone was asleep. The awkwardness between her and Rose has been there from the first—how Elizabeth has hoped it would be otherwise. She knows they should have a strong bond: in the whole community, they are the only ones to have slept in a man's arms, pushed in labor, held infants to the breast. Rose has borne two children, a daughter who died, a son who is in Emmitsburg, attending Mount St. Mary's now, along with Elizabeth's boys. Elizabeth knows Rose has suffered as a wife, as a mother: married at fourteen, widowed young, losing a beloved child. Like Elizabeth, in her widow-hood Rose had turned for comfort to the Church: to the Sulpician priests of Baltimore, to an admired mentor, a Father David. And she found more than comfort, she found a vocation. Now she is the most capable sister here, valuable to the community and to Elizabeth: she is, in fact, assistant to her superior. But Rose remains distant, correct but aloof. Those agate eyes of hers keep watching, watching. She is kind to the children, even affectionate—but at certain times, times like this, Elizabeth sees her disapproval of their lark-ing; a disapproval that is clear, sharp, deep.

If the two of them could talk of this, Elizabeth thinks . . . She knows it isn't possible. She is used to being able to charm, to disarm with warmth. But Rose resists, stolidly, consistently. With this woman, her lieutenant, her second, Elizabeth feels helpless. And, she must admit it: threatened. There is an instinctive sense of competition between them, she knows; they who are a little older, a little more seasoned, a little more capable than the rest.

"Then turning to God—Blessed be Thy name, shall you say, Who thus graciously discovers and prevents the snares of my enemy. . . ."

Now the sky begins to shift and roll with fast-moving late-summer storm clouds; they send swift shadows over the grass and the washing spread upon it. The sisters glance up, their movements quickening. The air sharpens with the sound of a bell—the bell from St. Joseph's Church in the village; Eliza-beth recognizes its tone. For funerals it tolls a stroke for each year of the departed's life: sometimes the tolling reaches into the eighties, the nineties. With each stroke now, the clouds seem to drop lower, darker; a rush of wind catches at the nuns' skirts, lightning flickers. A moment later it has be-gun to pour rain. They struggle with the wash, some of it still heavy with water from the tubs; they wrench and pull at the yards of dark cloth that now seem like loads of tar to lift, to drag back to the house. Another flash of lightning; an exchange of sharp words—everyone giving directions, getting in one another's way. Sheets of rain blur them, clothing sticks, washtubs collide. They straggle into the farmhouse, dripping, still snapping different orders: *hurry, wait, watch out, not there, stop.* Clustered by the hearth, jerking at the loads of wet wash, they look to Elizabeth like a group of bedraggled and quarrelsome schoolgirls engaged in a game of tug-of-war. Their habits are plastered to them, clearly outlining their figures, the differences in size and shape; the smell of black dye rises from them. The smell, and smoke from a greenwood fire fill the room, and the room itself seems to grow smaller; there are only two cramped chambers downstairs, one above, for all sixteen of them. Water puddles on the brick floor. The children whine and sneeze. Cecilia crouches, coughing, near the fire. Elizabeth, arranging a clothesline before it, knocks a piece of crockery off the mantel. It smashes on the floor; the clothesline sags, then snaps. Sister Rose suddenly turns on her heel and walks out, alone, into the rain. As Elizabeth climbs the garret stairs to get more clothesline, she feels an oppressive sourness in the room behind her, as tangible as a visiting tramp.

How little it takes a shake them, she thinks. How little it takes to shake her. They are so fragile still, so freshly hatched; so lacking in patterns of how nuns should be and how a community should live. They are so cooped up with one another in this little house, elbow to elbow, soul to soul— and literally nose to nose at night when they drag their mattresses out of the cupboards and lie together on the floor. The garret smells of damp down from the stored pillows. A splash of water strikes Elizabeth's nose. The roof leaks. In winter, if they cannot get a bigger house built, snow will sift down on them as they sleep.

Elizabeth finds the clothesline, tangled. At the window she tries to unknot it, her fingers impatient, ineffective. Below, she sees Rose pacing in the rain. Doubtless Rose thinks she could have managed that last half-hour differently. Doubtless Rose thinks she could have made it smoother, easier, less dispiriting. Doubtless . . . Elizabeth hears the cutting edge on those thoughts. And under that edge, propelling it: fear. What if Rose indeed could—and Elizabeth could not? She allows herself to stride back and forth across the garret floor, twice, three times, recalling suddenly the release she had felt, long ago in the *lazzaretto*, jumping rope. She looks at the clothesline. No. Nuns don't jump rope. Or do they? Yet another question about this life to which she has no answers.

From the other window she sees her sister-in-law Harriet struggling to cover the woodpile; a moment later Father Dubois is there to help her. Elizabeth feels an inner lifting at the sight of him; at the same time, she wishes he hadn't come. The woodpile should be sheltered in the first place. He has seen another mistake, another sign of bungling, and she wants him to see none. She likes John Dubois: strong, short, stocky, he is often there to help. A priest whose passion is not only God but also building, he has, himself, built sections of Mount St. Mary's, the preseminary school he founded up the road. His features are blunt as his speech and he has a directness, an energy that appeals to them all. And though he was born in Paris ten years before Elizabeth, he strikes her as an American—he has an optimism, a pragmatism that belongs here. He is happiest as a frontiersman: a circuit-riding priest, a horseman, a woodcutter—and just now, the protector of their little settlement. But for all his goodwill, Elizabeth senses, he needs to be shown that this settlement has the mettle to survive and grow. And as she stands muttering at the tangled clothesline, Elizabeth again feels unsure of this herself. She has already gotten into conflict with the Baltimore priests; she has already made dozens of other blunders, obvious to her if no one else. She sees so many times she could have been firmer, warmer; more forceful, more hopeful, better at stabilizing this small group around her—as she could be doing right now. Elizabeth sighs, and with the clothesline still half-tangled in her hands, she turns to go downstairs.

Voices below drift up to her. Fragments of conversation fall into place, making a pattern that stops her on the highest step. She pauses there, quiet, tensed, listening.

"She should have known. . . ."

"She couldn't have. . . ."

"But look at us. . . ."

"Mother was right, she knows. . . ."

In the corner, by the hearth, she sees them gathered, wringing out their drenched skirts: Sally, Susan, Maria, Cecil O'Conway. The others have gone into the next room to change clothes, leaving these three together in discussion. A discussion clearly centered on Elizabeth; and clearly centered on something more than whether she should have gotten them indoors sooner, before the rain.

"Mother doesn't always know everything. I *wish* she *did*." Sister Susan's soft quaver holds a wail at its core. "Sometimes I think she doesn't know much more than *we* do about all this, I just don't." Her chin trembles. "Otherwise she wouldn't have fought with Father Dubourg like that."

"She didn't fight with him." Sally's broad face is impassive, her voice firm.

"She questioned him. She protested—he'd still be our director if she hadn't." Maria's hands tap the air as if to underscore each word. "You know it's true."

"And we need a director. . . ." Susan's voice quavers again.

Elizabeth stands very still on the top step. A few weeks before, Father Dubourg had written from Baltimore, telling her that the sisters must have no more communication with Father Babade. Elizabeth had immediately protested. Babade was not only her friend, he was the priest most of them felt closest to. He had planned to visit them, to hear confessions and give counsel; the thought of this had been sustaining. Though Dubourg was formally director of the sisterhood, Elizabeth knew they needed the older man's added support, but her protest had hurt Dubourg: he had resigned, leaving them without a priestly director at all.

"She was right," Sisiter Cecil is saying now. "She shouldn't have given in."

"She should have offered it up." Maria's hands tap the air again. "A good nun is obedient."

"A good superior stands up for the rest," Sally says flatly and folds her arms. "We needed Father Babade."

"What we needed was *peace*." Susan touches the spinning wheel beside her with a nervous hand; her plump face tightens.

"Mother was too attached to Father Babade." Maria's long thin nose reddens at the tip; the sharp angle of her jaw juts toward the others.

"We were all attached to him." Cecil's large brown eyes soften behind her wire-rimmed spectacles.

"Not like Mother," Maria cuts in. "She wrote to him constantly, I happen to know. And I happen to know who reported that—quite rightly, too—to Father Dubourg."

There is an instant of silence. Maria reaches out and gives the spinning wheel a turn; it creaks in the stillness. "It's the one who'd do us better as mother, in my opinion," she says then.

The door opens. Rose comes in, dripping. She nods to the others, then makes her way to the next room and dry clothes, her shoes making small wet sounds in this second sudden silence. As she passes, Maria nods again.

From the stairs, Elizabeth sees the room in a strange clarity: a place of sharp shadows. She sees the dinner dishes, set to dry on the mantel: the white bellies of the bowls in a row, the one that still lies smashed on the floor. The spokes of the big spinning wheel between her and the women, divide one head from another; in the next room she hears her children fighting. She hears Rose's voice, soft and calming. The sound of it makes Elizabeth's face hot. Rose: a tale-bearer. Maria: a troublemaker. Tale-bearer, troublemaker—schoolgirls' words. But in a community this small, this new, schoolyard plots are perils. Rumors could shake them. Discontent could splinter them. Rivalries could break them. And in that moment Elizabeth, frozen on the stairs, is not certain she can keep that from happening.

Gloria in excelsis Deo, et in terra pax. . . .

The silver candlesticks on the altar were hers: they had lit suppers on Wall Street and Stone Street and State Street, and now they lit the eucharistic meal in the little chapel of the new log house—the new Mother House, not yet finished, moved into anyway at the beginning of this new year.

Laudamus te. Benedicimus te. Adoramus te. . . .

Above the candlesticks was the picture of Christ she had hung on the walls of her three houses; before the picture, sprays of wild mountain laurel and paper flowers Sister Sally had made—a poor little altar, an altar of hand-me-downs: the sight of it irritated Elizabeth and moved her to tears, all at once.

Gloriam tuam, domine Deus, rex caelestis. . . .

She looked at the flea bites on her clasped hands. The

carpenters and plasterers were still at work on the house and in the hair used for the plaster there lived a plague of fleas. The sisters were bitten purple—under the lilt of Father Dubois's *Gloria* she could hear the persistent sound of scratching. Outside the fanned front door there were still blocks of wood instead of steps; there were piles of wood shavings in the yard, and upstairs there were piles of mattresses on the floor, as in the smaller farmhouse. They still had only two cots, and nightly they dragged these mattresses from room to room to stay clear of the workmen . . . and the fleas. Elizabeth's mind wandered briefly from room to room now, making worried inventories—it turned away at the kitchen. The night before, in a crashing storm of rain and wind, its chimney had blown down, taking most of the wall with it, and Sister Rose had run into the house with a pan of frying fish in her hand. Sister Rose: Elizabeth's eyes had strayed to her again.

Deus Pater omnipotens. Domine Fili unigenite, Jesu Christe. . . .

Elizabeth brought her mind back to the altar, the Mass, the moment. It was unusual for her to let her thoughts drift at such a moment. It still seemed a privilege to be hearing Mass, a joy to sleep in a house with a chapel, an altar, the Blessed Sacrament—to have them always so nearby. But this was an unusual time.

It was hard to overlook the empty places in this chapel. There were two bent heads that Elizabeth's eyes still searched for: a dark one, a fair one—Cecilia and Harriet, both dead within months of each other. Harriet had gone suddenly, quickly, of a brain fever; Cecilia had gone more slowly in the Seton way, gasping for air. A death at Christmas, a death at Easter, and the community graveyard was begun; Elizabeth could remember Harriet selecting the site one windy afternoon, making them all laugh. "Drop me in there," she'd said cheerfully, tossing an apple core against an oak. The rest of the sisters remembered that too.

Agnus Dei, qui tollis peccata mundi, miserere nobis. . . .

Elizabeth had thought to rely on these two loyal sisters; and now she needed support more than ever before. She could not be sure she would be hearing Mass in this chapel next month, next summer, next year. She could not be sure because of Rose and Father John Baptiste David, the order's new director.

Father David: she could feel his unbending presence all the way from Baltimore—a tall stiff stalk of a man, an émigré from Nantes and fifteen-year veteran of classrooms and missions in Maryland. He had begun to direct Elizabeth as he had always directed others—handing down rules like edicts, orders like papal bulls, ignoring the line between his and the mother superior's authority. Without consulting her, he had begun to set down regulations for the sisters' fledgling school; Elizabeth had already clashed with him over it, by letter, worse than she had with Dubourg. She also knew that with this man, she could do nothing else. David's eyes, slate-gray, had a way of staring people down, even in ordinary conversation. His jaw, set slightly ahead of his thin hard face, had the appearance of being cast in some heavy mold. He did not smile. He did not banter. He did not appear to sweat. He reminded Elizabeth of her father in his younger days; she could not shake that impression from her mind. Still, on his rare visits to the convent, she had seen David unbend with one person—Sister Rose. She had been his spiritual protégée in Baltimore, as Elizabeth had been Carroll's and Babade's. And now it was clear that David wanted a more cooperative mother superior to work with. He wanted Elizabeth removed, relocated, replaced by his preferred sister: Rose herself.

Suscipe deprecationem nostram, qui sedes ad dexteram patris . . .

Priests. Protégées. Politics. Of course it could happen here: not only in vaulted Vatican hallways, not only among princes of the Church. And politically, Elizabeth realized, she had been weakened. She had lost her patron, Babade, in Baltimore. Rose had gained hers. In addition, Elizabeth saw, the presence of her family in the convent had made her vulnerable. It had been Bec and Anna who had written to Babade so often that Rose had noticed. It was during Cecilia's final illness that Rose was first proposed as mother of the house. Elizabeth had sent letters to Carroll, trying to explain; trying to find some solution. But Carroll was being noncommittal himself just now; he took no clear side, only urging self-sacrifice for the success of the order. What did that mean? She wondered at it, prayed over it. Should she remove conflict from the order by removing herself from it?

Quoniam tu solus sanctus, tu solus dominus. . . .

Elizabeth looked around at the people from the village who had crowded into this little chapel, this half-built house, for a Mass lit by supper-table candles. The sight of them filled her eyes with sudden tears: the smiths and tanners, the tailors and coopers and farmers' wives, heads bent, hands clasped, grateful just to be here. She remembered how they had crowded into the little farmhouse too, kneeling amid the sisters' cots and mattresses, cooking pots and washing tubs. She thought of the classroom across the hall, she thought of the school—still so small, but growing, changing as she wanted it to change. It was her hope that it would become a free school, a parish school. She had already welcomed the first three pupils from the village; she hoped there would be more. She wanted to be here to find them, to welcome them, to teach them herself. The community had just emerged from a winter of sickness—she wanted to be here to see it enjoy some good days, some healthy days; she wanted to watch it spread out in the new house.

Jesu Christe, cum sancto spiritu. . . .

Her sisters were needed here. She was needed here. For this she could maneuver; for this she could fight. She would not think otherwise. *In gloria Dei patris.* Not yet. Not quite yet. *Amen.*

"See Washington, born of humble parents, and in humble circumstances—born in a narrow nook and obscure corner of the British plantations! Yet lo! What great things wonderworking industry can bring out of this unpromising Nazareth. . . ."

Through the schoolroom's open window, Elizabeth could hear Sister Cecilia O'Conway's voice reading the history lesson aloud to the class. The steady voice was like the smell of good thick soup on the air: nourishing, strong, rich. It could get you through till dinner, that voice. Elizabeth heard the scrape of chairs, the classes change; she let her mind go to the schoolroom, to the calm rows of desks and inkwells and letters on the board. She had been taken away from this orderly one-room world all morning by the correspondence piled on her own desk; she would work back into this world now by observing a class. One of her most important duties was this: listening carefully to the lessons, sometimes with eyes closed in concentration, re-designing, readjusting, reworking the classes with the teaching sisters, and with the laywomen who taught French and music. Elizabeth felt an inner brightening as she went through the fanned door of the house and heard Mme. Guérin's voice beginning the French lesson.

"*J'entre dans la salle de classe,*" the children recited.

"*Bien—continuez.*"

"*Je dis 'bonjour, madame. . . .' *"

Odd. It sounded different this morning. Too perfect. Too shaped. Almost staged. Elizabeth went to the doorway. She saw Mme. Guérin at the pigeonholed desk at the front, one finger raised, her enormous lacy bosom heaving with cadenced breath. She saw the spread of blackboard behind Madame, chalked with the sentences to recite, the letters curling like white ribbons. She smelled the good scents of ink and paste and chalk. And then, at the back, behind the rows of pupils' heads, she saw a black bonnet that didn't belong there: Sister Rose, notebook in hand, her eyes on the teacher, her head cocked intently to one side. Standing in the doorway, Elizabeth felt a narrow flame of anger rise in her chest. Sister Rose was observing this class. Perhaps the history class as well. Perhaps all the morning's classes. Sister Rose: making notes, quick, jabbing marks in her book. Sister Rose doing this task she had not been asked to do— not by Elizabeth, not by anyone here at St. Joseph's.

"*Je prends ma place . . . j'ouvre mon libre . . . tiens, livre . . .*"

Mme. Guérin stumbled; the class stumbled with her. The gaze of these two chief nuns, superior and assistant, was altering the rhythm of the lesson, the rise and fall of the voices. Elizabeth looked at Rose, forcing her to meet her gaze. She nodded toward the door. For a moment Rose did not move; then slowly, color coming into her face, she followed Elizabeth out of the classroom and out of the house.

"Well, Sister. Is Madame satisfactory this morning?"

Rose did not reply.

"Is she?" Elizabeth could not keep the edge from her voice. "Is she up to your standards?"

Rose said nothing.

"That class is our best," Elizabeth went on. "I just watched it Friday. It disturbed the lesson to have it watched again."

"The lesson was disturbed only when you came in." Rose's voice was tight and still. "I was doing what I was supposed to do."

"You took this upon yourself?"

"No."

"You were told to do this?"

"Yes."

Around them the grass rippled in the breeze, their skirts rippling with it. A pair of cardinals alighted, cheeping, on the fence. Elizabeth kept her eyes on the birds until she could trust her voice. She did not want to ask Rose who had told her to observe this class. She did not want to ask which others of her duties Sister Rose had been asked to assume. She did not need to ask. Father David's presence was with them on the grass, conjured by their thoughts. She could see him there, hard-eyed, stiff-shouldered, that perpetual shadow of a heavy beard on his long jaw. The two women circled the building in silence, thinking of him, each unable to break from the other's pace, the other's silence.

"You both can't wait, can you?" Elizabeth blurted the words despite herself. "You can't wait for me to leave before you start doing my work." Her face was hot. Control, control, she'd lost it again—her voice had risen anyway.

"It's quite reasonable," said Rose, maddeningly cool. "Quite reasonable of Father David to want a superior who understands him."

"I understand him," Elizabeth said grimly. "If Father had his way, we'd have no say in anything—the entire order would be run from Baltimore."

"That's hardly fair."

"Is it? And if we give up control, it doesn't stop with us.

Rose! We're the pattern. If we plan badly now, sisters here in twenty years, fifty years, they'll feel it."

"Frankly, Mother . . ." Rose stumbled on the word. "I doubt there'll be sisters here in twenty years if this order doesn't get some peaceful guidance."

"You think we're that fragile?"

"I do."

"And you feel you can give that guidance?"

Rose didn't reply.

"Answer me, Sister. You feel that?" Elizabeth heard the sharpness of her voice and could not stop it.

Suddenly, surprisingly, Rose's eyes filled with tears. "Maybe I could. I'm not being used—you don't know how much I can do."

"But you're my assistant, my second, you—"

Rose shook Elizabeth's hand off her arm. "You *don't* use me," she said again, her anger showing now. "You think you can soothe me with titles—you're afraid I'll be too good, you're afraid I'll outshine you—"

"That's unfair."

"Sometimes I think . . ." Rose walked in silence for a while. "I think you don't see what I can do, what others can do . . . not out of malice. Simply because your mind's so taken up with your children. Your girls. Your 'darlings,' always, always your 'darlings.' "

"I thought you, you of all people—I thought you'd understand about them."

"I understand about children. I play with your girls. I feel . . . affection for them, it hurts me sometimes. But I also understand a convent's no place for them. A superior can't have two jobs, two sets of needs to answer. And I think it's presumptuous to try."

"And I know I have to try. The archbishop knew all about my situation when he chose me, he . . ." Elizabeth broke off, her voice starting to shake. In the silence they could hear the French class finishing with its customary chorus of voices: "*Je dis 'au revoir, madame. . . . Au revoir! Au revoir!*' "

A stream of children moved sedately from the building

for recess; sedately down the steps, down the path, then eddying like fast brookwater, they moved, laughing, between the two women. Elizabeth and Rose looked at each other over their heads, then looked away. In a few moments they would go on to other duties, other concerns. They would see each other in chapel, and at dinner, and at twilight they would see each other over children's heads again. Tomorrow and the next day and next week they would see each other a hundred different times, and these words would stretch between them, taut and connective as clothesline strung across the mountain air.

In the next weeks, lessons were chanted and Mass was sung and the clothesline tightened. In the next weeks April became May, the month of Mary, and the house was cleaned and purged of fleas and the tension went on. In the next months the weather was hot and the house was finished and the sisterhood's first anniversary was celebrated; the tension remained unchanged.

To leave this valley, Elizabeth thought, looking out at it, that autumn from one of the attic dormers. To have to leave now. She had gone up to get her knitting; people were somehow less awed by the Mother Superior, she'd found, when she had wool and needles in her hand. She had gone up and glanced out and been held by what she saw. Long low light lay across the fields and fenceposts; from the woods the maples blazed. The shadows of clouds moved handlike across the grass, and beyond, the mountains arched their spines in the sun like sleek-backed cats. Whenever she looked at them, especially the nearest, St. Mary's, Elizabeth saw in her mind the rise of Montenero in Livorno; its curve of road, its church amid the umbrella pines. She had never expected to live in the lap of another mountain. Her mountain. She had begun to call it that, she noticed. She had begun to feel a bond with it as with a friend. A city dweller for most of her life, she was amazed at the country dweller she had become—as if she had only been waiting to come here.

Across the fields she heard the faint lowing of cows. The convent had its own now, and pigs, and chickens. There were tomatoes and beans and lettuce in the garden, and in the air, the clear voice of its own bell. Around her she felt the spacious house branch, its thirty neat cells complete, the dormitory for the students stretching across the second floor; its soft sounds and voices were familiar to her now. In her head there was always the sound of the day's lessons, and the sound of the day's Mass, and the sound of the day's simpler words: *pass the salt, lovely morning, mind the step.* She thought of the crowded smoky farmhouse they had come from; it seemed a long way off now. She thought of the other households she had run, her pleasure in their stocked larders, their orderly cupboards. Those households were small, compared with this; their pleasures seemed smaller now as well. To leave this, to leave now: she could not imagine it.

Looking down from the dormer, she saw Anna's black skirt and bent head. Her daughter had, these past few months, thrown herself into the religious life around her; it had begun when Charles du Pavillon had written of his engagement to someone else. The change in Anna pleased Elizabeth and concerned her at the same time; now she noted the girl's measured walk and downcast eyes, so different from her previous demeanor. She noted that and she noted something else: the sheaf of letters in Anna's hand. In her quest for useful chores, Anna must have taken this one upon herself today: bringing in the mail. Elizabeth felt a tightness in her chest. Every day she waited for this time of the afternoon, the time that the mail arrived; every afternoon she waited for the letter that would remove her from this valley.

Elizabeth was down the steps now, at the door. She was thanking Anna too quickly. She was moving too quickly toward her desk with the mail in her hand. The letter from Baltimore, from Carroll, thrust itself forward. Her fingers fumbled, opening it. Her penknife sliced it jagged. She read the letter through, read it again; put it down, read it once more. And then she asked to have Sister Rose sent to her.

There was that deliberate pattern of steps Elizabeth had come to know, to listen for. There was a rustle at the door. There was that almost imperceptible lifting of Rose's chin, that straightening of the spine Elizabeth knew came next. Rose sat down, her eyes lowered—but not before they had swept the blotter. She had seen the letter with the archbishop's seal. Her face was flushed, expectant. Elizabeth realized that Rose waited for the daily mail as anxiously as she did.

There was some news, Elizabeth began, trying to keep her voice colorless, flat. There was news that would affect them all. Bishop Flaget, newly appointed by Carroll, had brought back from France a religious rule for the order: the rules and constitutions of St. Vincent de Paul's Daughters of Charity. Having those guidelines should make things smoother.

And there was something else; Elizabeth took a breath. She knew she was stalling, working to keep a note of triumph from her voice.

There was this: Bishop Flaget, after he was consecrated in November, would be taking Father David with him to the new diocese in Kentucky; it would be a great opportunity for them both. There would of course be a new director of the order appointed by the archbishop.

And there will be no more talk of my being replaced— Elizabeth did not add.

And Carroll, after all my letters explaining, asking, reminding, has committed himself to me—she did not add that either.

And *Hallelujah*—she did not need to add that, it was in the air.

The silence thickened between them. For a moment Elizabeth felt a flash of pity for Rose. She had lost this struggle; she had lost her mentor, too, as Elizabeth had lost Babade.

But Rose sat stonily, never changing expression, never shifting her gaze from her hands. She murmured something appropriate. She bowed herself out. Elizabeth felt her pity recede, worry return. David's departure would make her secure here, she knew. But it might also deepen this rift. And however Elizabeth wished to hymn this news to her mountain, she knew that if she could not heal this breach, she had not truly won. However orderly the new house, however safe her position within it, this household was not yet secure. It was still disordered, on the edge of winter, as long as this rivalry persisted.

The fire started the week before Christmas in the hem of Sister Susan's habit.

No one noticed at first.

Elizabeth was giving a holiday talk; sisters and schoolgirls had assembled before her. The smell of singed cloth was not instantly discernible in the crowded classroom, redolent with pine trimmings, damp cloaks, mulled cider, and sweat.

Sister Susan, in her chronic shyness, had stepped too close to the hearth. She herself did not realize her skirt was smoldering until after Elizabeth had talked about the Virgin's maternity. Susan's plump tremulous face had been transfixed. She had never heard anyone speak of Mary's pregnancy, of Mary as a nursing mother. Elizabeth's empathy and earthiness were arresting. The room was quiet. The voice was clear. The words pulled Susan out of the low-grade anxiety that she could seldom overcome. But only for a few minutes. Then she smelled the smoke.

To Elizabeth, standing nearby, it looked at first as if Susan were suddenly taken ill. The girl had gone white, then bolted in panic for the door. I hope I haven't made her sick, Elizabeth thought, half-serious; then she saw the fiery streak on Susan's black skirt. In a moment Elizabeth was following her, Sister Rose close behind. In the hall, Susan was running for the door, her skirt shimmering now with a forking snakelike flame. A high whimper came from her—*ohnono-nonono*; she flung the door open and rushed outside, beating at her skirt with her hands. In the same instant, Elizabeth and Rose snatched up the rug from the hall and rushed outside into the gray December afternoon. Susan was still ahead of them, galloping, lowing—trailing light like a torch. She dashed into the small toolshed, the nearest outbuilding at hand, desperate to put out the fire alone, mortified that she was on fire at all; terrified of burning anyone else— especially the person pursuing her: Mother herself.

Elizabeth saw the girl fling herself into the shed; saw

the fire leap from skirt to sleeve to wood shavings on the floor—reached the shed with Rose and, gasping, threw the rug over Susan. Swiftly, silently, still breathing hard, they rolled her on the ground outside, while behind them the shed began to bloom with flame. *Never mind the shed, never mind*, Elizabeth hissed to the heavens, *the girl, the girl*. Her hands moved, quick and capable, as if independent of her. Then she hesitated. Rose hesitated. Elizabeth guessed they shared a fear: that they would unroll the rug and find Susan badly burned, perhaps dead. At the same time, they felt the presence of the community gathering, panting, pushing around them. They unrolled the rug: Susan made a mewing sound and sat up, teeth chattering, tear-streaked— but only mildly burned. Looking into her face, Elizabeth realized for the first time how blue her eyes were.

Elizabeth stood up. She saw the circle of black bonnets, the wide shocked eyes. There were girls here among the students who would now cry out in their sleep, dreaming of fire. There were sisters here who would have the same dreams. Elizabeth had to say something. She had to diminish the incident, move them past it. For a moment she could think of nothing. Then she felt Rose's eyes upon her; that gaze concentrated her mind.

"Well," she said, dusting her hands against her skirt. "I've told you all we must blaze with love of God. Let me add one caution. This isn't quite what I had in mind."

There was a ripple of laughter: nervous laughter, relieved laughter. Laughter to go on with. Elizabeth heard that laughter all evening, even after Susan was put to bed, the fire was put out, and the stir through the community was stilled in sleep. Even in the midnight silence she heard it, sitting up in her room, her bed untouched. Sometimes, Elizabeth had found, a crisis rallied everyone, set small problems at a distance, drew the community tighter. And sometimes a crisis rattled everyone, shook problems loose, broke links in the community that had weakened. This evening, between fire and bedtime, Elizabeth had had two visitors to her room: two women, jarred into speaking. Their presences, dissimilar, disturbing, lingered here now. Thinking of them, Elizabeth left her room and walked slowly through the house. As she had often done in her own private households, she walked with her ear tuned to the breathing, the sighing, the shifting of the sleepers here. She moved past the nuns' attic cells, through the students' second-floor dormitory; her candle streaked the dimness, the floorboards creaked beneath her. She paused, listening to the girls' dense, even breathing, rhythmic as crickets on the dark. Sarah Blackburn Taylor slept among them here, though tonight she had told Elizabeth it wouldn't be for long.

"I've told my father to take me home," she had announced this evening, slouched up against Elizabeth's bookcase. "The letter's gone, you can't change my mind." She glanced at her nails. "Mother," she added, belatedly.

This girl wasn't a beauty, but she was long-necked, graceful, groomed. Her hair was the color of fine-grained dark wood. Her face was flat but delicately boned and fair, like pale silk drawn across an elegant oval embroidery hoop. She looked custom-crafted, well-wrought, expensive. Her only crudeness lay in her chin and eyes: her father's chin, too strong, too square; her father's eyes, sharp, imperious, a bright hard blue. The only daughter of a prominent Baltimore merchant, she daunted most of the nuns. Her insolence didn't daunt Elizabeth, who had known many Sarahs in New York. Under slightly different circumstances, Elizabeth thought, she herself might have become a Sarah. All the more reason to have empathy for this girl, to see past the insolence.

"I'm not *happy* here." Sarah's eyes flicked Elizabeth's face. The eleven-year-old voice had an older inflection, bred in adult company. "I'm not. I've *told* you. I read those verses you told me to, they didn't help. They don't change anything."

"No?" Elizabeth said dryly. "Even your state of mind?"

"The same things are still wrong. All this theology, I don't see the point. *We're* not going to be nuns."

"You might be a wife, a mother."

"So?"

I'd like to shake you, Elizabeth thought. "So," she said instead, "you're being prepared for that, then sent back over the cities like good leaven."

"That's what you always say."

I'd like to slap your face, Elizabeth thought.

"I'd learn better in a city," Sarah went on. "Not up here away from everything. Including libraries. I want to be someplace that isn't a glorified farmhouse, either. Someplace you don't catch *fire* just listening to a *lecture*. You don't even have screens for your *hearths*." She glanced up, a glance showing more than scorn; some question, some need Elizabeth could not decipher.

"We have screens. That was an exception."

"Even so. I wrote Papa. . . ."

Elizabeth sighed. Sarah's papa had had these letters before; they had sometimes brought him to St. Joseph's Valley. The last time, he had been incensed over the continuing presence of Protestants in the school; Elizabeth would not bar them. The time before, he had been irate at the presence of children from the Emmitsburg parish; children who could not pay, educated in a special section called St. Joseph's class. *On my money*, he had spat. But he still did not seem to want his daughter home. He had stamped off with the same thrust of chin Sarah used now.

"I wrote Papa. He'll come . . ."

"Sarah."

"You'll see—who'll pay for your precious orphans if the rest of us leave?"

"*Sarah.*"

Elizabeth crossed the room and carefully shut the window, sending her mind into the gesture and away from the girl. It was true, the school was different from its original plan. It would never, Elizabeth knew, be a school only for poor country children: it simply lacked the financial resources. It had become a boarding school for urban girls, often wealthy girls; girls with old Maryland names and old Maryland money. Within it, there would always be St. Joseph's class, but Elizabeth knew she was mainly educating girls who came from her own background. She wasn't disappointed; she often glimpsed her younger searching self among them, here in the place that self never had. It was only at times like this, with the few Sarahs, that she felt a twinge.

"Papa, he'll take me home, this time he will." Sarah's voice trembled. "When I saw Sister Susan today, running, I knew it—that's what I wanted to do, run, run."

And abruptly, without another word, she was out the door. Elizabeth heard her quick footsteps fading down the hall. Sarah would go to bed angry, not pacified, not comforted. Elizabeth had not been able to find the words.

Nor had she been able to find the words for Sister Sally, who had come in shortly after Sarah had flounced out. The appearance of Sally, polite, forthright, smiling, had been a relief to Elizabeth—until she had begun to speak. This sturdy country girl, the community's *procuratrix*, was one of the order's best nuns. In Elizabeth's mind she bore a resemblance to Amabilia Filicchi—dark, green-eyed, quick, her face in an abiding kindness. She had seemed to adapt easily to community life and to an inner life of prayer. If Sister Maria—withdrawn, stern, sad Sister Maria—had come to say she wanted to leave, it wouldn't have been surprising. But to hear those words from this young woman was, to Elizabeth, a shock.

"Mother, I knew it when we all ran outside, when we saw Sister Susan on the ground." Sally studied the candlestick beside her. "I wasn't thinking of her, all I could think of was someone else. What if this . . . someone else was in danger. And I wasn't there to help. What if this . . . someone else needed help. . . ."

"And this someone else is . . . ?"

"His name is . . . Tim. We were friends before I entered. He . . . he's here in town. I see him when I market, I . . . Mother, I thought I could overcome this."

"You had thought of marrying?"

"I had, but . . . nothing was ever spoken. And then I . . . heard about you. I felt . . . I thought . . . a true vocation . . ."

"Not just a wish to hide, escape?"

"No, Mother. I wanted to come. I didn't miss him right away—it sounds so strange, but . . . it was after the first year. After we moved out of the farmhouse, after things stopped being so hard . . . that's when I started to think of him again."

"And now?"

Sally's broad face flushed; her rawboned frame seemed to contract in tension. "Now I wish . . . Mother, I wish you'd give me a very hard penance, I . . . wish you'd tell me if I should . . . just go away."

"Is that what you want, Sally?"

"I don't know, Mother, truly I *don't.*" Her voice split on the word. "For the first time I realize . . . I don't know how to say it, I won't . . . ever . . . be . . ." She broke off, took a breath. *"Held."* She forced it out, her voice low. "Sometimes I just . . . want . . . that."

"I know." Elizabeth looked at Sally. "That's one of the hardest things, I think. Not to have that. Affection—it must be one of life's best joys. And being loved specially, singled out, that too. Until the feeling of God's love comes strong, that lack is strong, I know. But it doesn't mean you should leave."

"But my vocation, it must be so weak . . ."

"No. Not weak. Just tested, I think, Sally."

"Oh, Mother, I don't think so, I think it's false. *I'm* false, I . . . Send me away, Mother."

"Sally, I think we should wait, I—"

"Please, Mother, you were married, you know how it feels. I . . . I want to be a nun, but I . . . I can't bear to see him in town anymore, to stand inside this habit and . . . want, Mother, *want.*" Her last three words were whispers.

Again Elizabeth had felt her lack of experience, her lack of seasoning. She wished she could, like Carroll, pluck metaphors off an inner tree abloom with more. She remembered how he had focused her mind that day in Baltimore. He had been, that day, some thirty years older than she was now. He had been a priest for most of his life. She had been a nun for just two years. And she had had no wise words for Sister Sally, except to pray over it. And to offer her own prayers. And now, passing Sally's cell, Elizabeth heard the girl's bed creaking—a wakeful, worried sound that was not unfamiliar.

Elizabeth hesitated a moment. For a moment she had an urge to waken her middle daughter, Kit. This was not the child to whom she felt closest, with whom she felt the tightest kinship. But this was her calmest child, a child whose presence often calmed the others. Sometimes it even calmed Elizabeth herself. But she couldn't awaken a child for that. She mustn't lean so much on these children altogether, Elizabeth told herself. Her eyes on her candle, she went back to her room. Sleep had fled her like a cutpurse in a crowd. Often when this happened, she would sit up with her Bible, underlining passages she discovered and rediscovered. But not tonight. Tonight she needed air. She took down her cloak, took out her shoes, and went down the stairs.

Outside it was colder now; she could see her breath. The moon had set. The lantern in her hand cast yellow squares on the ground ahead. In its sallow glare the land, the house, the fences looked stark and harsh. She saw herself moving among them, as if from a distance: she looked small, feeble. Today she'd had a chance to come closer to Rose. She hadn't used it. Tonight she'd had a chance to reach Sarah, help Sally. She hadn't. A sense of discouragement penetrated her like damp air.

The rubble of the toolshed rose up before her, giving off a sour scorched smell. The wreckage had stopped smoking. Now it was just a heap of charred wood, the blade of a hoe, the prong of a rake protruding here and there. Elizabeth sifted through it, as if for a key.

Kneeling there, she felt the press of this many-chambered, many-acred household around her. Even from a distance, even from outdoors, she could hear it breathing, turning in its sleep; she caught its drowsy murmurings, she sensed it dreams. She realized that she understood its cries and shifts, even if she didn't yet know all the ways to quiet them. And that was how it went, raising a family. Sometimes, she recalled, she'd been able to hush an infant's squalling with a note in her voice; sometimes she'd walked the floor all night. She had learned as she went. She was learning all over again now.

She knew she still lacked the inner resources, the spiritual depth she needed here. The order and the school were stronger now, and so was she; she knew, in her case, this was not enough. She would ask to be deepened, honed in the way she knew she must be. And in the meantime—in the meantime crouched by the rubble of the shed in the dark, reaching for the right notes in a lullaby, rocking this great cradle of a household in her mind.

18

I *have to admit it.*

She did okay.

And after that year, according to my notes, things settled down for the order. It got a new director, a pleasing choice: John Dubois, president of nearby Mount St. Mary's. It got approval of St. Vincent's Rule, a rule which allowed for this Reverend Mother's children. And it gained stability. Elizabeth Seton's position was not challenged again. Under her guidance, school and sisterhood continued to grow— and, you might be tempted to think, she lived happily ever after. If you weren't looking closely, you might say that. If you followed the public thread, ignoring the personal: this line that runs like counterpoint against the clearer, more hummable melody. Another counterpoint of suffering.

Suffering, we are told, purifies. The Hellenic Greeks told us. The Christian martyrs told us. Jesus showed us. And we believe them. We believe that wisdom and compassion and caring are carved from us by pain, as if under some accurate surgical knife. But I also believe that suffering can sometimes warp, not hone; twist, not teach. This is, in fact, what I fear may be happening to me.

I dreamed of Michelle last night.

My sister. My charming noisy younger sister.

A sister I steadied, shepherded, worried over. Perhaps too much. Not unlike the way Elizabeth Seton was with her children. Her conflict between family and vocation—it's uncomfortably familiar to me.

After I entered the seminary, Michelle started to drift: the perpetual student, the eternal traveler. I can see her fair hair, bleached lighter by the sun; the sun on all those beaches she returned to. I can still hear her voice, shredding, speeding, on the phone. All those phone calls. All those false starts, false hopes. I couldn't help her anymore. I was too busy, too rushed; too impatient. Too important. I was a priest now. Other people needed me. I didn't really hear the desperation in her voice then. I didn't hear it till she was dead.

She cut her wrists two months ago, in my old room; in my old bed. No accident. No question: suicide. And I, the canon lawyer, ruled out her burial in hallowed ground. I could have given her the benefit of the doubt; I could have given her a Mass. Law or not, these days, the Church rarely turns a suicide away. And this is what I did. I was too afraid to do otherwise. Too ambitious to do otherwise. Afraid to give the appearance of favoritism. Ambitious for myself, ashamed for my sister. And, I suppose, angry at her as well. Now that anger is gone. The only anger left is at the Church, its laws. Easier to lay blame than take it. The ambition is gone; none of that left at all. What's left now is guilt. And pain. The kind that warps, I think. The kind that twists and teaches nothing.

I try to sidestep anything that touches this; that wakes it. Even Grief Workshops. Even Elizabeth Seton's children: her conflicts, her guilt. This line of counterpoint is one I'd just as soon not hear: her inner music, that year of 1812. Her mental melodic notations, as the conflict grew and the cadence shifted and the way got harder ahead.

On the way to Mass: no road.

On the way to Mount St. Mary's, Sunday morning, through the woods, over the creek, keep an eye out, don't get lost.

Let us meditate, my sisters, on the Joyful Mysteries of Our Lady, going; on the Sorrowful Mysteries, coming back. Let us be prayerful—let us be careful, too, let us try not to fall in the creek. *Hail Mary*, stay together, *full of grace*. Rosaries in fingers, feet slipping on wet stones. Patterns of light and shadow, leaf-dappled, on black bonnets, black capes. Soft murmur of voices, *the Lord is with thee, blessed art thou;* all around the trees, tall congregation of them, rustling, leaning, *blessed is the fruit.* The creek sliding by, shining, underfoot, crossed stone by stone, sister by sister, a pause at each stone, a pause at each bead, *of thy womb Jesus, Holy Mary.* Dinners in sacks, sacks strung from belts, *Mother of God pray for us sinners,* sacks and knives and rosaries dangling, clinking, swinging in the air, *now and at the hour of our death.*

At the hour of our death: Anna coughing and falling behind, she has to be helped, singled out again. The cough in Elizabeth's mind with the prayers: *Hail Mary,* can't deny it anymore—the cough, the breathing, the heat of her skin. Not Anna. Yes: Anna. The Seton complaint, the Seton curse. I should have sent her to my sister Mary, she offered to take her, to have Wright help—I didn't, too late. *Full of grace,* when Charles du Pavillon threw her over, that's when it seemed to come on. How religious she's become now, how dedicated, so devout it makes me proud, but is it real? Or is it rebound? Of course it's real, why shouldn't it be. *The fruit of thy womb,* if only she weren't so much worse, so white—but she's young, she's strong, she can recover, of course she can. *Mother of God pray for us now,* and on Wednesday nights when the boys come over from the Mount, *and at the hour of our death,* Anina, lean on me, that's right, keep together everyone, not much longer now. *Hail Mary,* forgive my straying mind; these are certainly sorrowful mysteries I've meditated on, not joyful ones—mother's mysteries. *Holy Mary, Mother of God,* I know you understand.

In Anna's cell, as in all the cells, there were a bed and a table and a chair. On the wall, as on all the others, there were a crucifix and a clothes peg; on the table a breviary, a Bible, a quill. But in this cell, unlike all the others, there were also a rag doll with a china face, and a stove sent up from Baltimore, and the constant sound of labored breathing which changed the walls, the bed, the cell, and set it apart as the province of the consumptive.

The decline, once begun, had been rapid. Now the disease was not only in Anna's lungs but also in her bones; her spine protruded at the thorax. Projecting from her side was a strip of linen on a silk cord, threaded through her skin and pulled to help drain her lungs: the cord's medical name was "seton," a dark pun Elizabeth could not bring herself to speak. Before prayers and after prayers, before class and after class, before and after and sometimes during meals, Elizabeth was there in this cell, listening to the breathing, smoothing the hair—averting her eyes from that cord, that festering side.

Anna seemed to be bearing this better than she was, Elizabeth thought: no tears, no night terrors, great patience with the pain. Her new devoutness was helping her, it seemed; she clung to her renewed faith as she used to cling to that doll on the table. It filled Elizabeth with pride to see this daughter's piety. Of all her children, Anna was the only one who had shown any interest, any aptitude for the religious set of mind. It pleased Elizabeth—it made her uneasy. After Anna's romance had ended, she had become so eager for mortification of the flesh—washing at the pump in bone-chilling rain, eating foods that sickened her stomach . . . too eager, perhaps. Perhaps these acts had hastened the progress of the disease. And perhaps, Elizabeth feared, she hadn't directed her daughter properly. She'd been so pleased by the piety, she had perhaps praised Anna too much; encouraged her too much on this new path. Elizabeth wondered how she could ever balance her feelings about this child; this child above all. All she wanted to do now was spoil her: she'd had this stove sent in, and a carpet, and oysters, when Anna longed for them—the only longing of the senses she had shown, these past bad months.

The cord in Anna's side needed to be pulled now; Elizabeth had grown adept at this, adept too at not watching as the flesh strained above it. She took the cord in her fingers; she wanted to cry out herself, almost wished Anna would. But Anna set her mouth and gripped the bed and said nothing until it was over. "My penance, Mama, my penance," she panted, "for so often drawing my waist small with my stays, for vanity, vanity." Again Elizabeth felt a stirring of admiration—and uneasiness. This child was too good. Perhaps it was true, as Anna said herself, that she was relieved to be free of Charles du Pavillion; that she'd secretly dreaded the involvement. Perhaps it was true, as she insisted, that she had at last found her true calling. Some of the sisters said she was an angel. Maybe it was true. Maybe it was genuine. And maybe it was an adolescent craze that had sapped her health—and Elizabeth herself had encouraged her.

Elizabeth could not keep her mind from turning again and again to the *lazzaretto*. She saw it in dreams, she saw it clearly in waking moments in Anna's cell: the brick floor, the damp walls, Willy coughing in the smoke from the old man's fire. The father on the bed, that elegant bed. The wife beside him, watching, murmuring Protestant prayers. And the child, this child, jumping rope from the chest; this child watching too. Thinking back now, Elizabeth saw how scared Anna was. How small—a witness, a confidante too young.

This "Seton complaint"; this Seton curse. It seemed to be a recurring family penance. Elizabeth suspected she herself was started in it: there was no more chest pain, as she had experienced in Baltimore—no expectoration, no cough; only a continual low-grade fever, despite worsted stockings, lamb's-wool shawls, early bedtimes. But with her, it was slow, it was mild, it could go on like this for years. With Anna it was quick: the consumption was blazing through her now. And now they were not isolated together in a *lazzaretto*, in a foreign country, with no one to think about but themselves.

All around Elizabeth, as she sat at Anna's bedside, the convent turned on its axis, on its office of prayers, its order of lessons. She could hear the chant of sisters and students, she could hear the creak of stair treads and the click of doors, and the cows, the bell, the wheels on the drive. As she sat with Anna, her office became that bedside, that cell. A dozen times a morning she turned from the child to the figure of a nun in the doorway—a butcher bill that must be paid, a request for a Mass that must be answered, a pupil to punish, a pupil to comfort, a need for new cloaks, new shoes, more prayers. Like a large family, it turned to her with everything, for everything. Mostly when the nuns came in, Anna leaned forward, listening, interested, concerned. This past year she had worked hard with the sisters, helping to prepare pupils for First Communion. She had looked forward so much to joining the sisterhood herself; it was still her wish. It was her wish to be with her own sisters too, but Bec avoided the sickroom now; this laughing woodsprite of a child grew silent anywhere near it. Kit, sensible square-jawed Kit, used to come and sit quietly by the bed, her smooth dark head bent over an endless weave of cat's cradle. But even Kit couldn't stand the vigil since the seton cord had been inserted in Anna's side. Mostly now, Elizabeth watched alone.

Now Anna moaned in her sleep, murmuring something. Elizabeth leaned closer, trying to hear. Unable to make out the word, feeling helpless, she reached for the doll on the table and tucked it into her daughter's arms as she would have done years ago. Elizabeth looked at the child with the doll in her arms and thought of herself with this child in her arms—tried to think of Mary with her Son in her arms: the mother offering the child, the child offering the mother. Anna waked, pushed the doll away. Her eyes picked out Elizabeth's tears, her finger traced them.

"For me, Mama? Should they be for me?"

"Anina . . . shouldn't they be?"

"Shouldn't we rejoice? It'll be just a moment, a moment— then we'll be together, reunited for eternity. Eternity, Mama, I know it, eternity."

She was fevered, repeating that word over and over; Elizabeth recalled how Willy had repeated words, sung them, stammered them in the last of his fever. And now his daughter, their first baby, was repeating words like "eternity." Saint's words. Words of grace. Words that again filled Elizabeth with uneasiness. Was this some desperate imitation of herself? Was this some role played to the death? And if this child were not in a convent, would she be playing it at all—dying at all? Elizabeth, rocking Anna in her arms, saw another tear splash down on the child's face.

There was a rap at the door. The long gentle face of Father Bruté appeared there, above his purple stole, above the holy oils in his hands. Dubois' new assistant, he had come to give Anna the Last Rites; Elizabeth could not put it off any longer. Anna looked up eagerly, offering her hands at once to the young priest. As he moved through the sacrament, saying the prayers in his broken English so that Anna would understand, the girl's face shone.

"Through this holy anointing and His most loving mercy may the Lord forgive you whatever evil you have done through the power of sight . . . through the power of hearing . . . the power of smell . . . the sense of taste . . . the power of speech . . . the sense of touch. . . ."

Anna held out her hands to the chrism, like a girl greeting a suitor; she smiled up into the stream of prayers.

"Anina, Anina . . ." Elizabeth tasted the salt of her tears on her lips.

"Laugh, Mother," the girl caroled. "Laugh, laugh, Jesus."

For several months after Anna died, Elizabeth expected to lose her senses. Her head was so disordered, without her daily tasks she did not know how she'd get through the weeks. Something within her felt stunned, stopped, stricken in a way she had not known before—even in Livorno when Willy died; even on Staten Island with her father. "Thy will be done," she said clearly, fiercely, at the grave; she would not consciously deny this. But she was unable to keep herself from a desolation so terrible, so all-encompassing, that the community felt it with her.

Every day she moved the sisters through the round of classes, prayers, meals, recreation. Every Wednesday evening she sat at the kitchen table with her remaining daughters and her boys visiting from Mount St. Mary's; every Wednesday she held a family supper. Every Sunday she received Holy Communion and every Monday she began a new week intending to rise above the disorder in her head. And every Wednesday the silence hung over the table; every Sunday her Communions were barren, and every Monday she seemed to sink lower into the mist in her mind.

Every night now, at two or three or four, when the house was still and the trees shifted in the dark, Elizabeth would move down the hall and open the door to Anna's cell. The bed was stripped. The mattress was bare. The clothes were gone from the peg on the wall. The crucifix had been moved elsewhere. But the doll with the china face still sat on the table. Elizabeth had asked that it be kept there. She had also asked that Anna be buried with her hands arranged as they'd been when she died—clasped, prayerful. If these things were wrong, she was not sure. If these things were improper, just now she couldn't say.

Elizabeth sat on the bed and looked at the doll. Anina, Anina. The body was under those loads of dirt; she'd seen the grave filled in. This disturbed her as much as the absence of Anna herself: the body underground, unwarmed, unprotected, in a box beginning to rot. She had never thought of this when the others died; now she could think of little else. This body had been within her own; she had held it, rocked it, bathed it—this body should not decay in earth. The last time she had visited the grave, a snake had curled upon it, large, ugly, dark. Elizabeth had watched it and felt something rising in her throat. Anna had been afraid of snakes—at four she had screamed when a small green one had wriggled over her shoe in the garden. Anna was there in the ground and could no longer shield this child from snakes. From cold. From harm. From the dark—Mary, Mary, pity a mother. In these moments Elizabeth could not imagine Anna's soul rising above that grave, that snake. For all her faith, all her prayer, she could not believe that she would see Anna again in eternity. She could not go back into the graveyard now, not without feeling the blood rush away from her head and a fainting sensation come on. Every day she walked to its gate and tied the gate shut, consistently terrified that Anna might be rooted at by the pigs. And every night she came up here. That was all she could do. She came up here and held Anna's doll.

Emma, Anna had called this doll—but that was long ago. She had called the doll Emma before she had ever come to live in a convent. Before she had ever thought of becoming a nun. She had wanted that so badly toward the end: the day after Bruté anointed her, Elizabeth had let Anna be received into the community as a sister; she was received from her bed. Again, if this was an indulgence, Elizabeth could not say. Her judgment, when it came to this daughter, this death, could never be clear; and she knew it.

Perhaps, she thought, smoothing the doll's gingham skirt, her judgment had always been wrong concerning Anna.

Perhaps she should have let her marry du Pavillon at four-teen, then and there; should have let her go off to the islands with him as his wife—perhaps in the island sun the con-sumption would not have taken hold. This thought was tor-ment. She had kept this child with her, taking too much pride in her, Elizabeth knew. And surely Anna had felt this —what if her faith was simply a desire to please her mother? What if her desire to please had hastened her death?

Elizabeth bent her head over the doll's impassive face. For a long time she sat that way, forgetting the house around her. She did not know how long it was before she heard footsteps behind her, felt a hand on her shoulder. The hand was gentle, the presence behind it was kind. In the dark, for a moment, she half-believed it was Anna's spirit some-how come to comfort her; to forgive her; to hold her one more time.

"I know," Sister Rose whispered. "When my girl died, it was the same with me."

She remained there in the dark, her hand on Elizabeth's shoulder. And in the dark, after an instant, Elizabeth's hand gripped hers.

"Mother Mother Mother!"

Rose hurried Elizabeth down the path.

"We just heard, Mother—how she screamed."

Elizabeth was running; their skirts skimmed the grass. They cut across the grounds, taking the fastest way, not speaking again until they reached a big maple on the edge of a field. A small group of sisters had gathered there: Elizabeth could see a cluster of black habits around the trunk, her youngest daughter, Bec, among them. Bec's face and the sisters' faces were all tilted, necks craned, fixedly, unswerv-ingly up. Elizabeth followed their gaze: it was impossible, though, to see more than the massy branches, the shifting greens of this tall old maple in full summer leaf. Beyond it, the fields spread open-lapped, genial, and the fences stretched out, basking in afternoon sun. It was only here, at the base of this tree, that the air was hushed and lips were tight and eyes were trained as if on a fire.

"Oh, Mama, Mama . . ." Bec turned, tears in her eyes. "It's my fault, he'll fall, he'll *die*."

From the maple high above, another voice spoke. Rich and deep, it might have been the voice of the tree itself: elevated, disembodied, it seemed to dispense gentle judgment on the little group below.

"Ain't so." The tree rustled, as if in thought. The voice of Joe, the groundskeeper, went on. "*I'm* to blame, fool I be. But don't you count on me smashed like no apple—leastways not yet." On these last words the voice shook, hollowing their bravery.

"I made him go *up*, now he can't come *down*." Bec's face streamed. "He almost *fell*, I screamed . . . Rose came . . . oh, *Mama* . . ."

Elizabeth glanced from the tree's green reaches to her daughter's face. This year the sight of Bec often misted her eyes; even so, just now, Elizabeth had to smile. The thought of Joe caught in that tree seemed, at first, faintly amusing— tall Joe, a crag of a man, his powerful arms and neck corded with veins. It seemed to the sisters he could do anything. He built fences, dug graves, fixed axles, lifted boulders. The strength of his back was matched by his quickness of mind: he solved problems of drainage and spoilage; he raised flowers, carved weathervanes. There was a tenderness in his large square fingers; they'd all seen it. His eyes, almond-shaped and long-lashed, were by turns arresting, exotic, gentle. His broad face, broadened further by a tufted beard, looked ageless, and sometimes, in concentration, fierce. It was a face they'd all come to watch for; a presence so indispensable that *"ask Joe"* was spoken almost as often as the daily *Amens*. The son of slaves, Joe had grown up in Emmitsburg's mountains, but he remembered stories from his African grandmother: tales of stones and ponds that could speak, could sing. He knew their names, and spoke them. He knew their songs, and sang them—but only to one person. Only to Bec. He made her laugh. He made her feel safe. He made them all feel safe, Elizabeth knew. It seemed impossible that anything could trap him, stop him, scare him—and danger no longer seemed amusing. The longer he was up there, the more alarming it became to Elizabeth; to them all. And especially, Elizabeth knew, to Bec.

Above them the tree rustled again. Bec's curly head jerked back sharply. Both hands gripped her crutch; she sat rigid in the little cart Joe pulled her around in. Bec was twelve years old now: an airy merry child, a child like a flash of light, filled with fast bright talk—it would take Elizabeth days to listen to her perpetual conversation. Of all the children, this one was the quickest, the most active, with the greatest need for room to move. And this was the child who could not run. Would never run. Would soon not walk.

Two years before, while Anna was dying, Bec had fallen on the ice; because of her sister she had kept her injured hip a secret as long as she could. The injury had worsened; the family tuberculosis had invaded that weak place, that bone. Bec had been sent to doctors in Baltimore and New York, even to the famed Dr. Physick of Philadelphia—no one could help. The disease that lamed her was starting to kill her. Bec had learned to get through the days with it; Elizabeth had learned to get through the days with it. And partly, they could because of Joe. He had become Bec's friend—and had become, as well, her walk, her run, her climb. He carried her around the grounds. He pulled her in a cart through the meadows, he drove her to Mount St. Mary's and back. He told her what he saw upcountry, downstream, and so the world did not move quite beyond Bec's reach.

This morning Joe had spied an abandoned bird's nest in the highest fork of this maple tree; Bec, sitting in the cart behind him, had followed his pointing finger with her eyes. She had longed to see that nest, hold that nest. In a moment Joe was climbing up to get it for her, moving easily till he'd reached the circlet of twigs. It was in his hands as he'd turned to come down—and was suddenly blinded by vertigo. He had waited. Bec had waited, down in the cart, her face upturned and patient. Joe had tried again to move. This time the earth had pitched, whirling, toward him—for a moment he'd lost his grasp of the branch. Below him he'd heard Bec scream. He had righted himself; he had cursed himself. He'd known he could not get down.

Elizabeth listened to this story now, told partly in the feathery voice of her daughter, partly in the deep voice that spoke from the treetop. She listened as the maple threw its dappled patterns over her, as others joined the cluster at its trunk. There were familiar voices, familiar whispers: her daughter Kit, Sister Susan, Sister Cecilia. And then, suddenly, the voices Elizabeth was always listening for, a little: the voices of her sons. Her sons—sending their husky shouts through this gentle murmuration, thrusting their shoulders and sharp-angled limbs through this soft cluster of black. William: the quiet one, the shorter one, looking so like his father now; and Dick: the noisy giant, the charmer, so unlike anyone in the family that Elizabeth sometimes wondered where he'd sprung from. They were here, sprung up without warning, their presences urgent, immediate, rakish, and rumpled—making everyone want to mother them and defer to them at once. Elizabeth didn't ask why they were away from Mount St. Mary's. She knew she wouldn't get an answer. At eighteen and sixteen, these boys thought themselves grown. They thought themselves men. They thought themselves independent forces to be reckoned with. To please them, she pretended this was so. To comfort herself, she pretended this was so. She knew better—not men, not grown, she knew, moreover, they weren't even reliable. William covered his unsteadiness with a reserve so seamless, Elizabeth couldn't guess his thoughts. Dick covered his with dash and banter; she didn't really know him either. She didn't know what delighted or disgusted them anymore, except for chocolates and spiders. She didn't know what moved them, what stirred them besides the pervasive restlessness they shared.

Now they were pushing toward the maple, Dick's voice crowing over them all. "Here we are, here we are, we'll get him down."

William, silent, shouldered along beside him.

"Get you down, Joe, no time flat."

Elizabeth watched her sons start up the tree, wishing they wouldn't. William moved stiffly, deliberately, like a middle-aged banker trying to be a sport. For a moment he glanced down at her; for a moment Willy's dark eyes appeared in a frozen version of Willy's face. Why was it so hard for this boy to smile? In manner he so resembled Dr. Bayley at his most aloof, Elizabeth often stared in wonder. And in love. Somehow, the chillier William was, the more her feelings for him intensified—but the more affection she poured out to him, the more he withdrew. She knew this; couldn't help herself even so. She would watch William and remember how he had cried desperately, at four, falling in the grass; she would remember the way his arms had come around her, at six, after a bad dream in the middle of the night. Now, in her own dreams, she saw him as a seminarian studying in nearby Baltimore. In reality, she knew, all he wanted was to escape: to war, to sea—and at the moment, up a tree. His head was disappearing among the maple's leaves. He still had not spoken a word. It was his brother's voice that floated out to them.

"Behind me, Bill? Easy, Joe, we're coming."

"Best you quit right there." Joe's voice was suddenly harsh. "Branches ain't strong enough, not higher, not for you both —git on down."

"Nonono," Dick's voice sang out, merry, condescending. "You're just scared, boy."

Elizabeth winced. Whatever people here called Negroes, slave or free, no one ever called Joe "boy." No one would even think of it—except Dick. Elizabeth had tried to overlook a certain streak in this son: not only of bigotry, but of lordliness over anyone he perceived as lesser than himself. And that was no small number. He was such a bubbling fountain of a boy, however, this was possible to forget. What showed most on Dick was his happy carelessness: the holes in his shirts, and in his shoes, the burs in his glorious fair hair. He always found someone to mend his shirts, lend him shoes, dust him off and put him right—for the next five minutes. Elizabeth watched now as a sprinkling of coins tumbled from his pockets to the ground, catching the light in a silvery shower. At least, she thought, he had some money in his pockets to spill. He was forever borrowing from friends, teachers—from Elizabeth herself, though what she had to give was precious charity, mostly from the Filicchis. She wondered when Antonio would run out of patience. She wondered what Dick found to spend so much on. And she wondered, just now, if this carefree, careless son would break his neck before her eyes, beneath this tree.

"Git down, Dick." Joe's voice came again.

"Easy, boy."

"Richard!" Elizabeth joined her voice to Joe's. "Come down right now, hear me?"

The tree still quivered, defiant; no answer came.

"Richard . . . William!"

She knew she sounded shrill. She knew she sounded unlike a Mother Superior; she sounded like a fishwife shouting out a window. As always, she wondered how her children would affect the community; how the community would affect her children. She hesitated a moment; in that moment there was a cracking noise from the tree, a shriek from Bec. The limb the boys had climbed onto could not support their weight; it groaned, it dipped, sending them down at a scramble. Elizabeth watched them, the blood thumping in her ears. She saw their faces, flushed, embarrassed, defiant still; shoulders back, covering their failure with a strut.

"Could've done it if you hadn't stopped us," Richard said, within the hearing of all. "Guess you'll just have to pray him down now," he added with a malicious wink and bounded away, his brother following.

Elizabeth's face was hot. She should have been tougher. She should have been kinder. She shouldn't have made a scene; she should have made a bigger one. So many times a week this happened; so many times she felt this inner rift between roles. If she let it, she knew, it could paralyze her. Since Anna's death, Elizabeth had learned to set this feeling aside, unresolved. She had learned to watch it from the corner of her eye, knowing she would have to look at it head-on another time. And in the meantime: turn back to what was at hand, as now—the tree, the man, the child.

"Best you keep folks down, Mother." Joe's voice, on the air, was stern. There was a pause. The voice gentled. "Bec?"

"Joe . . . yes!"

"You there? Can't see you through them leaves."

"Right here, right here."

~ 272 ~

"Be all right. Just my knees weak." Another pause. "Mother . . . sorry for the ruction."

There hadn't been many ructions lately; all had been so smooth for a while, Elizabeth had half-forgotten the feel of a crisis around her. Beyond Emmitsburg the country was at war; the British had burned Washington, Baltimore was besieged—but here in St. Joseph's Valley, war seemed distant. The school had gone on growing: more than fifty pupils now, eighteen sisters. The round of classes had become quietly routine, as had the sight in town of nuns with students. The order was expanding, too. Soon Sister Rose and Sister Susan would go to Philadelphia to run an orphanage: the sisterhood's first offshoot. Elizabeth's mind and desk were filled with names, figures, plans; with drifting scraps of paper. Even so, she found a sweetness, a serenity, in this chaos. This had helped to heal her after Anna's death—this and the presence of Father Dubois's assistant, Gabriel Bruté.

She could hear him behind her now. Just as her ear was tuned to the notes of her sons' voices, her ear had grown tuned to his. But unlike Dick's, it did not elbow into this gathering; it ribboned softly through, as always when urgent, in French.

". . . il peut tomber, c'est très facile . . . ah, Mother . . ." Bruté's face brightened at the sight of Elizabeth. There was also a flash of guilt in his gray eyes—he had promised her he would try to think in English. It was his difficulty with the new language that had drawn them together three years before, when he was a recent arrival from Paris. Elizabeth, speaking to him in French, had helped him learn English; now Gabriel still sent her his sermons for revision. They had become collaborators, partly because they were so much of the same mind.

"I was here to retrieve my sermon . . . our sermon . . ."

"You found it—on my desk . . . ?"

"Under the flower vase, yes, then I heard this . . . this . . ."

"Commotion?"

"Commotion, and I come, I knew how it would be with you . . . and Bec."

How could it be, she wondered, that Gabriel was five years

younger? They seemed to be exactly the same age. How could it be that they had grown up in different lands? They seemed to be compatriots. Over and over they found this, tramping through the fields together, finishing each other's sentences, talking, talking—light-headed, elevated, lifted along on clouds of talk. He was emotional, had sudden outbursts, "*coups de têtes.*" She understood, she had them too. Perhaps they looked like brother and sister, these two figures, walking in the weeds, waving their hands—both small, slender, dark-haired; her fine-boned face faintly French, his foxlike face more so. Their lives had paralleled in many ways: as she had sailed for Italy, he had embarked on a career in medicine; that year they'd both changed course. As she had arrived in Baltimore, he had been ordained. As he had arrived in America, two years later, he had been in the group bringing St. Vincent's Rule to her order. Now it seemed Gabriel had always been there. And now, as always, she was grateful.

At the base of the tree, Gabriel had taken out his sketchpad. This was a habit of his; it helped him solve problems, see more clearly. She had seen his drawings of St. Joseph's fields; she had seen his drawing of "his little woman of the fields": herself. Now she watched more fields take shape on the pad; not the tree, as she'd expected. Then she realized Gabriel was drawing Joe's view of the grounds from the top of the maple; the perspective made Elizabeth cringe. Suddenly, as she watched, Gabriel tore the sketch in half.

"I am stupid not to see it before." He smiled at Elizabeth. "The night." He smiled again. "Wait till the night."

As night came on, the wind died down. The tree ceased rustling. The birds quieted. Across the clear air they could hear piping girlish voices at recreation up the hill, and beyond them the bark of a village dog, the slam of a distant gate and, faint and high and sweet, a woman calling from some invisible veranda: *John-eee come on home now. . . .*

The sun had set. Most of the sisters had left the maple to go about their tasks; Elizabeth herself had gone and come and gone again. As she returned once more through the twilight, she saw the tree become a lacy silhouette against the dimming sky. Only the topmost branches were faintly touched with orange, illuminated by the sun's afterglow. Joe was still sitting up in the light; Elizabeth, standing below with Bec and Gabriel, was in darkness now. The sky had gone a deep shimmering gray. Looking up through the maple's leaves, Elizabeth could see the first sprinkling of stars. Until this vigil, she thought, she had never been so aware of the sky; never had her eyes been turned so continuously upward. As she watched now, the sky gradually drained. The tree grew indistinct, became a part of the dark.

"Look down now, Joe," Gabriel called.

There was a pause; then, from the treetop, a low whistle.

"Joe? What do you see?"

"Paradise, Father—no ground, no fields, no *nothin'*."

"You can come down now, feel your way?"

"I mean to try." Another pause. "Bec?"

"Here, Joe!"

"Sit tight, honey."

The tree began to rustle. Bec's hand tightened on Elizabeth's. There was a sudden skidding sound; a sudden shower of bark.

"Never mind—ain't *me*." Joe's voice floated down. "This easy now—now I can't see down." They heard him chuckle. "Just like leanin' on the dark."

His voice was closer. The tree seemed to shiver. Moments passed. In the dark there was a sudden creaking of branches, a shower of leaves. Then, with a whoop, Joe was on the ground and Gabriel was lighting his lantern. In its sudden brightness, they saw Joe, coveralls torn, face shining, swinging the child into the air. They heard her thrilled laughter as, from safe inside his shirt, he drew out the gift he'd climbed for: The bird's nest he'd claimed for Bec.

Soon after Bec died, Elizabeth took her cart and pulled it to that maple. She stood under it a long while. She remembered that trill of a laugh. She remembered the lantern light on her child's face. These were the things she would try to remember; not the sickroom, the sickbed that had replaced this cart.

She would try not to remember the fevered chatter, the

child's babbled fears of not going to heaven. She would re-member the way Bec's room had looked, pink and festive with the lilacs Joe had brought. She would remember the night of the tree.

Elizabeth, with the cart behind her, walked toward the little cemetery in the oak wood. She had feared visiting this grave. She had feared this death, the loss of this saucy little daughter; feared just as much the devastation of soul she had known with Anna's loss. Since Anna's death there had been other deaths in St. Joseph's house: Sister Maria, Madame Guérin; with each Elizabeth had mustered strength she thought she had been stripped of, with Anna. But these women were her spiritual daughters; not her children. She had never rocked them through thunderstorms, told them stories; tossed them, shrieking with joy, toward the rafters.

When Bec died, Elizabeth had been holding her; she had gone on holding her, perhaps ten minutes. She had held her and waited for the devastation to come. Instead, to her sur-prise, she had felt a deep sense of resignation. She had said a *Te Deum*, that great prayer of praise; she had waited for the resignation to pass. It had not passed. It continued to surprise her by its constancy.

Elizabeth reached the graveyard's gate. She remembered when Harriet had chosen this site with the flick of an apple core; she remembered when, after Anna's death, coming here had been nearly impossible for her. Rose had helped; Gabriel had helped. Archbishop Carroll's presence, however distant, had helped too. Now Rose was leaving. Gabriel had already left to become president of St. Mary's in Baltimore. Carroll had died the year before. All the other children were away: Kit in Baltimore, teaching piano and going to parties; Dick in Baltimore as well, apprenticed to a merchant there; and William, the farthest of all, apprenticed to the Filicchis in Livorno. Elizabeth was more alone now than she had been when Anna died. Perhaps she was spiritually stronger now; perhaps not. Hesitating at the graveyard's gate, she wasn't sure. Now it will come, she thought. Now it will come and crush me.

Within the cleared space by the newly mounded grave, Elizabeth saw a familiar figure: saw the denim coveralls, the heavy boots. She had thought she might find him here. Elizabeth opened the gate and went in.

Joe did not look up as she approached. He stood half-turned away from her, carefully folding into small squares the red bandanna he mostly wore around his neck. Elizabeth knew he had dug this grave. She knew too that he had not been at the burial. He did not look up as she came toward him now.

"That tree," he said after a while, his voice thick. "Up the tree—sick, scared's I was, felt better than this."

Elizabeth touched his arm; they stood in silence for a time.

"I can't believe she's anyplace but . . . there." Joe's voice burst out, angered, sudden.

"That's how it was for me with Anna," Elizabeth said. "I could hardly stand to come here then."

Joe glanced at her in disbelief. "And now?"

She smiled thinly. "I'm here." She touched the mounded earth with her shoe. "She's not. Anymore. I know that this time. I feel so . . . weary, Joe. Heavy. Clear to the bone. But I can come here now. Stay here. And I know I can come back."

"For you, Mother, with your faith—it must be easy. For me—ain't so easy."

"It isn't always easy for me."

He looked at her again in disbelief. There was a flicker of curiosity on his face; then it was gone, absorbed by the pain in his eyes. Elizabeth could think of nothing more to say; nothing to tell him for comfort that wouldn't sound formal, preached. There was only one thing she could do.

She placed in his hands something she had taken from the cart; something wrapped in a handkerchief, a handkerchief edged in lace. When he looked at it, he would recognize it as Bec's, her best. And when he unfolded it, he would see the treasure she had kept inside it: the bird's nest he had brought her from the tree, the night he'd come down leaning on the dark.

19

"*S*pit on it!"

"On the *altar rail?*"

"Sure—nothing works like spit."

The boys' voices echoed through the empty chapel on the slope at Mount St. Mary's. Elizabeth smiled in spite of herself and shut the door behind her. Within the brightness of this July afternoon, the church was quiet, shadowed, and smelled, not of incense, but of lye soap. The sacristan, she knew, was ill. His tasks had been given over to this pair down by the altar, surrounded by pails and brushes, mop and rags. The sight of them cleaning made Elizabeth smile again—a maternal smile, she realized, though only one of these boys was her son.

Dick had returned from Baltimore, this hot summer of 1817, his apprenticeship incomplete. A bad report had come from his employer: irresponsible, extravagant, unsuited to the work. Now, at nineteen, he was back at Mount St. Mary's, though not to study; just to fish and talk and tramp about with the seminarians while he pondered what to do next. While Elizabeth pondered that. While they wrangled over it. Elizabeth could see her son's fair hair in the dimness by the altar rail; she could see him flipping it out of his eyes. He was always doing that. He was always bursting out of things—rooms, clothes, Mass; buttons flew off him, keys and books sprang from his hands. Beside him, the other, older boy looked calm and still, his head bent in concentration: Pete Girot, the first-year seminarian with whom Dick had become tight friends.

"I think I'll stick with soap and water, Seton."

"You ever hear of spit and polish?"

"*You* spit, then—I'll do the floor."

Elizabeth's eyes followed Pete as he picked up the mop. She knew him well; he was her friend too. She often came here to the Mount to talk to the boys; sometimes they sought her out, looking for advice, encouragement, a little mothering—Pete had been one of those. She had been instantly in tune with him; more in tune, she knew, than she was with her own sons. Pete looked delicate, though he was not: it was his pale skin, milky, almost luminous here in the chapel's shadows; it was his red hair, his shyness. He was gentle, awkward, grave; she had seen his wistfulness, watching the faster-limbed boys play cricket. She had also seen those boys watch Pete wistfully in the classroom: Pete, in his quiet way, had a strong vocation for the priesthood. In that way he was unlike William, but something about this boy reminded her of her older son. Oh, *William William William*, she wrote to him in Italy, as if to draw him closer simply by repeating his name. She knew she thought of him too much, worried over him too much, fretted him too much about the state of his soul. Her anxiety for this son, Willy's namesake, was something she could not seem to control. She sighed, knowing it, impatient with herself, and turned back to the boys at hand. She guessed Pete had volunteered for this cleaning job, just to be in the chapel—and Dick had volunteered, not to be in the chapel, just because he went wherever Pete went.

"Richard," Elizabeth said from the aisle. She had begun wrong already: her voice edged with impatience, with urgency.

The boys rose quickly, seeing her. Pete's smile flashed white in the dimness. Dick flipped his hair back and tapped the altar rail with a finger, the rhythm casual, his face alert.

"Your brother's coming home from Italy," she said, and paused, not wanting to say much more. "He's on his way, it just . . . he wasn't—"

"Filicchi sent him back?" Dick's eyes were mocking.

"Perfect William? What happened, he didn't speak to anyone for two years and they got sick of it?"

"Don't talk about your brother like that." She wondered how many times she'd said that phrase in her life. In fact William, in his withdrawn way, had disappointed Antonio Filicchi as much as Dick, in his flamboyant one, had disappointed Luke Tiernan of Baltimore. "It's just wasn't right for him," was all she said.

Dick split the chapel air with a whistle. "Hallelujah— I'm not the only scamp in the family, then? Not the only failure?" His laughter cracked. "Thank you, Brother Will."

"Don't say that to him when he comes."

"Sure." Dick flipped back his hair and looked away. "We have to protect him, don't we? Doesn't matter what he did over there, just matters what I did—here."

"That's not true."

"Here where people know our name."

"I've never questioned you about Baltimore, I don't even know—"

"You want to know? What I did wrong? No you don't, it embarrasses my Reverend Mama too much, doesn't it?" In the sudden hush, she could hear Pete making himself busy with mop and bucket up the aisle.

"I came here," she snapped, "to ask if you would like to replace William in Livorno."

Dick looked at her.

"Your brother wants to go into the Navy." She went on quickly, trying to keep all emotion from her voice. She did not want to say that this seemed an unbearable choice to her; she did not want to think of the separations it would mean. She did not want to let this son know the depth of her love for the other.

"The Navy," Dick repeated, his eyes mocking again. "As far away as possible."

She ignored him, making her voice even again, going on. "I'll try to do what I can for him, and for you, you know that. And if Antonio's willing, I think you should go."

"William gets to choose for himself—I get chosen for, it's always like that." He flipped his hair back harder.

"Richard." Her voice was sharp. "It's a good position. And good people, your father's friends, and mine."

"Exactly." His voice turned lower, bitter. "No wonder William couldn't last there. Everyone looking at him, and seeing Papa. Seeing you too, Mother—finding God."

"Richard." She heard the sting she put into his name. She had heard the sting he'd put into hers.

"It's true. You know what that's like? Going everywhere as Mother Seton's son? Something in him had snapped open, he couldn't seem to stop it.

"Richard, this outburst, it's not the place—" Her voice, she knew, was cold and stiff.

"Where is?" His face was red. "You don't want to know, I'll tell you anyway—you don't want us to be merchants, you want us to be priests. That's right. You think I don't know? You think William doesn't?"

"I've never . . ." Her voice was shaking. "I've never said I want you to be a priest, either of you."

"Mother." Dick's voice echoed through the church. "Mother, you don't have to."

They stood facing each other for a moment. Then Elizabeth, still shaking, turned and walked up the aisle. At the door she glanced back. Afterward, she remembered that. She remembered the dark nave and the flip of bright hair and that all-pervasive smell of strong brown soap.

Afterward, Elizabeth wondered how long it was between the time she left the boys and the time of the accident. It seemed important to know exactly. She wondered what time it was when she went from the church to see Father Dubois in his office. She wondered how long it was that they walked under the oak trees, speaking of the boys, before seeing them again: the red hair and the fair hair, reappearing yards away.

Finished with work, the boys looked unpriestly, unguarded, prankish, free—calling to each other, tossing a pair of knives at a tree; a sport with all of them here. The knives flashed silvery on the air. The boys' voices lifted. Dick's aim was true, his throws strong. Pete's were fumbling, weak; Elizabeth saw his face flushing with frustration and effort. And then he made a sudden lucky hit. Elizabeth heard the *thunk* of the knife in the tree. She heard Pete's warble of triumph; saw him rush forward, wrench out the knife, turn to try again. She saw the joy light his face as he ran; even as he stumbled, even as he fell, the knife in his hand twisting under him. For an instant there was a stunning silence. Then she saw Dick bolt forward, crying out.

The trees blurred. Elizabeth was running, she was reaching for Pete, she was kneeling beside him; there was blood on her hands, blood on her skirt. She didn't notice when Dubois went to get the oils, when the others started to arrive. She wasn't sure if Dick, his face salt-white, spoke. She wasn't sure how they knotted his bedsheet around Pete, just below the point where his ribs diverged. All she saw at first was the rust-colored hair striping the skin under her hands, and the blood soaking through the cloth beneath them. Slowly her numbness dissipated. Elizabeth heard Dubois finish the anointing and begin prayers for the dying. Pete's eyes shifted from his face to hers. She returned his gaze with effort. A wave of nausea came over her; a wave of protest, disbelief. She groped for an inner reserve of strength; she seemed to find none—nothing but technique.

"Holy Mary, pray for him. . . . Every holy angel and archangel, pray for him. . . ."

Elizabeth had a sudden mental image of Sister Susan under her hands, rolled in that rug from the hall; spared, saved. Elizabeth had felt clearer, stronger then. Perhaps she had been.

"Every holy apostle and evangelist, every holy disciple . . ."

She heard Dubois's voice crack, falter. She could not help him. She knew he had been as close to this boy as she was; closer. She had thought that, even so, he'd help them all.

"Every . . . holy monk and . . . hermit . . . St. Mary Magdalen . . ."

Dubois stumbled on. His face was gray. Beyond his face, Elizabeth could see clusters of other shocked faces; half the school was there now. She turned her eyes back to Pete. The rosary in his fingers was taut. Sweat glimmered on his jaw, his lip. His skin seemed translucent. His hair looked shockingly bright against it; a cowlick, innocent, incongruous, stood up. She saw it and felt another wave of nausea. She saw his face and saw the faces of her sons.

"*Every holy virgin and . . . widow, every . . . saint of God . . .*"

The prayer trailed off, unfinished. Dubois could no longer control his voice. Elizabeth's mouth was dry, her mind empty of comforting words. Her sense of desolation seemed to broaden the distances among them. Dubois looked far away. Dick looked far away, across a vast expanse of grass. And Pete, this beautiful dying boy, seemed to lie across a sea space, a widening, darkening sea. The silence lengthened. Pete's breathing changed.

Dubois groped for the pyx, the small gold case that held the Host. Pete's eyes were unfocused now, his breathing harsh as Dubois held the Host before him. The wafer trembled in his fingers. His voice lapsed into Latin.

"*Ecce Agnus Dei, qui tollit peccata mundi . . .*"

Dick leaned forward. For an instant, as Pete saw his friend's face, his eyes cleared. Elizabeth closed her own. She heard Dubois's voice, very faint, "*Domine, non sum dignus . . .*" She heard a long windlike sigh from Pete. And then a different silence. She opened her eyes. Dubois was closing Pete's eyes. His hand shook; his other hand still held the Host. Elizabeth sat unable to move.

Suddenly she felt the jolt of an arm against hers, grabbing the rosary from Pete's fingers, knocking the Host from Dubois's hand—Dick, in a spasm of rage and grief, throwing the rosary on the ground.

"I'm damned now—right, *right*? I'm damned, well, I always was, ask anyone." He was crying now, face flushed, staring at his friend. "That's it, Pete, I'll tell you right now—I won't stay here, not now, not without you. I can't, you know that—oh, God, I hate God."

He raised his hand and with all his force struck himself in the chest. He raised his hand again, fist clenched, reeling from his own blow.

Elizabeth's fingers closed around his wrist.

She saw her hand, small and veined, against his harder, darker arm. She saw the distance between them contract, saw herself on that grass, under that tree, as if returning from afar. For a moment he struggled against her; in that moment, she was more powerful than he. All her pain seemed to fuel a furious stubborn strength—it caught his arm, held his arm; it caught him as his knees gave way, it held him fast. As he swayed, as he sank she was holding him; she was kneeling amid blood and beads, Dick against her shoulder. His tears wet her skin. His weight was heavy in her arms. She rocked him and wept with him and still she held him. A flamelike sense of love rose within her, sweet, hot, strong—love for this child and for the dead one; love for the children looking on, and for those beyond them, unseen: an eddying limitless love she'd not felt before, this sharp. This deep. She felt Dick growing light against her, though he did not move, did not shift. She felt herself slowly lightening, letting this boy go, and his brother; letting go the craving to hold on.

Dick stirred, lifted his head, shifted onto his knees. Elizabeth glanced up. She saw the stricken faces all around her. Dubois' was averted. The body was still exposed. The community was disrupted. The prayers were unfinished. Elizabeth wiped her face and handed Dick her handkerchief. She stood; she picked up the prayerbook and found the place.

"Go forth, O Christian soul, out of this world . . ." Her voice was muted. "In the name of God the Father Almighty . . ." The words' rhythm steadied her. Her voice grew clearer. The rhythm of the words seemed to steady the others; other voices joined hers. "May angels in their splendor come to welcome you . . ."

She saw Dick's hand moving in the grass. It retrieved the rosary. It paused above a white disklike form, the dropped Host. She saw the struggle on his face. No one but a priest must touch the consecrated bread; it still seemed wrong to leave it there on the ground.

"May Christ, the Son of the living God, find a place for you in the bright fields of paradise. . . ."

Over the prayerbook, Elizabeth watched Dick hesitate. At last he spread her handkerchief over his hand, picked up the Host with it, and laid it in Dubois's palm.

*". . . may you drink in the beauty of almighty God . . .
in bliss for all eternity . . . Amen."*
Elizabeth closed the book and laid her shawl over Pete's
face.

It was twilight by the time she left Mount St. Mary's in
the wagon with Joe. Under the seat his shovels clanked; he
had just dug the new grave.
"He would have been a priest," she couldn't help saying,
glancing back in the dusk. "A good one."
"Maybe Dick, he be one too."
"No." She shook her head. "No." She said it again,
noticing it didn't hurt as much to say it now. They rode
in silence for a while. The fenceposts of Saint Joseph's
began to appear, white and luminous in the changing light.
As was their custom when out together, they paused beneath
Bec's maple. For a moment Elizabeth saw the other tree
again—the tree with the boy and the blood beneath it.
For a moment she was seeing all the bedsides she had ever
stood by. The deathbeds. The empty beds of her children.
The stripped beds of her own childhood. She was seeing
them still warm with pain and love; seeing them through
the dark curve of this trunk, the spread of these branches
against the sky. Only through this tree did they finally
seem to make sense.
The maple rustled. Behind it the sky, still faintly lavender,
scattered its first stars. Joe watched them; then, with the
gesture of touching a child's head, he laid his hand against
the maple's bark.
Elizabeth thought of him coming down that tree. Leaning
on the dark, he'd said. Leaning on the dark for Bec. It had
been worth it to him then; it was worth it to him now. In
the rippling leaves Elizabeth could hear that daughter's
laughter again. In the shadow of this tree she could see all
her lost ones, present, immediate, laughing, comprehending.
It was worth it to her too, she saw: that vigil; all the vigils—
the risk of the climb; all of them.
Tonight she would return to her desk. She would right
the blotter, fill the inkwell, lift her pen. She would begin
putting into words what had happened today: sisters would

~ 285 ~

be summoned, the story retold. A letter would be written to Pete's parents. A coffin would be measured and made, blessed and buried.

Tonight there were children missing. Tonight there were children here. Tonight her family was gone to ash and oak and ocean. Tonight her family was here.

20

I have always found, to my shame, that wrestling brings me a measure of peace. Perhaps not the ideal recreation for a priest. Still, it releases something within me. And watching Elizabeth Seton's struggles with her children seems to be having a similar effect: I watch her wrestle with the guilt, the pain; I feel, just a little, my own guilt and pain loosen. It's her humanness that seems to unknot some of the threads for me. It's seeing that she was no Supermom. It makes it slightly easier to accept that I'm no Superman—and I'm not the candidate for canonization.

Perhaps some conflicts are never entirely resolved, some wars never completely won. But truces can be called: she's shown me that. Perhaps perfection's not the key. Perhaps the key is simply the willingness to go on wrestling.

But that far I may not be able to go.

I feel some ease from guilt, from grief, but not completely. And no ease from my urge to leave, to break my vows. To sever myself from my sister's death by severing myself from the Church—the church I neglected her for. I understand myself too well.

I wonder if Elizabeth Seton would have understood that. I believe she would have.

I believe, in those last years, she yearned to stop wrestling, herself. Those years when it must have seemed, as it were, all sewed up. Those years when the order was growing and the children were grown. She had, at that time, one more great struggle to face.

I can see her, facing it across her counterpane. I can see her there, in her room adjoining the chapel, her nearness to it a compensation for having to be so much in bed. In bed with the Seton complaint flickering on and off in her. In bed, at forty-three, she feels old. In bed, that late spring, 1818, she feels the Seton complaint starting to win.

Elizabeth opens her eyes and sees the leech on her arm. For a moment it seems to swell, filling with blood; then it blurs. Her mind is misted; nothing seems clear, or close. Carefully she turns her head. She feels the soft crinkle of the collar of her nightgown. She feels the gentle press of bedclothes over her. She sees that her arms are spread wide, sleeves rolled high; the leeches have been placed on the veins at the bend of each arm. It was done like this the last time too; she has been bled before. The pain in her lungs seems far away, like a splinter in someone else's hand: she understands how it should feel but cannot feel it deeply, just now, herself. Faces come and go at the bedside: Father Dubois, a sister. They seem as distant as the pain.

She lies back into the fever as into a warm bath, comfortable, accepting. Perhaps this time she will drift and drift and not come back. Thinking that, she feels a slow sweet sense of elation; it filters through her, stronger, brighter, like early sun through a curtain. Just to drift, to go, go now, how good.

Her mind passes quickly over the sheets folded in the cupboards, the copybooks stacked neatly on the shelves, the ten-pound sacks of meal and flour in the kitchen. Her house is in order. She lets her mind float over the classrooms, the nuns' cells, the students' dormitory. The sisterhood is in order, and the school. They can stand solidly without her now. She sees, as if from some height, the spread of fields and fences and the spines of her mountains; the strong white walls of the house she lies in and the rough stone walls of the house they'd begun in. She sees the lines of the creek and the graves of her girls and the boughs of Bec's tree. Again, she sees the rest through this tree; sees the tree as a cross with green green leaves—and then, as voices pull her back into the room, simply as a maple once more.

Faces hang in the room like pale globes. Among them she sees a streak of light: a candle carried in someone's hand. She closes her eyes. The darkness buoys her up like gentle water. She spreads her arms and lets herself drift on the dark, on the warm sweet air; she feels herself smile, drifting deeper still. There are candles in this darkness, she sees, pinpoints of radiant light. She allows them to float nearer, and they grow brighter; too bright. They become faces: they jolt her, they hurt her eyes. They grow larger, drawing her back, speeding her back—back to the room in the white house in Emmitsburg. Finding herself here again, she feels her eyes sting with tears.

Her children. Theirs were the faces that had needled her back. But William is in the South Pacific now, sailing with the Navy. Dick is in Livorno, apprenticed to the Filicchis. Kit is visiting friends in New York. They are gone, these three: they are raised. She has done them good, she has done them harm; she has let them go at last. She lets herself drift off again.

Her skin is light as parchment, an envelope bearing her upward; her head seems crystalline and clear as blown glass. She sees all the days, all the nights of all the years lining up before her now, like figures waiting patiently in line. They are moving away from her. She lets them go. How good it feels to let them go. She watches them with affection, imperfect as they are; she sees them from afar, like a mother watching her children go out the door to school. She drifts past the days and nights, past the mountains of Emmitsburg and the mountains of Livorno, and sees again the clearing near Miss Molly's house—it seems a thousand years since she has been here. Perhaps it is here that she will loose the threads that hold her back; perhaps from here she will go. Perhaps now: she has wondered so many times how it will be. Will she come face to face with Him in a field, or by a good fire indoors? Will she be in company, or alone? She has wondered; she has longed for that moment. She has strained to see it, yearned to touch it; and still she is not sure exactly how it will be. All she knows is that drifting toward it is like moving toward a lover; moving slowly, too slowly. It was this way when Willy had waited downstairs for her, his violin under his arm; it always seemed an eternity before she got down the stairs to him at last. Now she feels God's presence waiting for her like that: expectant, affectionate, a hand held out to help her down that last step. With this Beloved she would dance, skimming the air. With this Beloved she could weep and feel forever comforted; with this Beloved she could laugh and taste the laughter always. She feels the gentleness of this Presence now, near, very near, warming her like light. She reaches out to touch the light: an edge, a hem, narrow and bright, and she feels it draw her, taking her with it, and she is laughing now, laughing in the light, and she is laughing, laughing out loud, even as she hears the cry of a child beyond.

The cry is distant, dim.

She hesitates.

The light remains near, bright as before.

The cry comes again, faint, mewing, soft.

The light glows, ready for her, waiting.

Again she hears the cry.

Elizabeth hesitates again. And then, slowly, reluctantly, she forces herself to shift away from the light. As she had left her husband's arms so many nights to feed a wailing baby, she wills herself back into the room again: back into the house at Emmitsburg, back into the bed; back to the place where someone is waiting.

The room is dim and calm and someone is there: Elizabeth perceives a presence as she lets her eyes open again. It is dark outside, early morning; she hears the hall clock strike four. The house is still. She feels another flash of regret at being back within its walls; the feeling sweeps her like homesickness. In spite of this, her vision is clearing. She looks around to see who has come.

A candle is burning on the nightstand. The sister who has been sitting with Elizabeth has stepped outside; her knitting lies curled on her chair. Even so, Elizabeth knows she isn't alone. All the facets of the room have become real again, sharpening, precise: the edge of the windowsill, the outline of the crucifix on the wall. And sharpening with them, assuming a definite shape, is this other presence. Someone here—someone she cannot see, but sense: a presence that is needy, troubled, eager, disturbing. Someone breathing softly, concealed, it seems to Elizabeth, beneath the bed itself—the big feather bed the sisters had brought in for her, over her protests, when she began to be so ill.

Soft footsteps sound now in the hall beyond. Sister Sally returns, murmuring, retrieving her knitting. Elizabeth looks at her; at the broad freckled face, the big frame, the gentle hands. Is it only Sally, after all, she's sensed nearby? Is this feeling only fancy, bred by illness? Elizabeth waits a moment, thinking. No. Sally has resolved her conflicts long before; she gives no aura of trouble now. This is someone else.

Elizabeth touches Sally's arm, motioning her to bed. After a moment's hesitation Sally goes, with a backward glance, leaving the daily notes Elizabeth likes to see when she is ill: *First Communion class progressing/ White sugar running low/ Sister A's anniversary coming/ Sarah's disappeared again.* Elizabeth sits looking at the notes in her hand. Sugar running low: the banality of it assures her she is back indeed. She sighs. She hears a sigh echo hers; or does she? Foolishness, surely. Perhaps she's longing so for God just now, she's dressing His presence in human form; imagining sighs, imagining this soft breathing. *Sister A's anniversary . . . Sarah's disappeared again.* Sarah, missing—and someone here, someone seemingly under the bed. Elizabeth feels a distinct inner jolt. She knows now who is there, just beneath her mattress, hidden by the plain muslin bedskirt. She should have known before. She has seen Sarah other nights, other times, at hours such as this one. She has seen her and said nothing. She will say nothing now.

The first time had been a night a year ago, when Elizabeth had paced with a candle down the hall, listening as she often did to the sounds of the house at night. Most nights, pacing, her mind clicked with a dozen details: letters, finances, the need for more black cloth, white flour. This night, through the click of these thoughts, she had heard someone moving down the hall behind her. She had turned; she had seen no one. She had gone on down the hall and sensed it again—the presence of someone behind her, a disturbing presence: this same presence she feels now. Elizabeth had gone outside, into the moonlight, and then, all at once she had seen it: something white hovering near a fence, moving steadily toward her—a girl's figure in a white nightgown, arms stretched out, rigid and reaching, eyes open but unseeing, staring straight ahead. For an instant Elizabeth had felt a tingle of fear; then she had recognized the slant of the long graceful neck, the jut of the strong chin: it was Sarah Blackburn Taylor, sleepwalking toward her. Elizabeth had gone to the girl, led her back to bed. Sarah had not waked, had not spoken, and in the morning seemed to have no memory of the incident. Elizabeth had seen her like this many nights since, and had thought of her on many others.

"She should go," Gabriel Bruté had said, when she'd told him of this incident the next day. Gabriel, newly returned from Baltimore and back at Mount St. Mary's, was the only one to whom she confided it. "She makes the disturbance." He'd frowned.

"She didn't disturb anyone—maybe I disturbed her."

"*Alors*, she disturbs *me*. You need her papa's money so very much?"

"It's nothing to do with his money," Elizabeth had answered sharply.

Sarah Blackburn Taylor had been in and out of St. Joseph's school for the past seven years, going home to Baltimore, then returning again, packed up by a nanny and delivered like another piece of her expensive baggage. Her beloved papa did not seem to want her at home; she seemed to have no place else to go but Emmitsburg. Now she was one of the oldest students there, though her absences had delayed her progress toward the oldest girls' classes.

"She's one of the brightest students we've had here," Elizabeth told Gabriel.

"And? If she disrupts too much, still she should not stay."

"She just disappears sometimes—it's no disruption, really."

"She disrupts *you*."

"I wish I knew why that is."

She reminds me of myself, Elizabeth thought: rich girl, cold father, no real home. Sarah's haughtiness had faded with the years; faded with the repeated humiliation of being shunted around, unwanted. Now she was only deeply withdrawn; her silences, her sleepwalking, had increased, arousing the irritation of the school sisters. Periodically she vanished for short times, hiding somewhere in misery.

"She is unbalanced, perhaps?" Gabriel had asked.

"No . . . I think not," Elizabeth said slowly. "Troubled, yes. But unbalanced . . . I'd say no."

"You indulge her too much, I think. This girl, she worries me—she's not dangerous, you're sure?"

"Sarah? Only to herself." Then again, maybe that wasn't so certain, Elizabeth thought. Gabriel did not know about the incident in the classroom. Elizabeth had a way of overlooking that herself. She had, for an instant, a memory of rolling on the classroom floor with Sarah, the two of them locked together, it had seemed, for all time. Then the schoolroom returned to its usual serene shine in her mind.

She had been teaching a class that day: her class, religion class. Elizabeth remembered looking out over the students, seeing the orderly rows of wooden desktops and inkwells, gleaming shoetops lined up beneath them, brushed heads cocked above them. It was a pattern that gave her eye pleasure. Behind her, she had felt the wide expanse of blackboard stretching like a still slate lake. There had been a smell of chalk and bookpaste, stronger that day than usual. It was a smell she'd liked since her days in New York; since the days she'd stood teaching her children, with hornbooks, in the parlor. Those small schoolrooms were often in her mind when she stood here—kernels of this one. And this one, with its feel of peace and order, never failed to calm her, even on the worst days; even on days like that one.

Elizabeth had heard the first hint of trouble through her own words, through the lesson she was teaching: a lesson on contrition, she remembered.

" 'So let us confidently approach the throne of grace to receive mercy and favor and to find help in time of *need. . . .'* " Elizabeth was reading aloud from the Old Testament. She had noticed, glancing over the students' faces, that one face was missing: Sarah's. She wasn't usually late; she wasn't one to disappear at classtime. Elizabeth had listened for her step and had heard, instead, the sounds of a scuffle in the hall outside.

"We must remember," she went on, listening still, "that nothing can remove us from God's love. No sin can do that, if we are contrite. This is difficult for some of us to understand . . ."

The scuffling went on: the skidding of feet on the floor, and then the sudden sharp sound of a slap.

"There are many ways for us to seek that great love, to ask that forgiveness. . . ."

The door had flown open then. Sarah had slipped inside, taken a seat, her head bowed. Elizabeth had continued the lesson, watching her; it wasn't until the end that she had seen the fresh bruise on the side of Sarah's face, half-hidden by her hand.

" *'Have mercy on me, O God, in your goodness; in the greatness of your compassion, wipe out my offense. . . .'* " Elizabeth had ended with a psalm and dismissed the class, motioning for Sarah to stay. The room had emptied. The girl had stood silent before her, eyes on the floor. Sarah had been shaking; her breath, coming in rapid gulps, was the shallow gasping of hysteria.

"Sarah, tell me, what—"

"You won't . . . won't believe me."

"I will, try."

"No one . . . will."

"You had an argument? In the hall? With one of the girls?"

"One of the *sisters.*" This burst from Sarah; suddenly her voice unspooled into the room, fast and thin. "She hates me, says I won't answer her, says I'm . . . rude, queer, strange . . . she's watched for my mistakes, well today, today, I was late, she grabbed me in the hall, she . . . I pulled away, pulled away fast, she was hurting my arm, she . . . she hit me then, I just went numb, you don't believe me, knew you'd never. . . ."

Her voice trailed off. Her eyes darted around the room as if for a way to escape. In fact Elizabeth had believed her; in fact Elizabeth had a good idea which nun it was. She'd reached for Sarah, too fast, too suddenly, her irritation at the sister quickening her gesture. Sarah had flinched, gasping, grabbing at Elizabeth's hands to keep them back. Elizabeth had tried to hold on, and suddenly they were struggling on the floor. Sarah, like someone drowning in deep water, had alternately pushed Elizabeth and clung to her; Elizabeth had fought to get a calming grip on the girl. She had seen the classroom roll around them, a continuous sphere of floor and wall and ceiling, desks whirling by, blackboard skidding; she had felt Sarah's sweat like blood on her arm. How long they had crashed and wrestled there, she had no idea—she knew only that Sarah had the strength of someone in great fear, and Sarah, ultimately, won. At last Elizabeth found herself on her back, still gasping for words to tell Sarah she'd meant no harm. And Sarah, above her, tears on her cheeks, was whispering over and over, "Bless me, bless me . . . Mother, Mother, bless me." Her eyes had blazed; her tears had fallen on Elizabeth's face.

"Sshh-shh." Elizabeth had laid her finger against the girls lips, trying in some way to soothe her. "Easy, easy—I can't, Sarah. I can't bless you, I'm not God."

"But you *could*." Sarah had let her go suddenly, and just as suddenly spun away, running from the room, leaving Elizabeth panting on the floor.

After that, Sarah had been more withdrawn than before, disappearing more often for short periods of time. And now she has disappeared again, taking refuge, for some reason, beneath this bed.

Elizabeth imagines her there, crouching in the narrow dimness with the dust balls, the lines of the floorboards impressing themselves on her palms and knees. She thinks of Sarah roofed in by the bed slats and the bulges of ticking, like a child playing house on a rainy afternoon. Elizabeth cannot help smiling. She clears her throat. She sails her voice out onto the air of the room.

"I had a dream last night," Elizabeth says, as if to no one in particular. She knows that the sound of Sarah's name would send the girl plunging up through the mattress. "I had a dream last night that I was going back to old times. As if I were paying calls on people I used to know. Visiting them. As if to say good-bye. Goodbye and thanks."

Elizabeth pauses, listening. The girl below is silent, but now the silence has a wary feel; her presence has been recognized.

"I went back to Italy," Elizabeth goes on, keeping her voice light. "I went back to the house where I was happiest as a child. And other places, not so clear. My father's laboratory: I used to hide in the hall outside it. Every afternoon, the year I was fourteen, I was there. Younger than you, but not much." She pauses again. The room's darkness has thinned slightly, shifting toward dawn. "I wasn't supposed to be there. But I had to be there. I know how much they mean, those hiding places, I guess that's why I dreamed of them. But in the midst of the dream, I heard someone whimpering. Calling me. And then I was back here. In bed. And you were underneath it."

For a while there is silence in the room. Elizabeth feels the fear in Sarah: fear that if she speaks she damns herself. Outside there is a light showering of leaves against the wall. And then, soft as the shower, faint and scared and somehow brave all the same, Sarah's voice floats like smoke up from the floor.

"Last night I had a dream too. . . ." There is a long pause. "I dreamed I was walking through halls . . . and halls, halls, dark halls. I couldn't find my way, I didn't know where to go. At the end of one hall there was a city, a house, my father's house. I looked at it and ran away." There is a catch in Sarah's voice, a huskiness, as she goes on. "Then another hall, at the end of it these mountains, the school. I couldn't stay there either, so I walked, walked, I walked so far, all those halls, and there were dark things in the air, they were whispering to me." A faint but perceptible tremor goes through the mattress. "I started to run, run, I ran and I was crying, crying as I ran, trying to get someplace safe. . . ." She takes a breath, gulps it down like water. "And then I woke up. I woke up here. Here in

your room . . . under your bed. And I was too scared . . .
too scared to come out." A longer pause; her voice has faded
so low, Elizabeth stoops to hear it: "Are you . . . angry?"
"No," Elizabeth says, meaning it. "Are you still scared?"
"Yes." It is a whisper.
"No need. Nothing will happen."
There is a long silence, more companionable this time.
"Is it true . . . ?" Sarah's voice quavers again. "It it
true that you . . . they said you . . . soon you'll . . ."
Her voice breaks off.
"Is it true I'm dying?" Elizabeth's voice is dry. "Is that
what they're saying?"
The bed shakes slightly; Elizabeth interprets this as a nod.
"Are you?" Sarah whispers.
"Oh Sarah." Elizabeth hears the sudden intensity in her
voice. "I want to be, can you understand that? Does that
scare you?"
"No. Other things scare me. Not that."
"When I was your age, I thought about dying very care-
fully. The way you're thinking about it now. For yourself."
Elizabeth hears a small faint gasp. "You knew, how?"
How did she know? Elizabeth isn't sure. "But, Sarah," she
goes on anyway. "I was wrong. It seemed an escape to me
then. It's not, of course. Now I see what it really is. It's a
party in another room, I think. But only when it's time."
"Is it time for you?"
"I . . . don't know. How I hope so."
"But not for me?"
"No. Not for you. Not yet."
Beneath the bed Sarah weeps; the mattress gently shudders
with her sobs. "I'm not crazy, I'm not," she chokes out.
"Please don't think that, don't think I am."
Elizabeth leans over the edge of the bed and reaches down
into the graying dark. After a moment she feels Sarah's
fingers close around her hand: cold fingers, fingers pressing
hers.
"Stay if you want," Elizabeth says.
They drift together toward sleep and morning, layered
over each other like books in a shelf; woman and girl,

folded together in the changing light, bound by the mattress they share. They are like that as full sunshine fills the room, as the house around them stirs and wakes.

The wheel of the day begins to turn around them, Elizabeth's bed at its hub; Sarah nestled into that hub like a silent observant insect. Elizabeth sees the day with Sarah's eyes: the parade of shoes and hems across the floor, voices floating high above. The letters to be read, the letters to be drafted. The endless stream of small questions, permissions requested, advice sought, *Mother should we, Mother may we, Mother how can we, how can she, how can I?* Above her invisible companion, Elizabeth smiles. Sarah has fled to the place she considers the center of holiness—the very pivot, axis, nucleus of the house. Elizabeth locates that center in the chapel, in the tabernacle; Sarah locates it here in this room, under this bed. But as the day unfolds, it seems to Elizabeth that her bed is the hub of the ordinary. Its spokes pass through no mystically charged air, no hermit's cave, nor even the Gothic heights of a Benedictine cloister. Even if she were well, Elizabeth would lead no procession of cowled sisters, would ring no bell, carry no crozier. Her seat here is no abbatial throne; it is more like a chair in a sunny busy household's kitchen. Elizabeth wonders if, seeing this, Sarah feels less safe beneath it than she did the night before.

During the day there is no time to ask. There is only time, between business and visits and prayers, to pass food from the tray to the edge of the bed. Wordlessly, they share the supper, the chamber, the chamber pot. Their closeness makes Elizabeth think of the *lazzaretto* cell in Livorno, so long ago, shared so tightly with people she loved. She wonders what it makes Sarah think of. And I? Elizabeth thinks. Why am I sheltering her? Why have I told them not to worry about her, I know where she is? Why this pleasure in knowing she sleeps like a puppy under this bed? She wonders still as the day fades into evening, as the day's voices fade away.

Again the house quiets and Elizabeth drowses; again it is unwinding before her like a ball of bright yarn—the road up Montenero, threading and glowing along the mountainside to the church. She is on the road, she is on her way to the church—this time, it seems, to be married. There are bells on the air. There are white silks whispering around her. She is moving inside the church, down the aisle through the cool spiced air to the altar. She will leave her bouquet for the Virgin and go to her Groom—that is all she has to do. She is nearer now; the flowers seem to drift from her hands. But as she turns to look for the Groom, a voice draws her attention away. She listens. She hears it again. She sighs and turns around. The aisle looks narrow and endless: a long path back. Sighing again, she moves toward it, starts down it, walking slowly, reluctantly, back toward that voice.

"Forgive me," the voice is saying. "I know it's late, I shouldn't have come."

Elizabeth opens her eyes.

"I had a bad time getting them to let me in," says Samuel Sutherland Cooper. "I couldn't think where else to go."

For a moment Elizabeth feels confusion, like a cloud of gnats, circle her head. Has she returned to the wrong place in her life? Cooper's face clarifies. The wall behind it, in the lamplight, clarifies as well. Sam, here, of course: she finds her place in the evening again, remembers why he is here— appointed to the Emmitsburg parish a few months ago. His face hangs before her like a lantern on a scrawny tree; his black shoetops, she knows, are planted by Sarah's face.

"Forgive me," he is saying again.

"Sam." She puts her hand out to him.

"You're much improved, they tell me."

"Do they?" She feels a spear of disappointment. "And you?"

"Fine, fine." He runs his hands through his hair. "I don't know, I don't know. I'm in a box, a trap, you've heard?"

Elizabeth nods, seeing Sam for a moment as he had looked that day in the Washington coach, fencing with his umbrella: his face so ardent, so alight. Now he looks far more than ten years older, his face seamed, hair thinning, eyes pouched—and those eyes: their passion turned up too bright, to a frantic, manic gleam. It has taken him a decade to be ordained, his health erratic, his vocation a struggle.

And now, ordained and serving a parish at last, he has created new troubles, veering from brilliant sermons into a campaign against drunkenness: it has become an obsession. He has singled out members of the parish, reading their names from his pulpit, seating them in one section; finally barring one from the church itself. A furor has resulted. The new archbishop has had to intervene, forbidding public penance; stopping just short of removing Cooper, who, it is hoped, will remove himself.

"My authority, it's been flouted, thrown in my teeth—how can I stay?" he says now.

"You've decided to leave, then?"

"No!" The word is a roar, echoing in the quiet room; Elizabeth feels a jolt of fear from Sarah, under the bed. "I won't be forced out, punished like a schoolboy, *no.*"

"What happened, Sam?" Elizabeth touches his arm. "The public penances, why—?"

"*Why!*" His voice leaps, flamelike, into a roar again. "Drink is of the Devil, the Church must be purified—it's very simple. Everyone in this country thinks of Catholics as drunkards, you know that's true. How can America embrace our faith until it's purged? How can we face ourselves, as Catholics, until we've burned this evil out? I myself have wrestled with this demon, I know its power—drink, stinking drink!"

Elizabeth looks away from him, sudden tears in her eyes. Sam, Sam. The light had been so strong in him; it had helped to brighten her own. They had begun together. They had had such plans. It hurts her to see how he is now: a lamp with its wick fouled in its own oil.

"Tell me what to do." His voice has switched cadence: low, tight, fast. "Tell me. Elizabeth. You think I'm right, I know you do. You think I should stay, of course you do. Tell me how to convince them, tell me how to save it, say you'll speak to them, you'll see to it, you will, say you will."

"Sam." Elizabeth looks at him. "I know you, I know what you can do. Before this started, you stirred people to their souls, they told me. I've seen you at your best. And Sam, Sam, this isn't your best. The parish needs to heal now, so do you. I think you should leave, Sam. Start again some-where else, another parish. Let this thing go, this—"

"*You.*" His voice rises, cracking. "I thought you were different, a friend, my friend, *you!* You're like the others, against me, all of you . . ." He is on his feet, bolting from the bedside chair, his voice fragmenting. "You you *you,*" he cries out, louder; his hands shake the bed frame. And then his voice implodes in a choking sound—he pulls back, eyes shocked. Suddenly, appearing from he knows not where, wresting him away from the bed, is a spectral figure: white-gowned, very pale, hair tangled and streaming, eyes dark-circled and ablaze. For an instant he stares at what seems an apparition, an avenging angel—then he rushes from the room. They hear his footsteps pepper the hall; moments later they hear his horse whinny and start away.

Elizabeth looks at Sarah, who is shaking, her fists opening and closing. For nearly twenty-four hours they have been together; this is the first time they are face to face.

"I was scared he'd hurt you," Sarah blurts out. She glances, undecided, at the space beneath the bed. "You going to ask me to leave now?"

"No." Elizabeth looks at Sarah, her face so pale, so tight. She wants to reach out and push the tangled hair off her forehead; she motions toward the bed, but Sarah stays rooted where she is.

"Are you going to tell me what you told him? That I should leave here—not just this room: *here?*" Sarah's arm describes a quick arc.

"And should I tell you that?" Elizabeth feels the tension rising in the room.

"Yes. No. I don't know."

"Would I be right to say, 'Stay here under my bed, for always'? Or, 'Stay and let me make you into a nun'? Or would I be right to say, 'Sarah, you've learned all you can here, now you must face what's in Baltimore—' "

"My father."

"Your life."

"*My life.*" Sarah spits it out. "My life, you don't know—"

"But I do."

"You can't." Sarah's breathing is coming faster, beginning to build toward that dangerous edge.

"Mine was very much like yours. My father was very much like yours."

"Please let me stay." Sarah is gasping now, her face ashen; her eyes, so dark-rimmed, look enormous, imploring. "Don't make me go back there. I know I'm trouble, but please." Her breathing has reached the frantic pace of the hysteric, the asthmatic. "Back there the only thing . . ." She gulps air. "The only thing I ever liked was the dances, the . . . dances I learned so fast, could do them all . . . pink dress, I had one, I . . ." Her breathing, faster still, seems to whip the air. "Not enough, don't make me . . . Oh, God, *God*." She gasps, a harsh tearing sound.

"Sarah—listen to me."

Sarah cannot listen. The panic is spiraling through her; her breathing fills the room. Her eyes, rolling white, snatch at the walls, the corners, for relief. Half-falling, she reaches toward the washstand, grabbing at a medicine bottle there; she smashes the bottle against the stand. Elizabeth rushes forward but Sarah rolls away from her, gulping air, the splintered bottle held to her own throat. "You want to go— you should understand—so do I, *so do I*."

Elizabeth draws back. Her eyes do not move from Sarah's face, nor Sarah's from hers. She looks at this girl, so like and unlike her; she knows there are no words that can touch her now. There are no hands that dare touch her now. All Elizabeth can do is touch with her eyes; reach with her mind, her love. Again, she feels it—that love she'd felt amid the boys, that light she's felt in sleep, in dreams, the nearing, warming light; but now it is not drawing her, she is drawing it, she is warm with it, she is strong with it, and silently she calls to Sarah, Wait, hold on, I'm here, I'm here, for you, the others, only wait, hold on. She feels Sarah's fear, fear like flame, and takes it, crackling, within herself. She feels Sarah's despair, tidal, deep and wild as seawater; she takes it within herself. She feels the panic and the pain, the lungs tight as fists, within her own chest. She hears herself sobbing with Sarah, gasping with Sarah, twin anguished voices.

And then, only one.
Hers.
Only one rasping breath.
Hers.
For a moment, dazed, still locked within the storm of tears, Elizabeth is afraid that Sarah has stopped breathing in convulsion, or worse. She opens her eyes. The room is still. The girl lying across the floor is quiet; the bottle has rolled from her hand. Elizabeth moves toward her, lifts her into her arms. Sarah is warm and whole, looking up at her, bathed in Elizabeth's tears.

I can see them there, the woman and the girl, sitting up on the feather bed in the lamplight later that night—the woman, aged by illness, wrapped in a black shawl; the girl, aged by sadness, draped in a white nightgown, her fair hair shawl-like on her shoulders. They sit together, cross-legged, like a pair of girls preparing to play jacks. In the woman's hands are a pair of pink dancing slippers. Shyly, awkwardly, eagerly, the girl tries one on; the woman ties it expertly. Around them, flickering in the lamplight, the room seems to float like a sea, and the bed is a boat, and on it they ride the night together, whispering, heads bent. There is much to be said before the parting to come. In the morning the girl will be going; in the morning the woman will stay.

She smiles, this woman, leaning forward, touching the girl's forehead as if in blessing. But she is not blessing with the usual prayers. She is describing, in detail and with care, the best way for a young lady at a party to feign a faint.

The sound in the room is laughter.

21

*H*ere in the basement of the Cathedral of Mary Our
Queen, we are at last preparing our findings for Rome; our
tribunal has received its final instructions.

The transcript of our sessions must be typed three times
with an indelible-ink ribbon.

Each page of each copy must be stamped *"Concordat sum
originali."*

Each title page must be stamped and signed by each of
us, with our academic degrees after our names.

All copies must go by diplomatic pouch to the Vatican,
to be judged.

The original, sealed with red wax and tied with silk cord,
must go to our diocesan archives, to be kept.

Our notary is, at this moment, running all over Baltimore, looking for sealing wax and silk cord. He might find
the right wax. But there hasn't been a big demand, this
century, for silk cord. I'd bet this transcript goes to the archives tied instead with sensible twine. By the time it does,
we will have met here for the last time. We will have had
our last off-the-record discussion. And I will have made my
last recommendation. To compile it, I've gone over my notes
from the beginning, to see how they look now.

"Hardly a Joan of Arc. . . ."

True. She was Elizabeth, and her martyrdom was not by
fire. It was a subtler, far more enduring torment: that

conflict between family and vocation, as searing to the spirit as flame is to flesh—I can attest to that.

"I cannot see this woman standing with the stature of a saint. . . ."

Not at first; not the way I defined the word. I thought saints had to walk on water, stop floods—work only Technicolor miracles. I see now that the abiding miracles are quieter; so subtly threaded through the fabric of the ordinary, they're harder at first to spot in the weave.

"I cannot see the miracle worker in this miracle. . . ."

I couldn't then; but now I see the shimmer of this woman in the data. I see her burning through a near-constant fog of loss to me. Perhaps that's what saints do, after all. Perhaps they are not perfect beings, flawless icons. Perhaps they are, instead, lightning rods. Conductors. Conduits. People struck with, fired with, filled with something from beyond themselves: so struck, so fired, so filled, they channel it to others.

Perhaps she always had it: dimmed in childhood, clouded in adolescence, it seemed to flame up brighter with motherhood. The Filicchis saw it, fanned it. Her suffering, her searching, her losses somehow fueled it. And by the end, she had the blaze that makes things happen; even extraordinary things. I believe that now.

When I began this inquiry, I was so rational. I prided myself on that. I still pride myself on that.

Some things don't change.

And some things do.

I look back and see myself groping my way up the stairs of her life, resisting the slant of the steps, muttering wisecracks into the dark. I saw the climb through my own shadow —and a thousand shadows of anger, guilt, doubt. I cannot say, precisely, when the shift began for me. I cannot find, exactly, the turning of the stair. Perhaps it was the image of wrestling with her grief, and a lacy pillow, on the floor of the Filicchis' house. Perhaps it was her struggle with her sons and daughters. Perhaps it was her final struggle that lightened me at last. For I do now feel so lightened.

I think of her struggle to stay, to live on, despite her

longing for God, for peace. I think of her staying on, as long as there was someone in need of miracles. And there is always someone so in need. The O'Neill child needed a miracle. I guess I did too.

Watching this woman has helped me decide to stay, myself; to stay and go on struggling with my vocation. Perhaps in my case this is only remission, not cure. Perhaps not. But I've resolved to avoid self-diagnosis for now; to concentrate instead on the wrestling.

And in the meantime, I've a declension to make.

Elizabeth:

Convert.

Nun.

Foundress.

Lightning rod.

I rest my case.

Historical Afterword

Mother Elizabeth Seton died at Emmitsburg on January 4, 1821, and was buried near her daughters in the graveyard at St. Joseph's. Samuel Sutherland Cooper had news of Mother Seton's death in Augusta, Georgia, where he went after leaving Emmitsburg.

William Seton became a lieutenant in the United States Navy and died in 1868. He married a Protestant and fathered four children, some of whom were raised in the Catholic faith, some of whom were raised as Protestants. In 1846 Seton arranged for the construction of a small mortuary chapel at Emmitsburg for his mother's remains. Richard Seton failed in his apprenticeship to Antonio Filicchi. He died at sea, still unsettled, in 1823. Catherine Seton, the remaining daughter, lived a long life and became a nun, though not in her mother's order; she became one of the first Sisters of Mercy and died in 1891. Mother Seton's nephew James Roosevelt Bayley, also a convert, became an Archbishop of Baltimore.

The Informative Process of the Cause for Canonization of Mother Seton was begun in 1907 by James Cardinal Gibbons. In 1940 Pope Pius XII signed the Decree of Introduction of the Cause in Rome. In 1959 Mother Seton's life and virtues were proclaimed heroic by Pope John XXIII and the title "venerable" was conferred upon her. In 1961 the Vatican declared miraculous two cures effected with relics of Mother Seton, one of which was the case of Ann

O'Neill. In 1962 Mother Seton's grave was opened and canonically recognized. Her beatification was declared on March 17, 1963. A third cure was approved in 1974. On September 14, 1975, Elizabeth Bayley Seton was canonized, becoming the first American-born saint of the Roman Catholic Church.

Author's Note

This is a novel: by definition a work of fiction. It is based on historical fact, derived from plentiful primary and secondary source material. It is necessary to remember, however, that this is not biography. Because the responsibilities of novels and biographies differ substantially, it is important to distinguish between the two forms.

It is also important to note that this novel's narrator is fictional, not based on any priest who sat on the tribunal investigating the cure of Ann O'Neill. However, the recollections and materials of the Most Reverend F. Joseph Gossman have been very helpful in recreating the narrator's setting. Bishop Gossman was notary to the O'Neill tribunal.

The following notes are also appropriate:

The school attended by Elizabeth Seton in her childhood in New York is referred to as Madame Pompelion's in this novel, but appears in the sources as Mama Pompelion's: probably a corruption of "Madame."

The book of personally inscribed prayers was not present in St. Paul's Chapel as far as we know, but such a book does exist in St. Paul's in Boston, and the custom is common enough to permit this license.

The building which housed Mother Seton's order and school is always referred to at Emmitsburg as "the White House." Because that title has a different connotation for most readers, I have, for the sake of clarity, avoided its usage here.

It is impossible, in novelistic form, to include as a character every historical person whose life touched the subject's. Certain fictional characters, however, have been drawn from scanty details of actual people. Sarah Blackburn Taylor was developed, in part, from sketchy accounts of a student named Mary Goodloe Harper; the Peter Girot incident, in part, from the death of Theophilus Cauffmann; and Joe, the caretaker, from accounts of a similar historical person of the same name.

Mother Seton is credited with founding the Roman Catholic parochial school system in America. It has been argued that there were Roman Catholic schools predating hers, but none was associated with a parish in the way hers was. Although her school was primarily a tuition-based boarding school, it did contain St. Joseph's Class, drawn from the parish and requiring minimal tuition or none at all: this was the kernel from which the larger system grew.

It is impossible to state how much on-site research contributes to a book such as this. The atmospheres of certain places shape some books to some extent; this book, to a large extent—particularly those of Florence and Livorno (also called Leghorn) and Emmitsburg.

Acknowledgments

My thanks to John Dodds, Jacques de Spoelberch, Fredrica S. Friedman, Thomas Congdon, and for his cheerful assistance with materials relating to the O'Neill tribunal, the Most Reverend F. Joseph Gossman, Bishop of Raleigh, North Carolina. Thanks also to Margaret McAleer, manuscript processor, Special Collections Division, Lauinger Library, Georgetown University, and to the following: Jan Anderson of the New-York Historical Society; Phyllis Barr, archivist, Trinity Parish, New York City; John W. Bowen, S.S., archivist, Sulpician Archives, Baltimore; Rev. John L. Conner, S.J.; Hilda B. Jordan, treasurer and chairman, Mother Seton House, Baltimore, Maryland; the office of Monsignor John F. Donoghue, Archdiocese of Washington, D.C.; Marcus Hansen, luthier, Colonial Williamsburg; William F. Jacobs, M.D.; Sister M. Felicitas Powers, RSM, archivist, Archdiocese of Baltimore; Susan Stromei, Colonial Williamsburg; and the helpful staffs of the Arlington County Library, the Library of Congress, Lauinger Library, Pratt Library of Baltimore, and the gracious Daughters of Charity at Emmitsburg.

It is impossible to list all sources, but I gratefully acknowledge the most helpful: *Elizabeth Bayley Seton*, Annabelle M. Melville's definitive biography, whose extensive use of primary source material was invaluable and timesaving; "The Making of a Saint," by Thomas Congdon, *The Saturday Evening Post*, March 1963; *Mrs. Seton; The Foundress of the American Sisters of Charity*, by Joseph I. Dirvin, C.M.;

~ 311 ~

The Immigrant Church in New York, by Jay Dolan; "The Exhumation of Mother Seton," by Joseph Gallagher, *Ave Maria National Catholic Weekly*, January 1963; *History of Emmitsburg, Maryland*, by James A. Helman; *American Catholics*, by James Hennesey, S.J.; *American and Catholic: A Narrative of Their Role in American History*, by Robert Leckie; *Baltimore: The Building of An American City*, by Sherry H. Olson; *The City of New York*, by Jerry E. Patterson; *Living Water: Prayers of Our Heritage*, by Carl J. Pfeifer and Janaan Manternach; *The City of New York in the Year of Washington's Inauguration*, by Thomas E. V. Smith; *Forgotten Folk-Tales of the English Counties*, collected by Ruth L. Tongue; letters, notes, and excerpts from Mother Seton's *Dear Remembrances*, and from the diaries, notes, and letters of the Setons, the Carrolls, William V. Dubourg, Simon Bruté, and materials from letters to ledgers in the archives of Georgetown University.

Affectionate thanks to Kathleen Currie, Helen Eisenbach, Hanna Emrich, Susan L. Hartt, Sherry E. Joslin, Judith Lantz, Caroline Lalire, Frances MacCallum, Melanne Verveer, and especially, once again, Rev. Thomas P. Gavigan, S.J.